THRILL KINGS: FRAGMENTED SKY

The Birth Of Interdimensional Travel

THRILL KINGS: FRAGMENTED SKY

The Birth Of Interdimensional Travel

By
Rik Ty

SAMPLINGS FROM:
THRILL KINGS:
FRAGMENTED SKY

THE OPENING
(from the Beginning)

"Look at that Moon," Charlie said. "It's beautiful. Look quick, before it goes behind another tree."

"I've seen it," Rose said, staring at the road through the windshield, "It was out when we got in."

She continued watching the ground beyond the car, gazing at the moving swatch of gray the headlights created, looking specifically at the streaking white stones, and the long black lines their shadows made. After a moment, she gave in to Charlie's suggestion and took a second peek at the moon.

And Charlie was right. It was beautiful: full and round, and whiter than it had been when they started the ride. Thin clouds raced past it, painting its lower half violet, and making the little moon look as if it were wearing a veil.

The half-painted moon ruled an entire sky that seemed split to Rose. Wherever she looked, division announced itself. She saw rows of clouds with their promise of rain, and she saw fields of stars with their promise of peace. Every turn of her gaze showed her a sky riding the cusp between storm and splendor, as if it couldn't commit to a course of action either.

"Very nice," She said, burrowing her fingertips into the knit of her sweater, and again looking out her window at the black road beyond.

"You sound mad,"...

***

Speed.

Three hundred miles an hour maybe. *Fast* — roadside trees flying by in streaks and slashes. Nonstop's engine roaring, changing pitch with the changing terrain, shifting intensity as it answered Nonstop's moves, flowing in that insistent symphony of engine noise and wind shear.

He was still ghosting; everything he could see was awash in night-vision green. The white markings on the highway seemed like one continuous line, the spaces between them not even given the time to show up.

He could keep this ghost session going longer too, postpone committing between this world and the realmlines and just streak across the landscape like a howling green apparition. If there were a record for ghosting, he'd break it. If there were a record for ghosting, he'd already have it. If there were a record for ghosting, it would be named after him.

The readout display told him that the path and the road were about to part ways. He was on a steady left-ward curve, about to leave the asphalt for the grass.

He leaned, the bike banked gently, and he abandoned the road.

His tire registered the change in surface and grew toothy. He maintained his speed to keep in ghost mode, and slalomed between the thin trees with ease.

He whipped over the forest terrain and suddenly a massive tree appeared ahead of him — a classic — a twisted behemoth with limbs that were thicker than his shoulders were wide.

Don't stop.

He didn't change trajectory. He did nothing to avoid the tree or disrupt the ghost. With an electric thrum, green light swam over the rough bark and... he entered the tree. For a microsecond the green glow around him illuminated the interior of the living wood, showing the rings of its grain, and the tunnels of its burrowing insects — and then he was out again, rocketing across a bare strip of earth lined with tall grass.

The grass whipped as he passed, and the tips and edges of each blade appeared to burst apart in crazy pinwheels of molecular fireworks — a beautiful sub-orbital dance where tiny portions of grass flared and spun away in the air — changing shape and disappearing — only to reappear somewhere else in the air, following orbits not completely seen. The pebbling effect followed the bike along the entire strip of grass — a whirling mosaic of moonlit blades seen as if through textured glass. The effect weakened, returning the grass to its normal state: rooted, and merely swaying in the slipstream.

***

(from the middle)

...Done! Gone! Free! Suddenly flying through the realmlines at heart-leaping speed, his bike forcing gaps between systems of realities, between disparate continuums, creating spaces that weren't supposed to exist at all, propelled by the weight of neighboring existences like a wet bar of soap speeding through a squeezing hand.

The arc of lightning he followed closed to a ring and faded into the streaking blurs of color that surrounded him. If he knew of gravitons, or brane theory, he might have made comparisons, instead, he paid attention to the decontamination wave that flared over him, momentarily brightening the energy envelope that rippled around his bike.

***

Skyde stepped off the edge of the parking lot and onto the grass, a dozen or more white plastic bags hanging off each wrist. She carried them to the back of Krork's bike. Nonstop made a point of catching her eye as she stepped into the workbay. He smiled. "We make the papers? Anything good?"

Skyde laid the bags down on the floor. She nudged them with her foot, and hooked their handle loops over cabinet latches. When she looked up, she didn't look happy. "Nothing good," she said, "They say that the military is in Marin County because they've uncovered a terrorist cell."

VI

"That's Bloch." Varrage said. "If the Newspapers are calling us terrorists, it can only mean Colonel Bloch wants them to."

Skyde didn't look at Varrage. Instead, she stared out at the night. "This is just going to go on and on. We're not going to get any peace from him are we?"

"No," Varrage said. Then he revved his bike, leaned, and started driving.

"But..." Skyde said, as she watched Varrage reach the road and continue on. She looked at Krork. "What are we going to do about Bloch? Just keep running from him?"

"For a little while, maybe. Yeah. Until Doc gets things worked out. We're lucky. We're bulletproof right? At least Bloch can't hurt us."

Nonstop blinked. He turned to his friend, changing his grip on the bike's control bar to aim his recently bleeding forearms toward the floor. He started to speak, but then revved his bike to cover any noise his throat might have made.

***

..."Man, everything Varrage said to me tonight is true. I can't work the equipment. I don't know tactics. I'm impul... Dude. I'm going to jack everything up. I can't just sit around and wait for me to ruin the whole world. I have to do something!"...

***

(and from the end...)

...a tiny circular shape, like a dark snowman, and all along the rims of these holes, were smaller versions of the same patterns of holes, and all the edges of these patterns were moving, bleeding with smaller versions of themselves. Beyond them, in the darkness, grew tendrils of slow-motion lightning, tendrils whose paths stayed etched beyond the sky, spreading like some great network of capillaries, illuminated again and again as fresh flashes blazed around them. The sight made

Nonstop feel sick in his mind. What sky could show the sun like this? Not his.

An electric roar, like amplifier crackle, pealed across the field. At the sound, Grace threw her arms around Nonstop's chest and squeezed. The road shuddered. Rings of light, like waves upon a shore, began rippling across the sky, radar green where the sky was dark, smoky white where the sky was blue.

And then the white portal split...

From Reader Reviews of
Thrill Kings: Fragmented Sky

"The pace of this novel is unreal! I loved it. ...Honestly, I pride myself on fast pace and this is like a benchmark for action stories! I couldn't be more impressed."

"...There are surprises and twists and most of all the read is great and excellent fun. Highly Recommended. A book I will predict is destined for great things, it's seldom such works of depth and complexity which are also lots of fun come around."

"Slick, quick paced, fun and colorfully detailed (literally)."

"...The book's a little on the long side, and might be slightly overwhelming for those just stepping into this world, but it's a wonderful introduction to the characters and concepts. Definitely recommended. "

"Suddenly, in the middle section of the book everything came together and I got swept up in the plot and the world and finished the last half of the book in one sitting. It closes with climatic, world-shaking events and delivers a thrill on every page."

Why not add your review?

THRILL KINGS TIMELINE

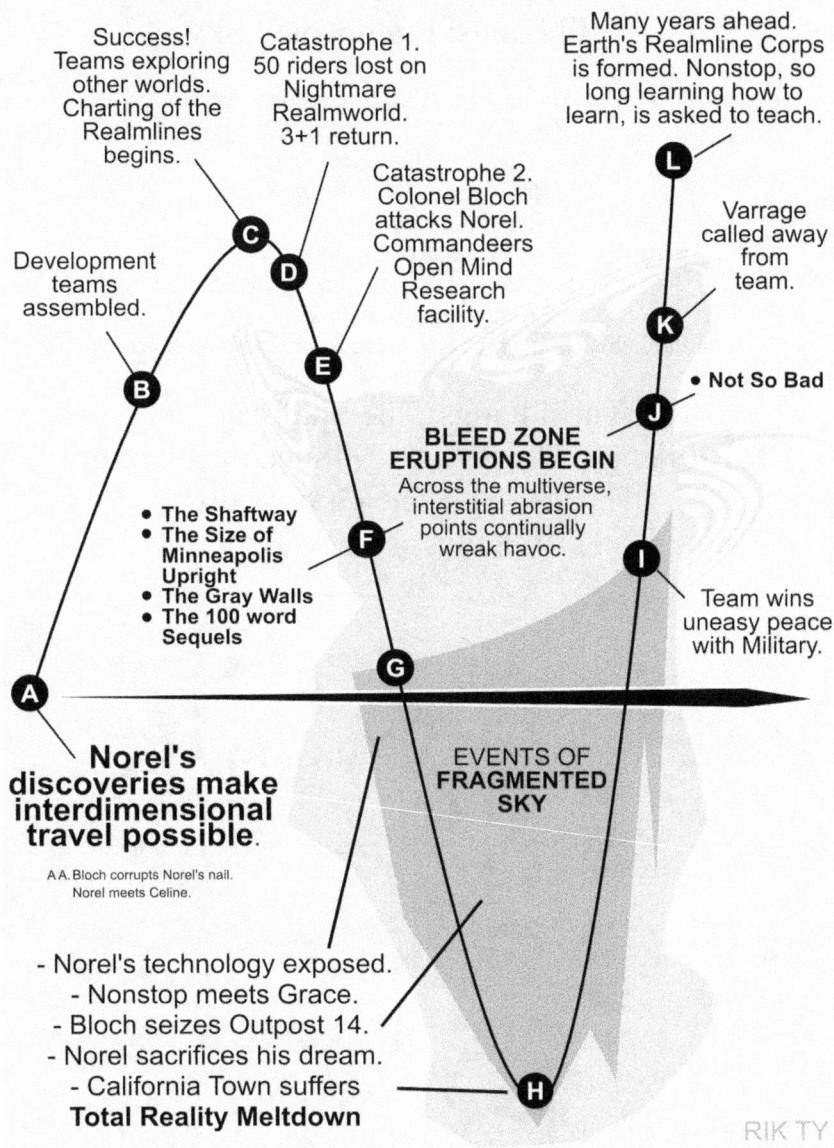

Success! Teams exploring other worlds. Charting of the Realmlines begins.

Catastrophe 1. 50 riders lost on Nightmare Realmworld. 3+1 return.

Many years ahead. Earth's Realmline Corps is formed. Nonstop, so long learning how to learn, is asked to teach.

Catastrophe 2. Colonel Bloch attacks Norel. Commandeers Open Mind Research facility.

Varrage called away from team.

Development teams assembled.

• Not So Bad

BLEED ZONE ERUPTIONS BEGIN
Across the multiverse, interstitial abrasion points continually wreak havoc.

• The Shaftway
• The Size of Minneapolis Upright
• The Gray Walls
• The 100 word Sequels

Team wins uneasy peace with Military.

Norel's discoveries make interdimensional travel possible.

AA. Bloch corrupts Norel's nail.
Norel meets Celine.

EVENTS OF **FRAGMENTED SKY**

- Norel's technology exposed.
- Nonstop meets Grace.
- Bloch seizes Outpost 14.
- Norel sacrifices his dream.
- California Town suffers
Total Reality Meltdown

RIK TY

Order Of Publication

Thrill Kings: Fragmented Sky

(6 Deluxe Excerpts from Fragmented Sky:)
The Kevin Woods Excerpt,
The Joy Ride Excerpt
The Brawling of Demons Excerpt
The Pinky Bet Excerpt
The Bonfire Excerpt
The Outrageous Nonstop Versus
A Parking Lot Excerpt
(Available FREE at Thrill Kings Now.com. And Kobo.com)

Thrill Kings: The Shaftway
Thrill Kings: The Size Of Minneapolis Upright
Thrill Kings: The Gray Walls
Thrill Kings: Not So Bad

Read By:

Date:

Thoughts:

Read By:

Date:

Thoughts:

Read By:

Date:

Thoughts:

XV

For Beth and For Kim,

and for you dear reader,

and for you.

In the folds of the trees of June, in the rushes of the grass, in the darkness 'neath the moon, far from building town or path, there came lights upon the air, small and sparkling, sweet and fair, arcs in darkness, breezes star-blessed, in the grasslands, here and there. By the highway, by the road, in the wild place, never strode, 'neath the spinnings of the stars, near the heat rush of the cars, in the night glade near the concrete, in the night glade free of scars. And these small lights kept to dancing, and these small lights shone and flared, and these small lights cried their warnings, to the witness,

Never there.

Rik Ty

THRILL KINGS
FRAGMENTED
SKY

Rik Ty

June
17th

10:45
P.M.

Rik Ty

**

"Look at that Moon," Charlie said. "It's beautiful. Look quick, before it goes behind another tree."

"I've seen it," Rose said, staring at the road through the windshield, "It was out when we got in."

She continued watching the ground beyond the car, gazing at the moving swatch of gray the headlights created, looking specifically at the streaking white stones, and the long black lines their shadows made. After a moment, she gave in to Charlie's suggestion and took a second peek at the moon.

And Charlie was right. It was beautiful: full and round, and whiter than it had been when they started the ride. Thin clouds raced past it, painting its lower half violet, and making the little moon look as if it were wearing a veil.

The half-painted moon ruled an entire sky that seemed split to Rose. Wherever she looked, division announced itself. She saw rows of clouds with their promise of rain, and she saw fields of stars with their promise of peace. Every turn of her gaze showed her a sky riding the cusp between storm and splendor, as if it couldn't commit to a course of action either.

"Very nice," She said, burrowing her fingertips into the knit of her sweater, and again looking out her window at the black road beyond.

"You sound mad," Charlie said.

"I'm not mad."

In the distance, the road slipped into a stone overpass, which, in the moonlight, looked like the wall of some grand, ruined castle.

"Ah Rose, don't be mad. It's *her* wedding and she wants crazy food. So what?"

Low concrete barriers lined the road that led into the overpass. Leading up to the concrete walls, rows of orange cones blocked the left lane and the road's shoulder.

"Charlie, we have family coming. They're getting on airplanes. They're bringing money. They deserve more than sprouts and bean curd."

"All right, so maybe we get her to offer something a little more traditional... In addition to all her sprouts and bean curds. Work your magic ."

"Yeah. Work my magic. It's always my magic. I wish people could get things right on their own."

"What about meatballs? Veggie meatballs?"

"Meatballs? Meatballs? I...I..."

"Over some nice pasta, with some nice sauce, and some nice vodka."

Rose laughed. "Some *very* nice vodka," she said, and she slapped Charlie's arm gently. "Grey Goose doesn't have any animal by-products in it, does it?"

"We'll use the house brand just to be safe."

"When you say 'safe,' you mean cheap."

"Nope, not me. I know better."

Laughing, they drove into the channel created by the road barriers, and both stole glances upward as the dark roof of the archway swept over their heads.

Inside the tunnel, their headlights threw leaping shadows across the concrete walls, the graffiti, and the skeletal frames of the grime-covered scaffolding.

"Besides, cheap is goo —"Charlie said. "What are those lights?"

"What lights?" Rose leaned forward and looked at the exit. Beyond the overpass, cutting across the road, she could see a line of jagged blue lights, moving and...

And even before the car emerged from the tunnel, Rose and Charlie were screaming.

Charlie stomped on the brakes but the car squealed closer to the line of creatures that blocked the road — hideous things as big as dogs, as big as lions, crawling over each other in long muscular knots, creating braidings of glowing jaws and glowing rib stripes. Forty. Fifty. Maybe more — with blue-lit teeth and blue-lit eyes and blue-lit liquids dripping from their jaws. The headlights hit the creatures and the beasts turned to snarl in unison at the oncoming car. Then the creatures quickly separated from each other, leaping away from the nearing machine, their fur and shadows flowing in front of the blazing headlights.

The car halted with the monsters flanking the vehicle in pools of blackness, eyes and fangs glowing, not leaving, not running away, studying the car as Charlie grabbed for the gear shift.

"What are they? What are they?" Rose screamed, pivoting in her seat, trying to look everywhere at once, and seeing only hints of the creatures, their heads below their heavy shoulders, their pelts ink-black without the light of the car hitting them. She continued to scream, covering her face with her arms, and was jolted in her seat as the car lurched backward.

Charlie, screaming and cursing, twisted in his seat to see behind him — looking for a way to escape back through the tunnel, flooring the gas pedal, swerving the tail-end of the car left and right until the rear bumper hit something — *hard* — hard enough to stop the car. Charlie thought they might have hit the concrete barriers, but he could see that it was a tree. *Had he swerved that far off the road?* No, they were still in the middle of the lane; it wasn't a tree.

And then another tree landed to stand behind the car, and another, and then the car bounced as something splattered heavily across the back window. Whatever the thing was, Charlie saw it burst, and then he saw little bits of the thing slide and wriggle back down the window and onto the trunk. Quickly and purposefully, the pieces slapped their way off the car and re-assembled into a pillar shape — *a tree — a tentacle.*

There was something crawling down from the overpass. Something big — made out of those tentacles. Something that was heading for the car.

Charlie shifted into drive and gunned the engine. Rose braced her arms against the dashboard and shook her head frantically as the car sped back toward the lion-things. There would be a second before the car hit the creatures. Full on. Hard.

The car plowed into the monsters. They bounced onto the hood as Charlie's face smashed into the steering wheel, and in the second it took for him to grab his nose, the creatures smashed into the windshield, whipping a white crack across the windshield's length, and filling the view through the glass with gnashing jaws and glowing streaks of saliva. Rose grabbed the steering wheel in the same second Charlie's hands returned to it, spiraling their arms in a twist of black and white sleeves.

The car slammed into the guardrail and lifted, flipping up off its wheels as its airbags deployed.

It hit the ground hard, bursting its windshield, and then continued down the slope, rolling and tumbling. The front axle ground over one of the creatures, and as the monster screamed, the air around it fought to reject the sound, allowing forth only a chopped, wavering emission, like a railroad brake heard underwater; a sound hardly noticed as the car jounced and bounced and banged down the rest of the hill.

The car slid on its roof and came to a stop in the grass, every window shattered, its headlights pointing back up the embankment. No creature braved closer contact. Many returned to the road's center, to the huddle, where they were equidistant from everything around them. A few moved to the road's edge, and for the moment, stood there squinting, their heavy shoulders swaying as they stared into the lights of the non-moving car.

Inside the car, upside down, hanging in their seatbelts and staggered by the impact of the airbags, Charlie and Rose coughed and thrashed.

"Don't scream. Don't scream," Charlie said as Rose gasped, gulping air, both her arms holding her weight against the ceiling. Charlie's own weight fought against his seatbelt, which dug into his neck so hard it felt like it could slice his skin. The belt wouldn't let go with his first press of the release and he had to push against the ceiling before the clasp would open.

"Can you get down?" He asked Rose, his eyes wide as he tried to look in every corner of the car. "We have to get out of here Love. Right now. Right this second. We have no windows." Charlie continued searching through each window in turn, each broken, some blocked by the deflating airbags.

He saw no feet.

He saw no creatures.

Not yet.

Charlie pushed along the roof and slid under Rose as she got her belt free.

"Charlie, how can we leave? What are they?"

"Honey. I don't know, but they'll get in. We can't stay." Charlie looked around him as Rose lowered onto his chest, but he saw only the ceiling and the upside down seats. Their first car had been a rat-hole — their first *apartment* had been a rat-hole, but their long ago car had weapons in it — a steel bar that locked across the steering wheel, a heavy flashlight in the glove compartment, a steak knife hidden under the driver's seat. This car was a thousand times grander, and there wasn't a weapon in it. Comfort had softened them — had softened *him*. He reached for the door latch beyond Rose, dreading the sound it would make.

"I don't want to go," Rose said, grabbing his shirt.

"I know. I know sweetheart. I don't either." His hand found the latch, strange in its upside-down orientation, and he pulled.

The door opened the barest crack. He pushed with his feet to slide them both out of the car. In the grass, they turned and rolled onto their bellies.

"Stay low," Charlie whispered. "And stay in the shadow of the car."

"Those bushes?" Rose asked, pointing. Charlie looked where she pointed, then around the rest of the hill to the field beyond. He nodded.

"Good idea. We keep the bushes blocking us. Look down the field. See all that construction junk? There are a whole lot of those supply things in the grass. We can creep behind them and get to the trees."

Rose nodded, but didn't say anything. She closed her eyes and drew her shoulders close.

"Come on," Charlie said, and they started moving.

They crawled in the shadows, not daring to look behind them, every second anticipating the pain of jaws clamping on their backs.

At the bushes, they peeked back up at the road where three monsters stood, still staring at the car. Rose and Charlie breathed, studied their view of the field, and moved on.

The grass on the field had been recently cut, and was shorter than the grass on the hill. Low concrete barriers, the same as those on the road, were scattered across the landscape, part of the same construction project presumably, and they gave much better cover than the grass alone. Rose and Charlie reached them, and then used them to creep to a pyramid of large black pipes, where they found they could stand, or at least crouch. They looked back up the hill.

The road was empty now. The headlights pointed at the broken guardrail and that was it. No creatures — at the road's edge or at the car.

"Where are they?" Rose asked.

"I don't know."

"Do you think they left?"

"I...No. Where would they go? What are they? Where do they even belong? I don't know."

Rose slipped her high-heeled sandal from her foot, and then removed her other one. "I guess that's good," she said.

"Do you have your phone?"

"It's in my purse. In the car. Airbag..."

"Mine is on the dresser at home — sorry."

She took his hand. He felt her wedding ring. He felt the slimness of her fingers, the trembling coolness. "Let's g..." Rose said, and then stopped, looking as a creature returned to the guardrail. The strange beast looked at the car, paused, and then paced toward the guardrail's other end.

Charlie looked behind him and whispered. "Okay, we stay low, and we head there," he pointed to the trees. "That will keep these pipes blocking their view." When the creature turned to pace in the other direction, Rose tapped Charlie's shoulder and they scampered to the tree line, daring to turn around only when they had reached its dark cover. When they looked back, they saw many more monsters on the road, testing the path down the hill, creeping to the car where Rose and Charlie had just been.

Charlie looked at Rose. Rose looked at Charlie. The moon painted leaf shadows across their terrified faces.

"We find a road. A car. A house." Charlie whispered, and they started to walk in the woods.

But the ground under the trees was carpeted with a thick layer of dead leaves and dry twigs. Each step was noisy, and instantly, in her bare feet, Rose thought of scraped ankles and sharp sticks, of broken glass and rusty hangers, of small animals and... "I can't see." She said, "and they'll hear us."

"Yeah, that's what I was thinking too. Okay, we just stay close to the edge of the trees. We just keep moving."

Up the hill, the car rocked as creatures tore at the air bags and the soft parts of the seats. More creatures walked past the rocking headlights, momentarily brilliant as they advanced to surround the car.

Rose smelled wet leaves and dirt. Worse, she smelled her own perfume. Did the monsters follow scents? Of course they did. Why wouldn't they? How easy could she make this for them?

"Charlie..." she said but trailed off, watching through the trees they passed. The car rocked up on the hill, and then started to pivot on its roof, its headlights moving too, and starting to point downhill.

Rose and Charlie reached a portion of field they hadn't seen from their hiding spot — with another depot of construction supplies. This stockpile included several huge concrete blocks — as big as rooms, with giant circles cut out of them. Junction boxes? Culvert supplies? Rose and Charlie didn't know, but beyond the huge blocks stood a giant construction vehicle — a payloader, or an excavator, and that they did know, and were excited to see.

"That thing. That truck. If we can get in it, we can hide. We can barricade the door," Charlie said.

"What? And stay in it all night?"

"Sure. Sure. I'll take that bet. We'll stay until the work crew comes. Maybe I can figure out how to hot wire it — We'll have all night to try."

"Can you drive it?"

"Not a bit — but even bad is good."

With their first steps beyond the trees, they could see a portion of their car, and its headlights, and after a few more steps they could see that several creatures were walking in a line down the hill, noses in the grass, following their scent trail.

"Go!" Rose said, pushing Charlie, and they sped toward the excavator. The car, which had been moving, moved again, and this time the headlight beams reached their portion of field. Weak, but not weak enough. Rose and Charlie could now be seen, and in that moment, Rose and Charlie Forrester began running for their lives.

He was faster. He grabbed her upper arm and tried to lend her speed. He turned to look behind them and saw the monsters galloping down the hill.

"We'll never make the truck. These things! These concrete things!" Charlie pulled.

"No! No! The truck!" Rose began to lean back, but then ran with Charlie.

"They're almost here! Now. This thing!"

Charlie sped ahead. He hit the nearest junction box at close to full stride, turning his shoulder at the last second to soften the collision. He bent, and laced his hands together, ready when Rose arrived a second behind him.

"Give me your foot." He boosted her up. She struggled to the top of the junction box and glanced at the field. The creatures were closer, more than halfway to them already.

"Charlie!"

Charlie stepped back, got a running start, and leapt for the top of the box. His fingers made the edge easily, but his muscles refused to lift him. *Too soft. Too comfortable.* He let go and tried again. Rose screamed again.

"Charlie!"

His fingers reached the edge of the concrete. Rose bent low and pulled at his jacket. She tried. She pulled. The jacket bunched tight around his armpits. It helped. It helped.

"Charlie," Rose called.

One of his swinging feet hit the rim around the cut out in the wall. He tried again. The rim helped tremendously. He could raise himself. He went up sideways and awkwardly, but he got there.

He rolled onto the roof and stood. The creatures raced nearer. Charlie took a step to stand in front of Rose, and saw that she had laced her sandals against her palms, creating three inch spikes out of the heels of her shoes. He nodded, and stripped off his belt.

One creature had pulled ahead of the pack, charging; it locked eyes with Charlie.

"Get back." Charlie glanced at Rose and then returned his vision to the field, swinging his heavy buckle low, getting a feel for its weight.

The creature leapt.

Charlie swung the belt with all his might.

The impact ran up his shoulder. It felt like the bones in his arms had tried to jump apart. He caught the creature right behind the jaw.

The muscular animal screeched and spasmed in mid air, twisting its body and changing its landing position. It tumbled off the concrete block, and instantly rebounded to leap away from the box, slowing only after it had acquired several body lengths of distance.

All the creatures in the field changed stride in that moment; they stopped running. They began walking slowly, their heads lowered, their steps steady and smooth.

The monsters that had followed the scent trail through the woods emerged from the tree line and joined the stalking pack.

The entire throng stepped forward, beginning to walk in sync, moving their heads in unison, all their eyes looking at Rose and Charlie.

A passing cloud drained the moonlight, and as the field darkened, the teeth and eyes of the creatures grew brighter. Glowing ripples passed between their shoulders, onward and onward, creature to creature, like chain lightning traveling through thunderclouds.

"Charlie, Charlie, what do we do?" Rose said, taking a step back, but having nowhere to go.

Charlie watched the creatures, his eyes wide, wild.

"I don't know, I don't know. Don't stop fighting."

* * *

**

Speed.

Three hundred miles an hour maybe. *Fast* — roadside trees flying by in streaks and slashes. Nonstop's engine roaring, changing pitch with the changing terrain, shifting intensity as it answered Nonstop's moves, flowing in that insistent symphony of engine noise and wind shear.

He was still ghosting; everything he could see was awash in night-vision green. The white markings on the highway seemed like one continuous line, the spaces between them not even given the time to show up.

He could keep this ghost session going longer too, postpone committing between this world and the realmlines and just streak across the landscape like a howling green apparition. If there were a record for ghosting, he'd break it. If there were a record for ghosting, he'd already have it. If there were a record for ghosting, it would be named after him.

The readout display told him that the path and the road were about to part ways. He was on a steady left-ward curve, about to leave the asphalt for the grass.

He leaned, the bike banked gently, and he abandoned the road.

His tire registered the change in surface and grew toothy. He maintained his speed to keep in ghost mode, and slalomed between the thin trees with ease.

He whipped over the forest terrain and suddenly a massive tree appeared ahead of him — a classic — a twisted behemoth with limbs that were thicker than his shoulders were wide.

Don't stop.

He didn't change trajectory. He did nothing to avoid the tree or disrupt the ghost. With an electric thrum, green light swam over the rough bark and... he entered the tree. For a microsecond the green glow around him illuminated the interior of the living wood, showing the rings of its grain, and the tunnels of its burrowing insects — and then he was out again, rocketing across a bare strip of earth lined with tall grass.

The grass whipped as he passed, and the tips and edges of each blade appeared to burst apart in crazy pinwheels of molecular fireworks — a beautiful sub-orbital dance where tiny portions of grass flared and spun away in the air — changing shape and disappearing — only to reappear somewhere else in the air, following orbits not completely seen. The pebbling effect followed the bike along the entire strip of grass — a whirling mosaic of moonlit blades seen as if through textured glass. The effect weakened, returning the grass to its normal state: rooted, and merely swaying in the slipstream.

Nonstop approached a small building, a maintenance bungalow of some kind, and again, did not slow down.

He ghosted through the maintenance building the same way he ghosted through the tree, glimpsing a succession of faint details — a wall that split a pair of rooms; a desk with papers on it; a table with a coffee pot — a few stacks of foam cups. In the far room, a simple window; on the far wall, a slanted copy of the window painted in moonlight — then he sped through a closed door and was out again, across a bare-earth courtyard, and through a parked pick-up truck — jacket on the seat, candy wrapper on the dash, and then back into the woods — still ghosting, still riding the great curve.

The trees thinned out. He could detect the moonlight growing stronger ahead. Then he saw two figures through the blurring trees, a man and a woman, standing on something — a small building? A van? The man was lashing his arm up and down — whipping at something. Nonstop banked, tightening his spiral in.

He saw the problem. A ring of creatures had trapped the couple on a big construction supply — *not a building after all.* Only a few of the creatures were facing the couple directly. Most of the ugly, four-legged beasties were pacing in two circles, from opposite directions, grinding their shoulders against each other as they braided one line out of two. The creatures had glowing patches on their bodies, and where they touched, the patches grew brighter. Together, the creatures looked like a wall, solid enough to keep the people right where they were.

He could put a stop to that.

He spotted a shallow dip in the land and revved his engine. He rode into the recess and up its far wall and instantly, he was airborne — and that was it for the ghosting.

* * *

Green light twitched across Charlie's terrified face, throwing the folds of his skin into stark shadow. When he turned his head to investigate, he saw a flare, like a green comet, shoot out of the woods and across the grass. What was it? It looked like a kid — a ruffle headed teenager on a really crazy... motorcycle? — the parts were all familiar, but they didn't look like anything he had ever seen before. The kid was on the thing; outside of it; it was rolling; it had a wheel, but it looked like a hot-rod — or a robot — or, what were those things called? — a centaur.

The kid sank out of sight and then launched up into the air, grinning like crazy. At the top of the jump, the green light around him faded away, and Charlie could suddenly hear the motorcycle — loud and blatty. Something sparked in the sky too — behind the kid, a flare of smoke-light, quick and spiral-like — like a wide letter S.

In front of Charlie, the creatures broke up their circle and ran to form one large cluster. Once together, they turned to face the rider and crouched. The kid took a wide turn out into the field, though still arcing steadily toward the creatures. The kid was off his seat, leaning his chest on some kind of upside-down trapeze bar — with all his weight on his right leg and with his left leg sticking all the way out to the back end of the bike — which was some kind of long disco chamber — or light chamber. Whatever it was, it pumped out swirls of colors — some kind of line pattern too. The kid wore jeans and a black leather jacket with the sleeves rolled up. Charlie saw riding gloves — there was an electric hum coming from the bike — under the blatty noise.

Charlie saw the rear creatures rise up. The bike got closer. The front of it might have been a robot, or it might have been an engine. It had a hot-rod air scoop where the head would be. It had two arms and a black accordion-style gasket that covered whatever attached the torso to the rest of the bike. Charlie saw caging around the single big wheel — a grated foot deck the kid was standing on, with an upright bar in front of it, and an extended bar coming off the back. The robot raised its arms — collections of hydraulic tubes and shock absorbers, with curved chrome blades on the ends where fingers would be. The chrome blades waggled, glinting in the lights coming from each of the engine thing's shoulders.

The kid headed right for the creatures and they started running back in the direction they had come from. The kid zoomed closer, and then right past the concrete block where Charlie was standing — the kid was laughing.

As he passed, Charlie saw him in more detail — there were protective pads sewn into his jacket — but maybe it wasn't a leather — Charlie saw some kind of folded netting bunched around the sleeve, and the kid had a gear harness too — with pouches on it. Across his back there was a coiled rope and a sword — maybe a sword — it was in a sheath — with stitches, but the grip looked like an ordinary motorcycle handle — brake lever and all. The shell of the disco chamber looked orange — hard to tell for sure in the moonlight. It had a spoiler on the back. He saw the rear view of the thing - *it had a tail light*. The slim rods attached to the foot deck had wheels on their ends — wheelie bars — yes - like you'd see on hot-rods, and there were metal things folded under the back end of the disco chamber — add Swiss Army knife to the list of things this thing looked like. It looked like it should make sense. Seeing all the familiar pieces told his brain that everything should make sense. He turned to Rose.

Nothing made sense.

*

Laughing under the moon, Nonstop chased the creatures across the field and away from the couple. The life-forms charged up a small hill and escaped into the tree line.

Nonstop crested the hill, verted it like the top of a half-pipe, and had Rattletrap apex on one arm for a second while he stole a peek into the woods. He glimpsed the creatures, retreating along the edge of the tree line, moonlight and leaf-shadow dappling their backs as they ran. That was good enough for the moment. He slipped back down the hill and coasted toward the couple.

That had worked out. That had worked out great. The couple was safe. The team could tap the creatures. So far, so... Nonstop slowed... what? Should he have started tapping the creatures? No, he got the monsters away from the couple. He... never mind, never mind; there were things to do.

He stopped near a brush-thicket several yards away from the couple. They looked scared and confused. The guy had his arms around the woman, and her hands were locked onto the guy's upper sleeves. Nonstop could see her eyes clearly, despite the distance, so intense that he had to look away for a second.

Data-box — that's what he should be doing, working his data-box. He fumbled at the buckle of his gear harness. The woman was calling to him; the box wouldn't come free. She was saying "Can you help us? Can you help us?"... it's easy, push the box down, then in, then up. She was calling to God. Nonstop looked up and waved to her.

"It's okay. Everything's okay — just a second," he said, and the box came free. Nonstop flipped the bike into whisper mode and the loud engine noises faded down to nothing.

Questions flooded out of the woman, and the guy started in too, same questions, only louder. Nonstop gestured to the couple, requesting quiet by raising a finger into the air as he looked down at the data-box. He jabbed at its screen a few times before raising it to the side of his face and speaking into it: "Hello?... Hello? This is Nonstop. We've got Inter-Ds — a lot. They had a couple of people trapped, but I chased them off. They're in the woods. No sign of portal. Hello? Can anybody hear me? Hello Varrage?"

Near the thicket of brush behind Nonstop, two glowing eyes opened. Nonstop kept speaking, oblivious.

"Krork?"

"Skyde?"

Nonstop's teammate Varrage stepped out from the shadows. The glowing eyes belonged to him. He spoke, and his voice was clear, betraying only the slightest impatience.

"If you don't know how to use that, turn it off."

Varrage was dangerous looking — regal. His musculature was a network of black, tectonic plates, sharp as chipped obsidian. From the fissures of their seams, volcanic lights glowed. His face was grim, set within a field of raw energy, dense enough to touch — an energy that burned yellow, but gave off very little light.

Still looking at Nonstop, he spoke again.

"Krork and Skyde, are they here yet?"

*

Seeing the black lava-man-creature made Rose feel like fainting. Another nightmare element, another monster. She sank to her knees and pulled at Charlie's arm, trying to get him to crouch down with her.

"I think it's okay." Charlie said, "I think he's with the kid."

"Who says the kid is okay? Get down here."

"You want to hide?" Charlie asked as he leaned forward, his statement more an offering than a question.

"This is so weird Charlie, This is..."

It got weirder.

Another green comet shot out of the woods, twice the size of the first one, quickly revealing itself to be another vehicle, something like a motorcycle-truck.

Rose pulled at Charlie's sleeve. He lowered himself slowly. They both continued watching.

The green glow evaporated around the truck-bike, best guess, its color was some kind of yellow. There were bundles and tools tied all over it.

Rose saw two drivers, in two different parts of the truck. There was a woman, young and beautiful, standing near the middle, not afraid, noble, short white hair free in the wind, head held high, dressed in a white uniform with a white gear harness and a white half-jacket with a fur-trimmed hood. A red cross was visible on one of the woman's gear packets.

As the truck-bike coasted to a stop, Rose got the nagging sensation she had seen the movements before. The idea was fighting its way through her brain, punching its way to the top, something from childhood, not her children's lives — *her life* — *her* childhood, all those long years ago.

A gold star, a reward, a paper. Yes — the young woman's stance — she had seen it in her mind: she was seeing Selene, the Greek Goddess who pulled the Moon across the sky, who drove a chariot pulled by two winged horses. Rose had written a paper about her in grade school. This young woman looked like that somehow. This young woman who stood at the front of a space-ship motorcycle-truck, and who held onto a rail like a woman driving a chariot. The surface directly under the rail featured a series of display consoles. Instrumentation seemed to line the inside walls of the chariot as well, surrounded by cabinets and tools. The outside walls were covered with zipper-bags and knapsack-things. The outside of the walls also held the vehicle's most prominent feature — long light chambers —

pumping out colors — just like the thing on the smaller bike, only these light chambers were larger, and flatter. Under the light chambers, holding up the chariot bay, were four giant tires, smooth, two to a side, with shiny hubcaps stylized with stark cut-out designs — just like the kind young men like to waste their money on. In front of the chariot, instead of a team of horses, there was another monster-man. Rose could only see part of him. He drove what looked like half a motorcycle attached to the front of the truck — low slung — with a wide front tire that had a handle wrapped all around it. The monster-man was huge — a muscular yellow creature in a blue uniform. He had giant arms, and there was a large piece of equipment harnessed across his broad back. His pants ended at the knee, and his feet looked like a dinosaur's; so did his skin: pebbly, like an orange. That's all Rose saw of the monster-man. She never got a good look at his face, so she never noticed that he was handsome, or that his heavy brow couldn't hide his bright eyes, or that his large jaw didn't stop his easy smile.

She did notice the large steel item slung over his back — two wedges with a channel down the middle like a big letter U. Her mind imagined it a lyre — appropriate for serenading the goddess when her long rides were through.

Charlie shook his head in astonishment when Rose leapt to her feet and started waving.

*

Krork stood by his bike and gave a quick look up to Skyde. She gave him a quick nod back, then leaned over the side rail to call "What have we got?" to Nonstop and Varrage.

Varrage and Nonstop both answered: "We've got —" and then Nonstop instantly silenced himself. Varrage continued without pausing or seeming to notice: "— multiple Inter-Ds," he said. "No obvious portal location. Skyde, go high and scout. Krork," Varrage said, pointing to an area on the field. "There's a rain basin over there — a deep one — the land dips extensively. Find a spot where you can get out of sight. Nonstop, you and I will start herding the Inter-D down that dip. Krork, let them gather, and then send them home."

Krork looked at Varrage. "Right," he said, "Where are the creatures now?"

"They're re-grouping in the trees."

Nonstop turned to look back at the woods. It was true. He could see the creatures sneaking in the tree line, regrouping from several directions. Varrage had his back to the trees; how did he know?

Nonstop turned back and saw Skyde hop down from the back of the big bike and crouch to reach under its workbay. When she stood up, she was holding her skyboard. As soon as she stood, the woman on the concrete block started yelling to her: "Hello? Can you help us? Over here. Hello?"

Varrage turned to Nonstop. "Tend to her," he said.

Nonstop nodded, gave his bike some juice, and rolled away.

*

Tend to her? Nonstop thought as he trundled toward the concrete block, *how am I supposed* — then he heard the woman start yelling again: "What's going on?" she said. "Tell us what's going on. Can you help us, please?"

Nonstop nodded to her as he slowed his bike to a stop and rubbed his forehead. "Yeah, Uhm, I, yeah," he said, and then looked behind him. Varrage was walking back to the thicket where he had concealed his bike. Krork was getting back onto the big bike, and Skyde was prepping her board. "Skyde, could you come here please?" Nonstop called over.

"Sure," Skyde called back.

As she stepped onto her board, bands of aqua-colored light activated within the channels along the heels of both her boots. The broad vortex chamber of her skyboard also blinked, matching the pattern in the channels, and once the devices locked fields, Skyde lofted the board a few feet into the air. A patch of swirling light spread on the grass immediately beneath the board, fading as Skyde gained height and started flying toward Rose and Charlie.

*

Rose shivered. The young girl was flying, on a machine, but flying, again like a goddess, like a goddess who was smiling, past thousands of years, back through antiquity, and here now, coming right to her. Rose worked it in her mind, and it could only come up with one explanation. "Are you from... *the f-future?*" she asked, cringing.

A bigger smile from the young woman. An Angel, Rose could cry.

"No Ma-am," the young woman said. "I'm from Texas." She brought the board level with the concrete block. "At least originally. You folks are in the middle of an Interdimensional Bleed Zone. Not a good place for you to be." She reached for Rose's hand. "How about I get you someplace safe?"

Rose nodded and accepted Skyde's hand. *She looks like me,* Rose thought, *same wide cheekbones, same strong jaw line. Her hair is white too, just like mine.* And while she thought that, some part of her mind saw, and looked past, the streaks of pink in Skyde's hair, and the long, thin braids at back of her head; Rose continued to think: *she looks like me,* and then added: *only younger. So many years younger.*

Rose was on the board before she knew it. She didn't ask how to stand, she simply hugged the girl, and then she had to stop looking at her. She had to turn away. Her breath came in hitches and she began to sob. She wept, and she didn't know why.

*

Skyde flew Rose off into the night. They sailed past treetops in the moonlight and Skyde kept her promise. Skyde brought Rose someplace safe.

*

Back in the field, Charlie scratched his head. He had just watched his wife go flying off into the sky with a young woman on a surfboard — had watched as they rose above his head and headed off over the trees, to the point where he couldn't see them anymore. *What else was going to happen?* He turned back to the field, feeling alone, and not knowing what to do next.

The kid. The kid was still here. On his bike, watching the tree line.

"What do we do now?" Charlie asked.

23

"Skyde will be right back. She'll find someplace safe for your wife, and then she'll take you there too. Everything's good. Don't worry."

"But —"

"— I know it's crazy, but don't worry." Nonstop watched the tree line. Two creatures rubbed shoulders in passing, and then turned toward him.

"They're coming." Charlie said, pointing.

"I see them," Nonstop said, and he undocked a device from a holster on his thigh. It looked like a shovelhead. With his free hand he pulled a bar on its top, and the shovelhead split open and extended down past his knuckles, glowing with blue light along its exposed edges.

Nonstop tapped the ground with the device, held it out for a second as his arm vibrated, then aimed at the approaching creatures.

"Kill them. Are you killing them?" Charlie asked.

"Just sending them home." Nonstop answered.

"Home? What do you mean?"

The lead creature charged. Nonstop fired. A distortion wave shot out from the device and enveloped the creature in a field of blue light. The creature faded in midair as it leapt for Nonstop.

Nonstop pivoted, and shot the second creature with the same result. Then he studied the creatures he could see grouping within the tree line.

"What was that? What just happened?" Charlie asked.

"They're not from here. I'm sending them back to wherever they came from — whatever realm-world. No harm. No Foul."

"What? What —?"

Varrage's voice came over Nonstop's data-box: "Half mile. North west," the voice said, followed by silence.

Nonstop lowered his tap and looked at the tree line. He had to go, but he couldn't just leave the old guy here alone. Where was Skyde? How long would she be? He turned to look at the man on the concrete construction thing.

And there was Skyde, off in the distance above the trees, beyond the man's shoulders.

"Here she comes," Nonstop said, and the man turned in time to see Skyde gliding toward him.

The man offered a small smile to Nonstop as Skyde pulled up alongside the junction box.

"Thank you," he said.

"Sure thing." Nonstop replied as he leaned forward and re-lit Rattletrap's shoulder lights. Then the man flew off with Skyde, and Nonstop drove toward the tree line.

* * *

Nonstop wanted the creatures to run, but he wanted them to run as a group, to become a predictable mass. That achieved, he could stay back, knowing his presence would make them run forward, and that if he kept to one side, he could keep them running in the opposite direction. It was the general principle for herding animals, and it usually worked for Inter-D as well — if you could get them to run.

He left the field and entered the woods. Under the trees, it grew dark fast, and Rattletrap's shoulder lights created small, stark stages along the brush — areas of over-lit greenery and heavy shadows that changed as the bike moved, and that made the darkness outside the beams seem all the more impenetrable. The forest was around him, tall and black, with all its thousand details hidden.

Nonstop saw two creatures in the process of pushing into the brush. That was good. They were moving.

He cut his lights and looked to see if he could spot any other creatures nearby. Patches of neon swaggered to his left and to his right, bobbing behind silhouettes of leaves and thin branches. The creatures were still close, but moving away.

He swept along the border of the tree line, looked for stragglers, found none and then faced the deeper part of the woods again, waiting for the creatures to find each other. After a moment, he popped his lights back bright and got moving, pushing through bushes, vaulting over logs, ducking under the husks of broken trees, and he smiled. Even when he scraped against a tangle of brambles, and a line of thorns raked across his right forearm, he glanced it off, grinned, and kept riding.

Ahead, the creatures ran in a wide line, their glowing ribs revealing their positions as they loped through the forest. Nonstop slowed to match their speed, and was rewarded with a rising sense of rhythm. The creatures did not choreograph their movements intentionally, but they all moved at speed. Several leapt over logs at the same moment their brothers ducked under them, and the line kept moving. Nonstop thrilled for a second to be part of it. He lingered. He grooved. He ran with the pack.

Then he shot to the eastern edge of the line, and started herding the monsters west, and out of the woods.

*

The creatures exited very near where Varrage lay in ambush. Once they reached open grass, Varrage hit them with the full beam of his headlight and the un-whispered jet-sounds of his engine.

Terrified, the creatures ran. Varrage followed .

He rode a vehicle the other Bike Pilots called Viablo. Red and sleek, it featured a rear vortex chamber that split into two points like a flying V guitar. Above its wide front tire, a console emitted swirls of light, and along the rim of its hollow rear tire, something like a mini-Tesla-coil spat bolts of lightning in the places where the wheel's spokes should have been.

Keeping the creatures terrified with his screaming bike, Varrage herded the Inter-D toward the rain basin.

He slowed, and spoke into his data-box: "Krork, they're headed your way." Then he returned the data-box to his belt.

Nonstop drove out of the woods and joined him. Once the creatures flowed into the basin, Varrage stopped his bike, and returned his engine to whisper mode. Nonstop paused next to him.

"I'm going to sweep the area for any we lost," Varrage said, and Nonstop nodded.

"Don't let them run back up the hill," Varrage added as he drove away.

Nonstop had the urge to blurt out "I know, I know," but resisted it. He trundled his bike to the edge of the land dip and started down.

*

Nonstop saw the creatures pacing down in the basin's center, grinding shoulders. None of them were running back up the slopes. Sitting ducks, but where was Krork?

"Krork?" Nonstop said aloud.

Krork's bike stood on the far edge of the basin, blocking the rim, acting as a deterrent — but it was dead: no lights, no sound, no activity. If Krork were there, he'd be here, well, he'd be in sight anyway, preparing to tap the creatures, or tapping them already.

"Krork?" Nonstop said again. Then he started coasting down the hill.

"Krork. Where you at man?"

The creatures snarled at Nonstop as he approached. Halfway down the hill he turned left, hoping to keep some distance from the creatures, to skirt them, and to keep a clear path as he looked for his friend.

The creatures, for their part, kept their faces locked on him, and turned to watch him as he moved. As he passed them, they crowded each other, jostling as they watched him leave. Those at the edges were pushed out far enough to watch Nonstop directly from behind. Seeing the bike's slow departure, they began to follow. Once following, they began to hunt.

Nonstop was aware that behind him, some of the creatures were spilling away from the main group, that the shape of the crowd was changing. A quick glance verified that the creatures behind him had begun stalking him, and that if he kept at his current speed, they would overtake him. He could speed up, easy, but then it was likely that the whole group would follow him out of the basin, and then this clean-up would be an all night affair.

He was going to have to make a decision though, and he was going to have to make it right that instant.

He turned the bike sharply, accelerated down the rest of the hill, and cut through the group of milling creatures below him. Using the lingering animals to slow down his pursuers was a risky strategy. He would either wind up with a riot of confused creatures, or a sudden field of hunters, all ready to make him their prey.

As expected, the beasts he drove toward moved to avoid his bike. What Nonstop didn't anticipate is that there was no room where the creatures were trying to go; they just pressed up against their fellow creatures — and then those creatures pressed up against the creatures next to them. Everywhere Nonstop turned, creatures spilled out in front of his bike. He had succeeded in creating confusion. Now he was getting stuck in it.

One of the creatures leapt at him. He dodged the strike, but the move lined him up with a second creature standing behind him, who also leapt, and who did not miss.

The creature slammed Nonstop into his steering bar, ramming its head into his back as its jaws worked furiously against the rope in Nonstop's gear harness.

Nonstop twisted. The bike shifted. The creature stayed in place. He aimed his tap behind him, but the creature shouldered the tap aside. He tried again, and the creature shook him. He snarled himself, growling "Mountain" over and over as he tried to improve his shot.

The creature freed its teeth from the rope and pushed its legs down on Nonstop's shoulders. Its breath smelled like low tide at the beach and it fogged Nonstop's neck, but through it, Nonstop could sense the position of the monster's head. He jammed his tap under his own jaw, slipping his neck deep into the open channel, and fired the device full blast.

A blue glow enveloped the creature. It turned to run, already fading. By the time its feet left Nonstop's shoulders, it was gone.

Nonstop, unhurt, shook his head.

He was surrounded. The creatures stepped closer, their eyes spasming with x-ray light. The light made it hard for Nonstop to focus on any one creature for very long. *Which should he tap? Which was about to strike?* He could shoot one or two, but what if that didn't scatter the rest?

He fired at the creature approaching his right knee. As he did, he heard the roar of Varrage's bike behind him, and even *he* shrank back at the sound. He turned as Varrage's bike, its lights shining full, came speeding down the hill.

*

Varrage kept his headlights fixed on the startled creatures, causing them to panic. Keeping the light on them, Varrage sent his entire machine drifting sideways across a bare patch of dirt at the bottom of the hill, spraying up arcs of dust and small stones. The stones hit the creatures. They hit Nonstop too.

*

The monsters ran. Nonstop coughed, grimacing, waving his arms to disperse the dirt that floated in the air. When he opened his eyes, he saw Varrage standing off his bike seat, firing at the creatures as they ran from the scene.

Nonstop fired too. Still coughing.

"I told you to hold the perimeter. Where's Krork?" Varrage said.

Cough. Cough. "He's not here." Cough. Spit. "I was crossing the dip to go look for him."

Varrage lowered his tap to his side and watched as the last creatures ascended the hill, marking their position. Then slowly, he began looking across the landscape. He raised his free hand and made subtle finger moves as he analyzed where Krork would have hidden, and where an attacker would have found a weakness. He pointed.

"That rise. Behind those bushes."

Varrage got Viablo rolling again. "Go see if you can spot him. I don't want the creatures getting too far. Next time call me if you change a plan."

"I had to help Krork."

"You can't help him if you're dead." Varrage said, and then drove off.

"Dead? How are they going to..." But Nonstop didn't finish. Varrage was gone.

*

Nonstop drove toward the bushes on the far side of the hill. He thought of Krork and grinned, happy to know where his friend was, and anxious to see him.

But as he drove, he saw no sign of Krork, and Krork wasn't supposed to be hiding. His mind showed him an image of his big yellow friend, dead on the ground and bleeding. He clamped his teeth together and sped toward the bushes, wide-eyed as he rounded them.

And there was Krork — standing, and Nonstop's eyes widened even more.

Krork was struggling in the grips of a huge pile of what looked like macaroni and cheese — some huge, tentacled creature, and while Krork wasn't having any fun, he wasn't dead. Nonstop smiled enormously.

"Euuuuuuuiiii" he said, stepping off his bike.

Krork worked to get free. With every tentacle he pushed away, a new one calmly wrapped around him. At some point Krork would become exhausted, and who knew what would happen then.

Slurking noises slipped and slopped as the tentacles moved over each other. Nonstop could see patches of white lather foaming in several spots where the tentacles touched — and something was odd about the way the tentacles moved; they didn't seem to curl as much as they seemed to *spill* into place. *Fish.* Nonstop thought. *They look like eyeless fish. Like a whole bunch of eyeless fish spilling out of a cargo hold. Like* — Nonstop cocked his tap and raised it at the creature.

Krork's eyes went wide, and he struggled to move a tentacle from his neck. "Don't shoot." He said, as the tentacle returned, and he had to pull again. "I... I don't belong here either."

Nonstop lowered his tap and took a step forward. "Well then brother, de-gloppify thyself," he said, leaning forward, and grinning.

"I'm... trying." Krork answered, not grinning.

Nonstop reached over his shoulder and pulled his sword from its sheath. The sword was a handcrafted oddity made of a motorcycle handle, a fused brake lever, and a long, whittled length of bone. He hunched over and took a step, holding the sword out in front of him cautiously. Krork's eyes went wide again.

"What... are you going to... do with that?"

Nonstop peered at a specific spot on the creature, and leaned in.

"I'm going to poke it," he said.

He did.

The monster tossed Krork aside, and snatched Nonstop up from the ground. Krork tumbled, and then lunged for the spot where his tap lay in the grass.

The creature lifted Nonstop, squeezing its coils around him, and suddenly Nonstop could do no more than inhale shallowly.

As he was carried through the air, he saw Krork fire into the creature, but he saw no resulting effect, just the distortion waves pumping into the moving coils of the creature's body. The creature turned Nonstop, and Nonstop lost sight of Krork altogether.

Coils slid upward over Nonstop's chest, rising and wrapping over his head, wet, sticky. He gagged; the slime on the creature tasted like garbage. He couldn't see. He could feel his feet go higher than his head as his body tilted — then sped up — and then he was tossed, thirty feet through the air, right between the bushes and Rattletrap.

*

Krork heard Nonstop's diminishing "AAAAAAAAAAAAAH" loft through the air and rolled his eyes. Impact diffusion would save Nonstop from the crash, but what would save him from himself?

Krork stepped back and continued firing. With so much mass to move, getting rid of the creature might take a while.

*

Nonstop hit the grass like a skier paying for a bad jump on the Matterhorn, pinwheeling in successions of blurring hands and feet, bouncing and rolling until he finally came to a stop. As quickly as he could, he righted himself onto his hands and knees, spitting to clear his mouth of tentacle slime. Thoroughly disgusted, he looked back up the hill — instantly perplexed and astonished by what he saw: Krork, busy tapping back the creature, with the creature starting to glow blue — and at the same time, he saw Krork up close, looking up at him and firing — seen from the creature's point of view.

The close-up image of Krork started to fade, replaced by two algae-covered boulders shining in a flare of sunlight. Nonstop saw that the boulders stood by a shore of lapping water in an open plain with a far-off line of trees — it was a pond, or an oasis — he saw a pale green sky... and then nothing, just Krork up on the hill. Had he seen the creature's home-world as it had arrived home? Yes, he thought, for an instant; that was exactly what he had seen.

He lowered his head and spat with new vigor.

*

Krork slipped his tap into the dock on his back as he bounded down the hill, giving a thumbs-up with each hand.

"Excellent plan." He said loudly.

Nonstop looked up and then returned his gaze to the floor, shaking his head.

"How'd it get you? Couldn't you talk to it?" Nonstop asked.

"It didn't have a language."

"It had some kind of telepathy-juice." Nonstop said as he crawled forward an inch and then collapsed onto his back.

Krork laced the fingers of his left hand around both of Nonstop's ankles and lifted him, stopping when they were speaking face to face.

"Yes," Krork said, smiling enormously, "It had some kind of telepathy secretion. Very impressive." Then, he stood to his full height. "I looked... *remarkable*," he said with his chest expanded, swinging Nonstop with every new syllable, "Distressed, yet rugged. A brave explorer, bravely braving the perils of a wretched and dangerous world."

"Hey. Hey. Put me down," Nonstop said, "And watch it. That's my wretched world you're talking about."

Krork looked at Nonstop as if he had forgotten he was dangling him in the air. Then he dropped Nonstop into a heap and asked: "So where are the creatures?"

Nonstop stood, brushing himself off, "What are you trying to do? Rip my knees out of their sockets?" he muttered.

"Your knees don't have sockets."

"Oh. Well pardon me, I just..."

"Seriously, where are the creatures?"

"They're eating Varrage. Or maybe Varrage is eating them."

"More of this? Nonstop. What's up?"

"What? Nothing."

"I can hear it. What's wrong?"

Nonstop considered for a moment, facing out into the night and squinting. "I don't know. Nothing — everything. I... I just wish things could be like they were. I hate this."

"Things are different. We have to be different too."

"How much more different do I have to be? Aren't we different enough already?"

"Pick up your tap. You can whine while we hunt."

"Hunt? You don't think Mr. Perfect already tapped —"

A stampede of creatures charged over the hill.

Nonstop and Krork, eyes wide, fumbled for their taps and started firing.

* * *

**

Skyde sailed her board along the treetops, skimming a few feet above the crowns, hugging close to the leaves in an effort to stay out of sight.

A few quick trips to higher air had given her a wider view of the area, but no hints of portal light, just trees and fields and roads. The readings on her data-box showed no particular strong point to suggest an epicenter in the haze levels — which probably meant that nothing new was being pulled through the portal, wherever it was. Good news in a way, but it meant there'd be no quick help from the device. She'd have to locate the portal on her own.

Considering that the portal light might be blocked by trees, she decided to fly over the denser collections of forest and look for any glimmers escaping through the layers of stacked leaves. Twenty minutes of flying on her skyboard should have been fun, and would have been if it weren't for the pressing tension she felt. She wanted results, and so far, she had none.

She skimmed forest-patch after forest-patch until finally, she saw a hint of light below her board and swooped down to investigate.

The light pulsed low within a stand of dark elms, shining across their trunks in pools of soft, pearlescent blue.

Skyde checked her data-box readings: brightness in the haze directly in front of her, dark eddies in the haze behind her. She tapped the com-link icon and called the team. "This is Skyde, 4 N, 17 E, off original position, I have Grandma. I'm going in to check. How're you guys doing?"

Krork answered with a "Hello," but his voice trailed off, replaced by engine roars and thumps. She heard Nonstop asking: "Where? Where?" and she heard Krork answer: "No. There!" and then she heard more thumps, and more engines, and then the screeches of creatures, Nonstop whooping, and then Nonstop laughing: "Look. I got him," and then Varrage's voice, loud, asking: "What are you doing?" and then more thumps, and more laughing.

Skyde rolled her eyes, traded her data-box for her tap, and flew into the tree line.

She was alone in the small forest. Ahead of her, amid hundreds of trees, a light flickered, small from distance, beating and pumping like a secret heart.

She approached, and darkness fell away. The trees around her stood vivid. Their rough textures pronounced by the strong pulsing light; their colors given lie to, transformed by the witch-light into iridescent blues and lavenders. Skyde stood among them, hovering on her board, likewise transformed by the unnatural light.

She stood, on a night in June, above a portion of American forest where in all the centuries of time that had ever been, no human dwelling had ever been constructed. She was one of few humans who had ever actually seen a portal to another dimension. She was looking at one now, and all that was on her mind was the speed with which she could close it. If that saddened her, and to a degree, it did, she swallowed it, to join all the other sadnesses she had swallowed in her young life.

The portal was mild. A steady, disk-shaped wall of light, maybe twelve feet tall. There were no major tendrils or branching capillaries, and no matter how Skyde shifted her view, she could see no coning. No weak spots, no strong spots. It was as run of the mill as you could get. Skyde raised her tap, and had the portal closed within minutes.

She checked the screen on her data-box. The percentage counter read zero. No Haze. No creatures. No infection. The Bleed Zone was closed. She could get back to the team, and they could set about leaving.

A sly smile emerged from the tiny motions of her lips. She had come miles from the team; she had accomplished her mission. There was no rule that said flying back had to be dreary.

She burst out of the tree stand at speed, closed her eyes as the wind hit her, and lifted. In a second, she opened her eyes and picked a target: old growth maples, spaced enough to let the moon in, twisted enough to spice some full-out torrent.

She slalomed in, weaving between tree trunks, stitching over low hanging branches, seeing moss, and ferns, and grass, smelling pine, whipping through the wind like a traveling lightning strike — *fast as fury* — enjoying, for every moment she could allow, the freedom that she loved.

As she burst from the maples, she saw something in the distance, between the stands of trees, and raised higher, slowing, then hovering to get a better look.

Trouble.

A squadron of Helicopters — Army — two flanking single-engine Kiowas and three large, double-rotored monsters — Chinooks in dark paint. They were approaching rapidly, sweeping searchlights across the ground. *Looking for us.* She thought. *Heading for the Bleed Zone.*

If she hurried, she could beat them to the team.

* * *

Nonstop, Krork, and Varrage stood near their bikes not far from the concrete junction boxes where Rose and Charlie had made their stand. Varrage swept his data-box at arm's length across the area, scanning for signs of other-dimensional elements. Krork, a few feet away, did the same. Nonstop, several feet away, also held out his data-box, and also swept it back and forth.

Varrage shook his head. "No haze. Skyde must have the portal closed," he said. Krork nodded in agreement. Nonstop nodded in agreement as well, glancing back and forth between his data-box, and his two teammates. Then Skyde's voice came over Varrage's device.

"Varrage. They're here," she said. "Three Chinooks and two support copters."

"The haze readings say —"

"— yes, we're done. I'm all set."

Varrage looked up at Nonstop and Krork. "All right. If Bloch's teams are here, then we have to leave."

"They're here already?" Nonstop said, turning to Krork. "That's crazy. *We* just got here."

Krork shrugged. Nonstop leaned closer to him.

"We've got to get these guys to knock it off. We have to change this."

"I don't know," Krork said, "So far, so good. Doc needs time. A stalemate is better than a defeat."

"But —" Nonstop said, and Krork raised a hand to quiet him. Skyde was talking over the com-link, and they were missing what she was saying.

"— Don't worry. I'll be there in a minute," they heard her voice say, "I have to help the couple."

"No." Varrage said, "We don't have time for that. Come re-dock your board. We have to go."

"I can't leave the couple where they are. I'll be right back. I promise." And with that, Skyde broke contact, and Varrage's data-box went silent.

Varrage tapped the screen twice and then re-docked the unit on his belt. He adjusted his gear harness slightly and traced his hand along the length of pipe strapped across his back.

"Come on," Krork said, waving to Nonstop, "let's get the bikes ready," and as he finished speaking, he turned and walked toward his machine.

Nonstop did not watch him go, did not watch anything. He simply looked out at the air and shook his head. After a moment, he tried to turn off his data-box, which was still stuck in com-link mode, nowhere near its haze-hunting mode. He tried to clip it in its dock backwards, so no one would see the light of its screen, but then wound up just clipping it into its dock, lit as it was.

As Varrage and Krork neared their respective bikes, Nonstop sat down in the grass near his. He let his back fall into the grass and breathed. He caught sight of a star that was peeking through the clouds.

* * *

Charlie and Rose huddled on the roof of the maintenance building where Skyde had dropped them off. They had spent the last half hour anxiously fighting its mild slope, propped near its chimney, and jumping at every twig-snap that announced itself in the woods.

Rose spotted Skyde flying just above the trees. She pointed. She stood shakily on the uneven roof, and Charlie joined her. Rose beamed.

As Skyde eased down, Rose peered at her.

"Selene?" Rose asked, "Would your name happen to be Selene?"

Skyde smiled. "Cynthia." She held out her hand. "Let's get you down."

"Is it over?" Rose asked.

"Yes. It is," Skyde said.

Rose took a few trembling steps onto the board, and then Skyde gestured for Charlie to come too.

"You can both come. We're just going to the ground."

Rose tensed. "You can't take us out of here?"

"I have to leave." Skyde guided Rose to the board. "Things are back to normal; you can walk over to your car." She ushered Charlie onto the board as well and spoke to both of them. "Listen, the Army is here. They're going to see your car, and they're going to want to talk to you. That's fine, but whatever you do, don't tell them we helped you — tell them you hid from us — that you thought we were monsters too. Any lie they tell you about us, you just nod your head and pretend to believe."

"What? I don't..." Charlie said.

"I mean it." Skyde said. "If you talk to them at all, just pretend that you're helpless civilians desperate to get rescued — unless you want to spend the next six months in an interrogation center."

"What?" Charlie asked.

"It'll be easy," Skyde said as they floated to the ground, "Just don't mention us. Play it that you're two frightened civilians; that you were scared by weird creatures, scared by crazy glowing motorcycles, and while you're at it, play it that you're scared of big army-guns and helicopters too."

"I am scared of big army-guns and helicopters," Rose said as they touched down. Skyde helped them off the board.

"You'll be all right," she said. "They're not really interested in you. Show them you're no threat and they'll push you away." Rose nodded. Charlie looked around.

"I'm sorry I can't take you further. Your car is a little over a mile that way." Skyde pointed to her left.

Rose looked into Skyde's eyes, and then squeezed Skyde's forearm. "Thank you young lady," she said as she stepped off the board.

Yes. Thank you," Charlie added. "It's really over? We're safe to go?"

"Yes. That's our job. You're safe." Skyde lingered, sensing there was something the older woman wanted to say.

Skyde hovered on the board. Rose shook her head. "We're being selfish."

"— The car —" Charlie started.

"— One second Love," Rose said, holding up a hand to quiet him, and then placing her hands on Skyde's arm, pressing gently. "You be safe too."

The two women smiled at each other, and Skyde flew away.

Charlie looked at Rose, confused.

"I don't think I want to go back to the car. I don't want to talk to the Army," Rose said.

Charlie watched Skyde: a white brushstroke sinking into the night's dark oil. He turned to Rose, who was also watching the young woman fly away.

"Rose honey, maybe we should just stay here until morning. The car's upside down. We 'll need a tow. If we go back now, we'll have to talk to the Army for sure; to ask for help if nothing else."

"I don't want to talk to them tonight," Rose said, still watching the sky, which now showed only the tips of trees.

Charlie sighed. "They're going to see the car. The license plates. The vin number. We're going to have to talk to them."

"Maybe," Rose said. "But not tonight. Let them find us."

"If we stay here, they'll find us tonight. There's a pick-up parked over there. We could see if the keys are in it." Charlie pointed toward the parked truck.

"No."

"No? What? Why not? What are you thinking?"

"I want to walk."

"Walk?" Charlie asked, "Walk? But —"

Rose pointed at the truck. "Look, it's on a dirt path. That has to lead to a road somewhere, right? I mean, someone drove it in here." She took a step. Charlie followed.

"If the Army finds us..."

"Then we'll know just how to play it." Rose looked up and smiled. Charlie looked at her, still wondering what she was thinking. Rose spoke.

"I saw Selene tonight. I want to walk in the moonlight."

"Her name was Cynthia," Charlie said, "and it's probably a good two hour walk to the nearest town."

She took his hand. "That sounds perfect."

They stepped onto the dirt road, walking under the trees, below the bright round moon.

* * *

The black Chinooks flew under heavy modification. Bands of gray equipment lockers ran along their sides, parallel to external fuel tanks. They bore few identifying marks other than the white unit numbers on their tail fins.

The copters formed a circle over a level section of field about a quarter mile east of where the ground turned hilly. They descended, landing in one unified movement.

In the hold of Copter One, soldiers moved into position, jostling shoulder to shoulder near the rear door. They wore non-standard uniforms, black, like their copter, and like their copter, their gear was heavily modified. The front halves of their helmets bore varied sensor arrays. Small red lights flashed in the corners of their visors.

The copter rocked as it settled, shaking the men. Without speaking, each raised his hand to his helmet and activated a small search-beam, throwing light and overlapping shadows onto the rear rampway door. Holding steady on the shaking floor, the men raised their rifles to their chests, and waited as the copter's hydraulics began bellowing. After a moment, the ramp-way lowered and the soldiers fanned into the field, sweeping the grass with their helmet-lights and hunting for the depressions tires would have made.

Above their heads, along the tree line, Skyde rocketed past them.

* * *

Skyde slid her board into the dock on the underside of Krork's bike. "I'm good. Let's go," she said as she stepped up into the workbay and walked toward the handrail at the bike's front.

Varrage drove toward a level portion of field. As he sped up, the air around him began to ripple; the ripples threw off colored bursts of light that stretched and coiled, trailing the bike like helixical phantoms. An electric arc of white plasma tore itself along the ground in front of his machine. Brilliant, the plasma arc rippled higher, until it rose above the bike, anchored on either side of the moving front wheel, jaggling erratically and continuing to grow. The effects intensified as Varrage drove forward. The electric arc expanded to a gateway that stayed a constant distance in front of the bike. The bike surged. Then the bike and the arc faded, disappearing as they drove beyond the Earth.

Tiny realm lights jumped and floated from under Nonstop's hair. He noticed them, and then tried to wave them away with his hands.

Krork powered up his bike and followed Varrage.

Realm-effects streaked around Krork's bike, surrounding him and Skyde. An Arc appeared, and they ghosted out.

* * *

**

Nonstop prepared to follow, and an urge rose in him that he couldn't define. This all seemed so stupid. Like pretend. He thought of the soldiers. *My age,* he thought, *those guys are my age.*

He looked around him. Deep in the woods to the east, he saw advancing lights, sweeping from side to side, eerie, and for the moment, silent. The soldiers were coming. He could leave though; he still had time to escape.

He started driving. He looked into the woods once more, and decided to take a chance.

He veered off the straight-away, drove back into the tree line and concealed himself behind a crazy overgrowth of brush. He'd play it out and see. *They're just people. They're my age.*

The soldiers took the field, all business. They fanned out in teams, and then those teams fanned out. Nonstop saw one soldier study the ground, searching for tire tracks, searching for whatever clue would lead him to Nonstop's bike.

Soldiers grouped at the strip of ground Krork and Varrage had just used to ghost out. They measured the strip of pressed grass. They photographed it, filmed it, and ran scanners over it. Other soldiers created a defensive perimeter, aiming rifles at the tree line, while dozens of scattered soldiers still searched the field.

One soldier reached the grass Nonstop's tire had just pressed. The soldier turned his head to sweep his helmet-light to the tree line and back, and then down the straight-away to the conferencing soldiers. Nonstop watched him. The soldier bent to study the grass again, rose, and returned to the junction point, bending to study the grass in the spot where Nonstop had turned the bike. *It'll be bent the other way.* Nonstop thought, and a chill came over him. *This was it then.*

The soldier walked the curved path toward the tree line near Nonstop. He walked slowly, his rifle held loosely, its muzzle pointed at the ground.

Nonstop watched the soldier enter the darkness of the tree line and stop. He saw him sweep his search beam at points along the ground and in the surrounding brush. There was no longer pressed grass to follow. There was no easy trail. Nonstop felt a twinge of something then, excitement? Fear? He would later flatter himself with mild wonder that it might have been doubt. In any case, he stepped to an open spot near a stand of thin birch and called quietly to the soldier.

"Hey my man. Over here."

The soldier whipped to face Nonstop, raising his hand to the radio-set on his helmet.

"Alpha-5. Contact. Sector twelve." He said into his helmet's mouthpiece. He then spoke to Nonstop directly, pointing his rifle at Nonstop's chest. "Give me your bike. Where is it?"

The soldier's helmet-light hit Nonstop, and Nonstop couldn't see much more than a vague impression of the soldier's gun, and a hint of the little red light on the soldier's visor. This had seemed easier in his mind. The words he wanted to say tangled, the end of his sentence jumped over to the beginning, and speaking at all seemed impossible.

"Yo... Hi..." Nonstop started, then the words came easier. "What are you guys doing? You're the Army, right? The U.S Army? Aren't you the good guys? What did we ever do that you're coming so hard after us? Come on man, talk to me."

The soldier didn't move, didn't lower his weapon, if he blinked under his visor, Nonstop couldn't see it. The soldier simply said: "Give me the bike, or I'll shoot you."

Nonstop grimaced. He had gotten exactly nowhere.

"Come on man; don't let it be like this."

The soldier fired; a solid burst headed straight for Nonstop's chest. The bullets never got there.

An inch before they slammed into Nonstop, they disappeared into shears of white light that jetted erratically around Nonstop's body.

The streaks faded quickly, as Nonstop ran back toward Rattletrap.

The soldier continued shooting, and the bullets continued running trace lines around Nonstop, creating streaks and whirls of displaced energy that were beginning to interfere with Nonstop's motions. He was getting tangled up. Running felt wacky, like he was pushing against the force lines of a gyroscope.

He had to reach Rattletrap before the bullets caught it unprotected.

A bullet sparked off Rattletrap's rear spoiler.

Nonstop stretched his hand to the end of the bike. He leap-frogged over its vortex chamber. His feet landed on the floor grates, and he fell roughly into his seat. He lit the bike. The engine screamed —*RRRRRRRRAAAAAAAARRRRRRRRRRRR* — as Rattletrap jungle-catted deeper into the woods. The soldier continued firing. The bullets streaked around Nonstop and his bike.

Nonstop looked over the dark portion of forest, searching. The stand of trees had to come out somewhere, he'd find some open ground, hit ghosting speed, and get gone.

In the woods, Rattletrap's shoulder lights gave only an instant's warning of the rough terrain. Nonstop crashed the bike through brush, hopped over boulders, and fought to keep his progress steady. Seconds later he saw the glow of moonlight through the trees — *open ground*. He pushed his engine. He had only to reach eighty-eight and he could put all this behind him.

*

And with that, he was out of the woods — night sky —open field — *there* — grass, guardrail — *go*.

Nonstop grabbed speed, the digital readout on Rattletrap's back rose to seventy five. He leaned left — then from somewhere unseen came the enormous sounds of hard-working turbines, coming from...

— Over the treetops. Nonstop spotted a team of two small craft — completely unfamiliar, and very fast. First glance told that they were single man V.T.O.Ls — vertical take off and landing rigs — quads — a barrel-like turbine on each corner, a pilot centered between them on some kind of saddle, and lots of light-weight equipment bolted everywhere. They were flying fast. He hadn't lost the soldiers in the woods; they knew exactly where he was and they were coming for him.

Rattletrap's speed display read 76, 79, 81...

Both V-TOLs powered up vertical light arrays mounted near their handlebars and shot broad patches of bright light on the ground. The nearer machine flooded the grass with a turquoise-colored light. The machine behind it fired a neon-green array.

The machines arced over Nonstop, jockeying along on either side of him, trying to catch him full within the light projections.

Unheard by Nonstop, the pilot to his left reported over his headset that there was zero atmospheric interference, and that he was continuing with stage one.

The pilot banked, caught Nonstop's leg in his light field and then lost him again. The VTOL dipped, and caught Nonstop square in the center of the moving patch of light, instantly firing a prolonged burst of machine-gun fire at Nonstop's back. The bullets thumped over him in familiar white-hot streaks.

"No effect on shielding. Moving on to Stage Two," the pilot reported. Then he swung back, and let the second V-TOL take position.

*

Nonstop drove, scared, and cursing himself for giving the Army the chance to try out new weapons on him. He tried to outrace the second V-TOL. He couldn't get any speed on the choppy ground. Every successful move that kept him out of the light-fields lost him speed and drove him further away from the open road. Every time he got caught in the patch of light, it seemed easier for the pilot to catch him again: first a foot, then an elbow, then the back end of the bike. *Get back into the trees then. Move.*

He veered toward the tree line, but the rig with the green light array had anticipated his move, and caught him pure in the patch of light. A second burst of machine gun fire hammered between Nonstop's shoulder blades. Still unhurt, he made it into the trees. He cut a rough diagonal and looked for a spot where there might be enough open ground to hit eighty-eight.

He spotted a clearing through the trees to his right, overshot it, then doubled back, hoping to throw off pursuit.

He hit the open field, increased his speed, and then almost cried aloud. Four V.T.O.L. swung around the tree line at the other end of the field, coming fast, right for him. *Okay. The field is big. Hit eighty-eight.*

The lead V-TOL slashed across the meadow toward him and fired a length of spiked chain across his path, well-placed to rip his tire to shreds. *This is crazy. This is crazy.*

Nonstop made Rattletrap slap the ground and the bike vaulted over the rip strip with a mid-air side-roll. As soon as he hit the ground again, Nonstop was caught in a moving square of intense rose-magenta light.

And this time he felt something.

Queasiness. A funny buzzing in his head and in his skin — and then the thorn scratches on his forearm split wide open and blood began to overspill the wounds. Bullets hit him, but they didn't reach him. *Get out of this!* his mind screamed as his nose erupted, and his blood flowed warmly over his lips. The taste invaded him, and suddenly no machine could move as fast as he wanted to go. *Don't let them get the bike. You can't let them get the bike.*

Nonstop slammed Rattletrap's right drive-claw into the dirt, tearing long furrows in the sod as he forced a direction-shift and shot back under the firing V.T.O.L..

Two craft, flying tandem, linked by a pivoting midsection, dipped lower to the ground. Four missiles fired from a launch pod suspended between the two pilots. The missiles separated as they flew, and a net extended between them.

Nonstop saw the missiles rocket across the field, and slammed his shoulder down into the ground, eating dirt to duck under the missiles. Rattletrap continued driving, cutting with the side of its wheel, grinding Nonstop's shoulder and face into the ground as an axis to pivot on. The missiles raced over Nonstop and lofted into the air, veering around to try again.

Nonstop spun himself upright. He drove.

Across the field by the silhouetted tree line, the V-TOLs approached in a tight formation, covering the grass with swaths of the rose colored light — the same thrumming rose-magenta light that had made his nose gush blood. *Move, flyboy move; you should be out of here already.*

The netted missiles re-locked on him, and crossed the field at a speed much greater than his. *No time. A second.*

Nonstop lateralled, and ran the outer ridge of the tree line. The missiles adjusted; he could hear them closing in. He slipped left into the tree line with the missiles behind him. The missiles' net instantly tangled around a birch sapling — *there, done* — but the missiles themselves slammed into the neighboring trees — shattering to pieces, freeing their burning fuel cores to chase Nonstop with erratic fire-balls of shrapnel that banshee-wailed in twisting flights of smoke and flame. Nonstop raced through the forest until the motorcycle and the burning steel all shot out through the other side of the tree line together. He twisted down to the ground, and the missile remnants rocketed past him to die in the grass. As his eyes followed them, he caught sight of a guardrail atop a small hill. Before he could form a thought, the team of V-TOLs arced over the stand of trees.

Get that road...

78, 81...

Nonstop took the embankment and vaulted over the rail, jolting back onto the asphalt — back down to 75. The V.T.O.L.s drew closer behind him — but he was back on hard ground, the road ahead as straight and black as the barrel of a gun.

Seeing his speed, detecting his inevitable escape, the soldiers fired at him all-out, light fields or not. He hit eighty-eight. He pressed a square button on his control bar and the fabric of the world opened.

An arc of lightning bid him come...

* * *

**

Done! Gone! Free! Suddenly flying through the realmlines at heart-leaping speed, his bike forcing gaps between systems of realities, between disparate continuums, creating spaces that weren't supposed to exist at all, propelled by the weight of neighboring existences like a wet bar of soap speeding through a squeezing hand.

The arc of lightning he followed closed to a ring and faded into the streaking blurs of color that surrounded him. If he knew of gravitons, or brane theory, he might have made comparisons, instead, he paid attention to the decontamination wave that flared over him, momentarily brightening the energy envelope that rippled around his bike.

He banked, smiling, and thrummed across a thousand mile expanse, faster than any jet, arcing happily across the enormous pocket of red, and black, and beautiful.

He swooped, barrel-rolled, and arced-back as the color around him changed, stretching beyond his sight, trailing to a distance beyond perception. No soldiers, no danger, no jobs undone, just the mighty realmlines: the most open of open roads.

Soothed, yet not sated, he checked his instruments and steered, paying loose attention to Rattletrap's main display, and drove on. The display showed a graphic representation of the realmlines, and off to the side, a series of digital rings bouncing in and out of a concentric alignment. The game was to keep the rings in at least a rough balance while he was free-riding; they would zero in on their own if he gave them half a chance, but where was the fun in that?

He rose over a wide vault of blue, and leapt in a lazy 360, enjoying a long free-fall — banking until the surrounding orange and pink zebra-striping could catch up to his wheel and ride under it. He allowed the bike to slow, and the striated bands began to darken, black against vivid greens and blues. He slowed even more, and the rings on his display slid into even alignment. The black striations around him widened and grew high above his head. Within them, on either side of him, razor thin gray lines began expanding into dim, compressed images of moving trees that flew by Nonstop as fast as he was driving, and continued expanding, growing upright, moving closer, rising and rising until...

* * *

... He was ghosting on a roadway: an empty two-lane at the base of the Rocky Mountains, streaking through the night like a drunken warlock's miscast spell.

He had to slow down to stay on the road, but he didn't want to lose the fluid speed of ghosting. His skill allowed for prolonged entries. He could stay in ghost mode, riding the edge between committing to a world, and not being there at all.

But finally he did enter, and the joys of the world flooded over him. Colors became vivid; the moon painted the mountains in sapphire blues and stark whites. The wind shot over his face and shoulders, noisy and cool. His ears filled from the elevation of the mountain road, and above all, he could taste the brisk air with its perfume of hill-forest pines. From ghost to coast, all smiles.

Cruising at highway speed, he pulled a tool rag from his gear harness, examined it for cleanliness, cringed at its blotchy nature, and wiped his nose and arms as free of blood as he could. After a few moments he could see lights in the road far ahead of him: a small gas station with a mini mart, still open for business. He neared it, pulled in along the dark road shoulder, and slipped into the grass of an open field.

Varrage and Krork waited for him there, where it was dark and they could stay out of sight.

"I could see you coming for miles." Varrage said.

Nonstop coasted in, "We're in the middle of nowhere. The army is ten states from here," he said, stopping his bike.

"This is Earth. You're a fugitive. Act like you realize it." Varrage turned away and watched the scene in the mini-mart. Through the gaps between the paper signs taped to the windows, several people, their heads and shoulders bobbing up and down, could be seen as they walked toward the front entrance. The front door, clear glass, opened, and Skyde stepped out. She turned with the door still opened, and smiled at the small crowd following her: the check-out boy, the night manager, the stock clerk, all bobbling and bumping as they crashed together in the doorway, each holding plastic bags full of Skyde's purchases.

Skyde smiled broadly as she collected the bags, and thanked the workers, each of them returning her smile, nodding exuberantly while talking over each other. The manager, too old for such things, slicked his hair back with a few swipes of his palm.

"And you're worried about them noticing me?" Nonstop said, a tiny point of realm-light floating out from under his hair.

"Even this will have to end." Varrage said.

Krork looked over to him, and then back to Skyde.

"Morale has its place." Krork said.

"Yes it does." Varrage stated, "It's after survival."

Skyde stepped off the edge of the parking lot and onto the grass, a dozen or more white plastic bags hanging off each wrist. She carried them to the back of Krork's bike. Nonstop made a point of catching her eye as she stepped into the workbay. He smiled. "We make the papers? Anything good?"

Skyde laid the bags down on the floor. She nudged them with her foot, and hooked their handle loops over cabinet latches. When she looked up, she didn't look happy. "Nothing good," she said, "They say that the military is in Marin County because they've uncovered a terrorist cell."

"That's Bloch." Varrage said. "If the Newspapers are calling us terrorists, it can only mean Colonel Bloch wants them to."

Skyde didn't look at Varrage. Instead, she stared out at the night. "This is just going to go on and on. We're not going to get any peace from him are we?"

"No," Varrage said. Then he revved his bike, leaned, and started driving.

"But..." Skyde said, as she watched Varrage reach the road and continue on. She looked at Krork. "What are we going to do about Bloch? Just keep running from him?"

"For a little while, maybe. Yeah. Until Doc gets things worked out. We're lucky. We're bulletproof right? At least Bloch can't hurt us."

Nonstop blinked. He turned to his friend, changing his grip on the bike's control bar to aim his recently bleeding forearms toward the floor. He started to speak, but then revved his bike to cover any noise his throat might have made.

"A terrorist cell," Skyde said, looking down at her feet, where a white plastic bag drooped. She nudged the bag back upright with the toe of her boot. "Something else for Dr. Norel to worry about."

Krork rolled his bike out to follow Varrage, watching to see that Nonstop was rolling too, and then turned to look back up at Skyde. "We did good work tonight," Krork said, "We can feel good about that." He looked ahead again. "Things could have gotten hairy, but you got us that warning. We can feel good about that too."

Nonstop looked at the trees as Krork gave his cheerful assessment, and didn't look at either of his friends as they reached the road.

"I'd say," Krork continued, smiling big, then smiling enormously, "We could take a long way home. Sample some worlds for Doc's charts. You know he'd like *that*; and if we find some place open and easy, we might like it too - get this taste out of our mouths."

He turned to Nonstop, "What say we motor, brother-man?" And with that, he revved, and ate up the road in earnest.

Nonstop followed. Driving, he felt better. He let his engine sound — in the middle, not silent and not screaming, just enough to monitor, maybe a little more, and he sped ahead of Krork. After a moment, their bikes caught up to Varrage's. Then Nonstop pulled ahead, reached eighty eight, and rode point for the team as they ghosted.

*

Within the realmlines, energy folds streaked around them, beat-boxing in waves and pulses of leaping colors. Nonstop, thrilled immediately, felt relief wash over him. This was familiar. This was excitement without threat. He stole a glance at Skyde and Krork and could read on their faces that they were charged up too. He banked over to Krork and raised an arm. They banged the sides of their fists together and whooped like idiots. Nonstop slowed, held his control bar with one hand, and hopped up onto his seat. Half standing, he offered Skyde the chance to bang fists as well. She leaned and gave the side of his hand a good solid whack. They both beamed. Nonstop pulled ahead, picked a realmline at random, and ghosted in.

*

The team followed him. A realm-world expanded around them, revealing a flat landscape in bluish, pre-dawn light. The ground seemed to be a plain of burnt ice, cracked into a network of mesas that extended to the horizon. The land hissed. Steam clouds rose from the gaps between its ice shelves. Nonstop looked at the long, lumpy ground, translucent in places, and thought it might be a great place to slalom, and he looked at the deep ravines, and thought they might offer fantastic jumps.

Still ghosting, he turned back to Skyde and raised his eyebrows high. She shook her head slowly, grimacing, and emphatically mouthed the word "*no*". Nonstop relayed the "*no*" to Krork with a shake of his own head, and the team continued the ghost toward the first ravine.

As they took the jump, a wall of bright blue lava thundered up from the canyon floor, engulfing them as they exited. For an instant, the world roared with the screams of flying liquid rock, and then the team was gone.

*

They ghosted safely onto a sun baked realm-world where the ground was parched and yellow. Ridges of wind-carved sandstone channeled the landscape into a maze of wide avenues — a landscape that begged for the invigoration of speed.

The team streaked down a long straight-away, their ghost light burning purple and clear on this Realm-world. The colors they saw of the landscape were true, though interrupted with ripples of violet distortion.

The rippling turbulence increased as the bikes zigged and zagged along the straight-away. Nonstop became intrigued and delighted with the effect, and was eager to see how it would behave in a full turn. He saw a wide patch of sunlight ahead, a gap in the canyon shadow, and decided to find out.

He sped ahead of the team, lifted his left arm in a turn signal, and leaned his machine around a stratified butte. The violet lines of turbulence multiplied, darkened, and sailed spectacularly across the field around his bike. The effect was better than... Nonstop swung his head left to right, suddenly driving through an outdoor market place — *people* — tall, purple Inter-D, were running to escape him. He

51

could hear them yelling, though they sounded far away. He saw colorful awnings stretched between tree-limb poles. He saw bins and blankets and baskets of goods. He saw light blue teeth in the screaming mouths of the Inter-D, saw their elongated bodies, their elongated heads, saw their black, rectangular eyes, opened wide in the rectangular eye sockets that extended past the sides of their heads like handles. He saw the Inter-D run. He saw their children run. He looked for a place to get out of their way, but there was no place to get out of their way — no place that wasn't crowded with people.

He ghosted right through one of the Inter-D, its fabric-wrap clothing slipping inches past his ear — *stop ghosting, and you'll hit them for real.*

The crowd deepened ahead of him. A thick, green, lizard-creature reared up above the massed people, held back by guide ropes. A second creature rose as the first one fell. Nonstop passed them. He saw teams of Inter-D with small silver helmets straining to control the ropes, while behind them, two cloaked figures grabbed a bound and kneeling Inter-D and ran off. A green-pepper-thing flew past Nonstop's head. A melon exploded on the ground in front of him. All the market-goers had cleared to the sides of the path and were throwing their goods at him, screaming and yelling in terror. The fat lizards charged, pulling their handlers behind them.

The team.

Did they make the turn? Were they in trouble now?

Nonstop swung his head to look, saw Varrage in the near distance, and saw Krork right behind him. Krork started to laugh the second their eyes met, and then Nonstop laughed too. A shower of round blades hit the ground in front of Nonstop; he laughed explosively, and raised his arm high above his head, opening and closing his hand twice.

He ghosted out. Another world sampled. His team was right behind him.

* * *

52

**

They entered a realm-world where the sun was shining and the air was cool. They hit a meadow, green and wide, and felt invited by the landscape to come and ride. They ghosted in completely, zooming along the clover, and accepted the invitation.

Nonstop felt the grip of his tire improve as it adjusted to the new surface. He banked left and Krork kept pace alongside him. Varrage hung back, eyes darting, observing the flanking positions on the field, watchful for every potential movement.

Nonstop leaned back in his seat, lifted his chin, and gave his chest to the air. He laughed, and called to Krork. "Hooooooo— those purple people gonna talk about us tonight."

Krork chuckled, "We are legend," he said, and then launched his bike forward, setting it free.

The land offered a long flow of gentle swells, and they rode them high and low, enjoying the tip and pull of their rolling flight.

They entered an orchard of small, blossoming trees, and stirred up clouds of fragrant petals as they drove. Nonstop saw Skyde smile through the flurry of white and pink blossoms, and smiled himself.

"You gotta love this," he said.

"It's like medicine," Skyde agreed, and then she leaned back and happily watched the petals float through the dappled sunlight.

The trees thinned, and the land returned to meadow.

Krork smiled broadly, leaning into the open breeze, wanting more of it, getting more of it. He was surprised when a dragonfly-ish something smacked up against his teeth and beat its wings against his lips.

It took some measure of control for Krork not to yell, or laugh. He stayed mindful, and kept his teeth clamped together as his smile grew gigantic, and then he turned to show the bug to Nonstop.

Nonstop saw the bug for a second before it got pulled into the slipstream of Krork's bike. He was surprised into laughter, just as Krork knew he would be.

The bug tried for a second to keep pace with them, beating its wings furiously, but soon gave up and was lost into distance.

The riders continued across the fields. They spotted a second orchard across the meadow and steered for it. As they rode, Nonstop noticed a dark patch in the middle of the grass ahead of him and it made him jumpy. *Where's that coming from?* He looked up and spotted the source: an enormous cloud in the enormous sky. The cloud was under the sun, its top bathed in golden light, its bottom painted in violet dusk. It cast a shadow upon the ground.

There were other clouds under the sun, roaming like lazy buffalo; a secret herd in plain sight, giant bison, floating in the sky, and on the field beneath them, the shadows that they cast. What was surprising about that? Clouds cast shadows on the land, of course they did. Big, fat, buffalo clouds? *Oh well,* Nonstop mused, *it's nice to have company.*

He pulled alongside Krork and said the first thing that came into his head. "Did you see the rig Rake was making? It's got wheels on the roof, big fat ones. Can't flip, or if it does, he can just..." The sound of Varrage's engine announced his approach, coming up fast behind them.

Varrage drove out in front of Nonstop and Krork, raised his right hand high, and closed it twice. Then he sped forward.

Nonstop, Krork, and Skyde looked behind them.

"Somebody's mad." Nonstop said, looking back at the sky and seeing the black cloud of pursuing dragonflies that filled it.

"Whoops." Skyde said.

They laughed and ghosted back into the realmlines, heading for home.

* * *

June 18th

12:00 A.M.

Rik Ty

**

George Lafleur drove the Daisybrook Rehabilitation Center's ambulette inland from San Francisco as the night's rain finally began to fall. The vehicle, despite its impressive paint job, was simply a modified van. It brandished no sirens or official capacity, and was merely a means of transporting patients. Sometimes those patients traveled seated, and sometimes, as was the case with this trip, on gurneys. On this particular assignment, George was transferring a patient to a new facility, taking the young man south; and as the rain fell and the miles ticked by, a gloomy haze crept over his thinking.

The patient had been a soldier — what the man was doing at a private rehab center like Daisybrook was anybody's guess. He couldn't move, couldn't speak, couldn't participate in rehabilitation of any kind — so how'd he get stuck in private center like Daisybrook? They must have had an open bed, George supposed, and some insurance company, somewhere, was paying. Perhaps the money was used up, and that was the reason for the transfer. George didn't know; the owners of Daisybrook hadn't discussed it with him.

George's feelings for Corporal Steven Jennings, the young man in his care, were protective. George himself had a bad leg, from a bicycle accident in his childhood. After the accident, he had taken a lot of bus rides with his mother to the local clinic. Those bus rides, plus the disinterested, overworked doctors who took care of him, told the story, round and round, of the summer when a necrosis had developed in his lower right leg — a plain *nasty* idea — some linkage to his Achilles tendon had died — *or had been allowed to die* — inside his body. The operation that removed it, the operation that somehow hadn't cost his family any money, managed to keep his leg functioning — yes, his calf still raised his heel, but his leg was weaker. And over the years it stayed weaker. He couldn't have served in the military even if he had wanted to. You had to run a lot in the Army, and that left him out.

But wasn't that just an easy excuse? If his leg had stayed fine, would he have been brave enough to serve? This young, young man,

Steven Jennings, had been brave enough to serve, and he had paid a price for it — dear Lord, he had paid.

Through the swinging windshield-wipers George saw the exit for Marin County. He put on his blinker and got in the right lane.

*

Twenty minutes later George was at the entrance of a private road, dark under a lining of tall trees. Beyond the rain he could see manicured hedges, and bordering the road, a line of small white stones that reflected his headlights back to him.

The road wound along, nestled within more trees and hedges. He rounded a bend and saw three crane trucks parked at the paving's edge, big as sleeping dinosaurs, set end to end behind each other, their left tires grabbing space on the roadway itself. George steered into the on-coming lane to avoid them. Next to the doors on the cranes, above the rear vent panels, white numbers stood out against flat green paint: *19*, then *04*, and then *07*. *Army,* George thought. *The Army had called for Steven Jennings; the Army was taking back its own.*

He could get with that. He could definitely get with that.

Passing the cranes, he returned to the correct lane, and found that the road still had a share of surprises to offer: stacks of huge concrete slabs with grooved sides lined the grass. He passed two piles and then two more. He saw muddy puddles at their bases, in the spots where the heavy slabs cut into the lawn.

He approached a turning circle, and saw banks of white lights shining through the trees on his right. *Okay, what's this? What's going on?*

*

At the turning circle, two soldiers sprang from a jeep and crossed a grassy median in hunched runs, eager to finish their task and get out of the rain. In the center of the median, a black plastic sheet partially covered a granite monument.

The front half of the sheet hung loose, and rippled loudly in the wind. The soldiers reached the tarp and stooped to where portions of it lay bunched on the ground. They raised it, releasing the rainwater that had collected in its folds, and then fixed the tangles in the sheet. As they did, they exposed the granite structure the tarp covered — an address marker — a series of sculpted letters that read:

Open Mind
Research Facility

The soldiers re-covered the monument and collected the thin steel rods that had pulled free of the ground at its base. As they did, the Daisybrook ambulette passed their parked jeep and continued driving along the entrance road.

The soldiers opened a satchel of tent stakes, heavier than the steel rods, set them into place, and one by one, hammered the stakes into the earth.

*

Straight ahead of him, George Lafleur got a better look at the work lights. Immediately, he expected them to be the gatepost he was supposed to sign into, but they weren't. They were attached to scaffolds built upon flatbed trucks, providing light for a work crew — soldiers using cranes to slide huge concrete slabs into position. The soldiers were building a wall — a giant pre-fab thing, long and high, using the same concrete slabs he had seen by the road. Suddenly the tongue and grooved edges he had noticed made perfect sense to him. They were how the wall fit together.

George noticed teams of soldiers installing razor wire along the tops of the walls. *What were they building here,* he asked himself, *a prison?*

He drove on, and finally came to the gatepost. Not a building, but two trucks parked end to end, blocking the road ahead of him. The truck on his left had a guard booth bolted behind its rear wheels. A small, striped gate-arm extended from the booth — which had to be symbolic, because it didn't look strong enough to actually stop anything. That clearly was what the second truck was for: any car traveling on this road would be stuck until the second truck moved out of the way.

George stopped obediently at the narrow gate and waited. Through the gap between the trucks he could glimpse a building, only partially lit, but beautiful, with dark windows and sweeping walls. A wave of lightning shuddered through the clouds behind the building, and for an instant George saw the silhouette of a glass tower. *Let the rains roll on,* he thought, *that building looks like it could sail.*

The driver's door opened on the truck to his left, and a soldier in a rain poncho stepped out. The soldier entered the guard booth and turned on a ceiling light, which threw his hood into stark shadow. As George rolled down his window, he flinched; inside the hood, he saw just a dark void, subtly shifting its movements to stay focused directly on him.

"I'm here to drop off a patient. What is this? Some kind of a hospital?" he asked the soldier.

"You should have gotten a form labeled C-12-A. Do you have it?" the voice from under the hood asked.

George had it. It was in the clipboard on the seat next to him. He picked it up and handed it to the soldier, who pulled back his hood to avoid dripping rain water on the form. *Normal,* George was almost relieved to see, just a normal, corn-fed, crew-cutted boy. God bless him. The soldier handed the clipboard back to George, then turned, and took a phone receiver from a radio box that was bolted to the guard house wall.

"Just a moment sir." the young man said, as he began punching buttons.

* * *

There were over one hundred labs at Open Mind, several grand and majestic. The North Lab had been one of the largest. A team could have built an airplane inside it, or, as was the case now, scores of workstations could be arranged within it. The workstations branched to a central hub, where a visualizing matrix could project their files in full dimension. But what had been projected? What, specifically, were these stations designed to do? Could you tell what they had built by deciphering their capabilities?

This was the core idea behind the tasks the soldiers were currently performing in the lab: constructing partitions around some stations, pulling other workstations apart, removing inner workings delicately, and in some cases, not so delicately, photographing and chronicling everything of interest, and everything existent. It was grand-scale dissection, an attempt at intellectual vivisection. Dr. Norel, if he were present and could see what was being done to his work, would have openly used the word *slaughter*.

High on a wall toward the rear of the lab stood a glass-enclosed observation room. Blinds had been recently installed behind its transparent walls. The blinds were closed, dark, but rim-lit. Behind them, a light was on.

* * *

Rik Ty

**

Colonel Bloch sat at a large desk within the dimly lit observation room, a room he had ordered be retrofitted into a private office for himself upon taking possession of Open Mind. The Colonel was in his fifties, bald, his head shaven clean. He stood six foot three, broad in the chest, heavy of bone and brow.

His hands worked at a flexbook computer docked below a wide array of devices and monitors situated on his desk. He sat with a corded phone receiver trapped between his shoulder and his ear. Ever patient, calmly listening, he lifted a courier package from his desk and opened it. On the base of his phone, a small square button began to blink, signifying an incoming call. He ignored it.

While he listened to the voice on the phone, he removed a pen drive from the courier package and inserted it into a port hub already crowded with other smart-pens. That done, he unfolded a pair of reading glasses and slipped them on as the files loaded. With his hands finally free, he gripped the receiver and spoke:

"Yes. That's right Colonel. I did have Dr. Norel's facility designated a restricted area," he said as he looked at the blinking light on the phone cradle, and then turned his gaze to his computer monitor, where a photograph of one of Norel's agents filled the screen. The photo showed "Nonstop" driving on his strange machine. The screen refreshed, and a tech-drawing scrolled down over the image, offering a wire-framed version of Nonstop and his bike made from polygons.

"I managed to get it restricted," Bloch continued once it was his turn to speak, "because it warrants being restricted."

A rendering of an armored bike, bristling with weapons and additional wheels, formed over the image of Nonstop and his bike. Gun pods formed over the bike's fore-arms. Grenade cannons ran along the edges of the bike's vortex chamber. Ramming spikes extended beyond its front wheel.

The image of the weapons-bike multiplied to fill the screen. The Colonel's hand hovered over the blinking phone button. He spoke again.

"Colonel Wyatt, I have followed Dr. Norel's work for years. Every item on this campus requires intense study, by teams designed for that purpose. I cannot allow the site to be compromised."

The monitor's image of armored bikes reflected in Colonel Bloch's glasses, replaced by a slide show of similarly designed tanks and troop transports: heavier vehicles, with heavier weapons and more robust vortex chambers.

A map of the world appeared on the screen. Blue circles formed over key cities across the Northern Hemisphere, across the US, across Europe, across Asia. Red diamonds formed over key areas of the remaining countries. Graphically, the result was obvious. The red diamonds surrounded the blue circles and blanketed Africa and South America.

Colonel Bloch sat up, moving toward the edge of his chair. "Yes I said 'compromised' Colonel. I understand your curiosity, but for the moment you'll have to be satisfied with the issued reports. Yes, that's right. I'm sorry. I'm going to have to say goodbye now. I regret that I can be of no further assistance."

Bloch calmly disconnected the call, and hit the incoming call button at the base of the phone.

"Colonel Bloch speaking," he said, and then, after listening for a moment, continued, "The van is here? Excellent. Have it escorted down. I'm on my way."

Bloch shut down his computer and placed his glasses on the desk. He pulled the pen drive from the hub and slipped the pen into his shirt pocket; then he reached into the middle left drawer of his desk and traced his fingers along its upper surface. When he found the flat-switch hidden there, he pressed it.

The side panel of his desk slid forward three inches, revealing a storage space behind the drawers. The Colonel undocked his flexbook, stored it in the compartment behind the drawers, and slid the side panel closed. There was an audible *click* as it locked.

Smiling, he turned to the phone and quickly punched in a number.

* * *

**

Lieutenant Alicia Camille had been placed in charge of the labs in the east tower of Open Mind. She had an office on each of the five floors, but spent most of her time in the third floor office, where she had two floors above her and two floors below her. She was outside that office now; the phone was ringing, and she was walking hard to go answer it.

Inside the office, she sped to her desk, tossed down the set of plastic folders she was holding, and picked up the phone receiver. She took a seat in her chair, turned it away from the desk, and gave her full attention to the call.

"Lieutenant Camille speaking." She said, not letting her back touch the rear of her chair, and giving her hair-clip a quick test as she listened for the response. In the fifteen months that she'd been in charge of the labs, her hair had grown beyond regulation length. She made a point of compensating by keeping it neat.

Colonel Bloch spoke on the other end of the phone. She listened as he told her that the van from the rehabilitation center had arrived, and then instructed her to join him as he met it.

"South Loading Bay 1. Yes sir." She said.

The Colonel said goodbye and hung up. Lt. Camille returned her phone receiver to its cradle.

Facing her desk, she saw that her tossed folders had had bumped against a small plastic model, almost knocking it to the floor. She leaned forward and rescued the small structure. It weighed almost nothing, just a white, plastic shell — a rapid prototype, spit drop by drop from a computer-controlled printer. It featured a human figure in a framework of braces, with oversized boxes connected to its shoulders and hips. She set it back in its place, and adjusted its position until its edges were parallel with the items on either side of it. Then she picked up the plastic folders and tapped them into one neat unit.

As she did, the frosted covers pressed against the contents of the folders and the title page within the first folder became visible. It read simply:

Spinal
Bypass

Lt. Camille locked the folders in the top drawer of the file cabinet furthest from the door, slipped the key into the pocket of her lab coat, and then walked out of the office.

* * *

Two floors below, Colonel Bloch walked through a long, half-lit corridor. His footsteps echoed sharply off the walls and ceiling. He reached a pair of twin doors marked OFF LIMITS, and waved a plastic card in front of a wall mounted sensor. The doors unlocked and he continued along an extension of the hallway.

Louis Sinclair, a much smaller man, balding, and wearing a white lab coat over newly-fraying clothes, hastened from a connecting hall and efforted to catch up to the colonel. With his left hand, Sinclair held a white clipboard in front of his chest, and with his right hand he readied a pen above it, poised to write even as he trotted.

"Colonel. Hello," he said, catching up, fairly breathlessly, to the Colonel, who did not slow down.

"Hello Sinclair. Progress?"

"Uhm, yes, perhaps. Not in the way you were looking for, but, we've uncovered a fascinating project of Dr. Norel's — it's a strain of wheat. Horizontal matting, long range salt-water hydration. It shows promise. If developed further, it appears it will yield an edible grain — a starch. It could be made to grow in *sand*."

"Sand. I see." Bloch continued walking. "Has anyone uncovered anything regarding interdimensional vehicles? Interdimensional travel? Interdimensional theory?"

Bloch's heel hit the floor. *Clack.*

Clack.

"No sir, not as of..."

Clack.

"Trans-dimensional? Pan-dimensional. Inner-dimensional. Outer-dimensional. Was there no useful hint of the technology left behind?"

"I'm sorry sir, there's nothing to report. Perhaps we could concentrate on some of the other projects here. We're sitting atop a wealth of innovation and advancements. We..."

The footsteps stopped. The Colonel stopped. The clacking stopped. They had arrived at the south freight elevator. The Colonel pushed a button on the wall and turned to the smaller man.

"I want those bikes Sinclair. Machines that can drive in and out of anywhere — *undetected*. I want them before Command shuts us down, and I want them before Norel wises up, and drives through here with a machine gun."

Bloch turned to look about the loading bay as the approaching elevator made a rumbling noise above the ceiling. Set on the floor to his right were several wooden pallets, arranged neatly along the wall, each loaded with bulk-wrapped paintings — stacks of stretched canvases — abstracts, landscapes, portraits, all from local artists, and all worthless. As he looked at them, an old idea tried to form in his mind and he disallowed it — the paintings were trash; they should all be discarded; along with the insane room-sized instrument-thing Norel had left behind: the glass bowl lined with all the electrified guitar string units — crazy thing looked like a giant, round typewriter — without keys or — Bloch brought his gaze to the elevator door.

He had recently had the paintings evaluated, had collected them all into one room, had arranged for an appraiser to come and inspect them, and had found, not to his surprise, that they were of no significance whatsoever, a mindless indulgence, and of course, Norel, the fool, had displayed them all — in prominent locations across his entire building.

Idiocy. Idiocy upon idiocy.

The elevator door opened. Lt. Camille stood within. She saluted the Colonel when she saw him, and Bloch returned the gesture as he and Sinclair stepped inside. The Colonel stood next to the Lieutenant, the swell of his chest level with her eyes. He turned to face the door.

"Lieutenant Camille, will the patient do? Are both his eyes intact?'

"Yes, of course, sir. He's prone to infection as you can tell from the delay, and his wound types are going to be excessively vulnerable to corrosion from the derma-infiltration, but he's an acceptable replacement." She said, studying her reflection in the steel jacketed door as the elevator descended.

"Excellent," Bloch continued, "We have control of his medical records?"

"Yes sir," she said.

"Complete control? The new restrictions took effect?"

"Yes sir."

"Excellent."

The curl of a smile betrayed the corners of the lieutenant's mouth. "Pass enough restrictions, and sooner or later you can do whatever you want," she said.

"You wanted to learn."

The elevator rocked as it settled, causing the lieutenant's eyelids to flutter. Then the doors of the freight elevator opened, and the trio stepped through the hall, out of the building, and into the rainy night.

*

The ambulette sat parked on the loading bay's main platform, under a light pole. Rain bounced off its roof, creating a halo of pale light directly above it.

From the driver's seat, George Lafleur saw three figures pass under a roll-top gate and walk toward him. He climbed out of the van and pulled his hood over his head, hunching his shoulders in reaction to the rain. When the team from the building was within earshot, he spoke:

"I'll need a little help unloading him."

The Colonel made quick eye contact with George, and George took it as enough of an acknowledgment to walk to the rear of the ambulette and begin opening its doors.

Bloch quickened his pace and strode to the back of the van as George climbed inside.

Camille and Sinclair slowed and halted: if the Colonel wanted to handle this, the Colonel would handle it.

The Colonel extended a hand to the driver and introduced himself. Then he looked at the gurney in the van.

"All right. What do you need me to do?" he asked Lafleur, keeping his face amiable and smiling, even with the rain beating down on his exposed head and his exposed shoulders, even with the rain beating down on the exposed silver oak-leaf clusters of his uniform.

"Just grab those two handles on the edge of the gurney, and pull when I say okay," George said, clicking the gurney's rain cover into place.

George maneuvered in the tight spaces of the van to stand at the head of the Gurney and take hold of its handles. "Okay, go ahead," he said to the Colonel.

Bloch pulled. Once the gurney had passed the door, its undercarriage extended to the floor. George hopped out and began slapping latches along the narrow cot's perimeter, locking the undercarriage in place. "You'll have to sign for him." George said, though he did not hold a clipboard, or make any move to go get one. He held the corporal's rain hood against the wind, keeping the rain from hitting Steven Jennings' face.

George shifted two steps back toward the head of the gurney, but didn't move his hands, didn't allow the protective cover to fall, and didn't move any further. Bloch examined him, and then slowly raised his left arm, clamping the rim of the hood between his thumb and the first joint of his first finger. He continued to look at George as the rain beat down on his head. He did not blink.

Then he remembered to smile.

Nodding, George brisked away to get the clipboard from the front of the van. His leg weakened and he started to limp.

When George returned, Sinclair and Camille stood near the Colonel. George smiled, and presented the clipboard to the Colonel, who looked at the Lieutenant until she stepped forward and took the clipboard from George. As she signed it, George closed the van's rear doors and shook their handles to make sure they had locked. When he finished, Lieutenant Camille handed the clipboard back to him. He made sure it was signed, and thanked her. The lieutenant smiled back and nodded.

Bloch stepped back. Lt. Camille walked to the head of the gurney. Far beyond Bloch's shoulders the Black Chinook helicopters began landing, easy to hear in the rain, if not see. Bloch nodded to Sinclair. Sinclair nodded back and left, walking in the direction of the helicopters, pulling a white painter's cap out of his lab coat and working it onto his head.

"One thing," the driver said, "I know your staff will be right on top of this, but he gets bed sores easy. You got to move him. You know, shift him around every once in a while." George pantomimed the action of rolling a patient, rocking on his hips as he swung his arms — as best he could with the clipboard tucked under his left armpit.

Bloch smiled and vigorously shook George's right hand in both of his.

"Thank you," Bloch said, "We're going to do everything we can to help him."

"Glad to hear it," George said, and returned Bloch's handshake before leaving to get back in the van.

The ambulette's headlights came on, and in the shadows on the far side of the platform, the escort jeep's headlights came on as well. The ambulette drove away, and the escort followed it down the ramp.

Bloch caught up to the lieutenant and used his pass to open the entranceway. They rolled the gurney into the building and headed for the elevator. As the gurney's front wheel hit the small gap between the elevator and the main floor, the gurney jarred and sent a fusillade of water droplets falling to the floor. Lt. Camille slapped down the dripping rain hood, exposing the wounded soldier beneath it.

Corporal Steven Jennings winced at the bright elevator lights and closed his one remaining eyelid against their stark, fluorescent glare.

He listened to the rumbling steel doors as they rolled closed behind him, and heard the whine of the elevator as it prepared to lift his body, and carry it wherever it was bound.

* * *

**

Colonel Montgomery C. Wyatt of the United States Army liked things neat and tidy. This business with Bloch and the terrorist cell was not neat and tidy.

If what Bloch was suggesting were true: if this scientist Norel really had developed a way to interfere with people's brain functions, not one at a time, and not close up, but whole groups of people, spread out over large areas, it could be the basis for one of the most promising non-lethal weapons systems the Army had ever come across.

Bloch was good at ferreting out weapons systems; he'd been doing it for twenty years. Wyatt just wished that the man didn't put his radar up. Something about Bloch was off, a dead fish. Dealing with him was like watching a slab of meat try to act cordial.

Bloch seemed to be well regarded, steady promotions, effective track record — not that it fell within Wyatt's normal duties to run checks on his fellow officers. It's just that there was a scent in the wind, that's all, and like it or not, he had started to hunt.

"Whattya got Henderson?" he asked as he heard his support officer's footsteps approach from outside the open door.

Corporal Anthony Henderson entered, and took immediate note of the change of light in the room. The overhead fluorescents were off, and the two desk lamps were on, reflecting off the room's polished wood paneling and suffusing the area around the desk in a warm glow. The room looked quiet. Which meant the Colonel's mind was noisy.

Corporal Henderson placed a thin folder on the Colonel's desk, between the two lamps, and then addressed the Colonel: "Sir, a casual look on the internet yielded a few hits. The most recent article on Dr. Norel himself is over nine years old. His name comes up hundreds of times after that in tech articles — but those are only credits: identifying him as the source of component technologies within various other inventions. I printed a small sampling of the articles so that you could see them. I could print more if you'd like, Sir."

"Thank you Henderson. Not right now."

Wyatt opened the new folder on his desk, revealing a photo, a printout really, of Colonel Bloch leaving a recent graduation exercise. The image was an enlargement, slightly pixelated. It showed Bloch walking by a hedge — walking away from the milling families, but turning his head to look at the camera. How far away was the photographer? One hundred feet? Two hundred? Had Bloch detected a camera being aimed at him from that distance, and from a crowd of excited civilians? Probably not. But it looked liked he had.

One by one, Colonel Wyatt dragged the tech-articles Henderson had mentioned to a pile on the side of the folder, until he came to the printout of the old newspaper article featuring Dr. Norel. The photo in the article showed a lean, balding man with a pony tail and a goatee, holding his arms open in an expansive gesture, smiling like a proud papa. Next to him, and behind him, stood a team of smiling, hard-hatted, construction engineers. The shot didn't look staged. This guy Norel didn't look dangerous, or crazy — no crazier than the average college professor did anyway. The headline read:

Construction Begins On
Open Mind Research Facility

Wyatt glanced at the first few words of the article and set the folder next to a tall stack of photocopied forms. He leaned back in his chair and studied the stack of paper. As he spoke, he tapped a pencil on the desk.

"No more printouts, thank you Corporal. There are too many papers on this desk already. Taken together, these forms are like a fog. And the closer they get to Bloch, the thicker the fog runs. I can't tell if I'm filling out clearances or puzzling my way through a maze." He leaned forward in the chair. "Did Valdez find out anything regarding our two mystery men?"

"He said that twenty years ago Bloch and Norel both had a connection to an experimental bullet nicknamed the meat grinder. The technology was based on a nail Norel had invented, and Bloch was on the acquisition team that turned the nail into a bullet. Valdez said that Norel tried to get the project stopped. He failed, and wound up quitting his job over it. Eleven years after that, and Norel opens his own research facility." Henderson pointed to the article on the Colonel's desk.

Wyatt nodded, "The same research facility where Bloch is now. But what's the current connection? We've got a commandeered research facility, a mountain of red tape, and a missing scientist. Ask Valdez what sparked the seizure of Norel's facility."

"If you'd like, you'll be able to ask him yourself Sir. He's flying in. He'd be here already except for a maintenance delay with the..."

The windows shook, hard enough to rock the blinds. At the same time, a *whumping* sound assaulted the office. Wyatt leapt to his feet and ran to the window. The orange glow at the center of the blinds already told him what he would see. What he already knew. He yanked the blinds away from the glass, revealing the fireball still rising a half mile away.

Something was burning across from the barracks.

Wyatt left the window and passed his desk in four strides, catching up to Corporal Henderson, who was so eager to move he was practically hopping in place.

"That's Tesson's field." Wyatt said as they ran out through the doorway. "Copter base."

*

Corporal Henderson drove the Colonel across the base. Sirens blared from Tesson's field, and from speakers the rover passed as it turned and swerved, traversing roads teeming with running soldiers. Figures ran in the distance as well, far from the headlights' erratic path, silhouetted by the pulsing haze of flames.

When the rover arrived at the heart of the activity — a crash site, as expected, there was nothing to do: a fire team was already busy fighting the flames. The ruined copter would burn for several more minutes.

There would be no survivors.

Colonel Wyatt stood up in the open rover, locking his gaze to the center of the flames. The heat pressed against his face. He felt it drying his eyes. He did not allow himself to blink.

* * *

Rik Ty

June 18th

12:27 A.M.

Rik Ty

**

Nonstop ghosted in along a path of packed dirt about a half mile from base camp. The ground he drove was a natural straight-away, tree lined and level, and so well-used by the Bike Pilots it had earned the nickname the landing strip.

Above him, the sky rolled dark, with the trees blocking most of the glow from the planet's two moons. Ahead of him, his headlights sent a beam of brightness into the dark forest roadway, bleaching the overhead branches into a weave of shadows that looked something like a wicker-basket throat.

As he slowed, the path looked more like what it actually was: a lush arcade of small trees, with pools of moonlight revealing a wide lane of scraped ground.

He stopped at the head of a path that curved down the hillside and eventually led into base camp. At the path-head, he waited for Krork, who he thought should be only seconds behind him.

Looking down the hill and past the trees, Nonstop could see the twinklings of several campfires, silent from distance, suggesting calmness and rest. He wouldn't mind spending the rest of the evening by one of those fires, relaxing with friends, watching the flames do their crazy dance. It had, after all, been a long day.

Krork pulled up, and Nonstop perked up. Krork brought the big bike to a full stop, and grinned enormously. Up in the workbay, Skyde looked back along the landing strip, watching for Varrage. She didn't have to wait long.

Varrage ghosted onto the dirt path, phased into the world completely, and rode right past Nonstop, Krork, and Skyde, driving to where the woods rose into hills, and then slipping his bike into the tree line without saying a word or even glancing back in acknowledgment.

His team watched him pass, and then Nonstop looked back at the campfires.

"Dope," Nonstop said, and then he added, "Okay, let's go," and his bike and Krork's both rumbled down the hill toward camp. Driving, they swooped past the dark hulks of several mobile bike-labs — large rigs built to study and repair vortex bikes out in the field, most with long launch channels extending from their fronts and high gantry stations making up their backs — each lab an industrial collection of tank-treads and stairwells, sensors and cranes, gangways and consoles, all surrounded by exotic driving machines: sleek bikes, stripped down buggies, safety-caged work-bulls and other multi-wheeled-fever-dreams of gear-headed ambition, all pointing toward a great open meadow, where their work would continue as soon as the daylight returned.

Away from the meadow, amid the trees, past the bike-labs, Nonstop, Skyde, and Krork drove closer to the campsites, and as their engines announced their arrival, their friends stepped away from their tents and came out to cheer.

As a group, the Bike Pilots were made up of a wide mix of people: old and young, male and female, extroverted and introverted. Some were fashion-plate gorgeous, some were shy-flower gorgeous, and more than a few were broken-nose gorilla gorgeous. Their skin colors hinted at many regions of ancestry, their hair styles at many temperaments, but they all lived in the same place, at the same moment, and for the same purpose. They were more than community. They were family.

They cheered when they saw the returning team, and created a gauntlet of whoops and hollers and cries of "How'd it go?" and "What'ya see?" as Nonstop, Krork, and Skyde drove past.

Nonstop stood up on his bike and pointed further down the path. "We're gonna recharge." He called, and several of his friends nodded, downing their tools by their tech-fires, and spreading the word as they followed along.

Past the campsites, Nonstop approached the central fire, where a border of stones enclosed a broad fire-bed, set between a large collection of long tables on one side, and a series of improvised test tracks on the other. At the center of the far test tracks stood Outpost 14 — a short, round building covered with machinery.

Nonstop swung up to the fire and fit his bike between the rigs that were already parked there. Krork pulled up to the fire bed too, not exactly alongside Nonstop, but close. Nonstop dismounted and pressed a slat on the side of his bike. The slat popped open and revealed a tray holding a ceramic grid.

Nonstop removed the grid, reeled out a jacketed cable tethering the grid to the bike, and tossed the grid into the fire.

A band of recharge lights appeared on Rattletrap's back display, equalizer-like: little green rectangles bouncing up and down in columns. Fun to watch. Energetic.

Krork slipped his grid into the fire as well. The approaching rumble of a large vehicle grabbed his attention, and he smiled as he turned toward camp. Down where the hill met the clearing, he saw the bushes shake and watched as they spread outward to release a colossal bike-lab that pushed forward down the slope and out past the small scraping branches that seemed reluctant to let it go. The machine lumbered onto the open field and turned for the central fire, draped with laughing Bike Pilots.

"Skyde! What'ya bring us?" shouted Brickyard, who drove the lab in, standing astride its upper tier like a pirate manning the wheel of a ghost ship. She was old school Bronx, stocky and thick, with iron gray hair that she tied back in a frizzy pony tail. She wore a black patch over her left eye, a long vest, short sleeves, and an oversized pair of work-gloves so tough they looked like she could have cupped them together and held molten steel. As she grinned toward the bonfire, she returned a celebratory cigar to her lips, clamped it between her teeth, and took a long drag, causing the front end to flare bright orange. As soon as she had a full hit, she forced the smoke back out through her clenched teeth where it billowed around her head, thick and white. She smiled wider. Five foot three. Eater of dragons.

She drove toward the fire, and as the lab clattered along, the thirty or so Bike Pilots hanging from it cheered and laughed.

A rider named Slice shouted "Heads up!" as he threw something flat and round from one of the upper railed platforms, and as soon as he did, a hand rose behind his head and squeezed the top of his short, perfectly groomed afro. Someone made a smooching noise.

"Hey, hey," Slice reacted, turning with his hands not quite fists and his pinkies up. "Who dares? Who dares?" he asked, dancing and grinning as he glanced at all the innocent faces around him that were suddenly looking away and whistling.

The bag of flour tortillas flew above Nonstop's head, arcing like a touchdown pass and spinning like a saw blade. It threatened to sail into the fire, but Nonstop leaned back and snatched it from the air. The second he did, the tortillas folded heavily over his hand.

"Good thing they're fresh," he called back to Slice, "Or that could have hurt," he said, tossing the bag back sidearmed.

Wazzi, a young Australian rider with tousled hair, quickly grabbed the guard rail in front of him and stretched out to catch the bag as it sailed over the big rig's empty launch channel.

"Hey! Quit playing with the food!" cried a young woman with long black hair and lustrous brown eyes who went by the name Heartbreaker. "It's not like there's a store where you can get more of it."

"What are you talking about? The basement's got all the food we'll ever need." Wazzi said, still hanging over the guardrail.

"Yeah, but you have to risk your life to go get it," said Plush, a red haired bike-designer who sat next to Heartbreaker on a walkway at the edge of the launch channel, helping to keep a blue drink cooler steady.

Heartbreaker raised her hand and waved it dismissively, "Risk your life? In that case Wazzi volunteers to go get it."

"If I go get it, I'll keep it all to myself. And then you'll have to be nice to me if you want any."

"Hmf. You look like an orangutan hanging there. Do you know that?"

"ooooh...ooooh... ooooh."

Heartbreaker rolled her eyes. "Forget it. An orangutan's hair is neater." and then she offered another waved hand, another turned head, another dismissal.

Slice pointed at Wazzi in mock laughter, sticking out his tongue and bobbing his shoulders — frivolous behavior, but so what? Their friends had returned safely, they had dodged another bullet, and the mood in the air was defiantly festive.

The bike-lab banged to a stop not far from the central fire. The Bike Pilots spilled off, carrying crates and containers to the long tables.

"Bonfire!" yelled Wazzi, lofting a long flat crate above his head like a surfboard. "BONFIRE!" came the call from Ouchy Big Time, and from Slice, and from Floorboard, and from Knock Knock Robusto, as they all hoisted firewood and crates above their heads — offerings to the gods of playful nonsense. Floorboard, taller and broader than the rest, strode with a log wrapped under each arm. He stepped away from the crowd, and tossed one log high over his shoulder in a massive, hooked arc.

The log silenced everyone as it flew, and when it landed it sent up a fountain of sparks that crackled as it climbed the air. A cheer went up from the crowd — with the exceptions of Nonstop — who smiled as his gaze jumped from person to person, and of Skyde, who smiled as well, though weakly.

Krork, earnestly unreserved, cheered with the rest. Light the music, he was ready to dance.

A second wave of Bike Pilots walked over through paths in the brush, their eyes and smiles shining as the firelight found them.

Hanging back from the crowd, Rake, black hair and black t-shirt, walked steady and calm. Around him came two girls on blast-boots — realm-rocket units that fit over their lower legs, controlled by swing arms anchored at each knee, zooming them two feet above the ground on light-strobing pulse fields that were fast, bright, and impossible to ignore.

Diamondsong skied in the lead, slaloming past walking Bike Pilots, her hair a puffy cloud behind her blue helmet. She wore a blue body-sleeve, and leaned almost to the ground as she turned. Her friend Sunset swung in line right behind her, wearing bright yellow, her hair a whipping stream of shining black that chopped around her shoulders.

The two girls circled the central fire, didn't seem ready to give up their ride just yet, and blasted back into the tree line, smiling and whooping to their friends.

Bike Pilots drove a team of small buggies up to the fire. Dismounting, they tossed power grids into the flames. A barbecue grill lit on one buggy. A beverage cart lit up on the other. Wazzi brought a long, flat stasis crate over to the grill wagon and popped its latch. The crate instantly grew taller as its contents jumped from two dimensions to three — revealing small mountains of vac-packed nutri-steaks.

"Uh. Fake food," Wazzi said, his smile fading.

"What is it?" Krork asked, craning his neck to see over Wazzi's shoulder.

"Tofu-derivative," Wazzi said.

"What flavor?" asked Slice.

"Does that matter?"

"Sure. What flavor?"

"Looks like all of them."

"The seasonings in there too?" asked Brickyard as she strode over and started rooting through the steaks. "Yeah. There they are," she said. "Back up. I'll take care of it. You'll be begging for seconds."

Wazzi smiled at her "MMM, tofu derivative with a garnish of cigar ash, I think I'll eat my own foot."

81

"Yeah? Go bite your own elbow." Brickyard said as she gave his chest a light push. "Get outta my kitchen funnyboy. Hey Skyde, you got any treats for mister fine-dining over here?"

Skyde held up a few of the white bags from the roadside store. "Sure, I've got candy." There was a whoop from the crowd.

"Ahhh, great. Just remind him that the wrapper is not a side dish," Brickyard said, and then went back to selecting packets from the stasis crate.

Interested Bike Pilots gathered around the back of Krork's bike.

"I've got plenty. Whole cartons. Junk food galore," Skyde called.

"Whole cartons - wooo! Pass 'em out!" someone cried, and Skyde did. She quickly emptied several bags to outstretched hands. Cartons were passed around, and passed back to the long tables. They were examined; they were read aloud. Some were opened; some were emptied.

Wazzi got his hands on a package containing a caramel and chopped peanut monstrosity, ripped it open and tore the confection in half with one bite. He leaned his head back, his teeth gleaming white as he smiled with satisfaction.

"Ahhh, there's no taste like home." He said, to no one in particular.

Someone in particular was listening though, and she rolled her big brown eyes at the young man again as she responded — also to no one in particular, "Uhh- listen to him, making a commercial. With no cameras even."

Wazzi wasn't the only one who laughed at the line. He nodded with big giant wags of his head, chewed vigorously, and then smiled, making a grand display of teeth that were no longer anywhere near gleaming, and in fact, looked like they had been mortared with thick beige tar, beige tar textured with peanut chunks. He looked straight at Heartbreaker, and with great effort mumbled:

"Could be my big break."

Heartbreaker looked like she could faint. For an instant, her head seemed to short circuit, vibrating in an apoplexy of revulsion. Then she spun on her heel and stormed away, announcing "Dios mio. Disgusting," to a laughing crowd.

Slice threw an arm around Nonstop, dragging him close enough to hear as he leaned toward Wazzi. "Invite me to the wedding," he said.

Wazzi thrust out his chest. "Don't you worry. She'll be desperate some day. Can I get an Amen, Nonstop my brother?"

"Huh? Leave me out of your religious debates."

Skyde lifted a few more bags from the workbay. "I've got music and magazines as well."

Plush stepped forward, nibbling a thin chocolate. "Magazines? Really? What are the latest celebrity addictions?"

"Publicity." Someone in the crowd replied.

"She said the latest, that's the oldest." Someone else answered.

"That aint the oldest." A voice said, further back.

"Hey!" Plush snapped, turning to face the riders immediately near her, clutching a pair of magazines to her chest. "Celebrities are very brave people. They are constantly overcoming adversity, and if you insist on insulting them, I will take my candy bars and leave."

"You tell 'em girl." Someone added as Plush rushed from the crowd and back to the tables, pulling Heartbreaker with her, both of them giggling.

There were more takers for the magazines. The news magazines got snatched up, the car magazines got snatched up; there was even a tug of war over the latest copy of Scientific American. And while musical selections at road side stores are never extensive — if they exist at all — the offerings Skyde purchased got snatched up eagerly as well.

Diamondsong and Sunset returned to the party, sputtering their blast-boots to a stop near the rear of Krork's bike. They removed their helmets and smiled at Skyde.

"Skyde, you done? You down for a ride?" Diamondsong asked.

"Not right now, I want to create a report on the creatures from the Bleed Zone, plus I have to log my observations regarding the portal — but you know, there is something I wanted to ask you."

"I know. I know all about it. Do I want to go Blast-booting with you? The answer is yes. No. No, wait, you want to know about that fine boy Rake. Do he still have those muscles. Do he still have that dark hair, those tight black T-shirts, those stripey tattoos on his arms. The answer is yes, and yes — in fact, the answer really is 'yes, yes, yes.'."

"I wanted to ask you…"

"Girl, he's so polite to you. He's willing to be tamed. Rarr."

"I wanted to ask you… about… data-boxes. About their individual functions. Can we split them up into smaller devices?"

"You okay? You don't seem right."

"Just tired. I'm fine."

"Okay. Right. Smaller, single use devices? Is that what you've got in mind?"

"Yes, exactly. I'd like a com-link system up near my collar — hands free. And I'd like to get a haze scanner on the tap unit itself. I want to be able to fly as hands-free as possible. I swing my arms around for balance, and the urge to stretch the fingers is pretty strong. The fewer gadgets I have to worry about dropping, the better."

"Okay, I wouldn't have to change the data-boxes themselves, just create some auxiliary devices. Redundancies are not the issue — hands free access is the issue. Cool. We could do that. We'll do that for all of you. Have you hooked up in a couple of days. What about Varrage? He seems picky about stuff like that. Do you think he'd let me touch his equipment?

Skyde grinned, and opened her eyes wide at Diamondsong. Diamondsong scowled, then quickly slapped the back of Skyde's hand.

"You bad. You bad. Well? Would he?"

"Sure. I think Varrage would see the sense of it. He might grumble about the redundancies you mentioned, but he'd also see that was a fight for another day."

"Okay, so before we get to another day, you going to come riding?"

"Sure. Later."

"How much later?"

"A couple of hours."

"Woman, you gonna be sleepin' in a couple of hours."

"Probably, but give me a nudge."

"I'm not going to give you a nudge. If you're asleep, you're asleep."

"Just give me a nudge. We'll have fun."

"Mmm-hmm. We'll see." Diamondsong folded her arms and looked away, taking her best shot at looking serious and failing, a grin threatening at the corners of her mouth. She spotted Krork, "Krork, your riding partner here is too tired to relax. Maybe you need to install a bed in the back of that bike."

Krork was looking across the central fire to where Varrage had just pulled up on Viablo. Varrage was busy placing his recharge grid in the fire. Krork had caught the word "bed" from Diamondsong's conversation, and the emotion behind it. It wasn't a serious question.

"You want to know what sleeping arrangements there are on the bike? Uhm, eight hammocks, two stretchers, and a cabinet of shock blankets. If she wanted to, Skyde could make herself nice and comfortable." He watched as Varrage walked away from his bike, and headed toward the Outpost.

Diamondsong waved at Krork. "That sounds comfortable to you? That's right. Guys will tell you rocks are comfortable. 'Let's go camping. Let's go camping.'"

Back at the long tables, Floorboard stood up abruptly and slapped a newspaper. He was a huge man, and his agitation caught everyone's attention.

"Neuro-terrorists?" he said, as he turned to look at the faces of his friends. "Have you seen this? I mean, what does that even mean? 'Neuro-terrorist' What's that?"

"There are a couple of articles like that." Skyde said, and the big man started striding over to her.

"You've read them? What do they mean?"

Skyde recoiled at Floorboard's advance, despite the fact that he was a friend of hers.

And suddenly, there was Rake. What shadow he slipped out of, Skyde didn't know. But he was there, between her and Floorboard, with a friendly hand on the big man's shoulder, gently extracting the newspaper from his grip.

"What does it say?" Rake looked at Floorboard as he asked, and then started looking at the newspaper itself.

Floorboard spoke directly to Rake, and jabbed the newspaper with one massive finger. "It says here that Open Mind was a center for a terrorist cell. Us. It says we had some kind of brain scrambler, and that we used it on people."

"They're calling us terrorists?" Slice asked.

"Brain scrambler?" Rake asked Skyde, calmly, from twenty feet away.

"What?" Plush asked, turning from her magazines and chocolate. "What's going on now?"

Skyde advanced to the very edge of the workbay and used it like a stage. "There are a few stories in the papers, and the general idea is that they're trying to explain away our bikes and the Bleed Zones by saying we're a terrorist cell, that we've been developing devices, or systems — some form of psycho-tronics that would allow us to interfere with people's brain functions at crucial times. Confuse them. Cause hallucinations. Make bus drivers plow off bridges. Make pilots crash their planes. Make surgeons fail after crucial incisions — things like that. They say that we were almost to the point where we could cause hallucinations over large regions, whole neighborhoods, when the Army broke down our door and stopped the operation."

"And they say we escaped?" Rake asked.

"And they say we escaped." Skyde answered.

"This is a Colorado paper. What do the California papers say? What do the Marin County papers say?" Rake asked.

Skyde didn't move, didn't falter, but she felt all eyes on her, looking for answers. She was just the messenger. "We didn't get any local papers in California. Several of the stories you see are A.P. — from a news service. A variation of them in some form or another could be in every paper in the country — every news organization in the world. Varrage thinks that the planting of these stories is a direct tactic by Bloch."

Slice folded his arms, and then unfolded them, and then grabbed his hips. He didn't seem to know where to look. "First they drive us into hiding, now they're saying we're terrorists."

Diamondsong hopped up onto the edge of the workbay by Skyde and sat, her rocket boots swinging over the side. "Just tired huh?"

"That's not all, I'm sorry to say," Skyde continued. "There... "

"I think I've got it." Brickyard stood up from a table by the grill, "The glioblastoma thing?"

"Yes, the glioblastoma thing." Skyde said, and the word ran through the crowd. Glioblastoma? Accompanied by murmurs of Brain cancer?

Brickyard gestured with an open hand at the newspaper on the table next to her. "It says here that there's a glioblastoma cluster forming around Open Mind. They're spreading the idea that we not only scramble people's minds, we cause brain cancer doing it."

Slice turned to Brickyard. "Us? Cause cancer? That's stupid, and then what? They gonna show a bunch of people with brain cancer around Open Mind when there aren't any?"

Rake turned to Slice, "You can fake records — you can fool the news services, and if you wanted victims for the news cameras, you would just have to fake the records at a different point, before the Doctors saw them. You don't need people who have cancer; you just need people who think they have cancer."

"I still say it's stupid, and easy to disprove." Slice said.

Skyde looked at Slice. "Actually I think it's brilliant. Keep in mind that we're not there to disprove anything, and look at all it does for Bloch — if you want to deny what people see in a Bleed Zone, blame it on mass hallucination. If you want people to run from seeing anything at all, tell them that they'll get brain cancer. If you want to kill inconvenient people — us — call them terrorists. When we're dead, the public will cheer."

There was silence for a second and then Wazzi spoke. "I don't know if 'brilliant' is the right word," he said, lifting a paper, "I mean, look at this crazy headline: "FURIOUS BRAIN CANCER VICTIM: I WAS ABDUCTED BY THRILL KINGS.' That's almost hysterical. Thrill Kings huh? Not bad. That's you, right Nonstop? Excellent." He gave Nonstop a thumbs up, and then looked around at all the friends he had failed to cheer up, all the friends who were looking pretty grim. Nonstop gave him a smile and a weak thumbs up in return, but even he looked depressed.

Near Wazzi, Slice refolded his arms and looked at his feet. "If the public wants us dead, how can we ever go home?"

Skyde didn't know. "Like Varrage said, it's a tactic," was all she could think of to say.

"We have to tell Doc," Plush said.

"Are you sure?" Slice said, "I don't think... Dag." And then he looked away, at the fire, at the trees.

Nonstop stepped forward. "I'll tell Doc," he said. "I'm going in anyway."

Krork looked at him, and stepped closer. "You're going to the Outpost now?"

"Yeah."

Krork looked back at the small building. "Maybe wait a minute. Varrage just went in to report to Dr. Norel."

"Yeah? So what?" Nonstop scratched the back of his head, waiting for Krork to turn back and look at him.

"Maybe give him a minute to finish," Krork said, still looking at the Outpost as Nonstop stepped in front of him.

"What? Give him a minute to finish? No way. Listen, Varrage doesn't have special privileges. He may think he does, but he doesn't."

Krork looked down at Nonstop, met his eyes, and tried to calm him with his own calmness. "Special needs then," he said. "Look, just don't pick a fight with him okay?"

"Me pick a fight with him? He's the ex-commando. He's the one who's always criticizing. He's −" and then Nonstop noticed that Krork was not responding, was not picking up the cry against Varrage, was in fact, just staring at him. "Okay. Fine. You got it. I won't pick a fight with him."

Nonstop turned and started walking. He didn't look to see if his friend turned away from him or not. Within a few steps he heard someone approaching — too light-footed to be Krork, and from the wrong direction as well.

"Nonstop, hold up a second," Skyde called from behind him, and Nonstop turned, happy for the distraction. "Before you go," she said, catching up to him, "Do you have the data streams on the Bleed Zone creatures? I want to file them."

"Sure. Hold on," Nonstop said, suddenly not as happy as he had been. He reached for his data-box.

"What happened to your arm?"

Nonstop looked below the rolled up sleeve on his elbow. Three long scabs had formed across his forearm.

"Nothin'," he said. "I scratched it in the woods when I was chasing the Inter-D." He glanced behind him to see where Krork was. Krork's back was turned; he was walking toward his work bike, already at least ten feet away. "Yeah, it ain't nothing," Nonstop continued, "I just drove through some thorns."

"I could take a look at it."

"Nah, they're already scabbed over - no problem. Let me see what I shot." Nonstop said, undocking his data-box from his harness belt.

"Maybe cover those cuts. Don't pick at them."

"No problem, I won't," Nonstop said, and he tapped he screen on the small device and watched it light. Blank. A blank blue field. He tapped it again, and it stayed blank. He started hitting random buttons until finally the menu screen came up. He navigated to the data stream folder, and tapped the folder to look inside it.

Blank again.

"No. It looks like I didn't get them," he said. "Sorry. I... don't have the hang of this thing yet I guess."

"So no still pictures either?" Skyde asked.

Nonstop saw the look of disappointment on Skyde's face, and wished he could do something, come up with some record, some picture that the data-box might have taken on its own, some kind of timed interval shot, some automatic, sensor, back up, protocol-status-document-thing to make up for the pictures he forgot to even try to take. He tapped the screen a few more times, and did not speak, his face already broadcasting the answer.

"No. Sorry. Did Krork get anything on the Glop-monster?"

"He said he got a data-stream, yeah."

"Well, there's at least that. I'm Sorry Skyde." Nonstop said, and he poked at the data box a few more times before docking it back on his belt, backwards and still lit. He let out a long breath, looked at Skyde once and frowned. He looked away, and then, without looking at anyone else, or saying anything more, he walked off, heading around the central fire, to the other side of base camp, to Varrage, and Norel, and Outpost 14.

*

When you looked closely at the dirt in the tracks around Outpost 14, it was still just dirt. Hundreds of vehicles had taken lazy runs around the Outpost, their riders testing the results of adjustments they had made to their machines, or just riding a couple of laps for the fun of it. Bike Pilots used the tracks for exercise as well, riding standard bicycles, or, as increasingly was the case, testing designs of their own.

Some of the track runs were Bleed Zone related, where the "Thrill Kings" team had circled the Outpost as the scanners calculated the best sequence of omissions for reaching a Bleed Zone. Once the Outpost had the sequence, the roof would lock its position, the critical information would be signaled to the Thrill Kings' bikes, and the ramp on the Outpost's roof would lower.

Once at ghosting speed, the Thrill Kings would hit the ramp, jump dimensions, and head straight into the next Bleed Zone mission.

But the dirt of the tracks, when you got close, was still just dirt, it was hard-packed in some areas, and there were plenty of raised ridgelines of displaced soil as well. The lines seemed so uniform, so deliberate, that they looked purposeful, and therefore must be strong, or reinforced, or somehow made maintainable. But that wasn't true, as Nonstop's kicks were proving. The ridgelines were just inert piles of soil, staying in place through something like habit, staying in place until the next force acted upon them, and sent them wherever they would go.

One of Nonstop's kicks dislodged a small stone. He gave it another kick, and a small puff of dust erupted at his feet. He studied where the stone came to rest, walked over, and kicked it again. Again he walked over to where it landed, and again he kicked it, hard enough to lose it in the darkness, and then he went back to kicking dirt.

It wasn't like he hadn't *tried* to learn the data-box. He had opened folders and read dialogue boxes, he had poked and prodded and spun little digital wheels with the tips of his fingers. He just never remembered what anything was, or what anything was supposed to do. Stupid hunk of plastic or meta-ceramic or whatever the stupid little thing was made out of.

The Outpost stood an easy sixty feet ahead of him, a few steps and it would be thirty, then twenty. Did he really want to go in? Couldn't he avoid fouling up again simply by finding something else to do for five minutes?

He stopped and looked at the building: small and round, ghostly under the two half moons, its main door and all its windows dark. There were options: he could climb the terrace steps that framed the main door, inspect the mammoth gear ring that crowned the building, play up on the roof, press buttons, try his luck with the data-box's big brothers. He could bronco ride the robotic crane arm, perch himself up on the ramp, maybe extend the rampway down to the ground. He could duck into the pilot house under the ramp. He could climb over the outrigger gantry and sit in the scanning chair. Maybe steer the roof around for a couple of spins — no chance of fouling up with that idea. No soldiers to foul up with at least. No stupid things to have to admit to.

Or he could just stay on the ground and get in trouble there. Mess around with the outdoor work stations. Kick the support columns. Crack the windows under the portico arcade. Maybe open the swing wall, expose the bike lab. Peek into Doc's window. See if that flickering light was Doc working on a computer, or watching a late movie. Maybe Doc was staying up watching the Lovingtime channel, crying, like his own mother used to do, crying and crying any time two people were even nice to each other.

Except we don't get the Lovingtime channel here. We don't get any channels here. All we get to do here is decide what kind of world the people back home watching TV will get to live in — or if they'll get to live at all. That's what we get to do. And we get to hit the wrong buttons, and we get to serve ourselves up to soldiers and see if they have any new weapons that they want to try out on us. That's what we get to do. That's what we're good at.

Nonstop found another rock to kick. And then he pivoted a quarter turn and kicked another. Then he repeated the motions until he completed all four points of the compass, and was looking at the Outpost again. His old friend the Outpost, with all its climbing handholds and all its noisy, moving components, and its brand new ability to sit, and stare back in silence, waiting, under the moons, for Nonstop to do something.

He turned around, suddenly curious as to what the central fire looked like from here.

There. See? It was absolutely beautiful.

*

Inside the Outpost's round central room, Varrage undocked his data box from a workstation and re-clipped it to his belt. Safety lights in the tech-filled space made the room look warm, but shadowy, like a restaurant after closing time.

Varrage stepped to the walkway at the perimeter of the room, and left through one of the five gaps between its walls that functioned as doorways. He entered a curved corridor where the only light present was what spilled over from the central room — through the gaps between the columns, and through the gaps between the workstations and their overhead cabinetry.

Walking in the curved corridor was like walking in the shadows of a techno-Stonehenge, a dim patchwork where rectangular light-casts cut into the surrounding darkness, amplifying the after-hours feel.

Darkness didn't bother Varrage. He preferred it. Quietly, he made his way down the corridor, to the rear of the building, to Dr. Norel's private office.

* * *

Rik Ty

**

In the far end of the long, narrow room, Doctor Edmond Norel sat working at a jumble of computers. Most of the light in the room came from the main monitors — bolstered by the array of smaller monitors that were stacked onto them, and piled next to them, and nestled under them. Together, their jumping light flickered across the doctor, and across the piles of mess scattered in the room: the mounds of print outs, the cardboard boxes full of print outs, the cardboard boxes full of other things, the piles of piles that radiated out from the Doctor's desk, and spread to claim all the flat surfaces in the room.

In some of the cartons, loose jumbles of tuning forks, kaleidoscopes, and other treasures from Dr. Norel's last desktop jutted out in straw piles. Somewhere under these cartons was his current desk, a long counter that ran the length of the room. Behind the chair where he sat, ran another counter, equally misused. The walls of the office were a patchwork of cubbies, pop stations and exposed equipment — there was little un-utilized space in the Outpost; even the walls had work to do.

To Norel's right stood the room's short wall, covered to the ceiling with stringed instruments: guitars, mandolins, balalaikas and the like. There was a roll of duct tape on the desk, slowly in the process of getting buried. So far, Norel had only stooped to using a single piece — a long strip he had stretched across the small monitors on the top of the central tri-screen. The tape turned the small monitors into a single mass, and kept them from sliding off either end of the larger monitor. Truthfully, Norel didn't want the duct tape to get buried. He didn't want the duct tape in his office at all. It seemed much too much like an admission, or an accusation demanding an admission. He'd have to do something about it — he would. Later. He would.

Norel himself was an absolute mess: gaunt, circles under his eyes, a pain under his shoulder blade from too many hours hunched over the keyboard. He had taken a shower just a few hours ago, but felt like he'd like to take another — just let the hot water dance on his skin, soothe the thrumming flesh around his eyes, fill his mouth with moist steam, allow his senses to control his attention — allow the act of showering to wash his mind. Oh Lord, that would be heaven. And he could have it. He could take another shower. No one would stop him. He could have heaven if that's what he called it. He just couldn't stay. Sooner or later, heaven would be done, and he'd be back to this.

At the moment he was superimposing data from several realm-scans over an image of Earth. The result was alarming. Together, the scans revealed a distortion field churning around the planet. A great double-helix distributed across several realmlines, pulsing when seen together, most likely invisible from any particular realm-world. Was it new? Or had it always been there? Was it even really there now, or just an illusion created by incomplete data?

Whichever it turned out to be; it was an additional area of concern, only minimally connected to the work he had tasked himself with: the creation of a vortex detection system — some protocol that would warn of approaching movement within the realmlines — the equivalent of a radar system to announce the approach of his vortex bikes.

A way out.

A way to win the current stalemate. Something that would create a contingency where if Bloch succeeded in stealing the bikes, they would be useless to him.

Norel had exhausted everything he knew, pushed every technology at his disposal, and the results were still feeble.

He watched the double-helix image, spent a moment simply observing the rise and fall of its curves, and then decided to run the data through a different filter. He heard footsteps approach from the doorway to his left, but didn't look up, even when the footsteps halted.

*

Varrage entered the doorway to Norel's office and stopped there. He saw Norel working at the far end of the room, so intent on his computer screens that his back was essentially to the entrance.

The man had designed this building himself. His office had only one door, no rear exit. No escape. He would be so easy to kill. Four or five steps, and any act of violence would do it.

Varrage could not redesign the building. He could not redesign the man. *He* would have to be Norel's escape route. He spoke.

"We're back sir. Do you have a moment?"

Norel kept his attention on the monitors, his fingers attacking the keyboard. "Of course Jaquon. The distortion around Earth is back. Stronger. We'll have to get a series of direct readings." Norel turned to Varrage. "Did you notice anything at the Bleed Zo…"

*

It was only for an instant, but Norel was jarred. It was happening again. In the doorway, Varrage's silhouette stood in stark contrast to the diffused light coming from the central room, and there was an image hidden in the effect.

Light filtered through the space between Varrage's arm and his ribs, creating a void where a ghost arm seemed to rise, upside-down, and made of light. If you continued down this imaginary arm, the silhouettes of the distant workstation monitors allowed enough light to come through to suggest an upside-down shoulder, then a neck, and then a head, and then another shoulder. The edges of the workstation's walls and ceiling aligned with the frame of Norel's own doorway, and together, cut out a shape that matched Varrage's silhouette nearly exactly, only upside-down, and made of light rather than shadow, a shape that wasn't there, but one he was looking at anyway.

Norel rubbed his forehead to hide his face, which he was sure looked frightened. His wedding ring flashed in the computer light as he moved his hand.

Secure that his eyes were covered, he stole a glance at the wall space across from the door, to one of the personal items from his office at Open Mind, one that had been too oddly shaped to stay in a box, and so had been casually hung on whatever latch or valve head had been conveniently sticking out from the wall. The item was unusual, and he once prided himself that its manner of display revealed a touch of resourcefulness. The memento was a scrap of T-shirt from his college days. The best part of the shirt, the graphic, was stretched within a wooden embroidery hoop. On the remnant were the faded shapes of a simple yin-yang image; the dark shapes of the symbol were created by ink, and the white shapes of the symbol were suggested by the raw fabric of the shirt, once a warm tan, now faded to near gray.

Norel looked back to Varrage in the doorway, and the yin yang effect in the light was still there, staring at him. He ignored it.

"I'm sorry. The glare hurt my eyes," Norel said.

Varrage turned to look behind him, saw no sharp light, paused for a moment, and then turned back to look at the doctor, taking a side step into the room.

"The Bleed Zone was very easy," Varrage said, "A few creatures, minimal spread; the area remained isolated. We were done with our work quickly — and yet as quick as we were, Bloch's teams still had time to show up. Their arrival junctions are simply too good. I think Bloch has copters in the air before any satellites have pictures of us. And unless he has sentries on every inch of the planet, he must have some way of detecting Bleed Zone events — also, there is something new: he's begun feeding the media the idea that we're terrorists."

"Terrorists," Norel said, dragging his hand down the back of his head, "Of course. We had to get to this point sooner or later. Bloch cannot attack us while we are here, so he attacks our future. Just as we cannot defend against him, so we attack *his* future."

"Attack his future?" Varrage moved his arms in front of him, gripping the wrist of his left hand with his right. His voice measured. "I don't see it. What attacks are you referring to?"

"Bloch wants the bikes so that he can penetrate defenses and attack with complete surprise. When we perfect the early warning system, we take that future away from him."

Varrage tensed.

"That's true," Varrage said, "but unless something has changed, that's months, or years, away. Bloch is a problem now. Bloch is expanding his attack now — and we can count on him to continue expanding it. Sir, I can end this. I can take Bloch out."

"Jaquon, I will not kill."

"It's not a question of what you will kill. It's a question of what you will protect. An assassin with vortex technology could change the world in an hour. An invasion force would be unstoppable."

Varrage looked along the desktop for an item he had seen before: a paperweight. He spotted it: a bronzed block featuring a standing nail and a standing bullet, both with deep seams running down from their tips. He walked over and picked up the item.

"Sir, he turned your nail into a bullet. He must not be allowed to steal your crowning achievement." Varrage set the sculpture down on the desk near the keyboard, pushing a few printouts aside with his wrist as he did so.

Norel looked at the paperweight, and then at Varrage. "Jaquon, we cannot solve this with force. Not really. Any violence against Bloch will make us a legitimate target of the entire United States Military. At that point we could never win, or hope to return home."

Varrage had considered this, and personally had his doubts about how far the military would go to avenge Bloch, but there was a possibility Norel was right. The Military might make a show of punishing any direct action against one of their own.

"Understood. But it's a standing offer. What about the Bleed Zones sir? How might Bloch's teams be detecting them?"

"I... don't see how they could be."

"Creating them? As a means of luring us back?"

"Creating the Bleed Zones? That's a troubling idea. If they've developed any technology that can create portals, then they're only a half step away from creating bikes of their own. I —"

Beyond the doorway, from deep in the corridor, came the sound of the main door opening, followed by the sound of Nonstop's voice.

"Yo Doc, can I talk to you a minute?"

Varrage looked toward the door and then back at the Doctor.

"Will you think about it sir?"

Norel let out his breath, "Obsessively," he said.

Nonstop entered the room and walked right by Varrage. Varrage tensed, and walked toward the door.

As Nonstop heard his teammate's departing footsteps, he smiled, but then shook his head and squeezed his eyes shut.

"Wait Varrage. You should hear this too."

"What?"

Nonstop stood across from the door and half-turned so that he faced both men. Varrage turned fully around, and re-entered the room. Nonstop addressed him directly.

"Before, when I was late to the meeting point, I wasn't joyriding." Nonstop said. "I confronted the soldiers. I felt "

"You What?" Varrage moved chest to chest with the young man in a single step.

"I thought if I talked to them —"

The glowing energy field at the forefront of Varrage's face tensed as what passed for his lips pulled back and revealed his clenched white teeth.

"You are the most impulsive — you're going to get someone killed. If it's *you*, Bloch gets the bikes." He turned to Norel. "Doctor, he has to be off the team."

"Off the team?" Nonstop said, rising on his toes, "Who are you? Off the team."

"Off the team," Varrage said, "You're one of the bullet-proof true enough, but you're reckless — if you compromise a Bleed Zone mission, you invite dimensional infection. Gravitational recognition. Do you need a refresher course? How about baby talk? Planet A becomes aware of Planet B. They recognize each other's mass, each other's gravity — then 'wham' — instant orbital collapse for both worlds."

"Jaquon, that's a theory." Norel said, placing a hand on each man's chest and actually moving them apart.

Varrage allowed himself to be moved. He took two steps back, but his eyes never left Nonstop's. "I'd say let him work aftershocks on other realm-worlds, but he's too impulsive even for that."

Nonstop launched forward; Norel's hand shot back and stopped him.

"Impulsive?" Nonstop said, jabbing a finger at the air. "You mean reflexes? At least I'm still fluid. You were stuck in the past when you got here you goosesteppin' Nazi."

"Lance!" Norel said, trying to catch Nonstop's eyes. Nonstop wouldn't look his way, but he stopped pressing against Norel's hand and set his heels back on the floor.

"Well, that's what *everyone* says anyway," Nonstop said quietly, keeping his eyes locked with Varrage's.

"Listen. Both of you." Norel said, "This..."

*

Outside the building, Krork stood at the main door, leaning in and listening. As he focused his hearing, the small rectangular cap his skin formed over his eardrum vibrated in short hops, calibrating as he focused in on the voices at distance. When he heard what the voices were saying, he entered the building and walked quickly toward Norel's office.

*

"... Look," Nonstop said, facing Dr. Norel, "I'm not a soldier. No one here is. He keeps pushing for me to be some kind of make-believe field marshal. I'm a test driver."

Varrage took a single step toward Nonstop. "You *were* a test driver. That is not enough for the duty you now hold." Varrage's voice, already grave, began to alter, to *shred*, as if a portion were peeling away and going somewhere else. "You won't learn tactics. You won't learn your equipment. All you're willing to learn is what you already know."

"What are you talking about?"

"Driving," Varrage said, taking another step closer.

Krork's voice boomed from the hallway. "Yo Doc! Can we borrow a guitar?"

Krork entered the workspace and passed between Nonstop and Varrage, close enough that his hip sent Nonstop crashing into the counter. Nonstop managed to avoid hitting the floor by grabbing the counter's edge, but with the move, his forearm knocked over a cardboard carton and several piles of paper.

At this, Varrage closed his eyes, turned, and left the room.

Krork paused until Varrage passed the doorway, and then leaned over and helped Nonstop stand. "Gah. Sorry," Krork said, and then he looked to Dr. Norel, who was watching them both, and seemed puzzled. "We're getting a bonfire going," Krork said to the Doctor, "Can we borrow a guitar?"

Norel looked at the mess on the floor, and then took a small step toward the back wall. "To play, right?" he said as he turned.

As Norel moved to face the instruments, Nonstop scooped up papers from the floor. Krork crouched to help.

"What'ya knock me down for?" Nonstop whispered.

"I was testing those fluid reflexes you're so proud of," Krork whispered back, reaching for a voltage meter.

"Yeah, well, look what you made me do," Nonstop gestured to the papers, the tuning forks, the calipers. "This is Doc's important stuff," he said, grabbing at the items with both hands.

"It'll be okay," Krork said, picking up a small wedge of glass whose interior seemed complex and folded. As he moved it to the carton, it trailed a rainbow on the floor and he smiled. Next, he noticed a brass kaleidoscope, capped with a collar of faceted glass jewels. He reached for it, eager to see what trick it might offer. Nonstop reached it first.

"They're talking about kicking me off the team."

"I got that impression, yes."

"You know? You heard — sssh,"

Doctor Norel pulled a guitar down from the wall, holding it by its strap. Nonstop found a spilled tweezer-vice to reach for.

"Here you go," the Doctor said.

Nonstop put the tweezer vice in the carton. Krork stood to accept the guitar.

"Thank you," Krork said.

"It's likely out of tune."

"It'll be perfect. Absolutely great, thank you," Krork took hold of the instrument and turned it in his hands, admiring it. A patch of reflected light slid back and forth across its surface, and he admired that too. "This is very nicely made," he said.

Behind him, Nonstop continued gathering the scattered pages, as well as the large tuning forks, and the small tuning forks, and the pencils, and the other scattered pages, quickly and carefully placing them all into the cardboard carton. As the conversation slowed down, Nonstop did too. He reached for a set of papers that were familiar to him: two pages, printed with bold patterns of black radiating lines. The set featured the same sun-ray pattern on both sheets — the top sheet printed on clear plastic, the bottom on white paper. If he remembered right, they had some kind of a French name, and when you moved them, the black lines would appear to spin and whirl — a great trick — no batteries, no motors — just a game of the eye, or the mind, or both, or whatever. Nonstop placed the sheets in the box, while Krork said something else about acoustics and guitars, and then Nonstop reached for the last spilled item — a big, cartoon-styled alarm clock - not even electric - a hand-sized, silly-thing with two big alarm bells on the top, and between them, one little bing-a-ling hammer waiting to make a racket. He tossed the clock lightly into the box.

"Oh, don't throw that," Norel said, and Nonstop froze.

"What? I —" he started to say.

"In fact, I'd like that to stay out."

"Sure, sorry, sorry. I didn't know," Nonstop said, cringing slightly as he plucked the clock back out of the box.

"Off the team," he heard some little bird sing somewhere.

Lifting the clock, he turned it. There was a photo on its face — of Dr. Norel and his daughter — circled by little diamond shapes where the clock's numbers should have been. The photo showed the doctor lying in the grass of a meadow, lifting his tiny daughter, barely more than a baby, with the trees behind them, and with a big patch of white-blue sky behind the trees. A very cute picture: Doc was nose to nose with the laughing little girl, holding her upside down in the air and backwards, so that her feet pointed out toward the clouds. The only other thing in the picture was a bird, way in the back, stuck in the pale sky. Nonstop turned fully toward Doctor Norel and raised the clock, offering it.

"Sorry. Here you go," he said.

"Thank you," Norel said, stepping forward.

Krork took the clock from Nonstop and passed it along to Dr. Norel, taking the opportunity to glance at the image printed on it. The Doctor accepted the clock, looked down at its face, and then continued looking down, slipping into memory.

Nonstop checked the floor for any items he might have missed, saw none, and stood with the carton.

"How old is she now?" Krork asked Norel.

Norel looked up as if startled, then turned, and quickly pushed aside a stack of papers. "She's... I should know that right away shouldn't I?" He set the clock down on the counter and stepped back to judge the stability of the amassed clutter. "She's seven," he said, "She should be in second grade." And with that, his smile changed slightly, locking around his lips, but shrinking from his eyes.

Krork watched the smile fade, and took a step closer to the Doctor.

As Krork and Norel spoke, Nonstop looked back and forth along the counter for a place to put the carton he held, but every space seemed to be covered with papers or print-outs or prototypes. He placed the carton half on the counter and half on a hill of equations, but the box started sliding as soon as he took his hands away, pulling the pages with it. Nonstop re-grabbed the carton and managed to stop the paper-slide before it could create a whole new mess for Norel to watch him make. He spotted a sturdy-looking group of papers near the back wall and decided to try putting the box there. When he moved it, a page that had stuck to its bottom dropped free, zig zagging all the way to the floor and making a second mess to deal with.

Was Doc watching? Did he see? Nonstop set the carton near the wall and let it go. It seemed to stand level, and he began listening again to what Krork and the Doctor were saying — something about a long time — spoken quietly and calmly. Something that had nothing to do with him.

He picked up the lost paper with one easy move and set it back on the pile it came from. Then he turned, and saw as Krork put his hand on Norel's shoulder. "She's safe," he heard Krork say, and then he heard Krork brighten and ask: "Coming to the bonfire?"

At this, Norel shook his head and looked downward, saying, "Doubtful. Sorry... I have something I need to speak to you about though..."

Nonstop held his breath, and was happy that he didn't actually gasp.

Norel took a step back to his workstation, "Here," he said, and he tapped a button on his keyboard.

Nonstop exhaled.

"There's a distortion around Earth," Norel continued. "It's sporadic, and distributed across several realmlines. Tomorrow, I'd like you both to start getting us readings from a few of these locations." Norel held out his hand. "I have a program I'd like you use. I'll have to load it for you. May I see your data-boxes?"

Nonstop stood still for a second, and then said "Sure." After another second, he looked down at his belt, to where his data box was still lit, and docked backwards. Krork slung the guitar over his shoulder, and with the move, turned to face Nonstop.

"Here, I'll pass it along," Krork said, reaching out his hand.

Nonstop handed his data-box to Krork, and Krork, with his broad back facing the Doctor, quickly tapped its screen and turned the device off. Then he removed his own data-box, placed it over Nonstop's, and handed both items to Dr. Norel.

Norel docked both data-boxes at his workstation, frowned, and removed one. Examining it closely, he tapped its screen a few times and then returned it to the dock.

Nonstop craned his neck to watch, but didn't catch what the Doctor actually did. He looked at Krork, who was already looking at him.

Norel typed at the keyboard. "This is pre-set with the omission sequences to several realm-worlds; each a good spot to take readings from," he said. "You can take your choice as far as which worlds to visit first, but I'd like at least three sets of readings by tomorrow afternoon." He undocked the boxes and placed both in Krork's hands.

"Absolutely," Krork said, accepting the boxes while Nonstop nodded in agreement behind him.

"Thank you," the doctor said, "Now go, go. The bonfire's waiting."

Krork smiled, and the Doctor shooed them away. Nonstop took a step toward the door, and they all said their goodbyes, quick and friendly.

Norel smiled at the two of them, then strode back to his desk and sat down.

*

"What was all that about?" Nonstop asked after they had taken a few steps into the corridor.

"You tell me."

"I did tell you — they're talking about kicking me off the team." Nonstop said, looking back over his shoulder.

"They're not going to kick you off the team. You're a great driver."

"Yeah, but, I have to be more than a great driver. I have to get into the game man... *more*. I have to do more. I have to — did you really come in to borrow a guitar?"

"Sure - that, and to make sure you didn't get killed by Varrage."

"We weren't gonna fight." Nonstop took a step in the dark corridor, then another. "Well maybe we were, but —"

"You're welcome."

"It's not funny. I didn't even get to tell them what I needed to."

"No? And why was that?"

"— that was just one foul-up after another in there — *Mr. Hip-check.*" Nonstop took another step, and shook his head. "I almost got caught back in the Bleed Zone. I wanted to tell Doc everything that happened, but it kinda matched what Varrage was saying about me, and I didn't want to help him make his point. I want to be a good part of the team; not a bad part of the team."

"What do you mean, you almost got caught? What happened?"

"I got hurt. I tried talking to the soldiers back at the Bleed Zone and they like, started to microwave me. I actually felt it. Some kind of beam. It hurt. Everyone's gotta know. Varrage too."

Krork considered this. "I'll tell him."

"You'll tell him? You're running between me and him a lot lately."

"Well... you know that linguistic chameleon stuff you like to kid me about? How I can pick up languages?"

Nonstop raised his eyelids and did not lower them. "You mean your special *'innate' ability to absorb languages simply by hearing them?* Why no, I completely forgot."

Krork ignored his friend, and began to gesture with his hands as he walked.

"Before I can grasp vocabulary, I catch meaning. Intent. Jaquon seems like he's hanging on to his humanity by will alone — particularly when he's talking to you."

"Me? What did I —"

"— I'm hoping it's part of the healing, that his humanity will set at some point." Krork looked directly at Nonstop for a second, then looked back to where he was walking, "You trigger something in him. At times he seems angry enough to rip your head off. If he ever gives in to that anger, there'll be nothing left of Jaquon but an interdimensional creature named Varrage."

Nonstop walked forward with sad-puppy eyes. "Poor Jaquon. Ripping my head off will cause him undue emotional trauma ."

"Jaquon..."

"'Undue' I say,"

"Jaquon is worth saving."

"Jaquon is a jerk."

They took the next few steps in silence. Then they reached the exit, and stepped through.

*

Outside, Krork paused to inhale deeply, and then took a long stride to catch up to Nonstop. "Are you okay with taking readings on your data-box?" he asked.

"I am if you'll script me another shortcut."

"Oh. Okay." Krork paused again. "Yeah... maybe," he said, looking at his feet.

Nonstop took a few steps before he realized Krork was no longer walking with him. He turned around and saw Krork step to one of the outdoor workstations, slipping under the shadows of the roof's gear ring.

"Where are you going?"

"I've got to get something."

Krork emerged a moment later, holding a clipboard. "I wanted to find you some actual paper - listen, I'll make you a deal. You draw those Bleed Zone creatures for Skyde, and I'll script you that shortcut on your data-box."

"I can't draw. I..."

"A diagram. How many feet. How many heads. She needs it."

Nonstop reluctantly traded his data-box for the clipboard. They started walking again.

"Boy, oh boy, oh boy. How did YOU get stuck with the job of interdimensional cruise director?" Nonstop asked.

Krork stood up taller, beaming.

"Let every flower bloom," he answered.

They walked on. A breeze blew, and after a few moments, they saw their friends, waving for them to come and join the party at the bonfire.

* * *

Louis Sinclair's commandeered office in Open Mind was the most well equipped facility he had ever worked in. For one thing, there was elbow room; you could turn around without knocking anything over, or bumping into other lab technicians. It was beautifully lit too — outrageously lit actually. Opacity controllers were built into the floor-to-ceiling windows, and with a few drags of a finger you could change the shape of the window's transparent space, the size, or the amount of light that was let in. The clear spaces could be huge, razor thin, round, or any combination of shapes — including painterly squiggles you made up on the spot. The windows also shared a library of preset forms that allowed the glass to mimic dozens of conventional window styles — or pieces of art. You could have a twenty foot Mona Lisa on the wall, if you didn't mind it being in stark dark and light - no dot-screens yet. The windows could even be used as an artificial light source — solar collector by day, adjustable light source by night. Within the next few generations of the technology, the light produced wouldn't be the florescent cool it was now; the windows might advance to offer a range of light options, all the way up to bright sunshine. The coming iterations might even let you choose your view. Tired of the tree outside? How about Paris?

That pre-supposed that there would *be* coming iterations. When Sinclair informed Bloch of the window's capabilities, the Colonel's reaction was immediate: he ordered the windows run at full opacity. Letting in the view was now an act of insubordination — or would be if Sinclair were military. Any discovery that wasn't connected to the motorcycles was an act of insubordination it seemed. And so Sinclair started squirreling away the interesting things he was finding, Norel's notes on innovative solar collectors, ocean surface farming, synthetic fuels, meta-ceramics — an amazing collection to have come from one mind, and the collection kept growing.

What kind of mind made all this possible? This building, these projects? Norel had to be rich. The rich have extra hours in their days. The rich can augment. The rich can augment their brain power simply by hiring more — uncredited servants, disposable geniuses, thousands of drifting, rootless flowers — not even flowers — the means to flowers — pollen.

Oh well. The rich boy went too far didn't he? The gifted received too much. Norel had called the lightning. Norel had called the attention of the Colonel, and the Colonel had come and taken it all.

Still... still, what kind of mind could have done all this?

When the soldiers had called to request a meeting with him (an odd formality, since he couldn't refuse them) he had about two minutes to place Norel's various binders back in their rosewood cabinets and sweep his own muffin crumbs off the counter and into the trash can. The paper thing that wrapped the muffin, he folded tightly and stuck into his pocket. Then the sounds of the soldiers' footsteps advanced up the hallway, and a three man team arrived with the data-stream he needed to pre-view for the Colonel.

Sinclair was required to tag all important science elements of the field data-streams for the Colonel's easy review. Corporal Vega would prescreen a separate copy of the data-stream and tag it for military elements — strategy, team performance, equipment performance and the like. The Colonel also required the original data-streams themselves.

What elements did Sinclair screen for? Whatever was portal related: how the lens behaved, how the portal behaved, what, if any, life forms were observed. Most of his work was related to portal location analysis. The lens was activated nearby — originally within the campus's southern habitat preserve, but surprisingly, the portals never manifested anywhere near the launch sites. The first event location was three hundred miles south-east of the campus, the second, two hundred miles north. Sinclair suspected it was a field repulsion issue, but he really didn't know what he was working with, so his suspicions were akin to guesses. He was working with trial and error. Through adjustments in the laser catalysts, he was able to get the events to manifest much closer — ten to twenty miles in a vaguely northerly direction — maybe local on the next shot. Then again, maybe not; he was just launching salvos. The lens had every right to surprise him.

But Vega wasn't here to drop off a data-stream. Corporal Vega had something he wanted Sinclair to see immediately, and it wasn't portal or life-form related.

After pleasantries, Corporal Vega handed a pen-drive to Sinclair, and Sinclair inserted it into a port in one of his lab's workstations.

Sinclair and the soldiers clustered around the workstation's large central screen as the data-stream came up. As Corporal Vega had mentioned, the data-stream pertained to the VTOLs' attack on the young rider from earlier in the evening.

The image was mid-range resolution, not choppy, but not film quality either. It showed the landscape sweeping under the flight of the VTOL. In the images, trees flashed by, and rectangles of light dashed across the uneven ground. The scene had a certain excitement level all its own, when you considered the vehicle that had made it. But the flight was not the point.

"Right here is where we see it," Corporal Vega said.

On the screen, the lean rider on the crazy motorcycle passed through the patch of magenta-colored light. Sinclair touched a button on the controller and the imagery slowed down. The patch of light moved across the ground to recapture the young man. Bright white flares spat from the machine gun cannon at the front of the VTOL as the bullets and tracers headed for the rider.

Sinclair saw the now-familiar sight of the bullet trails wrapping around the rider and his bike - like instantaneous spider silk, he thought. He had prescreened many other bullet-impact data-streams for the Colonel, but this, he had been told, was different, and so he paid close attention. The bullet trails blazed hot around the driver and then faded — normal, at least status-quo, and then the rider bucked and twisted in his seat, as if in pain.

That got Sinclair's attention. That was new.

Corporal Vega spoke again. "This jamming frequency does not short out his shielding, but it appears that he feels it."

"Yes," Sinclair said, "it does look that way. I'll enlarge the image, does the camera stay on the target?"

"For a time. The target is evasive, as you know."

"Mmm-hmm." Sinclair nodded, as he worked the controls.

The image enlarged and panned until Nonstop's head and shoulders filled the screen. The frame rate continued slowly, showing as the shoulders of the rider jerked upwards and his head tilted radically to the side.

Sinclair slowed the rate further.

The head was seen turning, chop, chop, chop, until it presented directly to the camera — fear on the young man's face as he looked at his attacker. Then the face winced, and blood erupted from its nose. The young man's eyes widened, and he brought a gloved hand up to the skin above his lip and wiped blood on the exposed patch of skin on the back of his hand. He looked at the blood. His eyes widened even more. He turned his head away from the camera, and within three progressions of the data-stream, was gone.

"Is that it?" Sinclair asked.

"That's what's out of the ordinary," Vega said. He handed Sinclair a clipboard. "The frequency data is all here sir."

Sinclair nodded, and said "Thank you," and then picked up the hand set from the phone on the workstation. He punched in a number and after two rings, got a voice mail prompt.

"Hello Colonel," he said. "This is Sinclair. Please come to my lab as soon as you can. There's been a breakthrough regarding the riders' shielding."

* * *

Nonstop crumpled a sheet of paper after an embarrassing start at a drawing, and looked for a place to throw it. He had no trash can. He had the impulse to toss the paper-ball on the ground, but they were guests on this planet. He thought of shoving it in his jeans, but he was in a hammock — so he un-crumpled the ball and placed the wrinkled sheet under the stack of papers already on the clipboard. That done, he got back to work drawing Skyde her space-dogs — as he was currently thinking of the creatures from the Bleed Zone — though when it came time to actually write something on the drawing — *title it*, if that was the right term, he might try something more official sounding: Inter-D specimen, or maybe something cooler-sounding, like Inter-D wolf pack, Inter-D panthers, Inter-D cougars. As for the creature that attacked Krork, he was still stuck with the Inter-D macaroni and cheese idea — maybe Inter-D *bleech*-pile. Whatever. He could worry about titles after he had finished creating these wonderful master-pieces.

He touched his pencil to the paper, but something still didn't feel right. For one thing, the shadow of his hand was right where he intended to draw. Well, he could move the light.

He reached over his shoulder and pulled down on the power cable that was draped over one of the branches above his head. A caged light on the end of the cable raised up toward the branches, and the shadow of his hand moved down the page. How was that? That was good.

He applied pressure to the pencil, and made a mark on the middle of the page, up near the top. His feet felt hot — weird to be in a hammock and have your shoes on. He put the toe of one foot against the heel of the other and pushed off his shoe. He repeated the process with his other foot, and leaned forward to pull off his socks, which caused the hammock to start swinging. He'd need both hands. He put the clipboard on the ground next to the spot where his sword was stuck in the dirt — good and ready should he need it. The hammock moved, but was secure, anchored to the back of Rattletrap on one end, and his loyal pet tree on the other. Rattletrap's back-end, up near the spoiler, swayed a little bit, but Nonstop had the bike's claws dug firmly in the ground. The bike wouldn't tip.

He pulled off his socks, gagging theatrically as he flipped them over his head and up into the tree — where they came to land with the rest of his laundry.

When he picked up his drawing, the tree returned the favor, dropping two dead leaves directly onto his clipboard. He looked upward, raised an eyebrow, and brushed the leaves aside. You couldn't escape commentary it seemed; even though that was the entire reason he had excused himself from the bonfire and driven here to his campsite. Krork had handed him back his data-box with the shortcut written on it less than ten minutes after they had sat down at the bonfire. Krork expected him to do the drawings there, but he couldn't. He stalled for a long time, but finally had to leave. He'd have never gotten anywhere with people watching him. This was much better — despite the fact that he still hadn't gotten anywhere.

His campsite was small — a clearing within a stand of tall, slim trees. There were a few interesting boulders that were either the universe's most uncomfortable couches, or its lumpiest tables — depending on what you were using them for. Other than that, he had room to park Rattletrap, an expanding pop-locker for his gear, a fire grid, a couple of sling chairs, and a great view of the sunrise — which, on most days, he slept through. The sun had a tendency though, he noticed, of rising steadily all morning, and its continual nagging usually prevented him from missing lunch.

Back to the drawing, and — maybe he should give up on the space-wolves for now. Maybe switch to the spaghetti creature. It was all squiggles, so what mistake could he really make? Skyde had a bit of data stream of the pasta-monster from Krork, so did she really need a drawing? Maybe not, but the pasta-pile would be easy to draw, and might help make up for the fact that the monster-lions wouldn't be.

He turned the clipboard sideways, so that the pages were horizontal, and dragged the pencil softly around the paper. Around and around, creating a vague shape — not really of the creature — more of the over-all space it took up. This wouldn't be too hard. He knew he could draw — sort of. He had painted the nonsense on his shoes one morning in the bike lab, and had added to it since then. He had made the magic-marker Vortex—S on the red T-shirt he was now wearing, and he had suggested his share of wicked deco on the rigs at the bike-lab. He could draw a couple of monsters if all that was needed was a diagram or two.

He focused the swirls of his pencil tip toward the center of the page, twirling the lines until a vague curve-shape appeared on the paper. It could have been a lick of flame, or a cast off strip of baker's dough. All it was really was a series of black lines encircling white empty space; all it was really was a jumble of graphite particles trapped amid bond paper particles, but it easily could suggest a tentacle, if that's what you were looking for.

The tentacle looked excellent. The little drawing worked out so well Nonstop repeated the process a zillion times, creating a million wavy sausages — and that was perfect, because that's what the creature looked like. It had drippy lather stuff too though. And the drippy lather stuff had a mind-link element, how could you draw that? Ha — easy — you draw three bumps for the lather, and write the rest in the margin — and while you're at it, you stay far away from hard-spelling words like telepathy, and stick with friendly words like mind-link. Then you draw yourself some lines between the writing and the drawing. That's a good trick. Do that.

He did. He considered starting a new drawing for the creature's home-world, but that seemed easy to mess up. There was a blank spot in the corner of the page, he could draw it there. He drew a couple of bumpy rocks, and slashed a horizontal line under them. Under that, he drew a squiggly puddle, and wrote the word oasis — another weird spelling word, but at least with that one, what you saw was what you got. He wrote "mountains" by the bumpy rocks, though he wasn't sure what they had been. He wrote CREATURE'S

HOMEWORLD in capital letters above the bumpy rocks, and drew in a couple of bumpy trees. Not bad.

He changed papers and moved on to the harder drawing. The creatures that had the jaws and the legs and the glowing eyes. He repeated what worked, swirling the pencil tip across the page until a big fat sausage appeared in its center — a reasonable torso for the space-wolf — and then added four bent sausages for the legs. But the creatures had muscles, lots of them. Were they sausages too? He tried swirling sausage shapes on the drawing. But where exactly? High? Low? Left? Right? Nothing looked good. He erased, drew, and erased again until the paper started to peel under the rubber end of the pencil. Disgusted, he wrote "muscles" next to the leg and drew a line between the word and the picture. He added "Glowing Foot Pads" and drew a line that pointed under the creature's foot. Claws? He wasn't sure he had seen any claws. The creatures had blocky, rough wedges at the toes that might have sheathed claws, and he decided to write that too. "Sheathed" was another word that might betray him; he wrote "covered" next to the word claws instead. He added a question mark.

Glowing stripes. A bunch, but big, right? On the sides? He drew four jagged lightning-boomerang shapes on the torso. He didn't know where they actually went, so he just made it up. He wrote "glowing rib-stripes" above the creature, and connected it to the drawing with a line.

A float or two of realm-light escaped from under his hair as he worked. He didn't notice.

He was getting antsy. It would be good to ride. There was no way he could draw the head. Strong, muscle-y, full of, well, parts — sharp teeth, flat teeth, all glowing, with glowing saliva drooling everyplace, and glowing eyes, and more muscles — and some of the creatures had flabby wedges on the sides of their necks, between their shoulders and their jaws. How could you draw that? How could you even start? How could you draw that the creatures who had the flabby necks looked strong too — were full of muscles too? It was hopeless. He'd never get it. He swirled the pencil at the head area — lightly. What kinds of shapes? The creatures had glowing eyes — how could you say what shape they were?

Dark heads, glowing features — *ha!* — Varrage Monsters. He could draw Varrage's face instead. That would be a riot, black sides of the head, sharp edges to the cheekbones, burning yellow face-plate stripe down the center of the head, pulled to sharp focal points at the chin and eyebrows, white slashes for eyes. With the exception of the jumping wedges of energy at the top of his head, Varrage did look like these creatures. A riot. He could see Slice and Wazzi laughing when he showed them the drawing. They'd get it. And his hand moved to do it. He felt the impulse to do it. It was there. Right in his back. Right in his breathing, the pencil circling above the paper, a millimeter from making a mark, a millimeter from drawing Varrage and finishing this rotten drawing, but... Skyde was serious about this stuff. These drawings were for her. In some weird way, they were already hers; he was just making them.

His weight was wrong. The angle of the hammock was wrong at his thigh. He was compensating for the lack of balance and it was nagging at him. Rattletrap was a little crooked now that he looked at him. He hadn't parked him as well as he thought he had. He could light him back up, uproot the left hand, shift the unit over to the left a bit, and then replant the claw — straighten it right up — two seconds... two seconds... he shut his eyes. Why? What? Just finish the stupid drawing.

He placed the pencil tip on the point where the neck started, and stopped the pencil cold, left it planted on the paper. He didn't press. He breathed slowly. He would draw something. If it came out terrible, it came out terrible. He'd just do what he'd been doing — write what the parts were supposed to be. All he promised was a diagram. Skyde didn't know what the things looked like right? He drew a head shape and it looked like a pumpkin. He added jagged eyes, and it looked like a Jack-O-Lantern. He drew teeth. So what if they were wrong. He drew some kind of muscle lines behind the mouth, *who cares if they were wrong*. A line between the bony eyebrows, a line between the brow and the forehead, a line in a blank space, a line in another. A lie. Another lie. He didn't know what he was doing. He covered his lies with descriptive words. He drew lines between the words and the drawings. He felt horrible. He could try again, but his mind locked that thought right out. No. He couldn't try again. He had promised diagrams. He'd hand them over, and at least keep his word. If Skyde ripped the pictures up in front of him, he'd just have to take it.

How long had he been working? He had no idea. He had a great many *no ideas* sitting there in his dark campsite. He had liked the drawings, and now he hated them. Not long ago he had felt good. Now he had no idea how he felt. Blank. He felt blank. He had rushed here, to this spot he mischievously referred to as his *room*, or *home*, or sometimes as his *little perch in the woods*, because he felt good, and feeling good made it easy to believe he could do the drawings.

He looked around him. He saw tree trunks: stalks of growth harshly illuminated by the caged bulb on the end of his work-light. And beyond the trees, a great, engulfing darkness that seemed more than just the night. You could move in the night: by moon, by star, by lantern, by touch. But this was a darkness more complete, waiting to swallow his little circle of light. He wasn't on Earth. He wasn't home. He wasn't a good friend. He was a fake. They weren't safe. The things that made them feel safe were fake.

He made one last mark on the page and then stepped out of the hammock. He watched the darkness. He stepped into his shoes. He held the clipboard against his thigh so the pages would not flap. He unplugged the work-light from the solar outlet embedded in the tree. He gave the tree a pat. He stood in the sudden and total darkness, not surprised at all that he was still there, that the darkness had swallowed him, but had not ended him. He closed his eyes. The moons were out. His eyes would adjust.

Half a minute later they had. The moon light showed him where the trees were, and where the trees weren't. He walked off to deliver the drawings, and left his little perch in the woods.

*

The long tables around the bonfire were empty. The bonfire itself was a blue-gray bed of embers, sheltering coals that flared red as the breeze passed over them. It appeared his friends had called it a night not long after he left. Maybe the party had moved on. Even The night crew wasn't anywhere that he could see.

He kept walking. He took a dirt path up a small hill, and passed through a cluster of young trees. As he walked the path, he passed a few individual campsites, but he reached the clearing at the top of the hill without seeing anyone.

The Bike Pilots affectionately called the clearing "Girls' World". "Girls' World" was made up of several deluxe tents and pop-labs set around a central fire grid. Girls' World had comfort. Girls' World had its own shower and bathroom facilities. Girls' World had furniture.

It wasn't hard to spot Skyde's pop-lab in the collection. Hers was the one surrounded by tables, each stacked high with portable animal habitats.

A new table, with only one plastic cage on it, sat in front of the others, starting a second ring. Skyde's white vortex bike, now rarely used, stood on the far side of her pop-lab.

Nonstop took a step toward Skyde's pop-lab, and his foot-fall made a crunching noise — *gravel*. There was a ring of gravel around the camp-site. Something new. A tent flap opened on the pop-lab directly across the camp from him, and Brickyard stepped out, pulling on one of her gigantic gloves. She looked right at him. He waved, and she nodded.

"I just want to give Skyde something." He whispered, holding up the clipboard.

"Fine. Just keep it quiet," she whispered back, and returned inside the pop-lab.

Nonstop's feet crunched on the gravel one more time before he hit grass again. Then he walked over to Skyde's encampment.

There was no place to knock on the front of the pop-lab. The side and back walls were rigid, but the front and top were stretched fabric. Even if the front were rigid too, it would have been hard to find a spot to knock on — the animal tables blocked most of the entrance area. What path there was was blocked by Skyde's Blast boots, which were parked in the gap between the tables.

As Nonstop approached the pop-lab, most of the little animals in Skyde's Wee-Be collection scurried to the edges of their cages to investigate him, looking for food or maybe just attention. Adorable little things. One little fuzzball with long furry ears was looking right at him. In the cage next to it was what looked like a living orange, with two black dots for eyes and a ring of smaller oranges for feet. Nonstop waved to them. "Hey little guys," he said quietly, and then turned to knock on the lab.

Kaya, Skyde's pet Inter-D, blocked his way. Her small furry head rose level with his as she balanced on her very-long tail. It was hard to say what type of creature Kaya was. Her head was like a slim white coconut; her fur was thick, and very soft. She had two shiny black eyes, a tiny little mouth, and tiny little nostrils on the underside of her snout — the narrow end of the coconut. She had a very long tail, which was covered with the same soft white fur as her head. No legs that Nonstop could see. No difference between head and body — again that he could see. With her tail included, she was about five feet long. A soft, furry comet that glided over surfaces with serpentine grace. The little creature avoided the ground, though Nonstop had seen her travel it from time to time. Even then, he had never seen her dirty.

She anchored herself by gripping a table leg with the end of her tail, and hovered at eye level with Nonstop, looking at him quizzically.

"Hey Kaya," he said softly, and then stroked her cheek with the back of his finger. She made a churbling sound at his touch, and tilted her head toward his hand. He extended his arm and knocked on the lab. Kaya smelled the hairs on his forearm, and the scarred places on his arm where the hair no longer grew. She lingered on his long fresh scabs, which seemed to Nonstop, like a logical thing for an animal to do.

"Skyde, you in?" he asked, slowly turning his arm away from Kaya.

*

Inside the pop-lab, Skyde shook her head and blinked repeatedly until she felt awake. A quick look around re-oriented her — she was in her pop lab; the bed was made; the lights were off. Moonlight flowed through the small window above her workstation and through the glass bottle collection on her windowsill. She was still sitting at the small workstation, though she was leaning on the wall. Somebody had called her.

"Yeah?" she said quietly, more to the floor than the visitor, "Hold on," she added. Then she stood and pulled back the flap of the pop-lab's entrance. She stepped outside.

She was still dressed in her flight suit, but her feet were bare and she had let out her braids. As soon as she stepped out from the lab, Kaya sped from Nonstop and draped herself across Skyde's shoulders.

"Hey girl." Skyde said as she gave Kaya a few friendly rubs, and then stepped over to Nonstop.

"Something up?" Skyde looked around her, "I thought you might be Diamondsong."

"Nothing much really." Nonstop waved the clipboard for her to see. "I kinda have something for you. Just, I don't know, a couple of sketches."

"Sketches?"

"The Bleed Zone creatures."

"Really? Oh let me see." She walked over and took the clipboard, immediately looking back and forth between the two pictures. She smiled. She smiled enormously.

"Oh these are great. Thank you." She continued to examine one picture and then the other. "So, quadrupeds. And this other, the squiggly one, did all its little bits act like fingers, or were they all individual creatures?"

"Sort of like both. Like a tangle."

"Colony life-form maybe? Invertebrate?"

Nonstop shrugged. "I don't know. What's invertebrate?"

"A creature with no spine, like a snail, or a starfish."

"Oh." He thought for a moment, "I don't know."

"These are wonderful. Thank you so much."

"I had some trouble with them. The lines on the dog-guy's neck, some of them, I don't know, had like fat-pouches on the sides of their heads. I know it seems crazy, but some of them actually had it."

"It's not crazy. They might be skin-flaps, like on orangutans. There are lots of reasons they might have them — could be a male/female thing, could be fat storage — stored energy, could be a resonating chamber for a mating call, or it could be related to age progression, or rank within the group — it could be something we never heard of. But it's nice to know it was there, thank you."

"You're welcome. I'm sorry it's just a sketch."

"Don't be. Sketches are great. Sketches have value all their own. They're eyewitness impressions — they don't have to be totally accurate — in some ways they give more information than a photograph — they give an overview, a sense impression that's already been edited by a human being. Sometimes a photo just shows a flat plane of color, and someone has to tell you what you're looking at. Live 3-D scans will be better when we finish developing them. Though I think we'll get beaten to the finish line on that one."

"People back home?"

"Yeah, I would guess."

Nonstop looked around at the Wee-bes. "Any of these guys going home soon?"

"I just took a few back the other day. These guys are healing very nicely. It won't be long."

"What about those guys? They don't look like they're doing too good." Nonstop pointed at what looked like three giant raisins under a spotlight.

"Those are eggs. They're all right. At least I think so."

"Eggs, really? Wow."

"Their nest-site was destroyed during a Bleed Zone. I don't actually know what temperature to keep them. The cage is a little warmer than the site was. I didn't see any rotting vegetation, and the mother was nowhere to be found. I didn't think the eggs would avoid predation out in the open, so I gave them their chances here."

"And so far, so good?"

"Yes. In fact, one of them is starting to hatch. I have a bunch of zones in the back of the cage, warm, cool, dry, wet. The creature can take its pick. But I don't have any indigenous food, just the one plant, the soil, and the eggs themselves. As far as nutrients go, all I have is chemical guess work based off those three things."

"How long will it take to hatch?" Nonstop peered closer. At the top end of the egg was a small tear, within the tear, a tiny snout worked open and closed. "Oh dig it. He is there." Nonstop said.

"Yes, it probably won't be long."

Nonstop looked at the snout. The little creature was gasping. "He's having a hard time. Is he dying?"

"No. It's hard work being born."

"Poor little guy."

"And it may get harder. They may not be able to stay here. If it turns out that I can't feed them, then predators or not, orphans or not, they'll have to take their chances at home."

Nonstop straightened up, and looked around at the animal enclosures. "This is a lot of extra work."

"It is, but every day more and more people are helping me. Jo is helping me with the chemical analysis for the nutrient development. Diamondsong developed these habitat transfer units for me, and a friend just gave me two eyewitness field studies to file." She waved the drawings back and forth. "I have absolutely no complaints."

Nonstop smiled. Skyde liked the drawings. Krork was right. A diagram was all that was needed — at least better than nothing. He was surprised and relieved.

He spent the next fifteen minutes helping Skyde feed the Wee-bes, and then Skyde went back to work and he excused himself to return the clipboard.

At the edge of the campground he picked up a handful of gravel, and as he strolled back down the hill, he chucked the small stones, one by one into the stands of trees, listening as they hit leaves or bounced off logs.

How about that Krork? Imagine, an alien having a better idea about human nature than he did.

Yeah. How about that?

He had one last stone and he threw it hard. The moons were out. The treetops were rustling. He tried to get easy. What good did it do to keep feeling bad? And bad about what? Maybe he should just...

*

... there was a figure by the Outpost. Nonstop stood still among the trees and tried to see who it was. The person carried a box toward the long tables. Was it Doc? Nonstop moved closer, staying in shadow. It was. Doc put the box down on the table, and then picked something up. A piece of paper by the look of it.

Nonstop took a step and then forced himself to freeze — *don't interrupt. Don't mess things up. Just... don't do anything.* He watched.

*

Norel stepped to the beverage cart and filled a paper cup with coffee. He sipped. He looked at the newspaper page he had picked up, and then lit a work light tethered to his shoulder. He read the page, and when he was done, he lowered the page. He lowered the cup. He leaned his head back and stood swaying, looking up at the two half moons.

After a moment, he returned the newspaper to the table, replaced the wrench that held the paper in place, and poured his coffee down the cart's drain. When the last drop was gone, he discarded the cup in the proper chute.

He stood a long moment, then began walking back, taking step after step until he reached the Outpost's doorway, where he stopped, and took a last look at the moons.

Finally, he stepped within the entrance, and the little building swallowed him.

* * *

Rik Ty

**

Nonstop moved as soon as Norel was gone. He walked to the tables. The box Norel had placed down held six bottles of wine — not much more than a sip for everybody. Did Norel have to go into the basement to get it? The box also held a mandolin. Did Norel play? Nonstop didn't know. Next to the box was a page from a newspaper. Nonstop traded the clipboard for the paper. His young eyes had no problem reading in the moonlight. The headline read:

NEURO-TERRORIST CELL UNCOVERED

Nonstop looked around the long tables. He saw several newspaper articles placed here and there, held down by wrenches and small pieces of motors. He had no problem reading the nearby headlines either:

"MILITARY SILENT ON
MARIN COUNTY"
"NEST OF MIND KILLERS?"

And Wazzi's favorite:

"FURIOUS BRAIN CANCER VICTIM:
"I WAS ABDUCTED BY THRILL KINGS".

What paper had that one come out of? Why not just burn the nasty things? Throw them in the fire before Doc had a chance to see them. Doc didn't need this. How is it? How is it that Bloch can kick down their door? How is it that he can kick down their door and try to kill them, and keep on trying, and now just lie and lie and lie, and the papers keep on printing it? How could so much unfairness keep happening?
He didn't know.

He put the clipboard on the table. He looked at the trees. He moved his head. He saw the mandolin in the box and picked it up. He plucked a string — on an instrument he had never held before — and heard its pure note sound on the night air. He looked around him, turning his shoulders and his hips. He saw the moons. He saw his old friend the Outpost bathed in quiet moonlight, the old friend that had just received the old man, the good man. He saw the moonlight everywhere, in the air, on his skin, on the far trees.

"All right. All right." He said to the moonlight, and then he turned back to the table, returned the mandolin to the box, and picked up the paper Norel had crumpled.

He stuffed the horrible thing deep in his front pocket.

"All right. I'll fix this," he said aloud, nodding.

And then he walked away. Fast, even for him.

*

Nonstop was quick getting to his camp, and once there, he stayed quick. He slid his sword back in its sheath, slipped the gear harness onto his back, and didn't bother with the rest.

He unhooked the hammock and let it hang, jumped onto Rattletrap and powered him up.

RRRRRAAAAAAR!! Went the bike.

The stupid jungle-cat noise. He had forgotten to put the rig in whisper mode. He corrected that quickly, freed Rattletrap's claws from the dirt, and rode back up to the landing strip.

* * *

**

Krork came awake at the sound of Nonstop's bike and leapt out of his hammock — double-sized — hung between four over-worked trees, and wondered: "What's he up to now?"

He wasn't the only one wondering. From other campsites he could hear his friends asking each other: "Where's Nonstop going?" "What's going on?"

Krork crashed out of the brush and ran for his bike. Slice was running to his own rig as well. "What's going on?" Slice asked as Krork ran past.

"That's what I'm going to find out." Krork said as he jumped onto his bike's seat and started it up.

"Does he need help?"

Krork took a quick look at Slice. "If he's going to Earth, you can't come. You might get shot."

The answer didn't sit well with Slice, but he nodded.

As Krork began to drive, green light flickered in the trees up at the landing strip. He'd better hurry, or he'd be too late.

* * *

The realmlines were awesome. Krork caught a zone of high powder blue, an immensity incalculable, a gigantic vista gently churning under and above him. Driving it was like being a leaf supported by the highest, clearest wave, on the brightest, clearest day.

And far ahead of him, a distortion — Nonstop.

The omission pattern on Krork's display already told him they were going to Earth. Good to know, but Earth was a big place. If he wanted to catch up to Nonstop, he would have to maintain sight of that distortion. If the realmlines stayed friendly, he thought he could do it.

* * *

For the second time that night, Nonstop ghosted onto Earth. Earlier, when his team had answered the Bleed Zone alarm, he had ghosted onto the world a few miles from the Bleed Zone's epicenter — as an excuse to enjoy a longer ride. He had caught glimpses of buildings — a town maybe, a city — he didn't know what for sure, but by his best guess, he was driving in that cluster of buildings now.

It had rained. The streets were shiny.

The neighborhood had an industrial feel. Short brick walls and parking lots, cobblestone shining under streetlights in long stretches where the asphalt had worn away and never been replaced. At a spot along the road, a jungle of weeds pushed a rusty chain-link fence nearly out of the ground. Beyond the fence the land dropped away, and in the distance Nonstop could see train tracks. Black tower lights flanked every few sections of track, standing like great, meditating insects, their dormant lenses reflecting the light around them, but providing none of their own.

The neighborhood was probably as close to deserted as any other set of man-made structures standing in America. And that wasn't bad at all. Nonstop didn't know where he was, but he thought it was a good place to find what he was looking for.

*

Krork Ghosted in. He thought he was in the right place. He hadn't fallen behind the distortion, and he was on Earth. Nonstop was here. Somewhere.

He turned off his bike. He shut his eyes and bowed his head.

He listened.

His ears did the trick that Nonstop got such a kick out of, vibrating like high-powered car speakers as he searched through sounds. But there wasn't much sound here. The hum of the streetlights. Trucks and cars somewhere in the distance on all sides of him, the blare of televisions from places unseen, the base thump of a car stereo stopped at a light, and then yes, small, Rattletrap's engine. To the left, and then bearing eastward.

*

The strip of road Nonstop was driving suddenly divided into opposite lanes. The concrete median between the roads featured planted trees, grown enormous, some with crowns that spanned the entire roadway on both sides. The warehouses around him were silent, their windows black. Streetlights twinkled through silhouetted branches. The area was rich in its own deserted beauty.

The trees thinned, but the median went on. Nonstop spotted benches, graffiti covered, some with slats missing, and he noticed more light up ahead, a higher concentration of streetlights.

The approaching intersection offered a small park — graffiti infested. The sidewalks, the benches, even a few of the trees, were jacketed with a crazy sprawl of spray-painted loops and slashes.

A large, concrete building, huge as a prison, reflected the streetlamps and coated the intersection with a sickly yellow light. A train station. An excellent candidate for what he needed. He looked up and down the length of the sidewalks, saw dented trash cans, a fire hydrant, abandoned newspaper vending machines — and sure enough, there near a park bench, was one of what he needed: a pay phone, papered from top to bottom with advertising labels, and given a coat of spray paint for good measure, but seemingly intact.

Nonstop drove up to it, and fished in his jeans. He didn't have much money back at camp, forty two dollars in bills and three dollars in change. How much was a pay phone these days? Was it still connected to anything? Or was it just a house for squirrels, or a canvas for the local spray-can Van Gogh?

Payphones were dying, just like newspapers. The future was trading hands and they were missing it. They should be the ones making it. They shouldn't be hiding off-planet while the skunks went on ruining everything. The whole world should know what was possible, what was right around the corner.

While he was picking out change, he heard something in the air. Something beautiful, and he stopped.

Somewhere — *there* — on the other side of the train station, a bar door was open, and a woman was singing. Her voice un-amplified, though he heard a bass riff over a speaker — a sound check maybe, or a band packing up or setting up. But the bass came and went, and all that could be heard was the woman's singing — a stretch of notes that grew in strength and rose from low to high, from modest to soaring. The woman added lyrics, which he couldn't make out save for the word "love". The woman stopped singing words, and then sang using only tones for a second or two more, and then she stopped and Nonstop stood aching. He wanted more. He wanted the sweet gorgeous music. He wanted the woman — he wanted to take her hand, and run, under the music, in the grass under the sun, away from the soldiers and the monsters and the... he had things to do. He needed a pen. This is where the other guys would know how to do something with the data boxes, but he was gonna need a pen and paper. He was cool with pens, he usually had a couple of pencils or such tucked away in his gear harness — but did he have any paper? Dag, he had had a clipboard full of paper just a few minutes ago — had almost jammed a page in his pocket, but stuck it on the clipboard instead — *on another planet.*

You get used to things quickly. They'd have some paper at the bar. He could go ask. He took a step back to Rattletrap and felt the newspaper clipping crinkle in his pocket. Cool. He could just use the margins.

He huddled over the phone and started making his calls.

*

Krork didn't hear the bike anymore. Which was good, he supposed, because it meant Nonstop had parked, and he might find him. It was bad, because he had no real idea where to look. Every street he went down meant there was a dozen he didn't go down. Time was a factor as well. He could pick the right street, but miss Nonstop by a few seconds. He'd look a little more, maybe not think too much, maybe mostly listen for any engine restart, and just let the visuals lead the way in the meantime.

Luckily, there were railroad tracks to one side of the road, down a hill, on the other side of a fence. After a quick peak, he could ignore that side. He paused at every corner and looked up every street, but he stayed on the road he was driving. It had a powerful North/South layout to it. Maybe it was the row of trees in the median, or maybe it was the channel of open sky between the trees and the buildings, but it didn't seem likely that you'd turn off this avenue unless you needed to. So he stopped at every corner, but he expected to keep moving forward. He'd just have to remember to go slow, not get too involved with any clusters of thought, and stay open to the sound of Nonstop's engine.

In the end, it turned out he didn't need his ears to find Nonstop — Nonstop was at the end of the tree lined avenue, under a bright streetlight. Krork could have ignored the side streets and found him quicker.

Nonstop must have heard the approaching engine, Krork thought, because he turned to look. The surprise on his face was actually pretty funny. Nonstop hung up the phone, and Krork coasted over to him.

"What are you doing here?" Nonstop smiled as he shoved a pencil stub — pens stop writing when you used vertical pay phones as desks, into a pouch on his gear harness that was designed for his socket wrench but now bulged with additional materials. Krork grinned.

"I need more peanut butter," he said. "What do you think I'm doing here? I'm spying on you."

Nonstop grinned back. Krork raised up in his seat, awaiting a response. Nonstop grinned some more, tapped his foot, and looked at the interesting fire hydrant. The graffiti was somewhat legible — obviously the work of an amateur. It read *"Sin 7"*.

Krork leaned forward and rested a forearm on the bike's front vortex chamber. "So? What am I spying on?"

"Uhm, uh, nothing. Nothing man, I, nothing." Nonstop rubbed the back of his head and walked toward Rattletrap.

Krork stepped off his bike. *How wrong? How wrong was this going to turn out to be?* "Nonstop, what's up?"

Nonstop kept walking to his bike, but when he started to shove the news article back into his pocket, the dam broke. He spun and faced Krork.

"Man, everything Varrage said to me tonight is true. I can't work the equipment. I don't know tactics. I'm impul... Dude. I'm going to jack everything up. I can't just sit around and wait for me to ruin the whole world. I have to do something!"

"What are you talking about?"

"Doc is a good guy. He invented something amazing, and the world is trying to kill him for it. Someone's got to help him." Nonstop held out the newspaper page to Krork, and started jabbing it with his finger. "Bloch is planting these stories in the media so that the Army can kill us and no one will care. I don't know how to fight the Army. I freely admit I can't beat them. *But I know exactly how to beat that story.*"

"How?"

"I'm going to kidnap a reporter and *make* him tell the truth about us."

"— Kidnapping is impulsive."

"— Not kidnapping. Abducting."

"— Abducting is kidnapping."

"— Look, if you're going to be so negative about it, you can just go home."

"Right. I leave you alone, and then it's *my* fault the whole world gets ruined. How would you even find a reporter?"

"I tried calling in a tip, but the lady said there's already a news crew in the area. Fourth and Charlotte."

Nonstop unclipped his data-box and jabbed at it. "Now let's see. Where's fourth and Charlotte? Hmmm." Nonstop stroked his chin, and tapped a few more areas on the box's blank screen. Krork rolled his eyes and held out his hand.

"Here. Give it to me."

Nonstop handed over the data box. Krork glanced at the screen and then raised his eyes to look at Nonstop.

"You're going to re-start those lessons, right? — tomorrow?"

Nonstop was surprised to receive an admonishing look from Krork, his usual partner in crime, and so he found some other place to direct his eyes. He looked down the street at the bar, and looked away. He looked at the fire hydrant, and looked away. He looked at Krork, and looked away. He looked at the dark connecting street he hadn't noticed before, and finally said: "Yeah, yeah. Whatever."

* * *

June 18th

2:25 A.M.

Rik Ty

**

Loading bays jutted along the bottoms of almost every building on Fourth Street. The street itself was cratered, choppy with potholes, and lined on both sides with hulking gray warehouses. A few more blocks and they'd hit Charlotte. Nonstop and Krork both put their bikes in whisper mode.

***

On this particular night, at the last street along Charlotte Avenue to have its streetlights on, a large sign blocked the roadway. Beyond the sign lay a wall of darkness. In front of the sign, a news crew worked, setting up lights. The sign read:

ROAD CLOSED
EMERGENCY
DO NOT PASS
VIOLATION OF THIS ORDER MAY
LEAD TO IMPRISONMENT OR DEATH

And under that, the sign presented the same message in Spanish.

A young woman in jeans moved a lamp connected to a tripod, and placed it at an angle so that the sign received enough light to shine brightly, but hopefully wouldn't reflect directly into the team's camera and flood it. She looked back to Nick the camera operator to check her results.

Nick wasn't paying attention. He had his phone plugged into his ear and was staring at its display, scrolling for a song to switch to. The young woman found herself wondering if all the metal devil-skulls pinned into Nick's eyebrows and ears ever caused any interference with his phone. She could ask him, she knew, but that would mean talking to him.

"Nick. How's the light?" she asked him.

He looked up. He seemed confused, "What?" he said, and then he looked at the light, and the girl, and the sign "Yeah, it's fine. I told you, anywhere." He went back to his song selecting.

Another young woman, taller than the first, strode onto the middle of the street, her heels clicking. She held a microphone in one hand, and managed the unwinding of its cable with the other. "We ready then? Come on, let's go," she said.

Nick rolled his ample hips against the parked van he was leaning on, and worked up the momentum needed to actually stand on his own.

"Come on Nick. I want to get this story done. It's the middle of the night, and I still have to edit."

"Yeah, yeah. I got it. Don't worry." He lifted the ancient 550 camera and put it on his wide shoulder. He aimed it. A red tally light came on above the lens. "Okay, go," he said.

The young woman straightened and then whipped a finger through her hair to move a curl off her forehead, a practiced move she hoped would become her broadcasting signature.

She looked into the camera and spoke:

"This is Minky Russells. We're here on Fourth Street, practically in the middle of nowhere, and tonight, we've gone as far as we can go. The rest of these streets have been closed by the Army. To move beyond this sign is to risk arrest — and just what *does* lie beyond this sign? What tricks of the mind might be induced...

Grace, the shorter of the two women, turned, and said to Nick, "She's got a hot spot."

Nick's face went sour, "Yeah, but it's just a little one," he said.

"You want people to listen to her, or watch the dot on her head?" Grace said.

Minky's hand went to her hip. "What's wrong this time?"

Nick lowered the camera, "You've got a hot spot. The intern just volunteered to fix it." Nick grinned at his shoes, and went back to selecting songs on his phone. Grace looked at him, and then at Minky, saw she would get no assistance, and went to wrangle the lights.

*

All of Fourth Street turned out to be industrial — stuffed full of old squat buildings made of brick and concrete. The streetlights were on, but the buildings seemed to absorb the light, pulling it into alleyways and arches and vestibules, creating a visual rippling as Nonstop and Krork slowed their bikes.

The dark streets made it easy to see that up ahead, around a corner, someone was working with bright lights. Nonstop pointed as he slowed his bike down to a crawl. "That's got to be them,"

Krork nodded, "Yeah, looks like it."

They trundled silently closer, and saw the sign for Charlotte Avenue before they reached the corner. They pulled up close to the last building, dismounted, and peeked down the brighter street.

On the far end of the block, they could see the news crew: three people, working in the middle of the road.

"Okay, there they are. Let me think," Nonstop said. Krork rolled his eyes to the heavens. Nonstop stroked his chin and spoke quietly: "Okay, I'll approach them nice and calm. You stay here and don't scare them."

Krork could think of no contribution to make to this plan, and so said nothing.

* * *

Moving out was simple, but it felt strange. Nonstop just gave the bike a little juice and it rolled forward. He steered it down the new street and it went the way he pointed. He would stay in the middle of the road, and eventually the people at the corner would see him.

It was so quiet though. It felt like it should be different, like it should somehow be momentous, but the truth was that Nonstop traveled down the block so silently, that even when he got close, the three people at the end of the street still had no idea he was there.

"Uhm, excuse me," he sort-of called out to them.

Nick spun at the sound, and his eyes went wide. His knees bent, and when he straightened them again he went backwards instead of upwards. He slammed his back into the news van.

"Oh my God!" he cried, bashing against the van to get back on his feet. "It's them! Run!" He stumbled around the van and headed for the driver's door. Grace stood stunned for a second, but then ran around the back of the news van as well. Nick yelled "— Brain cancer Minky! Run!"

Minky, standing in the middle of the street, watched every move Nick made, astonished.

Nonstop also watched, shocked as well. Then he stepped off his bike and raised up his hands. "Hold on," he said.

Minky watched the van in disbelief. "Nick! You stopped taping?" Then, as the van started moving, she yelled "Nick, where are you going?" and then stared with her mouth open as Nick put on a batter's helmet that was covered with crinkled aluminum foil.

"Brain cancer Minky! You're in that psychotronic brainwave thing!" he yelled as he drove away, raising the passenger side window as Minky spun and screamed:

"Nick, get back here and tape!"

Nick crashed through the road closure sign, knocking over every light, and disappeared into the darkness, risking arrest or death without a second thought.

That left Minky and Nonstop alone in the street. Nonstop took a step forward, and Minky took a countering step backwards, her shoe-heel teetering on the uneven ground.

Nonstop took another step. He tried to catch Minky's eyes, but she wouldn't look at him for more than a fraction of a second. She was watching the street. "Miss, I need your help," he said. "I'm not a terrorist. I'm not a hallucination. I'm not a brain-cancer-thing. Please miss, you've got to help me."

"Stay away from me — *whatever you are.*"

Minky circled step by step as she retreated from Nonstop and looked for a way to get past him. Nonstop matched her steps, but didn't move any closer to her, only shifted and side-stepped to continue facing her. "Miss, please," he said again.

*

Back at the corner, Krork crossed his arms and smiled. "Ahh, not kidnapping — *begging,*" he said.

*

Minky kept moving. Nonstop saw her steal a glance at a sports car parked in the shadows. In a second she'd be in the car, and he'd have missed his chance. He took a step, both hands up. Minky backed away, her voice rising as she repeated herself: "Stay away from me!" she said, and seemed ready to say it again and again.

"Miss, it's dangerous to stay here," Nonstop reached out to touch her elbow. "Could we please..."

Minky gave every indication she was going to scream, but instead hissed "DON'T YOU TOUCH ME!" and then quickly looped her microphone cord around both of Nonstop's wrists. She pulled the cable tight, and brought his wrists together. As Nonstop looked at his hands in confusion, Minky kicked him between his legs with all the force she could muster. He doubled over, gripping himself with his bound hands. The air went out of him. Minky reached under her jacket, behind her back, next to the microphone's battery case, and pulled out a can of pepper-spray. She sprayed it back and forth across Nonstop's eyes, and he threw his bound hands up to his face, bellowing. She flipped the slender can in her hand so that the bottom end stuck out from her fist, and rammed it into Nonstop's forehead. He tipped backwards and yelled "OW" as he fell onto the street.

She ran to her car, started it up, and squealed a minor victory lap around Nonstop as he tried to get up. She headed back up Fourth Street and left — without risking arrest. She accelerated, and drove past Krork without knowing it, or even suspecting it.

Nonstop, practically in a fetal position, called out, "Come back! You have to help us!" He rolled onto his hands and knees. "If I *was* a terrorist, and you needed to sell *car* commercials, you'd talk to me!" he yelled as he unwrapped the cable from his wrists. He managed to stand, though not very well, and raised his fist to the empty street, "OH YEAH? YOU PRESENT OPINIONS AS FACTS! AND, AND— EVERYBODY KNOWS IT!

He put his hands on his knees and gasped. "So there," he said, and he heard Krork call from the far corner.

"Can I come out now?" Krork rolled his bike from the shadows, and into the amber light of the street lamps.

"Ungh... What happened to impact diffusion?" Nonstop said.

Krork stopped and answered, "There must be a relationship between the force of impact and the met resistance."

"What?" Nonstop said, and then, after a thought, "No, that *can't* be right."

Krork pushed the bike again, "Actually, I think it probably is," he said. "I think it has something to do with how the energy stacks up. If sudden, large-impacts force the fields on top of each other, and smaller impacts allow them to slip around..."

"No, no, no," Nonstop said, standing doubled over again, "Those were big impacts that just hit me. Big. Big."

"They don't compare..."

"You're real aren't you?" A voice came from behind Nonstop. He whirled around, amazed.

"Oh, hey," Nonstop said, and his jaw kept working, but the words stopped coming out. It was a girl, kind of good looking, curvy, lots of hair, wearing a tool belt, standing by a dumpster, holding a little silver video camera, and some kind of folded club — a weapon? Yeah maybe, a light stand, but maybe a weapon too. "How you doing?" Nonstop continued, and then added, "Uhm, great."

"What kind of help are you looking for?" the girl said.

Nonstop straightened up. He tried to stop squinting, and thought it might be good if his eyes would stop tearing, but since he didn't know how to control that, he just went on: "We're being lied about. I want the world to know the truth. Will you tell our story?"

"I'll capture it. You can tell it."

"You don't think I'm a hallucination? You don't think I'm a terrorist?"

"If you were a terrorist, I think you'd be more... competent, and if you were a hallucination, I don't think you'd show up on my camera."

Krork wheeled his giant yellow bike down the street. "Unless that were *part* of the hallucination," he called out.

"Said the big, yellow dinosaur," Nonstop said, laughing a little, but the girl was having none of it. Her eyes grew wide as she saw Krork. She raised the light-stand, trembling, and backed away. "Oh my God... Oh my God — it's true! You're making me hallucinate."

"No, hold up. We're not hallucinations... This is my friend Krork; he's a linguistic chameleon — sort of. We're interdimensional explorers — it's a new technology. No. No. Let's start this right. This is Krork, I'm Nonstop. Please, tell us your name."

"I'm Grace. Your name is Nonstop?"

"No. It's a riding name, an apelido. I don't know if it's a good idea for you to know my real name. Okay... No..."

"I don't care what your name is. You're not real anyway."

"Grace, we're real. I just look weird," Krork said.

"You look like a hallucination," Grace said.

"Well, wait," Krork said, "how do the buildings look? If you were under the influence of something, the buildings would look weird too. Wouldn't they? That's right. Isn't it?" Krork smiled to himself, delighted with his own logic. Grace looked around and moaned.

"They do look kind of weird. Shadowy, and the colors seem weird. Yellow — and gray" she said.

"Oh brother," Nonstop said, "That's the streetlights. Krork, you got her spooked now. Thanks a lot," and then he added, facing the young woman directly, "Look, he's okay, really. You a reporter?"

"Ah, I'm an intern. Your reporter ran you over. Okay. All right. I'll shoot your story."

"I guess a reporter in training will do." Nonstop brightened.

"She's not a reporter in training." Krork said, studying Grace, and then bowing to her slightly, "She's something else."

Grace smiled, vaguely charmed. Nonstop rolled his eyes to the heavens.

"That's right," Grace said. "I'm an independent documentarian. I'm working as an intern just to — how did you know?"

"We'll tell you everything," Nonstop said, looking around. "Just somewhere — *anywhere* — else."

"I'm not going anyplace with you."

"It's not safe here," Nonstop said, "The Army is after us. Look, you pick a place, and we'll meet you."

Grace looked around her. The streets were deserted, and very dark beyond the knocked-over sign. From that wide darkness, came the sound of a helicopter, flying toward them. She saw the guy who called himself Nonstop look toward the sound. She looked down both ends of the dark street, and then up at the dark sky.

"The Army is all over this neighborhood," she said, "Look, forget it. I'd better not."

The helicopter sounds grew louder.

"Nonstop," Krork said, watching the dark sky. Then he stopped watching, and backed his bike into one of the trash bays nestled between the two warehouses on his left. Nonstop grabbed his own bike and followed. He looked at Grace while he pushed the machine.

"All right. But get the story out: we're not terrorists. The Army wants to steal our bikes. They're trying to kill private citizens. Now *quick*, you should hide too."

Grace looked around her for a second, and then ran back to the dumpster she had used to hide behind when Nonstop first came down the alley. The dumpster was over-spilling with flattened cardboard boxes, so it would hide her from above — she hoped.

Krork tugged garbage cans from left and right and slapped them down in front of his bike. As soon as Nonstop pushed his bike close, Krork grabbed it and lifted it into the yellow bike's workbay, creating a tilted and imperfect fit that brought a questioning scowl to Nonstop's face — until Krork lifted *him* and placed *him* in the workbay too. Then Krork jumped onto his bike, held two trashcans in front of him for good measure, and hoped that the overhang would be enough to hide them from view.

The copter arrived, a small, single engined Kiowa floating out of the darkness at the end of the block, so close, its thumping engine and its chopping blades could be heard individually. It stopped just above the roof-line of the warehouses, and hovered, shining its searchlight down on the toppled warning sign in the middle of the street.

Then it inched closer, creeping its beam along the street and the sidewalks and the loading bays. Grace cowered in her hiding place, not daring to move, or to look out as the search-beam crept over the dumpster, and over the sidewalk around her.

The search-beam lingered on the trunk of camera gear that still sat on the edge of the sidewalk, abandoned by Nick in his haste to escape from Nonstop. White stenciled letters on the trunk's black surfaces read: "Property of K.A.L. NEWS". The copter's tail swung a bit as it hung in the air, and then the copter moved to the other side of the street, drawing its beam up and down the buildings.

Krork's toe was visible. So was a whole portion of his shin. His foot had wound up amid some papers and cardboard, and he didn't dare move it. What would the pilot make of it? Would he recognize it for what it was? Looking for a motorcycle, would he recognize a piece of an alien's foot? Would he think it was a twisted drop-cloth, or a broken bit of ornate plaster from the warehouse's hundred year old interior?

The search beam's light circle slid across the sidewalk toward Krork's foot, filling every chip and gouge in the cement with white-blue brilliance as it traveled.

The beam stopped, and reversed direction before it ever reached Krork's foot. The copter turned in the sky, rotating in the very tight space up by the roof tops, and then flew off, following the direction Nick took when he left the block.

When the sounds of the copter grew fainter, Grace ran to the trunk and threw it open. She perched beside it and began shoving its contents around. "Stupid hundred-year old gear," she said, as Krork removed Nonstop and the bikes from the trash-bay.

Nonstop gave Rattletrap a quick once over to check for damage, and then noticed Grace rummaging for batteries.

"So you'll come with us?"

Grace looked up at him. Most of the batteries in the trunk were for the 550. She took the few accessories that would fit her personal camera and shoved them in the zippered pouch of her tool bag. The mini-tripod didn't fit in any of her tool belt's pouches, so she flung it back in the trunk and then closed the lid. She closed her eyes and inhaled slowly. Then she relaxed her grip and looked at Nonstop again. "Yes," she said, and then, "I — No, forget it. I won't... Ohh... go where?"

"Himalayas? Australia? Hawaii?"

"Hawaii?"

"Hawaii."

"Really?"

"Sure, come on. Let's go."

Nonstop raised his hands toward Rattletrap, and waited.

Grace looked at the crazy bike: single wheel, robot chest, light thing, the word "Rattletrap" painted in script on the body near the seat. She continued to look at the bike, at "*Rattletrap*" as she stood up. She held her camera close to her chest, and then wrapped her other hand around the camera. She never made a conscious decision to accept Nonstop's offer. She simply looked at the bike, moved one trembling leg forward, and then walked the rest of the way as if things were perfectly normal.

Nonstop smiled broadly, said "Great," and sprang toward Rattletrap. He squeezed the release at the top of the seat-back and folded it down, turning it into a second place to sit. His hammock was back at base-camp, so he didn't have to slide it out of the way. He stepped toward the back of the bike and offered a hand to Grace.

"Thank you," she said as she accepted his gentle assistance.

"Sure."

She rose onto the foot deck, holding Nonstop's hand. She pivoted to swing her leg over the bike, and found that she couldn't do it. Holding Nonstop's hand put his body in the way.

"No. You have to let go," Grace said, and she leaned away from Nonstop to try and make enough room to get her leg over the bike. She leaned further, and started to tip.

Nonstop grabbed her hand tighter, pulling.

"Gah! What are you —"

"Sorry; you're falling."

"I am now."

And it was true. She was doing a kind of slow-motion, rolling lean, first away from him and then toward him. Her shoulder hit his chest gently and he caught the middle of her back with his free hand.

"Sorry. Sorry"

"It's okay ... just ... let go."

He didn't actually. He pushed her a little to help her stand and *then* he let go — fast, pulling his arm back as if she were electric.

"Sorry," he said with his hands raised. And he kept them raised as he stepped to the front of the bike — *so, now he knew: if you wanted to help a beautiful guest onto your bike, you had to stand in front of the seat, not behind it.* He'd know for next time. Great.

Krork watched, and waited on his bike as Grace took her seat and Nonstop climbed onto Rattletrap.

Nonstop got on, hit a couple of buttons on the control bar, and the bike purred to life.

"Sorry, I never helped anyone on like that bef—"

"I was there. I know what happened. Thank you." She bumped him on the back with the bottom of her palm, and when she did, a tiny spray of realm-lights drifted from the back of his head. She gasped.

"What?"

"Lights. You have lights in your hair."

"Oh. Yeah. That happens sometimes."

"uhhh..."

"Okay, listen —"

"That's interesting dandruff for someone who's not a hallucination."

"It's just a weird thing — listen — we're about to roll. My gear harness is full of straps. Find two, grab hold of them, and don't let go. You can keep your feet on the deck, or hook them under it, whichever you feel you need to do, — and there's nothing down there your feet will hurt, so if you want to wedge them at some point, that's cool."

"Okay." She found two straps and took hold of them. "I have the straps. Is that all there is to it? What does the machine do?"

"I don't think you'll feel much different," he said as the bike began rolling slowly. Then he reached down and touched something, and the bike got loud. Grace winced. Nonstop, not facing her, smiled.

"Does it have to be so loud?"

"What?"

"Does it have to be so loud?"

"No, but it's more fun loud. Okay, wait a second."

He put the bike lower on the whisper spectrum, and the engine sounds almost disappeared. "That better? Okay, like I said, I don't think you'll feel much different." They rolled smooth, and then he turned the bike around in a slow, lazy curve, not realizing that she already felt different, that she already had a tingling in her belly.

"The bike forces open a space between the realmlines," he continued, "then we ghost out, and we ride in that space."

"Realmlines," Grace repeated, not quite a question, not quite a statement, some manner of mental note her brain tucked away as she watched the world for what would happen next.

The bike faced the long dark straight-away of Charlotte Avenue. "Hold on now," Nonstop said, slightly louder than usual, as the bike began to speed up.

Grace saw the air around her distort, saw the spontaneous flashes of realm-light, saw as the flashes pulled into streaks and the reality around her began to twist, becoming tunnel-like. She began to groan. As they sped up, she groaned louder. The arc-gate appeared before them — white, erratic, wild.

"So Hawaii's what? South?" Nonstop turned and asked.

Grace screamed as the realm-lights around them flared and they ghosted out.

Krork followed right after them.

Behind them all, on the long straight-away, a twirling scrap of paper settled softly to the ground.

* * *

Grace's mind reeled.

"Oh My God! Oh My God! I don't like it!" she said as she squeezed Nonstop, and squeezed him harder, and practically tried to climb inside his back. There was nothing physically under her. There was nothing around her. She was surrounded by nothing. She could see

Nonstop and the machine and everywhere else she saw nothing but dark swirls of color.

Below her, maybe far, far below her, she saw a light distortion shaped like an amoeba. It looked as big as a continent seen from the air. They were passing it. Where were they?

Grace hid her eyes against Nonstop's back, pressing her forehead against the rescue rope. She cried. Her shoulders shook. Nonstop looked back at her, twisting as little as possible.

"I won't let anything hurt you," he said.

"Promise?"

"Sure," and then a smile, "Pinky bet." Nonstop reached behind his back as best he could and offered a bent pinky finger. Grace reached up cautiously and hooked her pinky finger around his. They shook.

"Keep your hands on the wheel," Grace said.

Back a few lengths, Krork raised his eyebrows, and smiled.

* * *

Colonel Bloch and Louis Sinclair walked briskly through the lowest level of the Open Mind research facility. The walls, bare concrete, reflected little light. Neither man smiled. Neither man spoke. Both looked straight ahead.

They reached a door with an electric lock bolted to it. Bloch held a pass against the lock's scanner, and the two men walked through the door.

They entered a dark antechamber where most of the light came from hooded security monitors. Two soldiers stood by their work stations, rifles in hand, raised but not aimed. They saluted the Colonel. Bloch returned the gesture, nodded, and the two soldiers left to guard the room from the other side of the door.

Bloch led Sinclair to the interior room, which was darker than the antechamber or the corridor.

Dominating the center of the small room was a waist high counter capped with a glass enclosure. A light moved somewhere low in the structure, glowing and fading in a continuing cycle. Small squares of reflected light circled the room's walls, its ceiling, and even the inside of the glass enclosure itself, like reflections from an underground aquifer. Approaching the glass box was like approaching a sarcophagus in a tomb, or a sleeping princess in a fairy tale.

Both men stepped closer to the case, taking opposite sides. Reflections drifted across the contours of their faces, mapping every hill and rut as they peered down at the lens.

The octangular lens sat within an array of sensors. It was slightly larger than a man's open hand, with a curved surface offering many facets: some deeply clear, some deeply cracked, and some deeply clouded.

Down toward the center of the lens, a haze of trapped light moved. The haze pulsed, flaring slowly across the interior facets of the lens. Half the lens shone brilliantly, throwing reflections into the room, and half the lens glowed only faintly, barely registering through the fogged surfaces. When the light traveled through the damaged portion of the lens, the lens appeared back-lit and shadowed, causing its interior to look burned, and changing what had been the lighter half of the lens into the darker half. It proved Sinclair's point. "You see? The lens is still cloudy," he said.

"Half cloudy," the Colonel responded.

"Fine. But it isn't clear. Not yet."

"But we can use it."

"You don't know that. You're guessing."

"And you're being timid. Sinclair, opportunity is here. Right now."

"We just used it. It was half-ruined to begin with, and now it's worse. I don't understand you sir. You say you want to know everything about Norel's interdimensional inventions. This lens is the only thing we have; it's the only thing that could teach us anything, and you're risking it."

Bloch looked at Sinclair. "We've learned the useful thing this lens can do. Tonight we learned a second useful thing. You showed it to me yourself, and here's what we're going to do: we are going to set every VTOL with the frequency that hurt the young male. We're going to use the lens again and get him back here, and when we do, we are going to *pound* him. You will have an actual bike to study — tonight."

Sinclair held the Colonel's gaze, though he had to muster the courage to continue. "You're being very cavalier about what you're exposing the world to — what you're exposing your men to. You don't have any idea what will come through a portal. It could be a virus. It could be another Army."

"Yes. Yes. Very imaginative. We will kill whatever comes through. Norel's people will still come to close the portal. Get a team together."

"I'm terrified to do it."

"Sinclair, I hate risk. I abhor it. But often it is the risk you don't take that punishes you. Do what I say."

* * *

**

They ghosted out onto a black field, dotted with palm trees they could barely see. Not far from them, the field ended in a cliff that overlooked the ocean. Krork smiled. Nonstop smiled. Grace looked around and said, "It's dark."

The moon sparkled gloriously on the water, but the young woman sounded disappointed, almost cheated. Surprised, Nonstop scrambled.

"Night probably just started here. Hawaii's west as well as south. You want to keep driving? I mean, it's daylight somewhere. Come on, look. The moon is still pretty isn't it?" He was looking at it. He sure thought so.

Grace reached out and stroked the edge of a fern leaf. In the weak light she saw a cluster of flowers that looked like pinwheels, growing on a nearby tree. She couldn't tell what color the pinwheel flowers were, only that they were lighter than the tree. *How could you see Hawaii, and still not see Hawaii?* — somehow she wasn't all that surprised that this was a riddle life gave her the answer to.

Spin, win, play again?

She looked at the dancing slashes of moonlight on the ocean, as white as any reflections seen in picture books, as pure as any moonlight seen throughout the centuries, and she smiled, as brightly as she could manage. Then she noticed the new smells, the perfume of the flowers, the moist tang of the ocean, the moist tang of the air itself.

She heard Krork as he stepped behind her. She turned, saw the alien, and recoiled slightly. He smiled, as brightly as he could manage.

"I know, I know. It's perfectly understandable. I'm making you nervous. I'm sorry... Whatever good that will do."

"It's so strange. It's so sudden."

"Yep. I know what you mean. If it helps, let me say this: when you go interdimensional, what's logical moves beyond what's ordinary — sometimes by a lot."

"And," Nonstop added, still looking at the moonlight on the ocean, "what sounds fancy, still don't make no sense."

Krork looked out with him, and drank in the view for a second. Then he put his hands on his hips and surveyed the world. "You know, I think I'll get some of those vortex readings for Doc. You two enjoy Hawaii."

Grace immediately fumbled for her camera. "Wait! Wait! You're leaving? You don't want to be on T.V.? You'll be great — the greatest thing ev..."

"I hate T.V.. It's like eating pictures of food."

Grace aimed the camera at him and began shooting. "Say that again. Say that again."

"It was a pleasure meeting you Grace," he said, smiling deliberately through the camera and directly to her. She watched him through the viewfinder, then lowered the camera a little sheepishly, and smiled back at him.

"Oh. Hey, likewise. It was a pleasure meeting you Krork." She stumbled on his name a bit, but she managed.

He smiled, and held up his giant knuckles. She smiled, and bumped them gently with her tiny ones. He walked back to his bike. She hopped off Rattletrap and caught him with the camera as he left. He waved goodbye to Grace, and to all the viewers at home.

Nonstop hit a button on his bike's control bar and a work arm swung out from under Rattletrap's vortex chamber. It held a small collection of tools. Nonstop got off the bike, selected a folded spade shovel, and walked closer to the cliff face.

"Why do you need a shovel?" Grace asked, as every slasher movie she had ever heard of flashed through her mind. "What are you going to bury?"

"I want to clear some ground for a fire — a little one."

He sank the shovel head into the soil, pushed down on the handle a few times, and then moved the shovel a few inches over and did it again. Each time the blade entered the earth, Grace could hear a ripping sound. She had never seen anyone dig like this; he didn't seem to be making a hole. "Are you making a crop circle or something?"

"Fire bed," he answered, and then he pulled up the circle of grass — and dirt — as if it were a throw rug, and dragged it a few feet away from the raw earth. He saw her confusion. "It's sod. Makes a comfy seat too." He handed her the shovel, and gestured for her to sit down. "I just have to see what I can find to burn." He walked over to the tree line, stepped into the brush, and rooted around, dropping out of sight every few seconds to pick something up, bobbing in the grass like a T-shirt-wearing stork.

He walked back with a handful of tinder and sticks, and Grace sat down on the sod: it was comfortable, though a little lopsided at first.

He peeled a piece of bark into shreds and made a little tumble weed in the middle of the dirt. He reached into his gear harness and pulled out a packet of tiny little seed things. He placed one under the tumbleweed, put away the packet, and then stacked a pyramid of dry branch-things on top of the tumbleweed. Grace watched with interest. He pulled something like a grill-lighter wand from his gear harness, stuck its nose into the tumbleweed and pulled the trigger. The fire started, and in two seconds, was burning perfectly.

"Wow. You're pretty good at that," Grace said.

"I've got a million ways to start a fire," Nonstop said. And then he looked up at Grace, and then sat down. "Where we drive, we're not going to find any gas stations, or power-plants. Our starter engines recharge with heat — the vortex chamber part runs on some kind of interaction with the realmlines themselves — which I can't tell you about — because it's a secret, and also because I don't know. Seems like anytime someone explains it to me, my stomach starts growling, or my eyes glaze over — I'm the best rider though. I can at least say that."

"If I had known you were going to say all that I would have caught it with the camera."

"No. No. No. Dag. We got to not say nothing about how the bikes work or anything. Just because I don't understand it don't mean some egghead won't. So please. Please. Please. Nothing about the bikes."

"Okay," Grace raised her camera, worked its buttons, and looked through the viewfinder. "Wow, full moon behind you, firelight on your face, Hawaiian palm-trees framing the shot — what? Have you done this before?"

"Done what? What did I do?"

"Nothing. Nothing."

"*You* picked Hawaii."

"It's nothing. It's just, you come out of nowhere, you act like you don't know anything, and then just like that, you set up this shot that makes you look all dreamy and stuff."

"What? I didn't set up any shot."

"You didn't? The moon just happens to be right behind your back?"

"What? I made a seat for you — facing the moon —because that's all there is to see here right now. I sat across from you because I'm talking to you. I didn't know you were going to film. I thought we'd talk here, and then go film in a studio or something."

"You have a film studio on Hawaii?"

"I don't have anything on Hawaii. I have a bike that can drive *anyplace, remember*? I figured we'd use *your* studio."

"I'm an intern. I don't even have a cubicle."

"So we're filming here? Oh, okay, cool. I had no idea it would be so easy. So, we'll just film, I'll take you back, and then mission accomplished right? You won't need anything else from me. Right?"

"Uh — I don't need anything from you *now* — this is your project. But yes, We shoot here and I can do any editing back home."

"Okay, so we're filming here."

"We're capturing here. It's called capturing. There is no film in a video camera. 'Filming' is a left-over term. 'Video' probably is too."

"Gotcha. Gotcha. We're not filming, we're not 'taping' either right?"

"Right. There's no tape in the camera either. It's recording to a chip."

They both laughed.

"But it's not chipping though — it's capturing?" Nonstop asked.

"Yes. It's capturing."

"Can I tell you something?"

"Sure."

"I'm just as happy with 'filming'." He chuckled. She didn't.

She raised the camera and began shooting.

"So. If you Thrill Kings are not 'Neuro-terrorists', what are you?"

"You're mad? I'm sorry. Aw, please, I didn't mean to make you mad."

"I'm not mad. Do you want to shoot or not?"

Nonstop rubbed the back of his head vigorously, and said "Sure. Sure." After a second, he looked into the camera. "We're explorers. Thrill Kings is just a goofy name I said to somebody and it's starting to stick. Sideways Mo' thinks the four of us should call ourselves the 'I.D.double C' — for 'Interdimensional Crisis Control', or something like that, but so far it's not happenin'. Most of the guys call themselves 'Bike Pilots'. We build all sorts of bikes and use them to chart the realmlines."

"Bike Pilots? How many of you are there?"

"Uhm. Let's see, we've got like ninety-nine guys — and by guys, I mean girls too, and counting Krork too. We're living off-realm in Outpost 14 — well, around it anyway. It's too small to live *in*. We're doing fine. We're doing okay."

"What do you want the world to know?"

"Aw man, the stuff I've seen is amazing. No. Wait. Hold on. We're not terrorists. We don't cause cancer. We're on the run because two years ago, the Army kicked down our door. We escaped in the Outpost and now the Army's telling lies about us. They're trying to kill us, and our only crime is creating a technology they want."

"So all these reports of monster hallucinations are lies?"

"Right. There aren't any hallucinations."

"Wait, are you saying that there are monsters?"

"Creatures."

"Oh my god, so it's true."

"No. No. The Bleed Zones are true. The details are all lies."

"The creature stuff is real? How do we stop these Bleed Zone things?"

"We have gear for it. We send everything back. No harm, no foul."

Grace looked up from her camera. "No. No. Not "How do we fix them.' How do we stop them in the first place?" She paused, looking at Nonstop. Nonstop looked away.

"We're working on it," he said, throwing a pebble into the fire. Grace quickly returned her gaze to the viewfinder.

Nonstop looked at the fire. "We don't know a lot about the Bleed Zones yet. They only started happening after we left Earth in the Outpost."

Grace lowered the camera altogether and said, "You see? You guys *are* putting the Earth in danger. That sounds like a crime to me. That sounds like a great, big, *giant* crime."

"No. We didn't kick down any doors. We didn't point guns at anyone. We didn't *shoot* at anyone. You want to call people criminals, pay attention to who did what."

"You invented something that causes monsters to come to Earth, and you actually believe you should be able to keep using it? You actually think this stuff belongs in civilian hands?"

"Better with us than with anyone! They came in firing. Doc saved lives. Doc is *about* saving lives."

"No way. The authorities should be in charge of things like this."

"What authorities? The guy who's trying to kill us is like king of the Army. How's that for authority?"

"No. The Army should control the bikes. Everyone would be safer."

Nonstop stood up, and started walking in circles. "This is horrible! I came to you to get the truth out, and you're gonna tell the world that the guys who are trying to murder me are right?"

Grace stood up. Still recording, but not looking through the camera. "I'm not saying they should kill you."

"They're not waiting for your permission!" Nonstop paced. "They're trying to *rob* me — of my *bike*, of my *job*, of my *life*, of my *future*." He jabbed a finger in her direction as he continued. "Before you *help* them, come see some of that future." He stopped pacing and faced her. "Come see the necklace."

"No."

"What?"

"No. The army should have the bikes."

"What? You just don't want to know. You're a reporter who doesn't want to know."

"I'm not a reporter."

"I don't know *what* you are, but I know you want to pass everything on to some imaginary authority and pretend everything will be all right. Wait. I do know what you are. You're a chicken."

"Don't you dare sum me up. You don't know me."

"Bwack. Bwack. Bwack."

Grace covered the ground between them in just a few steps and kicked Nonstop in his left shin. Her camera was still on. It recorded the grass. Nonstop was in front of her, hopping around like an idiot, holding his left shin and yelling "Ow. Ow. Ow," and she captured an unstable close-up of under-lit switch grass. On review, she didn't know which aspect of the scene embarrassed her more, that she kicked the guy, or that she missed the shot.

"Oh — oh, I'm sorry," she said, and as she covered her mouth with her hand, her camera swung on her forearm and recorded Nonstop rubbing his leg, and then the moon, and then the black palm trees.

Nonstop stood on both feet, rubbed his left shin, and grumbled "Impact diffusion. Impact diffusion," as if it were a curse. Then he mumbled "Dag. Little chicken's kicking my tail-feathers — *everybody's* kicking my tail-feathers." He took a step to the small fire and began stomping it out. "Ten minutes," he said as he stomped. Then he walked past Grace, saying "Ten minutes," directly to her as he did, and then he reached down, grabbed the circle of grass, and dragged it over the remains of the fire.

He tamped it back down with both feet, and said "Come on Grace. I'll show you the necklace. I'll show you the future of humanity. Just give me ten minutes."

Grace said "No... Ten minutes... No..." and then:

"Okay."

* * *

Dr. Norel studied the data on his computer, oblivious to time.

The helix distortion, from one angle or another, filled all three of his main screens. He was very uncomfortable. He felt hopelessly stupid and had for hours. It was a feeling he'd had before, many times, and it was a feeling he supposed he'd have again.

At some point in his life he had examined this feeling, this discomfort, and had changed its scale, and changing its scale had allowed him to push through these times of frustration and go on without quitting.

He had thought of a door. A closed door. If you wanted to go through the door, you would have to make contact with its surface, get it moving on its hinges. You'd use a hand, or a shoulder, or a foot, but most likely, some part of you would precede you and hit the door first. You planned on the impact, so it wouldn't bother you, but change the scale. Get close to it. Wouldn't that impact affect some part of you? Compress cells somewhere? Wouldn't some part of you feel the force of hitting a door that wasn't opened yet? Change the scale again, to the human encountering the unexpected, to the human frustrated by the unexpected, change the scale so that it is days of contact instead of microseconds, and you can find the faith that the frustration will end in insight, that an answer will come. The hand must hit the door before the door will open. It is possible, and it is often true, that discomfort precedes discovery. You might make the argument that the analogy doesn't work, that in our times of frustration, we don't know if we are pushing on a door, or a wall, or the face of a mountain. And that is also true. Though even if that proved to be the case, it wouldn't win you the argument with Dr. Norel; he had invented machines that drove through doors and walls and mountains.

151

He didn't know what to make of the data, or why he couldn't leave it alone until the data was more complete. In his frustration, he stopped looking at the numbers, and started looking at the shapes they made, watching the computer simulation of the effect as it undulated on the screens.

He peered closer. He ran the simulation slower. There was one aspect of the wave, from one angle, that attracted his attention. He zoomed in on it, froze the image, and used the program's tools to select the wave and copy it. He assumed he had seen the wave before, and he began searching through files to look for candidates to compare it to. He pulled files on light waves, and sound waves, and realm-charts. He pulled graphed representations of data, but he examined first what he feared most — the files pertaining to the hearts of the vortex bikes — the files regarding the alignment drives, and the charts representing the effects of the alignment lens.

As soon as he saw them, he knew that the waves matched. His mind raced. His heart sank. It took changing the horizon line, since the charts were aligned with the screen, and the distortion data was aligned with the axis of the earth, but when the alignments were made to match, the waves matched too — perfectly. Of course they did.

"What are you trying to tell me?" Norel asked the screen. "They have a bike? They have an idea? They have a..." Then the fabled door opened. Not a wall, not a mountain, a simple door, to a 30,000 foot drop. Welcome to Norel airlines. Where we really are stupid after all.

Norel stood up and in three hard steps was at the carton Nonstop had knocked over earlier. He pulled out items. When the items started to slide on the mounds of paper around the carton, he cleared away stacks of paper from the counter, placing them down again absently — wherever — on other papers, on other boxes, on the souvenir clock he had just rescued from the jumble. What he was looking for was not in the first carton. He moved other papers, glanced in other boxes, until finally, he found it, at the bottom of a carton, so important, it had gone in the box first, and had become buried by everything that went in the box after it. He lifted the object and brought it into the light: a wooden case, beautiful, carved and varnished. He opened it, and of course the case was empty, except for its felt lining, which revealed a vacant octangular recess at its center.

"Damn me for a fool."

As he strode out of the room he flung the empty case back onto the cluttered table. He was dimly aware that it pushed a small wave of papers as it bounced, but he was out of the room before things came to rest. He never saw the wave of papers hit the T-shirt. He never saw the yin-yang symbol start to swing.

*

Outside, under the moons, fog blanketed the campgrounds. Norel looked around, and for the second time that night encountered the long tables absent of people, this time half-buried by mist — as if some failed cloud had drifted down from the sky and become stuck in the ground, and in its failure, was now drowning in the quicksand of immobile soil. Norel turned right, and walked toward a small, tree lined hill.

*

The pipe is extended. The chain is coiled. The arc of the strike is foreseen.

Varrage whirled into motion, pivoting to the spot where his back had just faced, striking out with the pipe, and toppling a pillar of stacked rocks with a single contact. Taking no time to admire the strike, he withdrew the pipe, swung it around his back, pivoted again, and struck another pillar in the circle of stones, this one in the eight o'clock position. He swung the pipe, blocking the two blows he would have been vulnerable to had there been an opponent in the ring with him, and then he leapt with a roundhouse kick high, landed low, and took out the ten o'clock pillar with a sharp side kick, striking two of the falling rocks with the pipe before they could hit the ground. He pivoted to the center of the ring, swinging the pipe around his body with fluid precision. He took out the midnight pillar with a backward pipe thrust while locking his eyes on the six o'clock pillar — the pile of stones nearest his bike encampment.

With a sweep of the pipe, still looking at pillar six, he took out pillars two through four. He faked a vault to eleven, and uncoiled a kick to the one o'clock pillar.

The kick stopped an inch away from the top stone and froze there, locked in place until Varrage lowered his leg and returned to a standing position. He sheathed his pipe across his back as Dr. Norel crested the hill.

"Doctor," he said.

Norel stood a distance from the circle, absently rubbing his chin. "You asked before if Bloch might be causing the Bleed Zones," he said, "It's possible. An alignment lens might do it."

"They have an alignment lens?"

"It seems likely that they do. As you know, my indulgences tempt me into keeping things within arm's reach. The pre-alignment lenses were all failures, but I kept some in my old office. In our rush to leave, I may have left a few behind."

"If I retrieve them, the Bleed Zones will stop?"

"Before we go that far, let's make sure they didn't get thrown into stasis crates and stored."

"So we need to check the basement."

"It's safer with two people."

* * *

The black utility vehicle was perfectly normal, high and wide, it didn't seem like a military vehicle. It wasn't disguised as a California Department of Highways vehicle. It just looked normal. It could have been used to drive kids to soccer practice.

Two soldiers, dressed in white coveralls, got out of the utility vehicle and set up striped saw-horses at the entrance to the small parkway. The saw-horses had blinking reflectors bolted to their tops, and large reflective signs bolted to their sides. The signs read:

ROAD CLOSED
DETOUR
NEXT TEN MILES

It was already deep into the night. Nobody saw the soldiers. They got back in their utility vehicle, and drove to the next entrance on their list.

* * *

Every light in Bloch's office was on. A new coffee machine, taken from the cafeteria, sat on the bank of file cabinets by the wall. From it, the rich aroma of coffee — 100% Columbian blend, according to the little mylar packet the pre-ground beans had come in, filled the office. His second cup sat cold and forgotten on the corner of his desk. He studied multiple video feeds on his desktop's large monitor, and watched as his highway teams concluded their jobs.

He pulled a sleek, black handset from his pocket, unfolding it once from the top, and once from the bottom. He did this with the sure hand of a magician doing a card trick. The little silent machine looked like it could do many tricks, provided the operator were skilled.

Bloch spoke into the handset, already closing down one set of video feeds on the large monitor and opening another.

"All roads are closed. Proceed," he said into the little black device.

* * *

The black Chinooks moved into formation above the western-most field isolated within the network of newly-closed roadways. The grass flailed under the rotors. The copters began landing.

* * *

**

Proud to be one of Colonel Bloch's Prime Eagles, Kevin Woods stood in the hold of Copter Three with the rest of his gun-team, and kept his balance as the large machine descended.

Like several of his teammates, Kevin Woods came to the Prime Eagles after cycling out of the Army's Ranger training program. His dismissal from that program stemmed from his failure during the *Water-Combat-Survival-Assessment*. His problem couldn't have been simpler: despite giving it his best effort, operating underwater in full combat gear turned out to be something Kevin Woods could not force his body to do.

His dilemma emerged in the early rounds of training, long before the small boat testing, or the team mission drill. The training required him, and the other applicants, to fully submerge themselves underwater. First, wearing full uniform in the seven-foot section of the training pool, then, wearing full uniform-plus-pack in the twenty-foot section.

In the twenty-foot section, each soldier needed to prove they could operate underwater in full-pack without panicking. In real action, a capsized soldier would have only seconds to secure his or her survival, and it was crucial that the soldier keep his or her head, and not waste time thrashing, losing focus, or otherwise giving in to terror.

Kevin Woods won his struggle in the early stages of the test. He managed to stand underwater in full uniform without panicking. Panic was instantly close. Terror was instantly close, but he kept his head, and he managed to perform his objective.

That wasn't the case with the later stages. He couldn't remain focused while underwater in full gear. He'd enter the pool's deep end, and just as quickly as the water slipped over his body, panic would flow over his mind: total fear as his equipment pulled him down, blinding panic as his arms and legs slowed under the immense weight pressing on them. Deeper fears arose as the weight of his uniform increased, as its fibers soaked full; and as his mind screamed with the sudden knowledge, transmitted from each and every clamping fold around each and every joint of his body — that he was caught; that he was tangled like some ancient sailor in some ancient poem, dragged down by seaweed, never to see home again — and that he would be the only one to know the truth: that the sea's treachery flowed anywhere human lungs slipped below water, including the bottom of Army training pools.

Kevin wanted to complete the task. He wanted to do it calmly. But it turned out, even if it took blind panic, even if it took giving in to terror, his body would force him to survive. He was brave enough. He could function under live fire; he could face hardship; he could face deprivation, but he could not pass Water-Combat Survival Training. He could not become a U.S. Army Ranger.

Soldiers who cycle out of Ranger training have options: most are invited to train harder and re-apply. Some are offered training courses for other specialties. Some simply return to their regular units, personally disappointed, perhaps depressed, perhaps even humiliated.

Colonel Bloch's Prime Eagles offered a new option for Ranger candidates like Kevin, candidates who specifically failed water-combat training but otherwise met the physical and mental standards demanded. The rationale was simple: underwater exposure would be rare in Bloch's service, and he both respected, and had use for, dedicated young soldiers. Soldiers *exactly* like Kevin Woods.

After rotating out for the second time, Kevin accepted a meeting request from a young Ranger on the course's administrative team. The Ranger presented Kevin with the message that Colonel Bloch had *personally* requested Kevin begin training for the Prime Eagles Task Force, and that the Prime Eagles were very interested in having Kevin Woods join their team.

Thrilled, Kevin applied for the training, and eventually passed with high scores, becoming one of the new members of the Prime Eagle Task Force — quickly becoming one of the *devoted* members of the Prime Eagle Task Force.

The Prime Eagles, formed to combat the emerging threat of neuro-terrorism, worked under a code of secrecy. No soldier knew everything about the force's mission.

Even the Colonel, who knew everything there was to know regarding Norel and his agents, admitted that he didn't know everything about the new threat. What you don't know makes you vulnerable, and it was the job of the Prime Eagles to end the Nation's vulnerability at the hands of Norel — the demented scientist behind the current wave of neuro-terrorist events.

What Kevin had been able to piece together went something like this: Norel used un-registered technology to somehow induce mass hallucinations. Norel's agents were gearing up for major attacks, and were currently conducting test runs. These agents were extremely mobile, and possibly consisted of independent cells, or networks of cells prepared to go active whenever neighboring cells went active. It was too early to know anything for certain about their system of operation. Each of Norel's agents drove a vehicle that functioned as some type of hallucination amplifier, or light-bending projector, or perhaps both. You absolutely could not trust anything you saw when near these vehicles. Sometimes they could even fool cameras. There was some talk that the same projectors that made soldiers see odd things, could somehow transmit images to the chips inside cameras, or project images onto the air to the degree they could be photographed. The Colonel said the images were certainly fakes, of varying degrees of sophistication, but that the Army didn't yet know every trick Norel's teams were using — stressing again, what a danger that presented to the Nation.

You could feel how strange things were around Norel's agents. You had to fight for a normal thought. You'd see things that didn't make sense; you'd have contradictory instructions battling inside your head. Short exposures were best, but the Colonel wouldn't allow even those without a field bio-light and a ready back up. When you were anywhere near a Norel device, or a Norel agent, you had to have your bio-light operating within your sight-line. Designed to match your specific brain patterns, your bio-light could help keep you steady. When battling Norel's agents, your bio-light was your best friend. Your bio-light, and your commanding officer's instructions, would get you through. The worst price you'd pay would be a few days worth of headaches, and maybe a long bout of queasiness.

On the plus-side, the Colonel possessed a small piece of Norel's technology: a lens, and thought that Norel's agents probably used something similar to it, though a few generations further along in development. Even as the night's mission started, the Colonel announced he was developing a new piece of technology to aid the Eagles: a neuro-scrambler. A piece of equipment that caused some type of brutal feedback into whatever transmissions Norel's agents were broadcasting. The devices were being assembled, and Kevin's team would have their's in a few days. Tonight though, Kevin needed only his rifle.

Kevin couldn't say if Norel's agents used bullet proof shielding, or just had the ability to make you aim in the wrong place, but the new frequency scramblers promised to work over a wider area than any bullet. As long as you aimed your shot in the general area of your target, you couldn't be made to miss. It was amazing to think about: the Eagles had a need, and the Colonel had answered it. The Colonel, as always, had come through big time.

Copter Three landed. Kevin heard the ramp's hydraulics and stood ready. He activated the bio-light on his visor, and watched as more of the small red lights appeared on the visors around him. Together, his gun-team exited down the copter's ramp, sped into the field, and took their positions away from the copter's rotors, awaiting instructions.

The light-splitter team from Copter One disembarked, and took position in the center of the field. They un-crated lasers, and mounted them onto heavy field-tripods. "Point them at the tree line," their leader said, and the team set to work.

The lens team placed tripods between the lasers and the trees. They mounted robotic arms onto the tripods, and removed the lens from its isolation crate. Finally, they slipped the lens turn-table atop the robotic arms, and set the lens so it faced the lasers at a slight angle.

The gun-team leader signaled. Kevin's team split into formations on either side of the laser array. Operation Commander Goldman walked out from Copter Two, followed closely by Corporal Vega. Kevin stood on the left wing, and could see both men perfectly.

"We are about to operate Norel's lens," O. C. Goldman said. "Soldiers," he called out to his teams, "check your bio-lights. Are they operational?"

"Yes sir!" came the cry.

"I want to hear from you only if your light is not operational. Is there anyone here whose Bio-Light is not operational? Call out."

Silence.

"Excellent. Gun team, fall in."

Kevin and his team dropped to single-knee positions.

"We are about to activate the lens," Commander Goldman continued, "Typically some type of light disk will appear, or seem to appear when the lens is activated. This light disk is a call to action for the nearest of Norel's teams. Your Bio-Light will keep you steady.

Should the light effect appear here, watch for Norel's agents to step through it — disguised as something designed to unnerve you. Your Bio-Light will keep you steady. Your equipment will neutralize any threat. Do not be unnerved. Shoot whatever appears to come through the light. Do not hesitate. Do not shoot the lens. What will you do when something appears to come through the light?"

"Shoot it sir!"

"If it looks like your Grandmother offering cookies, what will you do?"

"Shoot it sir!"

"What will keep you steady?"

"My Bio-Light will keep me steady sir!"

"Good. What will you not shoot?"

"The lens sir!"

"Excellent. That is very excellent. Good job men. Prepare to fire. Full Auto."

Kevin switched his rifle from safety to full auto. His weapon ready, he looked at Operations Commander Goldman, who was looking at the lens.

"Is the field clear?" Operations Commander Goldman asked.

"Yes sir!" the lens team called back.

"That is excellent. Laser team, begin."

The left half of the laser team activated their machine. Glass chambers in its main body began to glow red. The machine fired, and except for the red dot that appeared on the lens, nothing seemed to happen.

Kevin watched the red dot on the lens. The lens looked even worse than the last time he had seen it. It looked scratched and chipped, with only half of its surface possessing the deep glossy quality he remembered. In the moonlight, its second half seemed to have a glaucomic haze to it — a reflected paleness he noticed even at a distance.

Looking away from the lens and the lasers, he checked his bio-light. It blinked rapidly. It calmed him. However the bio-light patterns worked, they functioned as promised. Kevin never felt bad for long when he wore his. He made use of it for another second. It was not recommended that you look directly at your bio-light. You were in-field to look at other things. A Prime Eagle was in-field to protect the world, not to retreat into its safety.

The laser light sank into the lens, splitting and strobing into its deeper facets. The edges of the lens began to glow. Kevin felt his stomach stretch.

Whatever was going to happen, it was starting.

The laser dot on the lens began to feed back into the air, slowly changing the invisible beam into a glowing red line that crossed the grassy field four feet above the ground — a creeping line with a jumping core of brilliant light that spasmed erratically every few seconds. When the glowing feedback reached the laser itself, the lens began to spin in its rigging. Once the spinning began, the blue laser team fired from the right side of the field.

The feedback effect happened instantly. The lens spun faster, and began discharging blue tendrils of glowing energy. The light grew brighter around the lens, creating a sky-blue ring of undulating haze. The haze grew, and then spread.

Kevin steadied himself and his weapon. He expected the portal-light effect to appear at the lens site. Seeing the lens spin, anyone would, but there was no guarantee of this. The portal effect could appear anywhere, or tell your mind it appeared anywhere, or tell your mind you had already seen it — *remember?* Confusion was the job of Norel's technology. Conviction was the job of the bio-light. Trust in your bio-light soldier, and do *your* job.

Kevin would. He would watch the lens until the light formed in front of him, or until spotters told him where it, or the concentration of brain-wave interference it represented, actually appeared. And it would happen soon. Any minute now, the portal-light would appear somewhere.

Something else happened first. Something that wasn't on the list of unexpected occurrences the soldiers had been briefed on.

Kevin watched the glowing lens spin, tilting back in its rigging until it spun parallel to the ground, and when it did, a second ring of haze appeared around it. The haze spread slowly into the air. When it reached the grass, the ground instantly covered itself with a carpet of blue light — as far as the eye could see, or as far as the mind could perceive, or as far as the mind held the concept of the ground, from tree line to tree line in any case. This blue carpet of light swirled under the soldiers, spiraling in great continuous sweeps across the region under the lens, faster and faster until the field appeared covered with a great, churning vortex Kevin could not feel.

And then the rim-light reaching Kevin's gun, the rim-light defining all its details, its rises and its recesses, began to dim. The light from the lens remained bright, but the light on the barrel went weak. The details on the rifle grayed. And then the details *moved*: the details, *all of them*, appeared to travel down the barrel of the rifle, rippling over its various surfaces as if the details had been mere projections all along, as if the projector was now moving to a new location.

Kevin looked at his bio-light. It looked dim. It looked alarmingly dim. He spun his head, just as the man next to him, his friend Wilson, began to scream. Wilson's screaming face, grayed and dim, rippled down the surfaces of his shirt, and Kevin watched it as it slid down to Wilson's shins, and then into the vortex on the ground.

Wilson's body dropped its weapon and leapt to its feet. The moving, black silhouette of Wilson's body began screaming, "What's happening?" over and over, his voice joined by the voices of the other Prime Eagles. Kevin looked at his own hand, a moving black void whose contours matched what his mind suggested he should see. He moved his thumbs, and waggled his fingers, and the contours of the void shifted accordingly.

His bio-light was nowhere to be seen and he felt a sudden rocketing of his senses. He was aware of the height of the sky and the fullness of his lungs. He felt very awake, very much as if he stood in a zone of hyper-reality — except there was a fading vortex under his feet where the grass should be — *except that everything in the field was blacker than the night sky* — except that the Prime Eagles had fallen into screaming chaos all around him — a black jumble of moving arms and legs and heads, a panoramic line of Kali-goddesses, removed, cut out from the fabric of the universe, windows into whatever void lay beyond. He felt the cooling breeze of the June night. There was the moon, right where it should be. There were the stars — *where was his face?* Who had stolen his face? The ground went black and he heard an enormous cracking sound, the sound a lightning bolt might make if it were two feet away from you. Rushing toward him, a shockwave of blue light barreled out from the lens site.

Inside the shockwave, the air burst into faceted walls of brilliant blue light. Kevin saw it for a second, and then the shockwave imploded. The collapsing light walls disappeared with a great *thwapping* sound, like the extinguishing of a candle amplified ten million times; leaving a blue double helix of light whirling around the twisted and ruined tripod array.

The lens. What happened to the lens?

He couldn't see it. All he could see was a great double helix of writhing energy, churning like two infinity symbols grinding together. Kevin heard someone call out that the lens was destroyed, and he heard Operation Commander Goldman yell "Steady up! Come on men! Steady up!"

Kevin could see Commander Goldman. Light seeped back into his body. He was gray, but nothing was traveling on him. All his features were where they should be. Kevin could see his own fingernails. Where they should be. Gray yes, but now tinted with his skin color as well. His bio-light was coming back too. He began to calm down. He raised his rifle and pointed it at the light by the lens array wreckage. Nothing had ever felt more real to him, but this couldn't be real.

The Prime Eagles steadied up. The Prime Eagles picked up their weapons and got back into formation. The Prime Eagles remembered to breathe. More was just about to happen. Their over-taxed senses told them so. The hairs on their arms told them so.

The massive portal effect appeared right in front of them, in the center of the blue helix. Spreading quickly, it stretched as long as a quartet of box cars before compressing back to the size of a movie screen. Maybe it looked like three round screens sliding over each other. It was hard for Kevin's mind to tell.

He steeled himself. He heard bits of chatter, mostly commands to quiet down and steady up. He looked ahead. Norel's agents were going to appear to come out of that portal — *that's what it looked like* — not a light effect — a hole — a hole filled with boiling light. He checked his bio-light. It was on. He felt his rifle's trigger, ready against his skin. Whatever came out of the portal effect, he was going to shoot it.

It was lightning. Lightning came out.

Bolts of ferocious energy leapt from the portal and into the ground. The earth rocked. The ground split; soil vaulted into the air. Laser-straight rays of twitchy, silver light shot up from the grass and out of the branches of the trees.

"Open fire!" Commander Goldman yelled.

Kevin fired into the light. Wilson fired into the light. The Prime Eagles let their rifles roar.

Wishful thinking. Wishful shooting — with the thousandth round as useless as the first.

The ground heaved in spots, pivoting up to the sky in great slabs. The men there tumbled. Other men yelled. Kevin heard someone yell

"Go! Go! Get out of here," as the grassland ripped apart and the silver lightning vented everywhere.

The copters powered up. Their rotors swung faster and chopped louder. Kevin ran for Copter Three. Men ran ahead of him. He saw two get close to the ramp, and then the ground rolled them all. A great wedge of bedrock pushed its way out of the land like a whale breaching the ocean. It hit Copter Three and toppled the copter onto its side. Copter Three's rotors hit the ground and shattered, sheering into the turbines and rotors of Copter Two even as Copter Two lifted off the ground. Crippled, Copter Two crashed back to earth, its own rotors chopping against the ground as the bedrock continued to move, and the ground rolled and crushed Copter Three beneath it. Kevin watched his Copter twist and flatten under the moving rock, as tragically predictable as the lamb rolled by the jaws of the wolf.

Copter One was in the air, away from the roiling ground. Kevin saw a side door open. He saw the engineer unfurl a rolled ladder. As the copter moved, he saw its last rung swing twenty feet above the ground and sway even further out of any soldier's reach.

Kevin turned and started to run, searching for a plan. The ground rumbled under him — not unfamiliar; it felt like the subway, rocking and rolling with the occasional jolt, except it wasn't the subway. It was the ground. It was the *planet*.

Kevin saw both transports bouncing across the field, heading for the road, slowing as needed for men to jump on — but never stopping, never waiting. He'd have to run much faster. He didn't have full pack. The gear he did carry didn't slow him down. His boots pounded across the ground and sent shockwaves up his body that were as steady and strong as any he would have felt on any of the copters. He angled to where the nearest truck would be in half a minute, and kept pounding.

Copter One was deafening, Copter Two burned and stank of smoke. The ground roared loudly as the soil ripped apart and boulders shoved out to the surface. Lacing through all these immense noises were the tiny sounds of men screaming. In hopes of being heard, Kevin screamed as well, opening his mouth and roaring "Hold it!" to the passing transports. He was seen by one of the drivers, who steered toward him.

Kevin caught up to the rolling truck, and grabbed the lowest slat along its sides. The grip wasn't good. Dirt slid between his hands and the painted wood. The beam offered an uneven surface. It had been chipped and painted, chipped and painted again, to the point where you couldn't be sure where its weak points were. The slat curved from his weight, but didn't snap. Soldiers reached over the side and began pulling him up. A forearm struck his helmet; another reached under his chin and grabbed his shirt. As all the clutching arms reached and pulled, his helmet was knocked from his head. His bio-light flew away with it, and his mind *reeled* — a sudden looping circle in his perception — as big as all the sky that he could see. His equilibrium suddenly failed. His body headed for the ground — which his mind accepted with calm fascination. *I am falling backwards. I will hit the ground. That is the proper thing to have happen when falling backwards.*

His teammates held onto him. His inner ear re-oriented itself. He grabbed the next slat, felt every fingertip, felt the bounce of the truck on its shocks as it powered across the grass, felt the wind as it shot over the skin of his bare neck. He grabbed the next slat. He wedged a foot on top of the truck bed. He held firm. Nothing was tossing him to the ground now. He was all right. He was leaving. The truck found the roadway.

He heard Copter One rise higher in the air. He looked back. The second transport slipped onto the road, every inch of it covered with men frantically banging on the truck's exterior, yelling for the driver to speed up and get them away from the erupting field.

Kevin looked at Copter One as it gained altitude. He heard a rumble, and looked back at the ground. The road behind him was moving. He saw its surface fold, and catch the moonlight. It continued to move, rising like a wave and getting closer. He was caught without his bio-light. The road moved like a liquid assassin, pursuing the truck, he could swear it *was* chasing the truck. Brain cancer. He was exposed to Norel's foul devices. Wasn't that the price? Brain Cancer?

It was so real — right behind him. He saw the white lines of the roadway as they traveled up and back over the surging mounds of blacktop speeding toward him. Could it be an earthquake? Could he be seeing an earthquake? Maybe under the influence of Norel's — he saw the road ahead of the transport ripple. He saw the road behind him rise to tsunami heights. The men in the second transport started screaming.

This was really happening.

The asphalt *was* stretching and rolling like a wave. Kevin started to scream.

The wave overtook the second transport and... *capsized* it. There was no other word for what he saw. It knocked the truck over, and the truck sank halfway into the road. Men flew from the truck, and landed half-submerged in the black asphalt. They fought and screamed as the wave overtook them. The wave submerged them totally, and then sped for Kevin's truck, causing the men around Kevin to scream even louder.

"This is happening!" Kevin yelled to his fellow Prime Eagles. Some of the men around him, also with lost helmets, were yelling the same thing, or very close to it. The wave hit them. He felt it. Didn't that mean it was true? Didn't it have to be true? The back of the truck rose up smooth, and steady, and fast, rising higher than the front end. The movement tossed men from the truck. They screamed. Kevin was thrown. *Real!* He landed in the road, and it couldn't be real. But he felt it. He was *in* the road. It swam over his legs, thicker than any pool water, heavier, and more restrictive. His pants pressed against his legs. He screamed. It was hard to move. The road oozed between his arms and his torso, burying his left arm and turning it into an anchor. He couldn't pull it free to roll over. It was pulling him down. Down away from the air. He was nowhere near water, but he was going to drown anyway. He saw the drowned sailor from the poem; he saw the seaweed entwining the sailor's arms and chest. He saw the roadside, twenty feet away. There was the grass. There was Wilson, screaming and screaming. There was the sky. His legs pumped, but there was too much weight holding them down. They didn't move. There was the moon, and the asphalt slid over his chest. *So heavy... he couldn't move...* He couldn't breathe. He gasped a last lungful of air, and clamped his lips shut as the road slipped over his mouth, his truck, and his teammates. He looked up, saw Copter One circling in the air, and then felt the road press against his lower eyelid. He squeezed his eyes shut as the road pulled him under, pulled everything under.

For a few seconds the roadway eased back to its natural level, and then a single ripple rode out across its surface and faded into the roadside dirt. The roadway solidified, and returned to normal.

At least that appeared to be the case.

There were no cars nearby to test it.

* * *

**

On the roof of Outpost 14, a flare of blue light rippled between a scanning post and a cooling vent. The light vanished, and then re-appeared several inches away.

Between the two points, an erratic helix of blue energy stretched into existence, thin but powerful.

The energy helix jumped along the Outpost's roof, sliding like buzzing mercury among the scanners and walkways and conduits. It reached the the long arm of the outrigger scanning station, and as soon as it touched the support anchorages, the entire gantry framework blazed with a coating of jumping blue light.

The energy surged at the control chair on the end of the gantry, and a monitor flashed with the message: BLEED ZONE COORDINATES before falling back to darkness.

Small flares of the energy spiderwebbed up an alarm post and into the horn of a loudspeaker, causing the amplifying mechanisms to crackle loudly. Before the siren could wail, the energy retreated, and the alarm returned to silence.

The crackling blue energy rose along other portions of the roof as well, and then faded, vanishing gently into the surfaces themselves.

*

Dr. Norel hit the enter key and then waited patiently for his selection to take effect. In the circular main room of the Outpost, surrounded by the black tech-henge of partial walls, he sat at the workstation nearest the basement door. Varrage stood nearby.

When the ceiling light flickered up by the pilot house, Varrage noticed. When Norel stood up from the workstation and the lights flickered from the pilot house down the tri-ladder right beside them, they both noticed. Norel frowned, watched, and when nothing else happened, shrugged. Hiccups in the power weren't unheard of, particularly in the instants before a Bleed Zone alarm. No alarm sounded. That was good. Two Bleed Zones in one night would be a new development, and this night had already had its share of new developments. Norel looked back to the screen, "Shouldn't be long. The path is written," he said, "Stabilizing code is 0527. It's not far."

A graphic appeared on the workstation's monitor, a simple line. The glowing line expanded into a rectangle, the rectangle into a box, and the box into an animation of blossoming rooms. Animations of rooms spread out from the edges of other rooms. Rooms pulled down from floors, giving the floors new duties as ceilings. The newly created levels created rooms of their own, which continued spreading sideways and downward. Corridors pushed open and flowed, creating a growing labyrinth, stairwells ascended and descended, rooms grew in width, in height and in length; sections rotated vertically, others rotated horizontally, until finally, the growth began to slow.

Norel stepped back as the animation ended and the stabilizing code appeared on the screen. He had a writing pad attached to the thigh of his coveralls, an old idea borrowed from the jumpsuits of Air Force pilots. He tore off a sheet and pulled a pencil stub from a pocket. Then he wrote the stabilizing code on the paper and left the paper by the screen, backing up some of humanity's newest technology with some of its oldest. He started writing a second copy of the code number on the pad.

"The basement seems to be behaving, but the errors could start at any point," he said, tearing off the paper and handing it to Varrage. "Please take this, just in case."

Varrage accepted the paper, folded it, and then placed it in his pocket without saying a word. Norel turned, and the two men walked to the bulkhead door that lead to the basement. Without looking to the side, or hesitating, they both stepped through, neither knowing what they expected to see.

*

Norel and Varrage entered a corridor of identical basement doors. A series of interlocking bulkheads that tiled together to form the walls, the ceilings and the floors. Within each bulkhead, the heavy, identical doors remained locked in their channels. The entire collection curved gently downward and leftward.

At the end of the strange corridor, on the left side, one door was open. Its light spilled across the nearby doorways, turning their recesses into shadowed pits, like the craters of the moon.

Norel began: one step down, one step across the door, one step up to the next bulkhead frame. Even he was not totally comfortable walking across a closed door, no matter how solid it felt. If a door should open under Varrage, Varrage would step, cat-like, to safety. If a door opened under Norel, the outcome was less sure. Varrage might pull him to safety, he might jump to safety himself, or he might fall. He could even fall and find that it posed no danger. There were no ceiling hatches in the programming. If Norel fell into an open door, he might simply re-align and continue walking on the floor. Still, there were too many "mights" in those thoughts, and human beings operate from their abilities to predict.

Norel and Varrage made it to the open doorway despite the odd terrain. Odd terrain was normal for the basement. The basement was an in-house Alpha test, take it or leave it.

They stepped into the next room.

*

They entered a large open space: a familiar, but astonishing knot of room elements swimming amid contradicting perspectives. No person who had ever seen an M. C. Escher drawing, ever walked in the basement of Outpost 14 without at least a nod of recognition, if not a rush of commentary. It overwhelmed most witnesses. It embarrassed Norel. He hadn't intended his dimensionally unfolding warehouse as a tribute to the left-handed genius, and felt personally tasked by every gleeful comparison made by well-meaning Bike Pilots.

Varrage looked around at the faceted spaces above him, "It's already shaky," he said.

"Catwalk," Norel said, pointing to a railed walkway that crossed the room, sometimes directly on the floor, sometimes across open space. A patch. As near as Norel could come to fixing the basement. For now.

Varrage and Norel strode along the catwalk, passing keypad consoles that were mounted on the railings, passing rooms beyond the railings, passing stairwells, and cubbyholes that all changed aspects as the two men walked; some elements seemed upright as they approached, and canted as they passed, some the reverse — a perception suggestive of the Doppler effect, where wave-cycles increase as the source of the wave pattern moves closer to you, and then decrease as the source moves away — the whole reason cars sound one way as they approach, and another way after they pass, only this seemed more a matter of existence, as if objects existed one way as you approached, and another way as you departed.

They came to a T in the catwalk and went right, then walked down a rampway toward more conventional structures. An open chamber, brightly lit, like a store in a shopping mall, stood expanded a few rooms down from them. It held several charcoal-gray storage structures and a long gray conference table with freestanding chairs.

Norel stepped into the chamber and walked to the nearest storage unit. He began sorting through the hanging stasis crates within it, pushing them along with a single finger.

"When Bloch's teams tore into Open Mind," Norel said, "I pushed everything on my desks into a stasis crate. We threw the stasis crate into the Outpost with everything else that couldn't stay." Norel said as he hunted through the hanging crates. "The crate was in the general pile for a time. Eventually, Slice and Wazzi volunteered to clear the main room. They brought the crate down here. But I don't see it. Strange." Norel checked through the entire upper level of hanging cases, and as he pushed the last one aside, he saw a stasis crate, rolled into a tube, standing against the storage unit. "Oh, that's right. Here it is."

Norel took the rolled crate, and Varrage watched silently as Norel put the tube on the table and removed a small red device from it. The device looked a little like a carpenter's level, only about the size of Norel's thumb.

The stasis crate unrolled, and covered the table. When it was flat, it became rigid, a three foot by four foot rectangle, less than an eighth of an inch high, silver, with rounded edges and black seams.

Norel placed his hand on the crate and Varrage spoke. "A stasis crate that rolls?"

"Another interrupted project," Norel said. He pushed the little red device forward on the table. "These adapters allow the deformation."

Norel opened the lid a crack, and as the contents transformed from two dimensions back to the classic three, the crate grew in height, gently raising his hand. When it stopped, it stood about as thick as a large piece of luggage, and Norel opened its lid the rest of the way.

Inside, hundreds of loose pages wove through tumbles of loose equipment, including several of the adapters and their predecessors. Norel pushed through the items, moving scales and calipers and notebooks, but no lenses, no elaborate cases.

"This is the crate; they're not here," Norel said as he sat down into one of the chairs, and looked up at the diode banks lighting the ceiling.

Varrage moved only his head, and looked directly at the doctor. "How will I find the lenses?"

"In my office suite," Norel said, looking up into the lights, flooding his retinas with vacant imagery. "You remember where my desk was? The array of picture windows? The lenses that weren't displayed were hidden in stasis crates slipped within the detailing of the window frames. The stasis crates should hold two wooden containers with pre-alignment-lens prototypes in them." Norel sat up as Varrage turned. The entrance to the chamber, which had been completely open, was now a split, four-way kaleidoscopic view of the rooms beyond the chamber.

"We're paradoxing," Varrage said, striding to the corner of the room, where a keypad console stood mounted on the wall.

"0527," Norel said. Varrage nodded, punched in the number, and the entrance returned to normal. Norel stood, and swung the lid of the stasis crate closed. The crate flattened to a sheet.

"All right," Norel said, "tell me what you'll need, and we'll put a team together."

"I don't need a team, Doctor," Varrage said as he picked up the stasis crate and slipped it into a slot in the storage unit. He turned back to the table and picked up the small red adapter.

"I need this."

* * *

Rik Ty

**

The news wasn't good. Bloch sat in the middle of Sinclair's lab-space. The overhead lights were off. Only the under-cabinet fixtures were on. The light they provided gave the room a mellow glow. Sinclair paced.

Bloch's elbows anchored on the room's widest table. He pressed his palms together, and rested his chin and brow against his thumbs and forefingers. He sat, absorbing the disaster, searching for the power to deny the disaster.

"All those men lost," Sinclair said, pacing up to the lit cabinets and then pacing away. "What do you do now? Call for reinforcements?"

"No," Bloch said, looking up, "No contact with Command. We'll handle this."

"Wait, no Colonel," Sinclair said, shortening the parameters of his pacing, staying nearer to the wall. "Whatever came through that portal is still out there. We don't have a lens. We don't have a clue!"

"Norel's people will still come. We'll get them. We'll get their equipment; we'll use it to get rid of the portal and whatever came through it. It won't be a problem."

"Colonel, we're down to the pilot and the engineer from Copter One and the micro-teams that are still out with the Kiowas. We can't continue."

"It won't be a problem Sinclair."

"Colonel, there's no one here to do anything. We don't have any men. It's over."

Bloch let his hands drift down to the table.

"We have men," he said quietly. "We just need to wake them."

* * *

The mist had crept a bit higher on the hill leading to Varrage's campsite, not enough to reach the hill-top, but enough to notice. The plateau, when Norel and Varrage reached it, was also made quiet by a layer of mist, blue against the blackness of the trees. There was not much left to say. They had reviewed the location of Norel's office back at Open Mind: top floor, down from the atrium. And they had reviewed the means of releasing the stasis crates from the windows: press on both edges, and the crates would pop out enough to grip. All that was left was for Varrage to leave.

There was something else nagging at Dr Norel. Something trembling just below the surface; he felt it in his back.

"Goodbye Doctor," Varrage said, "I will return soon." Varrage walked to his bike, which was parked across from a low, stone and branch building, not much bigger than a tent, built by Varrage during the long weeks when his body required no sleep.

Varrage powered up his bike and Norel walked over to it. "Thank you Jaquon. I'm sorry to ask this of you. Please be careful, but please, don't... kill anyone."

Varrage closed his eyes and turned his head away slightly, slowly raising his right hand from the bike as a barrier to further discussion. As his hand rose, his first two fingers extended slightly, as if pointing toward the horizon. "Your wishes are known to me," he said.

Norel nodded. Varrage looked at him and nodded back. Then he drove down the hill, and made a right onto the landing strip. Norel watched the green light of Varrage's departure flicker through the trees, and when it ended, he looked away.

He stood alone in the field of mist and hand-carried stone, looking up at the sister moons which had traveled further across the sky. Should he work? Should he plan? Should he sleep? Should he pray?

He stood.

* * *

Lieutenant Camille's face shone brightly on the large screen in Sinclair's office. All the lights were on in the room now. Bloch stood by the monitor, though the ideas in his head kept propelling him, causing him to pace a few steps every few seconds before stopping to speak.

Sinclair sat on a lab stool with his arm resting on the long counter. There were other stools, on the other side, behind the rosewood counter, and every time Bloch drew near him, Sinclair would wish he was sitting on one of them. On the other side of the counter he'd still be able to hear Lt. Camille, but he wouldn't be so close to a pacing tiger.

"All right Lieutenant, You've seen the information from the V.T.O.L., is it sufficient for imprinting?" Bloch asked.

"Yes. These are the ranges of frequencies that can be expected to incapacitate Norel's riders — seems simple enough. I don't foresee any problems," Camille said over the screen.

Bloch took only a single step, toward Sinclair, and then turned to him, facing him directly. "Is there anything else?" he asked.

I know the answer to that one. Thank God.

"No. That's all we learned tonight," Sinclair said.

Bloch stepped back to the screen. "Will you be able to incorporate this?" he asked Lt. Camille.

"It will be an easy adaptation. We'll put it right in with the synaptic disruptors. Yes, especially when..."

"I need it done now Lieutenant. Right now"

"Oh. All right. I'll do it myself then. I'll modify —"

"— What about the cognition overrides? Can we modify them? Secure more control?"

"Yes. We had to merge and stack them with the sleep governors. We'll, we'll speak later."

Sinclair slid forward on the stool, practically open rebellion; at least it felt like it. "Sleep governors? Disruptors? Lieutenant Camille, what are you talking about?" he asked.

"Nothing you need to worry about Sinclair." Bloch said, looking at the monitor's controls, and then at the screen. "Thank you Lieutenant," he said.

He shut off the monitor and the screen went black.

Deep in thought, he strode toward the exit. Near it, he turned and locked eyes with Sinclair. "I'll call you when I need you." he said, and then he left, closing the door calmly behind him.

Sinclair looked at the closed door.

He wore no shackles. No manacles. No electronic cuffs. All it took was that look from the Colonel to trap him.

* * *

**

The Sun, that happy maniac, blazed through a tall canopy of yellow leaves, back-lighting them into brilliance. The naked blue sky shone through multiple gaps in the leaves, and the sky itself also seemed brilliant, lush with the glory of the day's light. Nonstop drove Grace in, and didn't worry about keeping a ghost going. The sooner into paradise, the better.

Grace gasped. They were out of scale for this forest. The dominant trees were very tall, darkly barked, and had no branches for the first thirty feet or so. Their leaves were turning colors, preparing to fall, spraying the forest ceiling with autumnal shades of yellow and orange and red. Shafts of sunlight slanted in the distance, angel-white, long and bold. The forest floor lay wide, gifted with drifts of bright leaves, fragrant with fruit and flower. Grace craned around her to see it all.

"It's so gorgeous. It's so beautiful. It's so..."

"It's daylight. Figures. I thought it would be night. The necklace is more impressive at night."

"I'm on another planet, I'm impressed."

Nonstop smiled, "Pretty cool, huh?"

"Yes," she said, looking. The plants that grew from the forest floor were foreign-looking to her, but at least they were green; at least that element seemed familiar. There were a lot of plants: broad-leafed, frond-leafed, spiral-leafed, more than she could catch sight of.

Nonstop slowed. He knew the spot, but he couldn't see it well because of all the leaves. Under them somewhere was a clear lane to ride — at least there used to be. He'd drive easy, mindful that the leaves might hide branches or stones.

They drove alongside a hill that rose into a ledge. Trees hugged its rim at its beginning, but soon gave way to an enormous mushroom that also grew along the hill's edge, a gigantic half-circle of golden brown trampoline. Grace watched it as they passed it, and kept watching it as they kept passing it. It was huge, a beautiful sienna brown, almost rust colored, with white dots and a white underbelly. She'd seen deer that color. She'd seen *pictures* of deer that color, she'd seen pictures of *cartoon* deer that color, little cartoon deer with butterflies on their noses, and skunks for friends. She rested her cheek against the coiled rope on Nonstop's back, and watched and watched.

It wasn't long before Nonstop slowed noticeably, and started moving left. Grace looked over his shoulder to see if they had arrived anywhere, and for the first time, saw something beyond the trees besides more trees, something dark. It didn't seem to be anything specific. It wasn't a building. It was... a lot of rock. A lot of cragginess. A mountain? The foot of a cliff?

Nonstop drove sharply to the left and cleared the trees. Yes it was a mountain. Yes it was a cliff. The forest grew on a mountain. There were other forest-covered mountains in the distance, on the other side of whatever valley lay beyond the plateau they drove on. Nonstop stopped the bike and shut it off. Not far from where the bike sat parked, the grassy land began to fall away. Grace wanted no part of it.

"We don't have to go down there do we?" she asked.

"Nah. Up there." Nonstop pointed to the cliff on his right. Grace whimpered a tiny noise; it didn't look like a much better option.

"It's not as bad as it looks. It's easy walking, and easy climbing. It's not easy driving, so we'll leave ol' Rattletrap parked," he smiled. "Dig it. There aren't any people here. No one's going to steal the bike. We're free."

He started to swing off the bike, and Grace followed his lead, getting off first. They walked along a grassy incline and came to a rocky slope. Nonstop went up a few stones and held out his hand. Grace filmed the mountains around her and then tucked her camera into its wrist strap, holding it to the inside of her forearm so it wouldn't swing around and bounce against the rocks. She took Nonstop's hand. They began to climb.

"So," Grace said, "we were driving in the realmlines, right? What are they really?"

Nonstop raised the hand Grace held, lending her strength as she pulled herself up a tall rock. "Hhhuf, let's see, Doc says that the realmlines are sort of like a radio. You tune into subatomic frequencies. He says stuff about blood types too. It's way over my head. I get the part about the wet soap though. I get that."

She looked up, directly into his eyes. He continued.

"You squeeze a wet bar of soap and it shoots forward right? The bike opens up a space between realmlines, and the weight of them wanting to return to normal shoots the bike forward. That's where the insane speed comes from, sometimes you can feel it."

She brought both feet onto one rock, eyed the next rock she would stand on, and set a hand down to steady herself. "So is this like that string theory stuff?" she asked, "That we're on one membrane, and other universes are on other membranes, and that the big bang might have been two branes colliding?"

Nonstop looked up at the rocks, at the brush, at nothing in particular. "Actually, that sounds kind of familiar," he said. "Are you a science ge... person? Do you know that field theory stuff?"

"I had a boyfriend who was taking theoretical physics."

"So you... like science guys?"

"He was okay," she stepped over a series of little rocks. "He had a car. I had destinations. Seemed like a match made in heaven." She offered a weak laugh.

"Maybe you'd want to take him to meet Dr. Norel. I mean if you're still friends with him."

"I don't know, he switched majors. He says the future is in statistics."

"Statistics." Nonstop repeated to himself.

"So where are we? Where are the realmlines exactly?"

They reached another flat grassy walkway.

"Exactly *exactly* exactly? I don't really know," Nonstop said, "But that's true when I'm on Earth too. You know? The planet's moving. The Universe is expanding. Who knows exactly exactly where they are? But dig it. You are going to love this."

He walked backwards, facing her, gesturing with his hands. "If you took all the stuff in our solar system, all the planets, all the asteroids, all the dust, and all the people, they wouldn't take up one *trillionth* of the available space. There's room for a whole lot of other planet systems around our sun, and it turns out they're there! Stars are omni-dimensional!"

"What are you saying? That our solar system is full of planets?"

"Over a thousand. Probably a lot more," Nonstop looked over his shoulder, grinning big time. "Here we are, right around this corner. Let me cover your eyes."

"No. No one is covering my eyes on a mountaintop on another planet. You'd make me fall..."

"Hey. No I wouldn't, but fine, fine, okay. This is once in a lifetime though, so like, cover your forehead and watch the ground. I'll lead you, you can watch my feet. You don't have to walk anywhere I don't walk."

"I can just walk; you don't have to be so dramatic."

"You're going to see the necklace. It's dramatic."

"Okay." She placed her hand over her forehead, and watched her feet. Nonstop cupped her elbow with the very tips of his fingers and walked backwards, drawing her forward.

Finally he stopped, and stepped aside.

"Go ahead, take a look."

Grace looked up. Huge in the sky was another planet, paled by atmosphere, but beautiful. Across its face, blue swirled into green, and green swirled into violet, soft as breath. Above that planet's shoulder was another planet, paler, but fully visible, and beyond that, a third.

Grace exhaled. She had gasped without realizing it. She freed her camera, and caught the image.

"Wow," she said, "that's an incredible shot. You're right. But, okay, where's the necklace?"

Nonstop wrinkled his eyebrows. "We're standing on it." He gestured to the planets. "See? Look again. Try to see what you are really seeing."

"What? I'm sorry, I don't —"

"The necklace is a ring of planets, all in Earth's orbit. This part of the ring is all in one realmline — but our little sun is an omni-dimensional superstar! So many planets, across so many realmlines, and we all share the same sun. The necklace is made of all the planets that share Earth's orbit; Earth's the crowning jewel of course, but dig it, we've got neighbors! We've got new people to meet. New sciences to discover. There are new things everywhere you look — and that's just here! We're learning how to make serious shortcuts — once we do, all those exo planets they're discovering outside our solar system will be available to us — and keep in mind, those planets are actually *in* our realmline. We could stay on them — put down serious roots — new homeworlds for whoever wants one, overflowing resources, new solutions to every old problem. Just planets and planets and planets. You mentioned the future — there's so *much* future!"

"It's amazing."

"You really should see it at night though. That's when it's *super-beautiful*."

Grace raised her eyebrows, and then her eyelids, and repeated to herself, "Super-beautiful," as she nodded.

He took a step closer to her. "Maybe I could bring you back sometime, so you could really see it." If there were a high school hall-locker behind her, Grace was sure he would be leaning one arm on it. She turned slowly, and started walking back toward the bike, cradling her camera in front of her.

"That sounds very nice. This whole planet needs to be documented. We could bring a whole crew, we could bring a hundred crews, a thousand crews — it's a whole new planet."

"I was kind of just talking about you and..."

"How did you meet Krork? Is this his Planet?"

"No, Krork's place," Nonstop started chuckling a little, "you take a right at Saturn. It's far out, but the heat travels different there. The planet is nice." They walked.

"So how did you meet him? How did he come to be a *"Thrill King"*?"

"Ah, uhm." Nonstop took a step, and watched the rocks where he walked. He exhaled loudly. "A rescue mission went bad. Teams were attacked by, well, creatures. Voracitors. We couldn't hurt them. Normal weapons went right through them. We lost a lot of people. Varrage and I were both hurt. He rescued me and got hurt worse than I did. Skyde and this hunter guy kept us alive, but they couldn't talk to each other, so he brought Krork to translate. When it was over, Krork asked to join up. We healed crazy. That's why Varrage looks the way he does, that's why I have the lights in my hair, and that's why the four of us are bullet-proof.

"You're bullet-proof? What happened?"

"Varrage kind of explo — I don't really want to go into it."

They turned the corner and saw a vine move, toward the bushes, near very tall slabs of rock. Grace stopped. The vine stopped.

"That vine just moved," Grace said.

"It did?" Nonstop asked. The vine moved again toward the bush. "It did," Nonstop said.

As the vine dragged along the ground, it twisted, and a broad leaf rose into view, traveling with the vine, in fact, ending the vine. "What is that?" Nonstop asked.

Grace began to blubber, "It's a living v-ine. Where's the bike? Let's go to the bike."

"No. Dig it. It's a tail. Get a picture."

"What?"

"I owe Skyde tape of an animal. Shoot."

"What?" Grace raised the camera, pressed a button, held the button, released the button, and lowered the camera. "There," she said, let's go get the bike."

The vine slipped into the bush.

"We just shot its tail." Nonstop said.

"That's all there was."

"That's not all there is though."

Grace's shoulders slumped, "A tail made out of vine is good."

"Lend me the camera," Nonstop said, holding out his hand. Grace gave him the camera, and he stepped between the bush and the rock wall. He noticed a gap. The rock wall sliced into the ground at the bush's midpoint. A few feet behind it was a second rock wall, staggered, and continuing behind the first rock wall, with enough room for a path between them. It was an overlap you might not notice, especially at night. Nonstop crouched, and took a step into into the gap.

"What are you doing?" Grace whispered, "Don't go in there. If you get killed, I can't get home."

Grace looked at the rock wall, at the bush, turned to look at the plateau's edge with the mountains beyond, and quickly turned back to look at the rocks again.

"Grace. Grace. Come here," Nonstop whispered, "This is wild. You have to see this."

Grace shut her eyes and tilted her head back. She side-stepped her way around the bush and crouched between the two rock walls. The gap was very much like a twisting corridor, the kind you might see in a zoo or a museum, where walls were set up to hide things from view without using any doors, or attempts to block passage, you just had to walk a little maze-like twist, and you were in. She could see Nonstop crouched behind shrubs at the turning point, where the inner rock wall descended to ground level with a jagged staircasing. There was more light where Nonstop was than where she was — he wasn't looking into a cave. Nonstop was looking out into sunlight. Grace crept nearer, until she could look where Nonstop was looking.

And it *was* wild.

The rocks gave way to a clearing, perhaps a vast bowl shape within the cliff, perhaps just a continuation of the normal ground encircled by tall rock formations, either way, a very sheltered area. There were many tall trees, but the center was clear, and in the center, as real as the trees and the rocks, there was a dragon. A dragon made of living brambles, brambles spiked with thorns, and arranged in familiar animalistic forms by the sinuous twistings of sleek, dark vines. The brambles became decorative near the creature's face, ringing its flower-petaled eyes with thorns, rising in a crown above its head, a majestic interlacing of stalks and thorns and iridescent petals.

Grace and Nonstop watched as it brought down its great wings and rose slightly in the air. Its wings were brothers to the trees, branching out in supple capillaried networks of smaller and smaller branchings, feathered with leaves in autumnal plumage, backlit from the sun, as orange as you could possibly think, as yellow, as black. The creature raised these great, bat-like wings again, and brought them down to stay aloft in the air. The movement sent a spray of leaves from its wings, exposing black branches within the new bare patches.

"Oh, it's beautiful." Grace said, and she looked at Nonstop to share the moment. He was holding the camera ridiculously. "That's upside down," she said as she took the camera from him. "I mean it's clearly marked." She started shooting.

"Yeah, well I never read instructions," he said. "Thanks though. Skyde's going to love this."

Grace continued shooting, shifting her stance for a slightly truer angle. "Never read instructions? That's why you hold cameras upside down. Who is Skyde?"

"Skyde is the world's first Xenologist. She studies Inter-D — *alien*, lifeforms."

"Pfft, Xenologist? Where do you go to school for that?"

"There is no school for that. She did it herself — she says sometimes you just have to insist."

"Oh, is that all you have to do? Well she must be great at it then."

"She is great at it. What's wrong? You're mad? You're mad because Skyde doesn't have a degree in alien lifeforms? No. Because that would be crazy."

"What is she? Your girlfriend?" Grace aimed the camera as the dragon landed and disappeared into the tree line. Then she turned off the camera and lowered it. Nonstop looked at her.

"No, Skyde's in love with that hunter guy. What's wrong?"

Grace looked straight ahead, refusing the tears she herself did not understand. "Nothing," she said. "I'm on another planet, with a dragon and half an idiot, and I'm interning for some other woman who doesn't even have a degree — *again*."

"This is shock right? Let's get you home."

He tapped her on the shoulder and stood fully. They skirted the bush, walked back out to the grassy ledge and stood for a second as Grace returned her camera to her tool belt pouch. Nonstop stretched his back, and treated himself to another long look at the far mountains. Then they both walked back to the rocky hill.

They could see the valley from there.

They could see the bike from there.

They could see the dragon — perfectly — as it swooped down and grabbed the bike with its rear legs, and then returned to the sky with its prize, looping back over the trees.

Grace gasped.

Nonstop did too.

"... I'm going to die," Grace said.

"It can't carry the bike for long. It's losing its wings. It's okay."

"I'm going to be killed by a plant. I'm going to be killed by a plant with mange."

"It'll be all right."

"How do you figure?"

"Because it has to be all right."

Grace looked at the spot where the bike had been a mere second ago, turned, and kicked Nonstop in his other leg.

* * *

Louis Sinclair paced his office with his sense of security obliterated. Rooting around in his treasure trove of files was impossible. Relaxing was impossible. Ignoring the dread that was seeping into his bones was impossible. The first version of the Colonel's plan had failed, and now it looked like he himself was locked out, *cast out,* of the plan that was developing. Was he making too much of this? Should he just sit tight? Would Bloch invite him in? Was he already in?

He didn't think so. He certainly didn't feel so. He felt like a loose end. He had been miles from the catastrophe in the lens field, but he felt like a casualty of it nonetheless.

It was dark outside.

He sat in a little protected room, under buzzing electric lights, but the truth was, it was dark outside.

Waiting here was waiting for darkness to visit him. A little information, a little information would help. A little light to melt the darkness.

He emptied his pockets, a wallet, half a roll of breath mints, his keys, and his security pass. His pass gave him liberal access to all the science labs, though probably not to Lieutenant Camille's work areas, at least not directly. But he was already in a secure area. He was already past the card-lock perimeter. He had free access to every set of fire-stairs on the floor. There were no guards in the building. The camera stations were now unmanned. He might be able to get close enough to learn something. He might be able to gain a little fore-warning for himself.

He gathered his things. Clipped to his key-ring was a press-button flashlight, a mini LED device no bigger than his thumbprint. He freed it and squeezed it. It shone with a distinctly blue tint.

He left the lights on in the room, and softly pulled the door closed behind him.

* * *

Nonstop tugged at the creeper vine he held and pulled it taut. He tugged it harder, and it shook the bush it was tied to. He tied another vine to the bush as a back up, even though he thought one would be enough.

They were terrific vines, supple and strong, but even so, they only made a rope about twenty feet long, and that measurement would be less when he tied the loop at the end.

No creatures had moved when he took the vines from the ground, including the vines themselves: nothing had tugged back, or made a noise, and so he went back to the same patch and pruned four more lengths of vine.

He quickly added the new vines to the old, and worried they might trap the safety rope he intended to run through them. He cut a smaller piece of vine and used it to tie an independent loop onto the end of the collection — now, if he ran the rope through the loop, the long vines could cinch and squeeze all they wanted and the safety rope would still slide.

Worried he was sweating the details, he moved a little faster. *Shouldn't he sweat the details though? Weren't they only going to have one shot at this?*

He fed his rescue rope through the small loop until it was roughly at its midpoint, and then he folded the rope over neatly. That done, he picked up the entire collection and walked to the tree he had identified as a good place to change the rope's direction. He passed the rope carefully over a chin-high branch., and after that, he walked the rope in the new direction, feeding it out until he came to the spot where Grace was waiting and watching the resting dragon, and wishing she were anyplace else.

He handed her both ends of the rescue line. "Okay," he said, "you pull the ropes, the bush way over there shakes like crazy, the dragon checks out the bush, and I snatch the bike."

"What if the bush is alive?"

"Maybe you'd feel safer behind those rocks."

"What if the rocks are alive? What if the dragon eats you? Don't you have a gun?

"Doc is dead set against guns. I've got a flip saw and an axe hammer."

"What about that... thing on your back?" Grace waggled her fingers in the direction of his shoulder, "Your sword."

"It's a Voracitor rib, not super-sharp, but practically indestructible."

"What good is a sword that isn't sharp?"

"It's something a Voracitor will feel."

"What does that mean? What —"

"— Okay, okay, look. It's not going to get me, but if it does, then you'll have to drive the bike out of here. You j —"

"I can't drive the bike out of here."

"It's not that hard. Y—"

"— I couldn't drive a regular motorcycle out of here, let alone some crazy outer-space-robot motorcycle."

"Everything you need to drive is on the control bar, there are back ups —"

"Doesn't it have an auto retrieve button? — this miracle of science of yours?"

"Auto retrieve? What do you mean?"

"I mean your boss presses a button and the bike comes back."

"Nah. We don't have anything like that. The Outpost can't communicate with the bikes past the first Realm-tunnel - sometimes not even then, but —"

"Well, is there a button *I can press* that sends me back?"

"Sort of, yeah - that's what I'm trying to tell you — the bike will remember the last few steps it took, but you still have to drive it. And its not that hard, you start it, and you watch the rings on the display. When they line up like a target you — I wish I could show you, but —"

"Yeah, we don't have the bike."

"Look. You're smart. Steering and throttle are all on the control bar — computer stuff is all on the display — you have to hit eighty-eight in order to start ghosting. You might figure it out if you had to — but if you can't —"

Nonstop undocked his tap, cocked it open, and offered it to Grace.

"— Just tap this against the ground and shoot yourself with it."

"Shoot myself?"

"It'll send you home. If we came through a portal I'd do it now, but we didn't, so I'm not really sure where in our realmline it would send you — could be Saturn."

Grace looked at Nonstop, touched her fingertips against the forward edge of the tap, and pushed it gently back toward him. "Thanks. Thanks very much. Go get the bike."

"Okay. I'm gonna, but remember, when the dragon commits to checking out the bush, you let go of one end of the rope and reel the other one back in. Don't wait for the dragon to reach the bush."

"Which end?"

"Either. It doesn't matter. I'll be back."

*

The dragon lay in its clearing. The rock wall that surrounded it split open in many places, and offered many paths to the rest of the forest.

Alone, Grace found that she wanted a weapon. She reached down to her tool belt for the screw driver. It would make a good knife, better than no — except it wasn't there!

She looked down. All her tools were gone. The screwdriver, the pliers, even the pens! She had nothing left to stab with. Had she lost them? She checked again, already knowing she would find nothing.

Already knowing the tools would be in the back of the van —
borrowed by Nick at some point without asking — again. She looked
up and watched as Nonstop crept his way into the brush.

*

Nonstop's bike, tasted and tossed, was still in the clearing, a few
feet from the dragon, but in one piece as far as Nonstop could tell.

The dragon's most direct path to the bush was on the opening to
Nonstop's left, so Nonstop crept to the opening on his right. At the
rock wall, he looked back, raised his head slightly to see above the
bushes, and spotted Grace. He raised his arm and gave a thumbs up.

*

Grace let out her breath and closed her eyes. She pulled the rope.
Nothing happened.

She pulled the rope harder. She heard the bush shake. The dragon
didn't move.

She shook it longer. The dragon turned its head and went back to
resting. She shook it five more times before yelling: "GO CHECK
THE BUSH YOU STUPID DRAGON!"

The dragon rose to its feet instantly. Grace gasped and ran behind
the rocks and shook the bush like crazy, hoping it would make more
noise than her yelling had.

The dragon strode quickly out of the clearing. Grace shook the
bush as she watched Nonstop creep into the clearing toward the bike.

She shook the bush, turned to look at it and saw that the dragon
was just about on it. She let go of one end of the rope and started
reeling in the other.

She was yanked by the rope. Powerfully. One of her feet left the
ground for an instant. She recovered, kept pulling, and was yanked
again, this time crashing into the rocks right in front of her. She
absorbed the blow with her upper arm and avoided crying out. She
pulled in the rope as fast as she could.

She saw Nonstop push the bike toward a gap in the stone on the far side of the clearing, away from her, not the way he had gone in. What was he doing? Where was he going?

She felt the rope go free and heard the dragon at the bush, thrashing it. She looked at the rope coiling at her feet as she continued to pull. She looked at the trees all around her, at the alien plants, growing mutely, only a few feet away from her. Where was she? She was on another planet; she was alone on another planet. She pulled the rope. Alien rocks. Alien sky. The end of the rope. What was she going...

Nonstop whispered behind her, from the rock edge above her back.

"Grace, shhhh," he said, holding a finger to his lips. "Toss me some rope, come on."

Grace, relieved beyond measure, looked up, and without saying anything, nodded and pulled in the last of the rope. Most of it lay in a tangle at her feet, too heavy for her to throw at once. She tried throwing the end she held, but it was too light to throw overhand. Grace quickly tossed out a long length of the rope and whipped it up over her head in a great arc. It seemed silly, more effort than seemed called for, but the rope reached the edge of the rock with length to spare, and Nonstop stepped on it, trapping it before it could slide back down.

Nonstop picked up the rope and looped it around his back, trapping it under his armpits before squeezing both handfuls at arm's length in front of his chest. "Walk up," he said.

"Walk up? How?"

"Hold the rope, straighten your leg against the wall and start walking. I will too. Don't think too much about it."

It was easy until the first step. Then her weight transferred to her hands and the rope started to vibrate. It pulled her arms straight. The sore spot on her upper arm protested, but she could feel Nonstop's help in the rope. She took a step, and started to sway at the shoulders. She corrected by moving her foot, saw that she needed to keep her back straight, and called up in a whisper "Go ahead. Go ahead, I'm going to walk." He did, she did, and it was done in less than four seconds.

Nonstop coiled the rope crudely as they crept to Rattletrap. "You did great!" he said.

Rattletrap's seat was folded down for two person riding. Nonstop pressed a latch, and lifted the entire seat, which was hinged at the front like a trunk lid. He stuffed the rope into the small storage compartment, and started pushing the bike through the brush. "We want to be as far from the Dragon as we can when we start cracking branches," he whispered, and Grace nodded.

They pushed the bike over a log and saw a slope that led toward the lane-way they had ghosted in on.

"Okay, down there seems good enough. We get on. We get out. Let me make sure it's in whisper-mode." Nonstop checked, "Cool, we're good."

"We get on and do the ghosting thing right?" Grace said, placing her hand on Nonstop's back, pushing, but holding back too, not pushing as hard as she wanted to.

"Yeah, as soon as we hit eighty eight, we ghost."

Nonstop pushed the machine down the hill. The slope took the bike and it started to move easily. "We can't hit eighty eight here though; this ground is too bumpy. I'll..."

Grace stole a look back before stepping down the slope herself. She saw hints of the dragon deep through the trees. From what she could tell, the dragon was tugging at the bush, and then biting it from different angles.

"Let's go. Let's go," Grace said, patting the air as she turned from the dragon and stepped toward Nonstop.

Her foot entered a pile of leaves, missed a loop of root, and landed on a loose stone, which turned under her weight and launched her forward. Her hand found Nonstop's shoulder again, and this time it pushed it hard.

They toppled. Nonstop's ribs crashed against the bike's vortex chamber, and Grace's ribs crashed against him. The bike slid forward, rushing on a carpet of moving leaves.

Not quiet. Not quiet at all. The trio bounced a ways down the slope, breaking twigs, and adding to the shuffling roar of sliding leaves before the ground twisted, and they fell past a bush, and then through open air.

They bounced back upwards once they hit the giant mushroom below them, along with sprays of leaves, and twigs, and sun-brightened clouds of pollen. Grace heard a loud crack from the woods far behind her, and in the next second she saw Nonstop hit the mushroom's edge and bounce away from view. The bike hit the edge as well, at an angle, and simply slipped off the crown. Grace could hear it crashing its way down the slope, and then she tucked in her arms, and bounced off the edge herself.

Below was a slope to another giant mushroom. She caught sight of Nonstop as he bounced over its rim, arms spread wide. Grace was in mid-bounce herself when the Dragon thrust its head through the tight trees. She screamed as she launched over the mushroom's orange edge and passed through a curtain of young, leafy branches.

She landed in a huge pile of leaves and hit the ground — *hard* — but unhurt.

"Come on! Come on!" Nonstop called as he reached for her hand and pulled. "Anything broken?" he asked as he got her to her feet and dragged her.

"I'm —"

"That's good. Come on."

"I'm —"

Nonstop worked at the bike's control bar even as he pushed the bike through a wall of leaves. He aimed the machine for a spot where the slope met level ground, and looked to where the dragon was tugging its way carefully through the snagging bush and tree branches above the mushrooms.

"Come on," he said.

Grace reached the bike. Nonstop kept pushing and yelled "Get on!"

Grace hopped onto the foot deck and swung her leg over. Nonstop started the bike as he ran alongside it, and then he hopped on, stealing a look behind him as he revved the engine.

"It's coming!" Grace yelled, as the dragon pushed its way down the slope they had just left. The beast looked huge, overwhelming, a tangle of ropes moving under its own power, a supple locomotive, changing direction to align itself directly with their escape route.

Nonstop opened up the engine. The ride got very rough. "Hang on," he said as Grace bounced and jounced on the seat behind him.

The trees thinned, the ground grew smoother. They sped up.

The dragon pursued, crashing between trees, the forest too crowded to allow it to run freely, too crowded to allow it to open its wings.

Grace watched the trees recede behind her. She saw the dragon shoulder its way free. She saw it lock its eyes on the bike and charge. She saw two cycles of the animal's gallop; the animal terrified her, but the speed seemed good; they were leaving it behin —

The dragon reached the end of the trees. It lifted its wings, and running, rolled its shoulders forward to present a thin edge to the wind. The move was odd enough and deliberate enough to hold

Grace fascinated. She watched, and as the dragon's wings snapped open and took to the air without losing leaves, she screamed.

Nonstop turned to look and pulled his sword. He held it out, angled over Grace's shoulder and toward the dragon.

"You said it's not sharp," Grace screamed.

"Better than nothing," Nonstop screamed back.

Grace watched the dragon grab altitude. The creature watched them as it rose, setting up its attack dive. Grace saw its coiled frame pull tight, and she saw as the diamond-points of sunlight shining through its body squeezed down to knife blade slits. In the air, the dragon looked like living calligraphy, like a flow of brush-strokes. As it soared, it looked like a kite made of flower petals.

Nonstop pointed the sword toward a patch of green land ahead of them. "We can get speed at that meadow."

"It's too far. It's too far," Grace screamed behind him.

Nonstop steered to where the trees grew thicker. Grace shrieked, shaking his gear harness. "What are you doing? The meadow! You said the meadow!"

The dragon screeched.

Grace punched Nonstop's back, "I hate you! I hate you! I hate you!"

"Hey! Hang on with both hands!" Nonstop said, turning his body straight ahead as the bike raced for the trees. Grace gave him a weak punch as she grabbed the straps at his shoulders.

The dragon dived toward the riders, screeching. Yellow leaves ripped from its wings and trailed against the blue sky. Its jaws flew open, rows of thorns. ready to rip and tear.

Nonstop read the immediate landscape, saw the fastest slice of ground, and shot into the tree line.

The dragon rocketed toward the trees, but rolled skyward at the last second, avoiding the places its wings wouldn't clear.

Beyond the blur of stalky trees, Grace saw the meadow slip further and further away. As she started to speak Nonstop yelled "HANG ON!"

Rattletrap grabbed a sapling, and the young tree bent tremendously as Nonstop pivoted the bike. The bike slowed, and as the tree tried to straighten, Nonstop used its motion to slingshot the bike out toward the meadow, where he might reach eighty-eight before the dragon reoriented itself.

"AAAAAAAAHHHHHHHH" Grace screamed, as the bike zoomed in its new direction, swinging her nearly off the bike, leaning her *way* off her seat, straining her grip on the straps that held her to Nonstop.

"AAAAAAAAHHHHHHHH" Grace continued as she righted herself, and saw that the landscape they approached was green and lush, and without a single tree to hide behind. Was there anything she could do? Anything? She didn't have a weapon. Could she make a weapon? An idea flashed to her from film class: with a match and a can of hair spray, she could make a flame thrower — but she didn't have a match, or a can of any kind of spray, All she had was her camera, her camera and — maybe another idea from film class...

She wedged her feet tight against the bike. She found two little spurs in the frame, right where she needed them to be, right above the tops of her feet.

She let go of Nonstop and clamped her feet.

She unzipped her side pouch and took out her camera and an auxiliary light, which was just about as big as the whole camera, *stupid hundred-year old gear*. She began connecting them — rushing. Maybe. Maybe this was something.

The meadow was treeless, but it wasn't rockless, and it wasn't rutless. The ride was every bit as hard as it didn't look to be. She fumbled, but she got the light mounted on the camera. Where was the dragon?

Nonstop was getting the speed he needed, but each rock and dip cost him some of it. He turned to look behind him for the dragon, raising his sword — and the dragon was RIGHT THERE! "Grace get down!" he yelled as he locked his sword arm toward the creature.

Grace leaned away from his thrust, and suddenly didn't have enough room to finish what she was doing. Instinctively, she leaned all the way down to the bumping vortex chamber.

She raised the camera and looked through it, trying to find one of the creature's eyes, hoping that the halogen mini-light would cause the same reaction in the dragon that it caused in every person who ever looked into it — that the dragon would flinch, or turn away — or maybe, with no fore-knowledge, even be terrified.

It was only a second, maybe a fraction less, maybe a fraction more, but she had to work for the duration of that fractional moment. The dragon was moving at speed, the bike was moving at speed and bumping, and she would have to keep the irritant in the dragon's eye once she found it. She would have to man her post to do these things.

She did. The eye came into the viewfinder, and when it did, she activated the mini-light and the sudden brilliance stabbed the creature in its eye. Predators have no doctors; any mistake might kill them. A broken jaw becomes a death-sentence. The dragon, having all the meadow to attack in, veered away from the light, and rolled skyward to reposition its drop.

Nonstop whooped.

He glanced forward while he kept his sword held straight out. The speedometer's numbers blurred. He listened to his engine, nodding, glancing at the landscape, glancing at the dragon. Grace sat up, gripped Nonstop's gear harness, and used her other hand to hold the camera against her belly, hiding its light from view, feeling its warmth.

She watched the dragon swerve and re-approach, mouth open, eyes locked on her, on her hands, coming in for the kill. She braced herself, waiting for the moment to go for the dragon's eye again — when streaks of light flew past her own eyes. As she glanced at the streaks they elongated and stretched into coils, the air around them instantly darkening and distorting. She swung her attention back to the attacking dragon and freed her camera, swinging it out at arm's length. Her flash found the dragon's eye — but it kept flying closer. It jerked its head to remove the irritant, but *it kept flying closer*. Grace tried again — the dragon veered to prevent her success, and as its head touched the twisting air of the ghost tunnel it spasmed and recoiled fully, perhaps finding a sensation so alien in the swarming molecules, so unexpected, that pursuit no longer seemed survivable. It stopped itself with a great upward sweep of its wings and hung in the air for a moment, with the swirling clouds of its lost yellow leaves adding a royal extravagance to the escape of Nonstop and Grace.

*

Grace looked ahead of her, stunned. Suddenly there was a whole new reality around her that she had to sync up with: safety, swirling realmlines, Nonstop in one piece, herself in one piece, the bike in one piece — and *home*. They were going home! She hugged her camera and put it back in her belt. She zipped the pouch closed as a brighter swell of light enveloped her and Nonstop and the bike. A smudge of dirt on her forehead faded away as the decontamination light ebbed.

The world they left, where was it? Grace turned to look, but she was already too late. The vast, drifting realmlines filled her vision. This was her third time leaving a world in order to enter this strange inter-dimensional space, and she had yet to see the transition. What did it look like? Did it shut like a door? The next chance she got, could she film it? Sure! Absolutely! Didn't she just defeat a dragon? She gripped Nonstop's gear harness and stood up tall, her hair whipping behind her in the field turbulence around the bike. "Did you see that?" she screamed above Nonstop's head, "We did it! WOOOOO-HOOOOOOOOOO!"

"Hey! Hey! Sit down," grandma Nonstop scolded.

* * *

Rik Ty

**

Louis Sinclair stood in the dim stairwell and looked at the aluminum push release on the door. It spanned most of the door's width. It was basically a flat bar seated within an open aluminum box. There were probably a few springs in it somewhere. He had seen its like a thousand times before, and he was familiar with it. It would make a metallic clacking sound when opened, and it would open easily. It was designed to open easily. You could open it with your hand, your elbow or your hip. If you were carrying somebody, heroically rescuing them from a blazing inferno that was rushing down the very stairwell you were escaping in, you could open it without putting the person down. Even a corpse could open the door; it would merely have to fall the right way. Sinclair looked at the release, and couldn't bring himself to touch it. The door probably wasn't locked. He thought it would probably open.

But the second it did, an alarm might sound.

It was possible that the door was locked. Would Bloch lock a fire safety stairwell? Yes, Sinclair thought he might. Would Bloch set an alarm on a fire safety door? Yes, Sinclair thought, that was even more likely.

He had chosen this door because technically, it didn't lead to Lieutenant Camille's lab tower. It opened to a hangar space that connected to Camille's tower. Not that he had any good reason to go to the hangar either. What would he say if caught?

He could think of no lie he found convincing. He might just have to tell the truth — that he felt like he was out of the loop, that he was in danger, and that he just wanted to see what it was that was making him feel that way. Perhaps they could all laugh about it. Bloch could reassure him that it was just an oversight that he was left out of the conference with Lt. Camille, and then he could invite Sinclair into the planning session.

That was almost as nice a fantasy as rescuing someone from a burning stairwell.

But there was an idea there. He *was* in danger. They were *all* in danger. Something had wiped out their entire team of soldiers and they had no idea what it was.

There was nothing he could do in his lab. He could say he came down to the hangar space to look for outside inspiration — to see what equipment Norel had warehoused that might help with this current situation. Not that he knew what equipment that might be. You could offer him a catalog and an infinite credit line; he still wouldn't know what tool to look for. Perhaps he could claim he wasn't looking for anything specific, that he was just looking for something, anything, to jumpstart his thinking. This hangar-space, full of old equipment, was a possible place to find inspiration. In fact, if this fire-well door *was* locked, he could go back upstairs and issue a request for access to the hangar. Maybe looking pro-active would get him back in the loop.

Feasible.

He pushed the door. It opened. No alarm sounded. The door hit an obstruction when it was halfway open — no, less than halfway, and the opening revealed almost nothing — except the back of a waist-high piece of machinery and then blackness beyond that. Sinclair glanced at the machinery, and saw a sheet of metal backing, held to a blocky metal casing with little hexagonal bolts. There was a machine just like it right next to it, and his mind immediately supplied him with a whole row of identical constructions. What were they, washing machines? They could have been hot dog carts for all he knew.

He squeezed inside and immediately wondered how he would get back out if the door locked behind him. It might, and he couldn't leave it propped open, that would only announce that he was in the hangar. He held the door open with his shoe, pulled out his wallet, and leaned into the weak light in the crack of the door. He pulled two fives and a ten out of the wallet and shoved the ten back in. Then he folded the two fives and placed them over the locking bolt. He tested it: he held onto the edge of the bills, then shut the door and opened it. The door opened easily and he let it close for good. *Fingerprints? Yes, likely.* Sinclair pulled his lab coat sleeve into the palm of his hand and rubbed the handle and latch of the door, never once thinking he was overreacting. For the next few seconds he fretted about his fingerprints on the money, and reasoned that if he came back this way, he could take the money back, and that If someone else discovered the tampered door, they might pocket the money instead of reporting it. He considered replacing one of the fives with the ten to make that more likely, and then had to ask himself: *Who? Who's going to find them? No one's here. Why don't you just get on with this?*

He turned into the darkness of the room. His eyes could see nothing. He heard the sounds of quiet machinery running in the vast, dark space: hums and small clacks and water-valve sloshing noises. Maybe these things blocking the door really were washing machines. This could be a launderette for all the sounds he was hearing, just ahead, in the dark.

Sinclair took out his LED flashlight and lit it. He held it at waist level, and covered it with his left hand. He ran it along the backs of the could-be washing machines, and found that he had been right: there was a whole row of them. They went on for about thirty feet, ending where the wall ended. The wall turned left presumably. The row of machinery simply stopped. Beyond both, he saw darkness — presumably empty space. The LED was too weak to tell him more at this distance. He put his back against the wall and sidestepped slowly toward the far edge.

One step. Two steps. Don't knock anything over, don't scrape against anything. Don't invite any attention.

The wall did turn left. The machinery did end, and there was a cavernous space beyond both, but it wasn't empty. He raised his flashlight into the darkness. An array of glass rectangles — *coffins?* — *terrariums?* — reflected the weak blue light back at him. The grid of tabletops continued no matter which way he swung the light. There were dozens and dozens of the structures, all swooshing and clanking quietly. What were they? Generators? Water treatment plants? What?

He swung his light to the structure nearest him, and took a step toward it. The structure wasn't all glass. It had glass panels set in a stainless steel framework. The panel facing him had a handle, as well as seams, and rivets, and gauges and cooling vents. It was an industrial sized something — but an *industrial sized something what?*

As he approached, he remained aware of the darkness pressing in on him. Every step forward exposed more of his back. He would be silhouetted by his flashlight. He would be easy to see — *if* something were here with him. *Here, in the dark.*

He was moving forward, and he knew, naturally, that he would look into one of the cases. But as he stepped nearer, he found that he didn't want to. He didn't want to move the weak flashlight beam to the windows of the strange machine. He didn't want to look inside. But he stepped closer anyway; he voluntarily stepped closer to whatever was in the chamber of the machine.

His flashlight cut across the case ahead of him. He heard its individual compressors chugging, its pipes gurgling. He heard fluids rushing on and then off.

Was it a specimen tank? When he finally peered into the window, would something be peering back at him? A pair of white, hateful eyes? glaring out from an insane human face? Yes, it would drive you mad to be locked in this room: in this darkness, alone in a stainless steel box, hour after hour, locked helplessly in a water coffin, while around you, you heard nothing but the sounds of dozens and dozens of other specimen tanks, clanking and wheezing, keeping other things in half-life, maybe animals, maybe slurking, loathsome, interdimensional creatures, creatures who could seep their way out of their tanks — and then seep their way *into* other tanks, traveling from one to another, looking for tasty, helpless creatures to devour. Creatures like you, strapped down within industrial isolation tanks, listening and listening...

Silly. Silly. Still, there might be a specimen in the tank. There might not be two eyes waiting to look at him; there might be six, or sixty — some poor creature, whose face was a mat of seaweed roots, with every group of tendrils nesting an eye down at their junction points, and the water pumps keeping the poor thing alive, and hooks holding it down, and holding it open, and its green-pink organs throbbing as it breathed the misty air, wishing with all its heart that it were dead. And when Sinclair looked in the case, the creature would leap at him, and splatter against the glass, and the case would shake, and maybe topple, and the coiled tendrils would escape, and the coiled tendrils would capture him, and the creature would pull him to the sharp silver hooks, and *he* would pay for what the Colonel had done.

Sinclair reached the dark window. His eyes were opened so wide, that when he closed them, he had time to note the distance his eyelids traveled. He shivered, and looked inside the case.

It came as a shock, so mundane it was jarring: a robotic arm moved within the chamber, power spraying a beam of water over a metal disk set in a bed of water — a water jet, cutting a precision component from a billet of some alloy — too dark to be straight aluminum. The disk itself was becoming a complicated looking gear, about a foot and a half in diameter, with a standard gear surface along its rim, but with a center that was cut into many tooth-edged apertures. It looked like a component from some giant watch.

All these machines, running in the dark, making pieces of other machines night and day. What was the whole these pieces were making? What was its shape? What was its purpose?

Some part of Sinclair's gut was relieved that there was nothing frightening in the chambers.

Some part of his mind looked at the rows of machines, and he thought he would be frightened for the rest of his life.

A glow flickered in the darkness beyond the water jets. A light not much stronger than his LED. The flickering hinted at the edges of a massive doorway within the darkness, matched in scale with the large space of the hangar. The flickering came from beyond the doorway.

To see more, Sinclair would have walk past the rows of chambers. He wanted it to be yesterday, when the lights were on and the sun was out, and he had all those wonderful projects pocketed in his cabinets, waiting for the day when he'd claim one for his own, the day he'd quit Bloch and go off to make his *own* fortune from Norel's abandoned work.

He took a few slow steps, and as he did, the flickering changed. Its rhythm became uneven; some flashes brighter, some flashes quicker, and then the flashes intensified.

There's more than one light.

Sinclair kept walking, one tentative step after anoth — a hydraulic pump moaned somewhere ahead of him, and its dinosaur screaming caused him to drop his flashlight. Some chemical surged through his system and it seemed he could taste the fillings in his teeth.

The hydraulic kept sounding, joined by a steady thumping, a pounding, a big noise, an industrial noise.

Sinclair cringed as he bent, looking for his flashlight, now dark without his finger on the trigger. He spotted it in the pulsing glow on the floor, a little black grape set between the humming water lathes. It cast a shadow, even in the dismal light.

He picked it up and continued. He heard a new noise, very small, easy to miss amid the humming water jets: a buzzing sound. Insectile. Electric. He had visited a friend with a porch one summer, and when he was leaving to go home, he'd heard a similar noise. He and his friend had just stepped out onto the porch. The screen door hadn't even finished squeaking yet when they were hit with a steady buzzing coming from the trees and the bushes. It sounded like the inside of an electric cable. It was all around them, maybe like a swarm of crickets. "Cicadas," his friend had said. Was the kid's name Willy? He didn't remember. They didn't stay friends. When it was clear that he didn't know what a cicada was, "Willy" brought him over to a small dogwood tree his family had growing in the front yard.

Hooked into the bark was a very large insect. Sinclair had peered closer for a better look, when incredibly, his friend managed to snatch the insect off the tree. Of course, "Willy" was just a kid, and the next thing he did was thrust the insect in the young Sinclair's face. The young Sinclair recoiled and ran away, and must have looked good and scared, because Willy wound up apologizing and showing him that he was only holding a husk. The insect had molted, and had left an old skin behind. The trees were full of cicadas that had split open their backs, and flown their new bodies up among the branches.

Sinclair saw a live cicada years later and was surprised: it looked like a giant fly. His first thought had been "Mutant", mutant fly. Also, it wasn't the dry, caramel color of the husk he had seen. It was an iridescent green; its underside was fish-belly white. He had been surprised to learn that it was the same creature that had supplied that electric chirping.

He didn't like hearing this new cicada noise now, coming from the dark alcove with the weak pulsing light. He didn't want to see whatever split-back thing lay in the dark ahead of him. But he walked anyway. He passed the doorframe and turned.

It was eyes. He saw eyes.

It was men. He saw rim-lit heads and shoulders. He saw cannons. The split-back thing was all these things: ten feet up in the dark room, lights pulsing into eyes held open by clamps, and that's all Louis saw at first: blackness, and a row of clamped-opened eyes, with only hints at the rest of the faces: a tribunal of newly-awakened judges, high in their benches. Then Sinclair observed their impassive faces, young men as still as mannequins. As still as coma victims. His eyes scanned further along the row and he saw men with corroded faces, ruined, cable-embedded faces. Men in lines of stacked machinery, men amid heavy weaponry. They were men *in* something: vehicles? Medical chambers? Water lathes? Battle armor? And then a door opened somewhere far to his right, and a blade of light cut a bright line within the wall.

Louis turned to face the opened door.

Bloch was striding out of the bottom lab of Lieutenant Camille's tower. Lieutenant Camille stood in the lab watching them both, her hair undone.

"What is all this?" Sinclair asked the Colonel, "What has this got to do with National Security?" Sinclair looked around the walls at the soldiers flanking him. "I think I want to leave Colonel. I think I quit."

Bloch slowed. "It's just another weapons system," he said, and then stopped walking. "Norel's work is full of them. If you know how to look." He raised his slim black handset from his pocket. "Here. Let me show you," he said, and he tapped a sequence on the handset's touchpad.

Bloch walked again, moving past Sinclair on a course that blocked Sinclair from any exit through the water jet array. Sinclair watched every step the Colonel took, turning as the Colonel strode. When the Colonel stopped, Sinclair heard the insectile buzzing grow louder in the darkness right beside him. Slowly, he turned to look.

Another light, pulsing into another open eye, only this time, closer, and the view revealed so much more: the man was ruined. His hair was gone. It looked very much like his skin was gone. The man, arms spread wide, head lolling, looked like a blasphemy of the crucifixion; worse, much worse, he looked like a true echo of it: a sad, anonymous suffering. The corroded man's body hung immersed in a nest of wires and cables and circuit boards to the degree that it was impossible to tell where the apparatus ended and the man's wounded skin began.

Sinclair began to run.

Four steps ahead, Bloch was already next to him and had merely to extend his arm to stop Sinclair. Bloch planted three fingers on Sinclair's chest, "No. I want to show you," he said as he pushed.

It surprised Bloch, to a degree he instantly suppressed, how hard pushing Sinclair back to the Lifers proved to be. He didn't have to use more than his three fingers to get Sinclair where he wanted him; he didn't have to grunt. But it did take effort, and in truth, he had to suppress a grunt. He also had to suppress the urge to grab Sinclair's lab coat in a fist and use his entire arm and his entire back to throw the flabby little man across the room. He pushed those ideas away, and concentrated on the job at hand. He smiled, and pressed a button sequence on his handset.

The equipment around the corroded man activated, and a large, bulky arm, not yet attached to the Lifer suit's torso, sprang to life.

Delicate metal phalanges launched out of the arm's hand, as quick as vipers, and gripped Sinclair's upper arm firmly, then began reeling him back to the wall.

"Colonel, what are you doing?"

"Sssh. A demonstration."

"What? Don't."

The massive arm began to ratchet and unfold, reshaping itself, twirling and locking with inhuman precision.

"Don't. Colonel don't."

Above his shoulders, above his head, Sinclair saw a pair of huge wedges emerge from the arm, painted with hazard stripes, pincers — tongs — a massive industrial vice. Sinclair threw his leg against the heavy bracing that housed the corroded man and pushed with all his might. It didn't free him. He pushed again and again, straining to escape the machine as the vice descended slowly down the arm toward him. Not to his own arm, not to his shoulder — to his *head*. Sinclair screamed "No." at the machine several times, and then turned, sweat beading on his forehead, to snarl at the colonel, to lock eyes with the filthy monster.

"I Damn you! I Damn you!" he screamed as the cold metal reached him, and scraped insistently across his forehead, moving the skin in little jumps as it pressed his scalp against his skull. Sinclair tried to turn from the vice, to avoid its presence, but his neck would only turn so far.

And then Louis Sinclair, father of none, beloved son of Ellen Sinclair — who had changed his diapers, and had watched him learn to walk, and who had wept when the mop-water on the linoleum caused him to slip and crash his tiny knee into the table leg, who had marveled that a child of hers could excel at school, could work so hard, could overcome his adolescent woes and earn his place in a university she could never dream of sending him to, that boy, Louis Sinclair, began to scream.

* * *

June
18th

4:22
A.M.

Rik Ty

**

Open Mind was a large facility. In addition to its main building, it featured a few smaller buildings, a huge walled courtyard, a small lake, a concrete helipad, bike lanes, exercise parks, picnic areas, acres of eco-labs, eco-preserves, and one large parking lot at the head of the facility where, if curious, visitors could transfer from gasoline powered cars to a variety of alternatively powered vehicles.

Several paved roads laced through all of these areas, typically patrolled by Bloch's men, and by Bloch's security cameras. Currently, due to the episode at the portal site, Bloch's men were not available to patrol the grounds. Only the cameras monitored the campus, and no one was monitoring the cameras.

In the hour that gave him the best chance not to be seen, Varrage ghosted in along a maintenance road, sending green witch-light across the trees, the blacktop, and the surprising concrete wall to his right. The large wall surprised him because it hadn't been there the last time he was at Open Mind.

He ended the ghost the first second he could, and veered instantly into the trees along the road. With some cover, he reversed direction, drove for a bit, and picked a spot where the greenery would keep his visibility to a minimum. He stopped the bike.

Taking a quick look around the area and seeing no one, he dismounted and stepped toward his front wheel, pulling his battle pipe and a rolled stasis crate from the back of his gear harness as he walked. He set both items in front of the bike's front wheel. Then he unrolled the stasis crate and opened its lid. Next, he rolled the bike onto the crate, leaned the bike on its kickstand, and pressed the crate's activation button.

Two things happened immediately: the walls of the crate grew shin-high, and the air around its contents faceted. For a second, looking at the bike was like looking at a cubistic painting of the bike. It fragmented without separating. Each facet offered a different view of a portion of the bike. Then the arrangement of the views shifted, defying logic. Views of tire sections blossomed next to views of engine sections. Views of cowling sections folded next to views of vortex chamber sections, and then, as the fields of each affected atom skewed, as its height shunted to fit within its width and its length, the bike, and the walls of the crate, both flattened.

Varrage looked down. The crate appeared to be a life-sized hologram of Viablo in a metallic frame.

Though no thicker than a sheet of cardboard, the crate did not waver to match the grass. It sat perfectly level, a plane in the real world. By design, it had a degree of visible thickness, though by rights it could have been thinner than the human eye could see. Varrage lifted the lid on its hinge and felt the gyroscopic thrum of the lid changing orientation as he swung it closed. Varrage took the red adapter, placed it on the end of the stasis crate and activated it. With it, he was able to roll the crate tightly, then, with a second activation, — *very tightly*. As a result, he was able to hide a motorcycle in a rolled tube less than a half inch thick.

He unscrewed the spiked cap to his battle pipe and hid the tube within it. It was heavy, though not as heavy as the motorcycle alone would have been. When finished, he sealed the pipe, re-sheathed it on his back, and crept toward the tree line at the edge of the road.

He looked up at the new concrete wall; in truth, the wall angered him. He had no trouble understanding it, but he didn't refuse the idea that the people who put it there should pay.

He walked quickly across the asphalt work road and onto the grass in front of the wall. The moment he stepped off the road, a tiny swell traveled silently across its surface.

He didn't see it. He didn't sense it.

*

It took Varrage a few steps to reach the wall, which stood a good twenty feet high and was too smooth to climb without assistance. He reached into a pouch on his gear harness and removed one of the devices he had requested from Diamondsong's team over the past two years; in this case, a hand-sized grappling hook launcher.

Studying the wall, he set the launcher's charge for forty feet and aimed for the top of the structure, at a junction spot where the wall panels slid into the support columns; a place where there were more surfaces to catch.

He fired. A metallic pant escaped the handset as the hook flew into the air and over the wall, followed by a dim clanking sound as it hit the concrete on the other side. Varrage dragged the hook until it caught firmly.

The climb would require grip strength. His boots would protect the cable from his feet, but exposed, and bearing weight, the skin on his hands would likely shred the micro line's fibers. He reached into a pouch on his belt and removed a pair of black hand coverings, each made from networks of tiny meta-ceramic beads. He slipped the gloves on, and began climbing.

At the top of the wall, he crouched, studying the closest side of Open Mind as he re-set the launcher. He fired the device again, and caught a safety rail on Open Mind's roof. After testing the line, he jumped, swinging through the air, raising his feet at the last second to absorb the impact of hitting the building.

He landed above the lower-level security cameras, and hearing no reaction to his move, began climbing.

There was nothing to hear when he reached the top except quiet machinery hums and the mild breeze. There were no guards present. No alarms rang. The roof was relatively dark — with his glowing face, he supposed it didn't matter, but he was sneaking into a building — he'd stay within what shadows there were.

He removed his gloves and repacked the grappling hook, exchanging the near empty gas canister with a full one, making the launcher ready for the next time he needed it.

Inside knowledge helped him. There were doors he had the keys to, alarm boxes he had the old codes to, skylights he could pry open, but there were also three panel boxes, situated at different positions on the roof, that he had identified as weak points back when he was working with Norel's teams at the facility.

He walked to one of the panel boxes, not much bigger than a side by side closet, and opened the metal door with a key. Inside was a column of thick, insulated cables, terminating on the rear wall in steel mounting caps. In the floor next to them was a rectangular tile, covering an access panel — a pre-made passage should another column of cables ever be needed. Varrage crouched and removed the tile, revealing a flat plane of blue insulation foam. He jabbed the tips of his two pointer fingers into the far corner, and quickly dragged their sharp edges along the perimeter, creating a small trench that weakened the foam to the point he could push it away in one neat piece. He reached into the new opening, found the edge of a ceiling tile below him, and slid the tile out of its support tracks.

Looking around him, he removed his gear harness and shut the door. He hooked his harness onto the toe of his boot and lowered it into the opening; then slid through himself.

Landing by the wall outcropping that concealed the heavy cables, he paused. The light was dim and the hall was quiet. There was no one around. He saw no cameras.

He used his battle pipe to prod the ceiling panel back into position. Then he put his gear harness back on and re-sheathed his pipe. That done, he stepped quietly down the hall.

* * *

In Lieutenant Camille's basement lab, all the lights were on, the ceiling fixtures, the lamps, the lights under the cabinets; every monitor, every wallscreen, every flexbook. Lieutenant Camille worked at a half circle of flexbooks, each chief to a different system. Bloch watched over her shoulder, comparing the data on Camille's screens to the data on his hand set. Occasionally he checked other functions on the device, like the the status of the team from the surviving Chinook: all still in delta stages of sleep.

"I'm not sure of everything I'm seeing Lieutenant. What's the status on the Lifers, give me an overview please."

Camille continued to watch the screens, inputting commands as she spoke. "Ten teams of three, all functional, with varying degrees of chemical support. Two advanced systems, still alive, one functional. Two Lifers failing, death imminent."

"Ten teams of three? That's extraordinary Lieutenant."

"We've had over a year."

The second flexbook in Lieutenant Camille's arc of flexbooks beeped, as did the Colonel's handset, as did other consoles around the room.

Lieutenant Camille worked the keys on her second flexbook and the screen changed to a grid of campus views from different security cameras, both internal and external, showing corridors and stairwells and doorways.

One view panel was outlined in red. In it, a figure walked along a corridor. Outlines activated around two other view panels, picking up the figure from nearby cameras, now beginning to track him. Camille clicked on one of the panels and it enlarged to fill the screen, showing Varrage walking down the hall.

"One of them is here sir. It looks like he's heading for Norel's old office."

"Really," Bloch said. "Excellent. That saves us from inaugurating the Lifers out at the portal site. Send the Lifers that can fit, up into the halls to block his exits."

"You don't want to just take him now?"

"No. Let's see what he wants."

* * *

**

Varrage approached the end of the hall. Only one of every four ceiling lights were running; enough light to see, but not much more. He could see the doors to Norel's office. Around the doors, the space opened up, brighter, not from more lights, but from fewer walls blocking the lights that were already on.

As he walked, he passed abandoned conference rooms, some with their doors open, full of tables and chairs no longer in use. He continued passing conference rooms until he reached the circular space at the end of the corridor, where a round counter of polished wood housed a greeter's station. Three corridors terminated in the circular space around the counter. Any greeter would have a clear view down each hallway.

Circling the greeter's station, sets of double doors lead to majestic conference rooms. Each doorway was flanked by a pair of soft chairs. Each chair was edged by a potted plant. The space was arranged so that meetings could spill from one conference room to the central counter, or to any other conference room and back again. The plants were all dead.

The doubled doors directly behind the greeter's station led to Norel's office. They were the only doors with glass. They were the only doors that were closed.

As he walked, Varrage slipped a custom lock-override from a pouch on his belt, and when he reached the circular counter, he hand-vaulted over it without breaking pace. He headed toward Norel's office doors.

The blocky override had a single notch in its surface. A green light blinked in the notch.

The doors to Norel's office suite were a small set of treasures, bought at auction from a French hotel. They were old items, ornately carved in the grand Art Nouveau style, with burled walnut frames and large, frosted glass panels, personally loved by the Doctor. Varrage placed the override under the carved doorknob and set to defeat any newly installed locks.

But there was no need. The original lock was ruined, and no new lock had been installed. The door opened as soon as Varrage touched it. He didn't even have to turn the knob. He simply pushed the door and entered.

And found destruction. Inside the suite, the shelves from the walls lay scattered on the floor. The walls themselves had been hammered to dust. The ceiling-tile framework, ripped free, lay in tangles around the room. Violence, past, but now rewarming. In the alcove, the same: Norel's cot, overturned, its mattress sliced open. In the shower facility, the fixtures, ripped away and removed.

The door to Norel's private office lay open. His father's desk now so much firewood across the carpet.

Ghosts had held sway here. The ghosts of the Nazis, the ghosts of the Secret Police, the ghosts of the Ton-ton Macoute. They had performed the familiar steps. They had staged for themselves a dark ballet, current revelers, blind to the sweep of history.

There was a fine layer of dust across the floor, and his footsteps would be visible if he crossed it. So be it. Let his trampling of this work be marked.

He strode to the windows behind Norel's shattered desk, knocking aside an upturned drawer that stood in the way of the straight path in.

A series of finger presses at the base of the third window frame caused two small stasis crates to eject from a seam in the steel. Varrage laid the crates on the floor and returned them to three dimensions. Each held a wooden case. Each case held six small proto-lenses. Each lens unique; each lens damaged.

The bank of windows yielded two more stasis crates, but both were empty. Varrage closed each of the small crates, and slipped them behind his shoulders, into an inside sleeve across the back of his gear harness. He stood, and left.

* * *

A belt-fed machine-gun cannon, with its own attached ammo-pods and its own array of sensors, hung suspended from four thin, robotic, spider-legs.

The gun skittered from one pool of shadows to another, throwing its own long shadow across the floor whenever the light hit it. Behind it, an identical spider-gun scurried between its own nests of shadows.

*

Varrage passed the last of the conference rooms and continued back down the corridor, away from Norel's office.

The hallway stretched before him, long and dim, with a distance to go before he reached the next junction. As he made his way toward it, he became aware of small sounds coming from the end of the hall in fast sequences: faint sounds, insectile buzzings.

He studied the end of the hall as he approached. It appeared as he expected until he got closer. He saw a light pulse up by the ceiling — two light pulses, flanking the exit.

Something.

They knew he was here. Something waited for him at the end of the hall; the corridors behind him were probably traps as well. If he turned back, he'd run into a crossfire at the greeting area. *Best odds are right here. One team instead of three.* Fighting here right now would force both of the other teams to cross two corridors before joining the fight. By then he could be gone, or at least know what he was dealing with.

He didn't alter his pace. He didn't let them know he suspected their presence. He unsheathed his battle pipe and kept walking.

He neared the end of the hall.

In five steps it would start. Bullets? Nets?

Varrage lifted his pipe in both hands and changed his pace by running the last section of hall. He slammed his pipe into the floor, launching himself up near the ceiling. His feet connected with the corner of the upper right wall, and he pushed off instantly with the full force of both his legs. He would not be where they expected him to be.

As he vaulted, he managed the briefest of glimpses at the trap set for him. Not soldiers. Big things. Blocky things.

He fell into an open space, ample, but not huge: a T-junction, with freight elevators directly across from the two stacks of Army-green machinery flanking the hall he just left — *possibly cargo containers — laptop monitors near their tops.* White cargo boxes lay scattered across the space as well — pushed aside? By who? What was he dealing with? Who was behind the stacks of Army gear? Had they slipped around the gear so quickly?

Surprise them.

Attack.

Varrage charged at whatever soldier was hiding behind the cargo stack nearest him. He found a blank wall.

The cargo stacks moved, and when they did, they looked very different, nothing like stacks anymore; they looked like men wrapped in bulldozers. The laptop monitors were actual faces, shrouded in steel cowls. He saw the term LIFER 15 stenciled in white letters on one chest. Looking up, he saw that the lights he had detected were devices, pulsing inches away from the eyes of the men driving the machines — and he saw that both men were disfigured, and that directly under the pulsing lights, the eyes of both men were clamped open.

In the small moment Varrage looked at the faces of the Lifers, each of the Lifers raised their right arms. The arms divided as they moved, and Varrage saw glowing panels rise from them, tall, slim, and thrumming with electric, rose-colored light. He leapt toward the elevators even as the Lifers began to fire.

The beams followed him, a fraction slower than he was. The white cargo boxes would offer meager protection, and they were far away as well. Varrage vaulted again, this time backwards, between his attackers. Upon landing, he thrust his pipe against whatever hinge system passed for a knee on the thing to his left.

The Lifer reacted, the knee bent, and the great masses that made up its body suddenly made the machine-man struggle for equilibrium. The Lifer's arm swung errantly, and its attack beam hit its partner.

Its partner screamed. The man inside the armor rolled his head back. His free eye squeezed shut. His clamped eye continued watching the light in front of it. The entire Lifer unit, with the man inside it, staggered and fell.

Varrage used the moment to slip out of sight, ducking to the the wall behind the Lifer. As he moved, he noticed the hydraulic lines silhouetted against the Lifer's leg.

The Lifer swung its beam across the floor, looking for Varrage. Its left arm whirred and clanked as its shapes twisted and ratcheted into new configurations. A circular saw-blade formed, spreading like a

Japanese fan, and began to spin, traveling down a track to the Lifer's wrist.

Varrage hooked the tip of his battle pipe under the hydraulic line and leapt — slamming his shoulders against the back of the Lifer and both of his feet against the wall, pushing with all his might. The hydraulic line popped and the Lifer staggered forward, trying to compensate for the massive weight suddenly put into motion. It crashed into the freight elevator and the building shook.

Varrage leapt over to it, glancing at the other downed Lifer, who was beginning to move. Varrage angled his pipe into a set of hydraulic lines on the machine man's other knee and forcefully levered the lines free. Amber-colored oil chugged from the hoses and pooled on the floor.

The Lifer tried to get up, but could only twist. Varrage smashed what he could of its attack ray, and popped the hydraulic line off the Lifer's second thigh. Then he popped the hydraulic line off the jamming ray arm and the Lifer fell back to the floor completely, the man inside staring at the ceiling as the oil around the battle-suit spread and began to drip down the elevator shaft. What would a fire do to Norel's building now? Varrage leapt over the downed Lifer and broke the hydraulic lines on its other arm. He heard the whine of moving hydraulics behind him.

Grotesquely, the other Lifer, silhouetted in the weak light of the hall, sprang off the floor on all four limbs, chest up, looking like a huge, squared, and headless dog.

The dog-thing began walking backwards toward the wall. When its back legs reached the wall, they started walking upwards. When the back legs reached the top, they would be arms, and the dog would be a man again.

Now.

With its hands on the walls the armored suit would have no ability to shoot. Varrage had a second, if that, to act.

He ran, pipe held like a bayonet, and rammed the only hydraulic line he had access to — the one on the Lifer's front leg.

The line bounced when he hit it, and the pipe head slid down a foot before slipping between the hydraulic line and the Lifer's leg. As Varrage continued moving, the pipe head extended around the leg, giving Varrage a leverage point. He had only to continue moving and...

... The line popped. The leg became instantly immobilized; Varrage continued under and past the Lifer as it straightened and teetered. Next blow to the face.

Varrage ruthlessly thrust the pipe upwards to where he calculated the soldier's mangled face would be. The blow landed true, smashing the light housing, and ripping the delicate metal clamps free from the soldier's eyelids.

The soldier screamed. Both of his eyes blinked, and now one of them ran with blood. The soldier thrashed his head from side to side, having no place to escape to within the cowl of the suit, having no limbs of his own available to cradle his face, or protect it. The soldier screamed and screamed.

Chest level to Varrage was the arm with the attack ray. He smashed at the ray housing with his pipe. He smashed at what he imagined to be the beam emitters. He ducked under the arm, and rapidly popped the hydraulic lines located at the back of the suit. The unit attempted to move, and with the attempt, crashed heavily to the floor, landing on its side. Varrage leapt toward it, aiming to pop the exposed lines off the Lifer's arm.

Machine gun fire sparked off the Lifer's armored chest and Varrage altered his move into a side-roll to the floor, using the Lifer for cover. He allowed himself a quick look beyond the Lifer to see who was firing.

It was a machine gun. A machine gun on thin spider legs, firing steady bursts of bullets and phosphorescent tracers as it advanced between the white cargo boxes. In the moment Varrage looked, a second spider gun hopped onto the white cargo boxes along the wall and began firing as well. Bullets and tracers. Sparks and phosphor. With oil on the floor.

From the other side of the armor he heard the man within the suit start to scream a litany of his own private horror; "I CAN'T MOVE, I CAN'T MOVE," he called over and over again, oblivious to the bullets, oblivious to the monstrosities delivering them.

Varrage worked into a crouch and took a good hold on his pipe. He could run. Any exit would do, and if bullets were all the spider-guns had, he could withstand them — *probably*.

He sprinted toward the furthest hallway junction, feeling the vibrations as bullets thundered into him, seeing the white streaks trace riot over him as the bullets exhausted their energy.

He reached the junction to the next hall when he heard the folding *pwaff* of the oil catching fire, and suddenly the hall was alive with jumping orange light, and the men within the armored suits screamed anew.

The ceiling sprinklers came on — *would they help in an oil fire, or just spread it?* He couldn't move the men, not in the massive armor. Could he get them out? Had he seen any fire extinguishers? The most immediate solution that occurred to him was to flip the white cargo boxes onto the flames and try snuffing them out. Could he survive extended exposure to machine gun cannons? Should he worry about the soldiers? Should he just leave them to their fates? Should he escape, and leave Norel's building to burn?

He saw the spider guns eject their empty ammo belts in smooth, steady streams. They could have been cash registers spooling out receipts. The gun backs rolled and ratcheted as new ammo boxes slid into place, and in that momentary cease-fire, he could hear other sounds: the whooshing of the flames, the patter of the water from the sprinkles, the cries of the men in the armored suits — no, just one. Just one was crying out. Was the other one dead? Most alarmingly, he heard a sound coming from the next hall: a scraping noise. He stepped back, and looked down the corridor.

Something was deep in the passage. Something was deep in the passage and coming his way.

It moved like a nightmare given permission to exist. Seen for an instant only in black silhouette, it was a large central mass advancing rapidly on four spider-like legs that together spanned the entire width of the hall and scraped the walls as they moved.

Then it passed under a light fixture and Varrage saw the man, dripping under the ceiling sprinklers, a scarred, steroidal torso bulging with swollen muscles and veins, a snarling head, bald, with an iron visor bolted across the space once occupied by eyes — the border of the visor rimmed with split and scabbing flesh, a red light throbbing and scanning within the black slit of the visor.

This man-thing dangled buoyantly in front of a large mechanical gun platform. Its robotic spider-legs rooted at the lower portion of the platform, and below them, at the very bottom of the housing, a machine gun cannon swiveled.

"Welcome hooooome," the man-thing said as it raised a weapon with one gauntleted arm.

Pistol-like, the weapon was not a gun. With a slanted glass panel near its tip, it looked like a variation on the beam emitters Varrage had just encountered on the armored suits. Enough like them for Varrage to know it was dangerous. Whatever it was, it was obvious that his enemies considered it important enough to emphasize, and this was no place to find out what its effects on him would be.

He jumped back, and rolled on the floor as the first shot from the beam sailed over his head. He jumped again to change position and —

— The spider-gun was right there, and it fired directly into Varrage's gut. Varrage doubled over in reaction and staggered back toward the burning elevators. He felt only a fraction of the bullets wailing into him, but it was still terrible. He swung his pipe and sent the spider-gun flying. The second gun attacked, but Varrage side-stepped its bullets and hit its central mass with a full swing of his pipe, sending the spider-gun slashing through the burning oil and crashing into the wall between the elevators.

Varrage turned, with no escape time left, and raised his pipe to thrust at the nightmare-man who must be —

— entering from the hall right at that second.

*

Dangler — the Nightmare Lifer, stepped into the jumping firelight of the T-junction, his jamming ray leveled at chest height and already firing.

*

The ray hit Varrage full on as he attacked, glowing hot inside his mind. Dangler was able to block the pipe strike with the bladed gauntlet of his free arm, all the while continuing to fire his ray at Varrage.

Every synapse hit by the ray sent a signal of unrelenting pain up Varrage's nervous system.

Varrage staggered, and raised the pipe again. Dangler kept the beam on Varrage's chest, calmly twirling it round and round, torturing Varrage's heart, his lungs, his spine. More pain and more pain and more pain. Varrage made a move forward, raised the pipe a fraction more, and then could go not one step further. His nerves were all too busy transmitting their surges of pain to tell his muscles to move, his lungs to expand, his heart to beat. Amazed, Varrage looked to Dangler's eyes, and saw only the sliding red light in its track of darkness. Dangler raised one of his platform's spider-legs and punched Varrage in the chest with it.

Varrage staggered backwards and crashed against a white cargo container. His battle-pipe fell, rebounding once on the container lid, and Varrage continued falling, sliding until his shoulder blades hit the floor. His head landed against the container wall and became propped by it. His chin pressed into his chest. He could see the ceiling, alternating rapidly between orange and black in the twitchy light of the fire.

Varrage's medulla systems recovered. His heart pumped again. His lungs filled slightly. His eyes could move. His vision threatened to quit, but he saw as the robot-man crossed the space to him, lunatic in the thrashing light, grinning as he raised one robotic leg — the one he had kicked Varrage with, and placed its tip onto Varrage's neck, grinding into the throat below the chin.

"Well now..." the robot-man said.

"Get him up," Bloch said, entering the T-junction with Lieutenant Camille and two other Lifers. "Douse this flame," He said to the Lifer on his left.

The systems on the Lifer's forearm shifted until a nozzle array protruded above the back of its wrist. It sprayed a white foam at the flames and they died away.

"The elevator," Bloch said, and the Lifer inserted its fingers between the elevator doors and slowly tore them open. As it blasted its extinguisher down the shaft, its face was lit by the flames several floors below. The extinguisher had no effect. "Faarr," the Lifer said.

"Lieutenant," the Colonel said as he passed his black handset to her, "Have one of the Lifers from the hangar open the doors to the elevator shaft and put out the fire."

"Yes, sir," Camille said, as she began working the handset.

"Now, Dangler," Bloch said to the robot-man, the one Lifer who was not a neuro-drone, the one Lifer who functioned under free will, "get him up."

"I don't think he can get up... at the moment," Dangler said, looking down at Varrage.

Bloch looked at the green armored Lifer standing nearest him.

"Get him up."

The Lifer stepped behind Varrage, surprisingly quiet and quick. It bent at the waist, grabbed Varrage, and pulled him harshly. Varrage slid, and his back crashed into the Lifer's shins as it pulled him up to a sitting position. Then the Lifer grabbed Varrage's wrists and crossed Varrage's arms across his chest and lifted him until he could be flopped into a kneeling position. The effect was such that if, at any point, the Lifer decided to extend its arms fully, Varrage's arms would be ripped off at the shoulders.

As it was, Varrage just continued breathing, slowly improving.

Bloch pointed at Dangler's jamming ray. "Get set to use that again — on his legs." Bloch walked closer to Varrage. "We don't see your bike. When are you getting picked up?"

Varrage breathed, tried to speak, swallowed, and then said, "Should... be happening... right now."

"Dangler," Bloch said.

Dangler fired into Varrage's ankle. Varrage threw his head back in pain. Bloch lifted his hand. Dangler stopped firing.

"Where are the plans for the bikes?" Bloch said, eyeing the top of Varrage's head, and then eyeing his spiked pipe atop the cargo container.

"I...wouldn't know," Varrage said, looking at the floor. Bloch looked at Dangler. Dangler fired into Varrage's chest. Varrage strained forward, and then collapsed backward, held up by the Lifer.

"Dangler, would you hand me that pipe please?" Bloch asked. Dangler stepped to the container, seized the pipe, and handed it to Bloch.

"Thank you," Bloch said, accepting the pipe and then swinging it in small, slow arcs. "Ahhh, Heavier than it looks. Concrete center? Hmmm. Tough guy. You could do a lot of damage with this." Bloch touched Varrage's head with the tip of the pipe, then looked at the downed Lifers, and then back to Varrage. "Do you have any bones in this body of yours, or are you all shell? Are you some kind of egg, or walnut, or lobster? — you know, a little boiling water, crack the shell, pull out the insides and then dip them in butter. Yum; yum. — That thing Norel used in the courtyard. Was it a building? A generator? Some idiot's flying saucer?"

Varrage could look at the floor. He did.

"It was a building," Bloch said, raising the pipe a few inches. "The plans are there aren't they?"

"Out of your reach," Varrage managed to say.

"We'll see. What did you take from Norel's office? Dangler, refresh the torso."

Dangler ran the beam over Varrage's arms and shoulders, then down to his waist and thighs. Reflex took over and Varrage tried to stand, tried to extend his legs and escape the beam. But his legs wouldn't obey. He couldn't move them. He couldn't move his arms. He couldn't move his shoulders, and still, the pain increased. The beam traveled back to his chest and he ran out of air before he could scream. He gasped. He panted.

As Varrage struggled to breathe, Bloch put the pipe down on a cargo container and took the stasis crates from Varrage's gear harness.

Bloch put the crates down onto the container right next to the discarded pipe, pushing it aside to make room. The spikes on the pipe's cap pivoted across the container unevenly, at a different speed than its bar, and a line of the pipe's spiral threading became exposed, gleaming minutely in the fire light from the elevator shaft.

Bloch examined the rectangular stasis crates closely, ran his fingertips across their surfaces, and traced the edges gently. He raised one of the lids.

The crate expanded, and for a moment Bloch was stunned. He opened the lid all the way, and saw a wooden case inside the crate.

When he opened that, he was stunned again.

"Lenses. Excellent. Lieutenant Camille. New Lenses." He quickly opened the remaining case, and discovered the second set of lenses. "We... are... back in business."

He removed both cases, and beginning to walk, left the empty stasis crates and the pipe where they were. As he passed Varrage, he stooped to look into the white slits of Varrage's eyes. Varrage was just beginning to recover, and could do no more than look back.

"Thank you," the Colonel said, smiling mirthfully, and patting Varrage on the head as he stood up fully.

Bloch turned to Camille and handed both cases to her.

"Lieutenant, I am going to rouse the chopper team. We have a ten mile section of road closed off; I will extend the emergency order and have the surrounding towns evacuated immediately. Assuming similar distances in areas between lens activation and portal manifestation to those we've encountered, that should give your Lifers enough room to operate. I'll need you to assemble Lifer teams and equip them to launch these lenses."

"These lenses? All of them? On the same site? You don't..."

"Yes Lieutenant. All of them. We move now. We end this. Assume that the last activation site is compromised. Use the stretch of land closer to Exeter. Also, bring in the Kiowa team and see what assistance they can provide you."

Bloch and Camille turned, heading back to the corridor they entered through. Varrage struggled to speak, wheezed out a breath, and then fought to be audible.

"The lenses are unstable. Don't use them," he managed to say, lifting his head only slightly, and then letting it fall again.

Bloch stopped and turned. He looked at Varrage, and then at Dangler.

"Dangler, make sure he doesn't leave. Cripple him if it pleases you."

With that, Bloch turned, and escorted the Lieutenant out of the T-junction. Dangler watched them leave, and then his mechanical legs carried him in six quick, tapping steps to the space directly atop Varrage.

He took a moment and let his smile expand.

And then he aimed his weapon

and fired gleefully.

* * *

June
18th

5:05
A.M.

Rik Ty

**

When dawn hit, the first wave of armor-encased soldiers loaded onto the Chinook. The paralyzed men, their minds commandeered, moved steadily in the blue-gray light, slowly chumbering their hulking suits up the ramp and into the cargo hold of the copter. They stepped heavily, like industrial pressing machines somehow given the power to walk.

The copter's ramp pivoted upward and sealed closed. The rotors increased their spin and pushed away the morning's mist, exposing a great circle of grass that whipped and thrashed as the copter lifted off the ground.

The Chinook flew away from the campus of Open Mind. It veered northward, heading for the ten mile loop of closed roads near the towns of Exeter, Newmill, and San Rialoto. The closed-off roads within the loop encircled several isolated fields — places where the Lifers would be able to work without being seen from the ground.

As ordered, the pilot deliberately flew low over the tangles of evacuating citizens, giving the impression to the witnesses in the traffic-snarled pick up trucks, the crowded sedans, and the re-purposed school buses, that the authorities were on the job and fighting for the Nation's safety. The pilot stuck to the major streets, flying over the cars, and over the deputies directing traffic, and over the firemen waving vehicles along and answering frantic questions from rolled down windows. It flew over the crowded intersections, and over the thousand cell-phone cameras filming, keeping the copter as visible as possible, for as long as possible.

Once past the exodus of citizens, the pilot circled just outside the perimeter of closed roads where the fleeing people would not voluntarily go, and began stage two: nozzles on the underside of the copter released a spray of E-90, a chemical mixture designed for its lingering, unpleasant aroma: similar to a merging of sulphur, ammonia, and photo-developer, completely out of place with the trees and shrubs it was landing on. Every few seconds the flight team's engineer grabbed a handful of printouts from a cardboard carton, and tossed them out one of the copter's windows. The printouts featured a profile graphic of a skull with a leaking brain, along with the message: DANGER - CANCER ZONE - written in both Spanish and English. Every half mile, the engineer also threw out a small speaker pod designed to release the sound of far off gun-fire at random intervals. When the circle was complete, the pilot moved to the interior of the evacuation zone and began stage three. He positioned the copter over an eastern section of field and landed.

The first Lifer team disembarked and set about constructing a large, but simple, camo-net hide. As the copter departed to get the next team, the Lifers continued working, and once finished, set to work on the more demanding task of setting up the tripod and laser arrays, performing the delicate procedures competently, if not gracefully.

The lenses they used were untested, and so the first attempts to activate them yielded unsatisfying results. Sinclair was no longer available to direct the particulars of the laser adjustments, and so was no longer available to choose which facets of the lenses to hit, or from which angle, or in which sequence, and so the job fell, over com-link, to Lieutenant Camille. Through trial and error, she quickly improved her results: the light injected into the first lens began to do interesting things; on one try the light was made to ricochet; in the next attempts, the ricochets became prolonged. In time, the trials ended, and the procedure commenced in earnest: light was forced into the lens and made to ricochet; the careening beams of light, and the energies contained within them, continued skirting across the interior facets of the lens; and as these energies continued traveling, additional energies flowed steadily in behind them, moving steadily in the flow, splitting, careening, and entwining, until a current was born; and as the current flowed over the interior facets of the lens, it expanded its travels within the lens, and as it expanded its travels within the lens, it reached the lens's interior resonation facings, and as the current, and the currents behind it, and the currents entwining within it, reached the lens resonation facings, they excited the unstable components within the lens resonation facings, and as the unstable components became excited, sub-atomic asymmetries erupted within the resonation facings, and as the sub-atomic asymmetries erupted within the resonation facings, they demanded balance within the resonation facings, and as they demanded balance within the resonation facings, the currents continued, and as the currents continued, more asymmetries erupted, and as more asymmetries erupted, more asymmetries demanded balance, and as more asymmetries demanded balance, unseen energies, unsuspected energies, flowed up from behind the resonation facings, from behind the interior of the lens, from behind the spaces where there were no spaces; and from within these manufactured eruptions, these energies from unknown places, from unseen places, flowed into the lens to offer correction to the asymmetries, and as they flowed into the lens to offer correction to the asymmetries, they joined the currents of the lens — and were pulled by the currents of the lens — and entwined with the currents of the lens, and as they entwined with the currents of the lens, the currents swelled, and as the currents swelled, they began to surge, and as they surged, they began to siphon, and as they siphoned, they increased the currents, and as they increased the currents, they generated a field, and as they generated a field, they scaled a larger asymmetry, and as they scaled a larger asymmetry, they opened a negation, and as they opened a negation, unknown energies poured into the negation, and as unknown energies poured into the negation, they filled the negation, and stretched the negation, and strained —

— *a blast* of aqua-colored light erupted from the lens, ripping through the air in a wide, wild loop that traveled across the meadow like the passing arc of some great gleaming sword, uprooting the grass, thunder-clapping across the air before dissipating gently into the clear breeze like a wave sinking into shoreline sand.

And then, for a moment, all was still.

There were three more lens teams coming to the field.

* * *

In a narrow storage room, with the lights out, Varrage's body lay thrown atop a small printer table. The printers that had previously occupied the space lay tumbled on the floor.

Varrage's arms hung low, his own grappling hook cable used to tie his wrists to the table's legs. The cable laced back and forth under the lowest shelf, and around Varrage's wrists, and around the table legs themselves, twisted and knotted, ending with the grappling hook itself jammed through the launcher's trigger guard and bent for good measure — just in case Varrage wasn't dead.

If Varrage, alive, were awake, and his eyes were open, he eventually could have made out the objects in the room from the light coming in under the locked door. If he cared to, he might have noted the multiple stacks of printer supplies, and boxes of paper, and cases of binders and folders.

If Varrage were awake, he would have felt the jumping energy as it poured from his fingertips and from the seams of his boots. He would have seen its aqua-blue color as it rioted over his body, forming its writhing helix around his chest, and vanishing as it rushed past his forehead.

If Varrage were awake, he would have felt his fingers twitch.

* * *

A massive surge of energy erupted along the roof of Outpost 14, twisting and inverting as it formed a helix shape, collapsed, twisted and formed the helix shape again, cycling and accelerating until it finally branched into slashes of blue lightning that spiked along the sides of the building and then launched, tower-like, into the night sky, leaving a rooftop alarm to sound and roar.

*

Krork was tying back a strap on one of the packs draped over his bike when he saw the blue lightning crackle over the Outpost and launch to the sky. He heard the alarm that followed. He tucked the extra length of strap under the satchel, mounted the bike, and drove to investigate.

* * *

It wasn't the blue lightning that caught Skyde's attention, or Sunset's or Diamondsong's. It was the alarm. It cut through the roaring of the blast-boots, and instantly ended all the fun the riders were having.

Skyde twisted her hips, which cut her forward momentum, and then she cut the power on her boots until she was merely hovering in place. She looked at the Outpost. Her friends joined her.

"What is it?" asked Sunset, "Bleed Zone?"

"No. That's not a Bleed Zone alarm. Something's wrong," Skyde said. She pushed down on the power feeds and rocketed forward into a stand of trees, whipping the grass and brambles under her jets as she took the quickest route back to camp.

Diamondsong started to move, but turned to Sunset. "Don't worry about keeping up with her. Worry you don't hit a tree." Sunset nodded, and they followed Skyde through the brush.

*

Norel rushed into the central room of the Outpost as the alarm continued wailing. He sped to the master station where an upright monitor was blinking, and began working at its keyboard.

Several Bike Pilots rushed through the main door and ran to workstations.

"What is it? What's going on?" Slice asked as he entered the building and paused in the doorway.

Norel spoke loudly, his words meant for everyone. "Some kind of energy surge is hitting us from the realmlines. We're leaking power. Shut down..."

"We've got a firewall warning," Brickyard said, as she worked at a keyboard, eyes fixed on its monitor. "If we don't want the whole building to wind up like the basement, we'd better come up with an idea quick."

Norel entered instructions into the keyboard, fingers flying. The alarm persisted. "re-set," Norel said. "We'll have to re-set the whole building. Right now. No prep."

A sparkle of light jangled in the air high above the middle of the room. No one paid any attention to it.

"Signal the disconnect," Norel said to Slice, giving the young man something to do.

A murmur rose among the Bike Pilots as they shut down building systems from their workstations. The murmur resulted from the questions they were asking each other, questions none of them had any answers to. Norel might have been able to address some of their concerns; he heard them spoken, understood several clearly, and felt the continual impulse to respond to them — to soothe the minds he could. Instead, he kept his eyes on his console, his fingers at his keys, and his back to his people, concentrating as he entered the instructions that would begin the re-setting procedure.

A compartment at the end of the work station slid open, exposing a large throttle switch. Norel reached for it and found himself hesitating momentarily, struck with a feeling akin to revulsion. The split handle stood on two arms, perfectly poised in the center of a graphic that was white at the bottom and black at the top.

Norel would have to touch it; there was no option not to. He would have to touch the control and interact with the white and black graphic. Work with it. Commune with it. And as he reached out to the handle, silly as it seemed, silly as it certainly was, Norel felt... *tricked*.

He gripped the throttle, and waited for the right instant to guide it into the black.

* * *

**

Krork reached the exterior door to the bike lab just as the alarm stopped and the disconnect signal began. The sound went from a repeating siren to a steady, thrumming pulse, deep, like the lowest notes of a cello. To Krork it sounded like the throat noise of some truly giant frog, warning: *free me, free me (cast off your lines and pipes and tubes because I intend to jump, so) free me, free me.* As he pulled open the hinged wall, he looked up at the building, and the frog comparison, unflattering as it was, seemed to fit. He looked directly up the slope of the building's ramp, a huge angled back, and at the way the building sat squatly on its ring of support columns, and he thought it really did look like a frog. Though no mere pond frog. A great spirit-frog, a great *sphinx—frog*, sitting, and glowing whitely in the moonlight.

He opened the bike lab, rolling a hinged section of curved wall away from the building to make room for his machine to enter. He drove in and parked. As he went to close the wall, he saw Skyde and her party speeding toward him and he waved them in before resealing the building.

*

Rake helped Dent and Floorboard uncouple power lines from the building. He caught sight of Skyde and hesitated for a second as he watched her speed into the Outpost. Then he rejoined his team, pushing the heavy wrenches as they freed the equipment from the building's exterior ports.

A seam above the roof's gear-ring lit with green ghost light. Bright spots moved within the seam and raced laps around the building. Bike Pilots continued running to the Outpost's walls, rushing to disconnect cables while there was still time. An engine designer named Utmost pulled the final power-line just as the entire building began to glow green. She walked a few steps to Dent and took his arm.

He put his arm around her as the building wrapped itself in green strobing light and faded from view. When it was gone, there was nothing left but a huge, flat circle in the dirt.

Dent, Floorboard, Rake and Utmost looked at each other. This was different. A re-set had never been necessary with so little warning before. A re-set had never left them behind before. No rendezvous point had been established. They weren't taking part in a coordinated evacuation. It was done. There had been a breakdown in the Outpost, and now the Outpost was gone, re-linking to reality all over again. They were alone.

There was nothing left to do but conference with the other Pilots. And they would find that the existing contingency plan left no one happy: they were to wait two days. If they could not find the Outpost, or if the Outpost could not find them, they were to pack up camp, return to Earth, and destroy the bikes.

* * *

The Outpost tilted and rocked. It behaved as if it were flying, though it had no flying capabilities. Every inch of every panel and every inch of every girder vibrated with the messages of movement. Views out windows told the story of rapid traversing, though over no tangible landscape; instead, the windows revealed streaks of colors — red running into violet, violet running into purple, with every section of overlap inking into deep and absolute blackness, as if the combined realities of the realmlines equaled white light's opposite.

In the central room, with the lights flickering, the twenty or so Bike Pilots in the building fought to keep their feet under them. They held on to columns and workstations and any solidly planted item that would lend them stability. Skyde gripped the tri-ladder; Slice held tight to a workstation. Krork wedged his arms between a workstation and a wall, while Sunset and several other Bike Pilots wrapped their arms around Krork's forearms.

Outside the windows, the realmlines swirled. Pools of perfect black seeped into flows of vivid green; green expanses thinned into white stream-lines that seemed to spiral on for miles before coalescing into bright mandala shapes whose distance and size were impossible for the human eye to judge.

The narrow chairs of the building's workstations were slim and padded, like motorcycle seats with tall, ergonomic backs, mounted on swing arms that pivoted on the same posts that supported the work stations. Dr. Norel had to fight to stay on his, strenuously pressing his feet into the floor while he gripped a ridge under the master station's console. He had one hand free to work the keyboard and he fought to continue manning the station.

Brickyard fought on her chair as well. She looked at Dr. Norel, "Anyplace safe?" she asked.

"Not yet... wait, yes, here comes something," he said, and then louder, so everyone could hear, he said, "Hang on!" and then he grabbed the throttle bar and eased it to the white.

The realmlines beyond the windows whirled and stretched. Thin white lines appeared, and then grew until they filled the windows, percolating with violet pebbles of light which amassed to fill the windows, turned dark, and then unfolded to stretch into a blue, open sky. Something white and hard-edged slashed up from the bottom of the window's view, a mountain peak, brilliant in the light of the sun.

*

Slice bit the inside of his cheek when the Outpost jolted to a stop, and it hurt at the same time it surprised him. He pressed his hand against his face and looked toward the main door's window. They were here, wherever here was.

Three windows were directly visible from the central room. Each overflowed with snow-light, glaring and bright, which made Slice feel cold just to look at. He turned his head to check all the available windows, something everyone else was also busy doing. The views showed only blue sky, nearby rock walls, and the sun-lit peaks of other mountains. From the center of the building, the views offered no real clue of the ground terrain.

The glare seemed brightest through the main door's window and Slice stepped cautiously toward it. When he reached it, he placed his hands against the pane and craned his neck to observe the entire view.

"What do you see?" Norel called to him.

"A lot of snow."

Skyde stepped past Dr. Norel and walked toward the main door. Sunset and Diamondsong followed her. Norel stood up from his workstation as everyone around him suddenly headed for a window. Krork walked into the bike-lab to check the back-facing ports. Brickyard followed him. Wazzi headed for the main door, but then opened the door to the infirmary, where he could get pretty much the same view through a different window.

Norel walked toward the main door, curious about the view, but also curious about how the crowd was splitting up here in the room. What was causing each individual to choose the window they were heading toward? Placement of the fixtures? Light quality? Social connections? Unimpeded paths?

Forget it.

Ignore it.

First things first.

"What do we see?" he asked again, almost laughing.

"Well," Slice said, "we've got a short snow field right in front of us before everything starts to slope, maybe there's eighty feet of flat ground. Looks clean though. I don't see any rocks or trees."

Diamondsong looked around. She didn't smile. "A skier's paradise," she said.

"No fire place, no hot chocolate," Sunset whispered, and she *was* smiling, and as she bumped her elbow into her friend's elbow, she sent Diamondsong rocking on her feet. Diamondsong turned to Sunset, made as if to say something, and then just returned the elbow hit, smiling.

"What about the side windows?" Sunset called out, "What do you guys see?"

"About two hundred feet of plain snow, before you hit a rock wall," a rider called Tumbler said, craning his neck as he looked up the window on the right side of the building. "The wall goes up pretty high. It's covered with a bunch of snow. There's a rise to the terrain between us and it."

"Yeah, I've got the same thing on this side," a rider called Cosine answered. "A wide spot of snow, and a rock wall that sweeps to the back." Cosine pushed his glasses back up his nose and called out to the back room, "Hey, you guys in the bike-lab, you see the rock-wall too, right?"

"Yeah," Brickyard's voice answered back. "It's a headwall. We're sitting in a little bowl — or a great big bowl, if you want to really talk about it. What about valleys? Anybody see some nice comfortable valleys?"

"Can't say for sure," Slice called back to her, "We're sitting on some kind of plateau, but no, I don't see any, and I don't think we're close to any."

"I don't know, Norel," Brickyard called back, "A mountaintop? What kind of airline are you running here?"

Norel finished peeking out of the main door window and headed back to his workstation. "When it comes to re-setting," he called back to her, "all the Outpost's systems can promise is fairly-level ground on an Earth-like planet, and like it or not, that apparently includes mountaintops."

The Bike Pilots began walking back to continue their work.

"Well," Slice said, rubbing his cheek again, "At least it's not a swamp." His friends laughed, and as they did, the systems in the Outpost drained down to darkness.

* * *

Rik Ty

**

"Well, no wonder Hawaii was still dark," Nonstop called over his shoulder, "I mean, it's just getting light here, and Hawaii's at least a couple of hours behind the west coast." He said, as he and Grace ghosted onto a city street, which lay quiet in the early-dawn stillness.

Grace heard him, but didn't respond. She just nodded and looked around her. In the cool light, the gray buildings were almost lavender, and the spots of color in the storefront windows looked almost like morning flowers. Her black office tower, clearly visible, several blocks away, stood tall over the other buildings, like some robed commerce minister, standing imperious over a sea of concrete book-keepers.

"Which one is it?" Nonstop asked.

"It's that tall one over there," Grace said, and then she rested the side of her head on Nonstop's back, dreamily watching the ghost-residue chop the air alongside them. She reached a finger out to it, and her finger seemed to rip the air, wavering and pixelating the images of the buildings as if they were merely projections onto violated gelatin, shaking and chopping and cubing until they spilled away into the slipstream, blending like a stripe of cream stirred into coffee, returning to normal as the slipstream faded away.

"What are you going to tell them?" Nonstop asked.

Grace continued watching the air as the ghost effect faded. "That there's something new in the world," she said, "Something we're about to lose if the Army doesn't lay off. I think you're headed for Congressional hearings."

"Politics?"

"It effects all of us. We should all decide."

"I don't want politicians deciding what I do."

"Prepare to make that argument. It's better than getting killed."

Nonstop frowned. The black office tower, with its upward-curving entrance canopy, grew closer and closer as he slowed, and so Nonstop slowed his slowing further, as if to delay the stopping, and the parking, and the standing, and the departing. But time only permits so much delay, and those things happened anyway. They slowed. They stopped. They parked on the sidewalk. They swung their legs over the bike, and they shuffled their way to the doors of the building. "You were very brave you know," Nonstop said.

"I was? I was," Grace beamed, "So were you."

"We don't get T.V. How will I know how things turn out?"

Grace popped on her heels and clapped her hands, "Oooooo — you could come back. There's a park around the corner. When is it light in Hawaii?"

Nonstop smiled, "Let's say two o'clock in two days?"

Grace had beautiful teeth when she smiled. They were probably beautiful all the ti... Grace had beautiful lips when she smiled... Gra

"Pinky bet!" Grace said, shooting her hooked finger into the air in front of Nonstop's chin — an uppercut fueled by ebullience.

Nonstop stepped back down, not realizing he had risen to the balls of his feet. He looked into Grace's eyes and slowly entwined his finger with hers.

"Pinky bet," he agreed.

The Marksman on the roof across the street raised his rifle. Next to him, a kneeling soldier raised a radio and spoke into it: "Six and Five, this is Tango. Subject in front of building. Good to go. Out."

The first bullet hit Rattletrap's tire, Shredding a chunk from its rim, but not popping it, merely exposing a section of its air-cell interior. Nonstop grabbed both of Grace's shoulders and flattened her against the wall as he covered her. "The Army's here," he yelled, looking up at the rooftop.

"Go! Go! Don't let them get you!" Grace screamed, looking at Nonstop, and then looking where he was looking.

Nonstop spun back and looked into her eyes, and then incredibly, began to pull her. "We *both* have to go. They're here for *you!*"

"Me? Let go! I'm just an intern!" Grace locked her knees and leaned backward. Nonstop pulled her as if she were water skiing. "I'M NOT BULLET-PROOF!" she yelled. Nonstop kept pulling.

"You are when you hold onto me — so hold on to me!"

They jumped onto the bike. Grace grabbed hold of Nonstop tightly and then screamed, horror-struck as a bullet hit Nonstop's head, mere inches from her eyes — and in the same instant, white lines sped all around her and Nonstop and the bike. As her scream was still rising from her throat, Nonstop drove the bike away.

More bullets hit them. More white lines. Nonstop drove off the curb. As soon as he hit the blacktop, a VTOL came flying from around the side of the office tower.

Nonstop made rattletrap slap the ground, and they flipped into reverse, heading down the street the other way. Grace screamed and ripped at Nonstop's T-shirt, shoving her hands under it and grabbing his chest, trying to get closer contact with him. Nonstop's eyebrows rose very high as he sped forward.

His eyebrows lifted even higher when he saw the second VTOL speed into view ahead of them.

"Duck!" he yelled, and he rocked the bike onto the side of its angled tire, immediately changing the bike's trajectory and shooting them toward the building's glass doors. Bouncing off the curb he hit the outer door and broke through both it and the inner door using Rattletrap's arms and its engine pod as a battering ram, counting on impact diffusion to save him and Grace from the flying glass.

Grace screamed, yelling: "What are you doing," as she buried her face in his back. Nonstop spotted a bank of elevators inside the lobby, as well as a reception counter, and several sets of double doors. A set of doors to his right was capped with thin steel letters that read: K.A.L. NEWS. Nonstop bounced off the floor, raced along the reception counter, and hit those doors high.

Whatever lock secured them, it was no match for the juggernaut created by the bike. Rattletrap smashed right through.

Overall, they entered a long chamber partitioned by cubicles. Speed allowed only glimpses of the passing details: carpet on the floor, potted plants in woven baskets, blue wall paper with sponged tones, a row of windows, sets of blinds *in* the windows, rows and rows of little carpeted walls trimmed with black plastic strips. They shot forward. Their path was narrow and lined with cartons. Nonstop ducked down low on the control bar, had Rattletrap set his arms together like a high diver, and set to work threading the needle.

"Is there a back door? An Elevator? A Fire exit?" he asked loudly without turning his head.

Grace peeked over his shoulder, flinching from any of the thousand things poking out from the walls where they were driving: restroom signs, fire extinguishers, office name plates, bulletin boards, push pins, taller potted plants... "There's an elevator up ahead," she said, "but it's little."

The wall to their left ended. The space opened up, with glass enclosed offices on one side, cubicles where they were driving, and carpeted columns in between, where *more* cubicles took up space, mixed in with banks of copiers and supply cabinets.

The lights were on in the first office they passed. Two soldiers stood in the room, leaning over a tired old man seated at a desk, his complexion yellow-white under the harsh light of the fluorescents.

"Sholly! That's my boss!" Grace yelled, as the old man leapt from his chair and waved them on. One soldier shoved him back down, while the other soldier raised his rifle and ran forward.

The soldier crossed the columned space and fired. A sound like cannons within the office hall. Bullets streaked across Nonstop and Grace as they drove past the elevators, turned a corner, and crashed through a final set of cubicles.

Nonstop saw a door with an aluminum bar across it — some type of exit — and drove for it.

Rattletrap hit the bar, the door opened, and they were inside. The landing didn't offer much more space than the door needed to open, anyone opening the door from the inside would have to stand in the stairwell traffic just to make room for the door to open fully. The architects must not have expected much foot traffic in the space, much less a speeding motorcycle.

Nonstop clattered in and immediately ran out of room. Rattletrap's hands went up, absorbed the impact with the wall, even as Nonstop twisted the bike and drove it halfway up the narrow staircase, just long enough to swivel Rattletrap's shoulders, have it grab the banister, and vault back down to the lower run of stairs, now facing downward. Too tight to turn, Nonstop threw Rattletrap's hands to the floor, skipped the tire along the wall, and used the handstand to turn the bike in the tight space. One more set of stairs, and then hopefully some room, or some way back to the street.

No such luck, they hit a narrow path between walls of coiling pipes, which lead to another path of coiling pipes, and which looked like piles of tidy machine intestines. The basement looked like the boiler room of some old battleship.

"There's no room down here to hit eighty eight," Nonstop said as he slowed, looked around, and started driving through the maze of pipes.

"Other staircases?" Grace asked, mindful of the jutting valve-heads all around her. "But won't all the soldiers be in the lobby by now?"

"Yeah. And they'll be watching the elevators too, right — if we could even fit in the elevator. But we can't stay here. Okay, what's that?" Nonstop said as he spotted a door with an exit sign and a levered door handle. Wherever it led, he was taking it. He drove to the door and used Rattletrap's elbow to press down on the handle. He drove them through the door and found —

— a much tighter staircase, almost a spiral, only with right angles, low ceilings, and dead-walls instead of curves. There was no way the bike would fit.

"Mountain," Nonstop said, and he slapped the wall, "Mountain. Mountain."

"Mountain? Mount...what?" Grace asked.

"Well, it aint no salt flat," Nonstop said, as if that explained everything. "Okay. This foot on the deck," Nonstop said as he tapped her knee in her jeans. "This foot under the deck." He tapped her other knee. "Use your legs to hold on as well as your arms. Use your hands, wrap them in the straps. Use your teeth if you want to, just don't scream."

Nonstop trundled to the soft light in the stairwell.

"What are you doing?" Grace asked.

He looked up. Thirty floors at least. Grace looked up. Rattletrap grabbed the banister and hopped up.

"Oh my God. What are you doing?" Grace asked again.

Nonstop balanced the tire on the handrail, and had Rattletrap grab the next set of banisters. Keeping the robot's grip, he drove to the top of the handrail, and had Rattletrap grab a higher section of staircase.

"Oh God, what? What are you doing?" Grace said, and repeated "What are you doing?" shrilly, on the verge of screaming.

"Ssh," was Nonstop's quick response, other than that, he just kept grabbing sections of staircase with Rattletrap's arms, rocking and twisting Rattletrap's core section as he kept Rattletrap's multi-tire driving on the handrails, shifting it into reverse, into forward, into reverse again.

They were headed for the fourth floor of the stairwell when Grace asked "Can you really do this?"

"We're doing it," Nonstop said.

Grace looked down at the bottom of the stairwell, at the spot where they had just been, already shrinking with distance. There was a swinging dark portion in the patch of weak light on the floor. Their shadow. Grace looked back at Nonstop.

"You're amazing! What floor are we going to?"

"Amazing? Cool. The roof."

"The ROOF? Are you crazy? That's thirty stories! We'll —"

"— Just hang on. We'll make it."

Grace looked down at the patch of light. They were already much higher. She looked up at the skylight, growing closer as the bike twisted, and rocked, and spun; the bike picked up speed, hit the next floor, twisting, and rocking, and spinning; it reached for the next floor, twisting, and rocking, and...

"I'm getting dizzy," Grace said.

"Don't think about it."

"I don't want to throw up."

"Are you dizzy? *Are* you gonna throw up? We shouldn't stop, but we can if you have to."

"I can go a little m..."

Two soldiers rushed into the stairwell. They heard the soft clanking of the bike on the banister, and ran to the patch of light between the stairs. Looking up, they both saw the crazy sight of Nonstop's bike spidering its way up the stair well, already halfway up.

The first soldier waved the second up the stairs and then raised his rifle and fired.

The bullets streaked around Nonstop, and Grace, and the bike. Grace screamed. She could feel the bullets thumping, not against her body, but against something very near her body and it terrified her. With the ground nearly seventeen floors below her, she took the first volley of bullets. But when the second wave followed immediately after, she couldn't tolerate it, and began frantically trying to escape the impacts. Rising into Nonstop above her, she squeezed his ribs, then slid her head and shoulders under his arms to his chest.

"Hey! What are you doing?" Nonstop asked as she rose, scissoring her legs against the bike's vortex chamber. The bike swayed and shook from her motions. She found a foothold in the release notch on the top of the seat back, and pushed her way up onto Nonstop's lap. Her legs hung on either side of his waist and she brought them in close.

"They're shooting!" she yelled, burying her face in his chest and holding tight to the straps at his ribs.

Her hair was suddenly in Nonstop's face, in his eyes. He had Rattletrap reach for a banister he could no longer see.

Rattletrap lunged, reached, and missed. The bike swung with only one arm anchored, and Grace's body threatened to swing out into open air. Nonstop stopped her quickly with his right arm, letting go of the control bar, and holding on with only one hand as the bike slammed into the staircase and they jolted. Grace's screams rose and changed with every event until she ran out of air and had to breathe again. Nonstop pulled her close.

"Okay. Okay," he said as he made the bike resume climbing, faster, and even more recklessly than before.

The bullets had stopped. Both soldiers were racing up the stairs. Nonstop could hear their feet pounding, echoing in the tight space.

With the bike climbing again, and Grace panting to remain calm, Nonstop considered his next move, and realized he didn't have one.

"Grace, they know who you are. I can't take you home. Do you have anyplace safe?"

"What? No. I just moved out of my Mother's house. What about my Mom? Are they going to bother her? What about my roommates? What about Sholly — I DIDN'T DO ANYTHING!"

"I didn't either. Doc will know what to do. We're going to hit the top soon. When we do, you get back behind me okay?"

"Uh, okay. Yes."

Grace, trembling, concentrated on getting back under control. She felt cold. Her legs felt weak and watery, and her eyes felt full and heavy. There were guns coming. Men with guns were running up the stairs. She had to get herself together.

They came to open space under the skylight and there were no more stairs above them. It was bright and brilliant and every bit as stunning as climbing through a rain forest canopy would be — breaking through the leafy crown and gazing out across the treetops. The sensation was there, if not the open space.

Nonstop made the bike vault over the last banister, and there wasn't enough room between it and the door for the bike to touch the floor. The landing was only large enough for a person or two to stand on. The bike rested on the last handrail. Its arms and chest rested on the upper portion of the exit door. Its multi-tire stood more than a foot off the floor, and its vortex chamber hung suspended a good three feet out into open air. It was as if they were perched in the bucket of some giant, twisty, fire truck ladder.

"Go ahead. Get behind me," Nonstop said.

"No. No. Outside," Grace said, peering over Nonstop's shoulder and seeing only the light on the far wall, and the tip of the Vortex chamber pointing at it.

"There might be soldiers on the roof. Go ahead," Nonstop said as he pushed forward, squeezing Grace against Rattletrap's torso, but giving her as much room as possible to maneuver back onto the seat.

Reluctantly, Grace put her left foot firmly on the foot guard. She heard the soldiers' stomping feet. They hadn't slowed down. She pressed down on the foot deck and stood, slowly sliding her chest against Nonstop's, not wanting to expand the space she took up not even one inch. With her back against the motorcycle's display screen, her hip rose, and as she moved it slid across the inside of Nonstop's forearm.

Now she could see. Now she could see the open space on every side of her, the arched surface of the Vortex chamber glass, the tiny patch of firm footing offered by the landing and its border of railings. She felt like a trapeze artist, one whose first attempt would be thirty stories high, without a net, without even an audience.

"Put your hand here," Grace said, holding out her right hand as she stared at the wall ahead of her.

Nonstop placed his hand in hers, and she pulled it to the waistband of her jeans, leading it to the fabric's edge.

"Hold onto me," she said. Nonstop saw her point. He would be her safety line. Good idea. He inserted all four fingertips into her waistband, grazed the smoothness of her hip, and for a jolting instant, sensed the landscape of her skin. He made the tightest fist of his life until he felt only denim.

"Go ahead. I gotcha," he said.

She brought her leg over, and when both were on the foot guard, she pivoted on the ball of her right foot and swung her left leg back over the bike without looking at anything specifically.

And it was done. She was turned around. Nonstop had Rattletrap reach for the metal bar on the door and push it.

As the door opened, the bike slid off the banister. Nonstop tilted the bike so that the Swiss-army gizmos wouldn't stick on the railings as they passed. The wheel touched the floor and they drove out.

An Army helicopter swung immediately into view above them, loud, and growing louder. As Grace screamed out a warning, Nonstop twisted the bike, darting it sideways, not waiting to see what the Army team had in mind.

Grace watched behind her as a soldier jumped out of the copter and onto the roof. He carried a flame-thrower-thing — a big nozzle-cannon that he gripped in his hands and some kind of tank thing strapped to his back. The soldier activated an igniter and a small ring of flame leapt into view around the nozzle's tip. Grace screamed without words.

Her screams rose as the soldier fired a jet of jellied flame at her. Nonstop jerked the bike and dashed behind the walls of the stairwell shaft.

The flame trail missed. The soldier released the trigger and ran in pursuit.

Grace saw him reappear from behind the Stairwell and raise his cannon. She screamed and turned her head as the flame erupted from the nozzle.

Her view facing forward was worse. They were driving to the edge of the roof, and Grace screamed with an intensity previously unknown to her.

Nonstop jolted left. The jet of flame shot past them. He slapped the rooftop with Rattletrap's hands and launched them into a cartwheel that got them out of the path of the flame, at least mostly, the trail caught Rattletrap's forearm on the upswing, and the flame stuck, burning on the chrome. Grace felt sudden pressure in her legs as the spurs above her feet suddenly held all her weight and the bike spun upside-down. She saw the flame trail twist in mid air as the soldier redirected it, and thought, even as the bike hit the roof again and was already rolling, that the flame trail would catch up to them.

Then the bike lifted in a short hop, so smoothly, and so nonchalantly, that part of her mind disengaged upon seeing it, as if she were merely a witness, and not a participant. She looked under her, and watched as the edge of the roof passed by. It was happening. They were going over. She saw the tarred seams of the roof paving, she saw the gray-steel line of the roof's capped edge wall, and she saw everything beyond it, thirty floors of building surface, a line of pavement, the tops of trees. Did she have two seconds left? Three seconds? How long before impact with the street below? Would she even have time to feel the pain of her death?

The flame trail crossed above them, fanning inches above her head. A torrent of noisy heat wafted over her shoulders like dragon breath.

Drops of the burning gel followed them in their descent, matching their speed, like confetti in a motorcade, surrounding them with burning rain.

Nonstop's cartwheel allowed them to fall near the wall instead of sailing out past it. Rattletrap's forearm still burned; the jellied gasoline adhering to it stubbornly. Nonstop raised the arm and made it reach backward, behind the bike's center of gravity. Its new position brought the flame inches from Grace's hair, with both hair and flame twitching and whipping in parallel slip streams, threatening to touch, kept apart only by the force of the bike's falling motion.

With gentle contact, Rattletrap trailed its claws against the smooth surfaces of the building's windows and support frames. The ride became rough, shaky. Sparks flew. The fire-tar smeared off of Rattletrap's arm and onto the building, where it burned in a line behind them. They paid for the move with a descent as rough as a re-entry into the atmosphere, but Nonstop used it to put the corner of his wheel in contact with the building.

And then they shot forward, leaving the cascading flame droplets behind them. A shred of tire flapped violently on the edge of the wheel where the bullet had hit it. The flap ripped loose and flew away, leaving an open gash along the rim of the tire. Nonstop struggled for control — for continued contact with the building as the bike descended. He looked at Rattletrap's display – *110 miles per hour — too fast to ghost.* He adjusted, headed straight out — sideways along the black building, adding forward momentum to fight the pull of gravity. Grace reeled, everything around her was insane: the buildings switched directions; the air lashed at her from in front and from below; they were driving where there was no road, where there was no ground, all the time knowing where the ground actually was, knowing, and clearly sensing, the little cabs and car-tops she would see if she dared looked down.

The display read ninety five, eighty five, another adjustment and it read eighty eight. Another adjustment and the bike began to stream green contrails of whipping ghost-light behind it. Another second and the bike vanished along the side of the building, vanished, in fact, from the Earth itself.

* * *

**

Krork stood in the middle of the central room, holding up a large panel of grated flooring. Slice and Wazzi worked down in the exposed floor, inspecting the conduits and pipes first hand.

"The connections all seem fine in this one too." Slice said, as he stood and looked toward Dr. Norel, who was checking the connections in another section of floor.

"I don't know what happened to the power," Norel said, almost to himself, as he continued studying the conduit connections. "We have generators in storage, but with the building behaving this strangely, I don't think it would be safe to activate the basement even if we could find the power to do it."

Slice looked at the Doctor. "There are generators back at camp. What do you think? Could we go get one?"

"Sounds like the safer bet," Sunset said, as Norel nodded.

"I'll go," Krork said as Slick and Wazzi rose to stand next to him, dusting themselves off. "It's possible. All I'd need would be a star reading to course my way back," Krork considered this for a second, shifting the floor panel to his hip.

"That sounds very good. Thank you," Norel said.

Krork nodded and handed the floor panel to Slice and Wazzi, not noticing that their knees threatened to buckle from its weight. "I'll just have to find some night," he said. He began walking toward the bike-lab. "I'll be back soon," he said, raising his hand in a farewell gesture.

* * *

Grace held herself in reserve. She wasn't exhausted yet, but she was tired. She was especially tired of being amped up on fear.

The realmlines swirled around her, dark striations that stretched and spread and blended into shades of blue. Could she pick out teal?

Yes. Could she pick out aqua? Yes. One band of blue was so electric, she had to think of it as sapphire, though she had no idea what shade of blue would truly qualify for that name.

She saw the blues but refused to gape, refused to acknowledge their wonder. It had been a day of wonders, and it had brought her low.

Nothing was required of her at the moment except that she hang on to the straps on Nonstop's gear harness and that she remain stable on the bike. This she did. When she tried to imagine solutions for her situation, scenarios arose in her mind, and she found herself grasping for them with great eagerness, as if they were brightly wrapped presents offered just for her. But her ideas always ended with the Army seizing her and her family anyway. The gift in each of these presents was just a rising sense of panic, and so she stopped thinking. She rested. In a little while there would be new information, and then she would think again.

The realmlines thundered past, black to color, black to color, black to color, like a train speeding past pillars, or trees, or farms. Gone and gone and gone.

Eventually they slowed down. Eventually a set of striations spread on either side of her.

Eventually, they arrived.

* * *

"What Happened?" Nonstop asked out loud as they approached the base camp. Grace looked over his shoulder and saw a lot of people busy dismantling equipment and carrying boxes. She saw a muscular guy standing between two pieces of machinery, pushing on a yard-long length of pipe. The pipe was fitted over the handle of a wrench that was down by his feet, twisting a ring on a tube that connected the two machines. She saw two women arranging plastic crates on top of a sheet of flat metal spread out like a picnic blanket. Someone had scrawled *"To the Exoplanets and beyond!"* in black marker on one of the crates. Next to the words they had added a cartoon rocket-ship riding a motorcycle. In the distance, Grace saw someone drive a small truck with a row of robot arms mounted in the workbay. This was a lot of people to be living secretly on another planet. This was a lot of people to be doing things no one else knew about, or even suspected.

She saw Krork, carrying something big on his shoulder. Nonstop saw him too, and drove over.

"Where's the Outpost?" Nonstop called as they drew near enough for Krork to hear them.

Krork lowered the device into the work bay of his bike. The bike bounced a bit in reaction to its weight. Krork turned and looked at Nonstop.

"The Outpost got corrupted. Doc had to re-set without any warning. Now it's acting dead." Krork looked at Grace and nodded. "Hello Grace," he said, and then he turned back to Nonstop. "Nonstop? What's up?"

"Bloch is after Grace now too. We have to ask Doc what to do. Are you headed there? We'll follow you."

"Okay. Doc's busy though."

Krork turned to look back to where some of the other people were working, and began to walk toward Utmost and Dent. Nonstop watched him as he reached the couple and spoke with them. Grace watched Nonstop, and looked where he was looking.

"What did he mean 're-set'?" Grace asked.

"Like re-booting a computer. The building syncs up with a fresh reality."

"This isn't normal though right? He seems pretty glum," Grace said.

"Yeah, he does. You're right. This isn't normal."

With that, Krork headed back to the big bike. Behind him, Grace saw the lights from several campfires, some on the other side of the trees.

Krork sat on his driver's seat and leaned forward. "Lock your bike in whisper mode," he said to Nonstop.

"Already done. Why?"

"Lots of snow where the Outpost is. We don't want to start an avalanche." And with that, he sped up and did the ghosting thing. They followed. Grace said, "Snow? Avalanche?"

*

On the mountaintop a few minutes later, the cold hit Nonstop immediately. Goose bumps broke out along his exposed arms and he thought of the jacket he had left at the perch. Grace squeezed tight against him.

They drove within the shadows of the rocky cliffs, quietly trundling toward the Outpost, their tires paddling through the loose snow.

As they approached the rear of the building, Nonstop saw Wazzi's spiky hair move in the bike lab's window, and then the back wall of the Outpost swung open, and Wazzi waved them in.

The bike lab took up nearly a quarter of the building. In it there were tools and tables, bikes on rails up by the ceiling, a long stasis crate system on the inside wall that looked like a beefier version of a stationary-store poster rack, with actual bikes trapped in stasis frames like life-sized holograms, thin enough to flip through like shirts in a closet.

As Nonstop followed Krork's bike into the building, Grace looked at the strange room, and then quickly looked at all the young people crowded into it. The guy with the messy hair, who opened the wall, started closing it, and another young guy, with a short afro, walked to the back of Krork's bike before it even stopped. Then all the people moved to the back of Krork's bike. The afro guy hopped up into the workbay.

"Great. You were able to get it." he said as he walked to the other side of the cargo.

Grace leaned back quickly, almost recoiling, as Nonstop stepped off the bike and then looked at him, unsure of what to do.

"Let's help them hook up the generator. Then we can talk to Doc," Nonstop said.

Grace nodded, and they stepped over to help unload Krork's bike.

*

Minutes later, an amber safety light spun into life on the Outpost's central room ceiling and the Bike Pilots cheered.

"All riiiight," Brickyard said as the rotating light swept over her. "Let's re-set and get out of here."

"We have to stabilize and recharge some systems first," Norel said.

As he walked across the mis-placed floor gratings and back toward the master station, he passed through the sweeping amber light, and then, for a moment, became blanketed in the patch of darkness that swept in behind it.

Skyde noticed Krork and the other Bike Pilots step in from the Bike Lab. She noticed Nonstop too, and was surprised to see him. A beep from the work station she was manning called her attention, and so she didn't think of Nonstop long. Grace stayed to the shadows and Skyde never saw her at all.

Norel's voice projected as he leaned over the master station and addressed the group, his fingers working fast on the keyboard in front of him.

"The power systems will come back up in sequences. When the option presents itself, shut your workstations down. Skyde, as soon as you can, get diagnostics running. Brick, monitor the basement firewall please. Make sure it's regenerating. Call out if it fouls up."

Skyde looked up from her monitor. "Power is flowing back up," She said, looking in the swinging light for someone to address, and finding Krork. "I think we can close the floors back up."

Krork nodded, and walked to the open floor grates, Slice and Wazzi followed him. Norel stepped closer to the keyboard to let them pass.

"No. Wait," Skyde said, and Norel froze. "It's locking up. It says..."

Norel didn't move, didn't alter his gaze, didn't so much as breathe while he waited for Skyde to say what he feared was coming next. As the amber light swept past him and traveled on, he was again left in darkness.

"...system corrupted," Skyde read, "Initializing core re-origination. Return to..."

"No," Norel said as the amber light returned, and threw his face into a relief of stark and jagged shadows. He strode to the center of the room. "Kill it!" he said, "Kill everything!"

Norel stopped, dead center in the building he had designed and built, surrounded on every side by a sweeping pattern of light and shadow. People he knew were thrown into this pattern, staring at him, waiting for his next, impossible instruction. When the light threw them into harsh relief, he could see them. When the darkness covered them, he could feel their gazes. His eyes tried, and failed, to follow the light as it swirled around him, looping and looping over all the familiar faces that were looking to him for answers.

Skyde punched keys as instructed, and everything shut down: the amber light, the monitors, the L.E.D.s housed inside the power switches. Everything.

The room took on a blue-gray sheen from the snow-light reflecting in the windows. Norel ran a hand over his bare head.

"I'll have to check on this. Excuse me," he said, and briskly left the room, heading apparently, for his office.

Krork audibly pulled air in through his nostrils as he watched Norel leave. Krork's fingers eased open, and the floor panel he was holding set into place.

Nonstop noticed that Krork had noticed something and walked over.

"What is it man?" Nonstop asked, but Krork was already moving, and only said "I don't know," quietly as he walked. A step or two later, and Krork passed the spot where Norel had stood. As he continued, he turned to the group and raised his hands: a silent request that no one follow him.

* * *

Krork found Norel in his office, standing near the rear wall and distractedly shuffling printouts from one pile to another.

"Sir, what's wrong?"

Norel moved more papers, without really looking at any of them.

"Re-originating is not re-setting," he said, his hands finally still. "It means starting over again completely — from the initial programming *and* from the initial position within the realmlines. We have two choices - neither one good: we can choose our current location as our new origin point - our new default reality - our new baseline from which our system will make all decisions — a terrible choice considering we don't even know where we are — or we can return to our true origin point and start over — this is very similar to the simple difference between re-booting a computer and performing a clean install of its operating system. Sounds simple, but in this case, going back to our true origin point, performing a clean install if you will, means going back to Open Mind. Right back where Bloch is."

Krork let that sink in as he watched his friend, but did not retreat, did not give up on his question. "Okay. But there's something else."

Norel looked at Krork, studied him, but said nothing.

"I can tell, you know," Krork said, "Something's been creeping around your edges for a while now, and it seems like it just moved front and center. What is it? What's troubling you Doctor?"

Norel turned his back to Krork, looked at the empty space where his mandolin belonged, and hefted the stack of papers in his hand, as if weighing them.

"The truth?"

"Yes Sir. The truth."

"I can't say it Krork. It's ludicrous."

"That's probably why it's bothering you. You're faced with something ludicrous."

There was silence for a moment and then Norel surrendered.

"I feel... I feel I am haunted Krork. I fear I... am not sane. I don't believe in messages from beyond, and yet I feel I may be receiving one — and the funny thing is, with all that I have seen, all that I have learned — that within what we take for emptiness, lie things awaiting discovery, families of universes, invisible, undetectable, but there nonetheless. After learning *that* impossibility, on what grounds do I dispute anything? After that, how strange is a curse from existence?"

Norel dropped his arms and the papers crashed against his legs. He looked at the wall and breathed in slowly.

"A curse?" Krork asked, watching his friend gently, "I haven't heard that term before, but I take your meaning. Please go on."

"Yes. Imagine. A man of science, driven to considering these things. Now driven... to admitting those considerations. I... I... — Soon after we escaped in this building, an odd idea began occurring to me. It is within these walls that I have worked with phenomena that is absolutely stunning — subatomic resonances, paths of alignment, fabrics of existence, all unsuspected. But as puzzling as these phenomena were, the building itself began to puzzle me more." Norel stopped, and scratched his wrist.

Krork nodded. "This building is nothing if not puzzling,"

"It shouldn't be here at all Krork," Norel said, "Why build an Outpost when we are still perfecting the bikes? Why expend the resources? And yet, when we needed escape, the building was here. Some part of me — I allowed some part of me, to imagine that as a kind of sign from providence. A message that I was forgiven for my intrusions, and well, I... well, it seems, that if there ever were any messages to me from Providence, those messages have now changed." Norel pointed to the wall at Krork's side, to the yin-yang T-shirt, and he walked to it.

"My wife gave me this T-shirt back in college; once upon a time when we loved each other," Norel looked away, and then looked back. "The name of this symbol is the 'Yin-Yang', Krork. It's from China, and typically, it signifies the idea of harmony achieved through the balance of opposing natures: a curving teardrop of black flowing into an equal teardrop of white, each containing a little piece of the other nestled within its heart, and together making a circle that neither begins nor ends. Celine and I both loved the symbol, but I suspect, and here is my lunacy, I suspect a darker nature to it now. I think the idea is round because it wants to turn. Unless you control events, things turn to their opposites: passion into indifference, life into death, insight into madness. I introduced something into existence, I am not controlling the events around it, and everywhere, existence marks this fact, taunts me with the symbol's imagery, stabs at me with the ideas that success is turning into failure, that I am not a beloved son, that I am a monster, and that the machines I created will not deliver us into an age of discovery, but instead will usher us into an age of tyranny. And that as a punishment for my crimes, I will be forced to watch it happen."

Norel, already looking away from Krork, covered his eyes.

Krork looked at his friend, this man, strong enough to wedge open the world, and yet so fragile, weak as the shell of an egg. Krork put his hand on Norel's shoulder.

"What crimes do you speak of sir? You equate discovery with intrusion, but what if discovery were by invitation? What if you *are* a beloved son? I know you. You are a noble man Doctor. You have committed no crimes existence would seek to punish."

Norel chuckled a bit, still not looking up, "Ah, the translator inherent, you hear *existence* speak now do you?"

Krork squared his shoulders. "Sir, I hear existence *sing*."

The Doctor still looked away. Krork bent toward him. "And what you face, I will face with you."

Norel looked up, smiling weakly. "It's going to be everything we've feared."

"Then we'll face it together," Nonstop said, stepping out from the shadows of the doorway.

Norel turned, shocked.

And then Grace walked in behind Nonstop, and Norel's shock turned to bewilderment.

"Who is this?" Norel asked, almost laughing as more weight fell upon his shoulders.

Nonstop took a step to the side and glanced behind him, "Dr. Norel, this is Grace. Grace, this is Dr. Norel. Doc, we've got a lot to tell you."

* * *

In Exeter, early sunlight colored the buildings with golden tones and raked the streets with long shadows. No cars rolled. No dogs prowled. In the sequestered fields nearby, the Lifer teams worked steadily, their lasers hunting deeply within Norel's damaged lenses.

Because of this work, portals would soon appear — *somewhere, probably near*, and Norel's teams would arrive to close them. Norel's teams would then be dispatched, and Norel's equipment would be seized.

Within the work sites, the streams of light from the multiple lasers entered the lenses, but no portals appeared in the fields. Instead, surges of energy would either leap from individual lenses and flash across the acres of grassland, or surges of energy would flash from lens to lens to lens.

In four of the lenses, these flashes triggered greater siphoning, and the speed and pattern of the light-trails within the lenses began to match, aligning and synchronizing. As the resonations between the lenses intensified, lines of force rippled between the arrays in spreading rings of concentric distortions, zebra-striping everything that could be seen with waves of folded air. These waves interacted at their points of contact, sending rising spasms of distortion into the air, distortions that eventually made contact with each other, and created a field-wide energy ring above the first level of distortions. This upper ring began to siphon as well, pulling energies from the other lenses in the field. The merging energies pulled, and then pulled harder and then pulled faster, tugging even at the grass, standing it on end, and then pulling further still, until the tips of the surrounding trees began to sway.

And then rapidly, in a line, four lenses burst, flooding their energies into the center of the field, creating a swirling knot of visible energy that roiled in the field like a trapped storm.

Of the remaining lenses, half began to glow brightly. The other half began to throb darkly, their cores emanating a spreading absence of light.

The energy storm began to shriek as it whirled. It began to glow blue, and then a brighter and brighter blue. The glow revealed a helix shape churning within the storm's crashing distortions, and then, near its center, a countering helix, which also churned, and roared with rising power.

The lenses in the field gorged. Those lenses broadcasting white light thrummed as their emanations grew brilliant. Of those lenses broadcasting darkness, their blacknesses spread, seeping outward into the very air around them.

The lenses in the field continued to surge until their structures could contain nothing more and they shattered, thrusting raw energies into the churning helix, over and abounding, until it too burst, launching a shock wave across the grassy field that thundered in visible crests and troughs as the human continuum itself folded, rippled by forces no human could see. As the shock wave ripped outward and pressed against the reality in its path, thin lines of rioting light shot from within the valleys between each crest, riding outward with the wave, screaming unchecked toward the fields and the sky and the grass.

* * *

A massive, double-helix of blue energy erupted from the Outpost's roof and launched itself toward the snowcapped crags behind the small building. Racing toward open sky, the helix sailed up the cliff face, winding within itself as it rose, with each revolution of its coils multiplying its energies, until the surge could no longer contain itself and so split into two streaking columns that moved entwined, then separated, and then returned to entwinement.

The wild surges passed through each other at the top of the headwall, split apart, and continued on in opposing directions, each rushing back down the cliff's jagged surfaces until they reached the snow covered plateau. From there they circled the Outpost, crossed again in front of it, and plowed their way to the mountain's fore-slope, separating as they raced forward.

In their descent, the two massive energy trails spasmed, crashing through the gorges and the open plains of snow like two convulsing serpents. Wherever their energies touched down, the snow churned, and wherever they struck exposed rock, their interiors sparked with savage brilliance. They continued, crashing and roiling, flailing down the mountain like newly blind penitents, lost, beseeching... for guidance, for safety, for some pocket of reality where existence was not torture, and with every move, finding only more and more of the same, senseless terrain.

The serpents bashed their way nearer to where the mountain split away from its brothers, a rocky crevasse, ice blue and miles deep. The trails poured into this jagged descent, continuing their lunatic ride down through the open air, plummeting toward the harsh valley so far below, pulling plumes of spiraling snow behind them to freeze and frost and fall from sight.

* * *

Rik Ty

**

"Good Mother... What was that?" Brickyard said in the twilight-painted central room. Around her, Bike Pilots ran to the windows to see what answers could be found for that very question.

"Did you see that?" was a question asked by Slice and Sunset and at least three other Bike Pilots as they raced to get a look, though by the time any of them reached the windows there was nothing to see except the landscape and the two new channels carved in the snow.

"What's going on?" Diamondsong said at the window, taking a good hard look at the two trenches in the field. "Oh, I don't like this," she continued under her breath as a cascade of snow crashed down the cliff face behind them.

And then a crackle of energy swept over Skyde's workstation, and then several spasmic launches of energy crackled over the other workstations, crashing and driving in arm-sized leaping corkscrews before disappearing.

No one moved in the dark room, and no new energy bursts appeared. After a moment, the amber safety light blazed back on, swirling within the tight space.

"I think it's hitting us again," Skyde said, reading what she could of the green code on the black screen in front of her.

Norel rushed from his office. "What's going on? Why is the power back up?"

"It came on by itself sir," Skyde said.

"Shut it down. We're not ready to go back," Norel said, and then a tremor ran under the floor of the Outpost.

Nonstop ran into the central room as the rumble of a vastly larger snow cascade announced itself.

"Oh my god," Sunset declared at a rear window, looking out at a sun-lit mountain peak far beyond the headwall, and gasping as the snow collapsed along its upper shelves and fell down along its front slope. She looked back at her friends; the mountain they were on seemed to be humming.

Nonstop rushed forward. "Don't," he said to everyone in the room, "Don't turn anything off yet." He stopped at the workstation facing the front window where Diamondsong stood. "Can I run the scanning chair from here?" he asked Doctor Norel.

"We need to shut down," Norel said, uncertain.

"We need the outside. We need the chair. We need to shift weight," Nonstop said, as structural metal groaned loudly from some unseen section of the Outpost, and the building began a long, slow pirouette.

"We're sitting on snow!" Nonstop continued.

Norel raced over to the workstation and typed at the keyboard with blinding speed. "Diagnostics," he said, "diagnostics will do it. Go ahead, you can run the chair with the arrow keys." He pointed to the keys, and Nonstop placed two fingers on them, waiting.

"Everyone else, man a station. Keep shunting power to Nonstop," Norel said, and the building shifted again. "Don't let the building have any more power, and don't let Nonstop have any less. We need a plan before the Outpost re-originates."

"Re-originates?" was the response from several Bike Pilots, followed by a volley of other questions which fell silent as the views through the windows verified the stories their feet were telling them. The building was moving. The building was starting to slide, and there was only one direction it could move — forward, which also meant...

Down.

"Nonstop?" Grace asked as she stepped into the room fully. Nonstop hit a key and the rattling sound of the moving gantry-arm could be heard from beyond the ceiling. The Outpost slid, and then slowed, and then slowed a bit more. Nonstop watched the window.

"You're thinking you can drive a building Brother-man?" Krork asked as he put his arm around Grace and she hugged him back. He grabbed a hand rail on the wall. Wazzi stepped over and grabbed it too.

"I can get us to a flat spot. I can do that," Nonstop said as he wedged the toe of one foot into the floor grate. He raised his elbows, poised over the keyboard, his fingertips kissing the arrow keys.

He heard a rumble outside the building. The sound grew louder, and he felt the rumbling in his feet.

"Nonstop? Nonstop?" Grace said, turning her head back toward the approaching sound, looking for a window, but finding only the door to the basement.

That wasn't the case with Sunset. She had the rear window to look out of, and her eyes were wide with horror. She screamed.

And the wall of snow hit them.

The building jetted forward, no more anchored to the ground than a fallen leaf. Round and squat, the building tilted forward as the rushing snow wedged under it, propelling it toward the mountain's fore-slope. Nonstop swung the gantry arm around the building and the building spun as it raced. With this move, he countered the forward momentum slightly, allowing much of the snow-wave to pass under the building. The Outpost was still swept along, but it was no longer the wave's battering ram. Pushed, the building continually threatened to tip, and Nonstop continually had to swing the gantry-arm in order to keep the building right-side up. The Outpost hit the mountain slope full-on, and its speed increased dramatically.

Grace screamed as the building spun, and the view out its windows went from white to blue to darkness and then back again, over and over. Not only did Grace scream, but Wazzi screamed, and Sunset screamed. There were a lot of screaming Bike Pilots in the central room, all of them clinging to something.

Nonstop hugged the workstation. It dug into his ribs. His left hand clamped the back of the console. Only his right hand was free to work the keypad. Still, when the avalanche cut across a ridge wall, he kept the building skipping along the top of the wave. His moves kept the building from capsizing, kept it from burial, kept it from getting locked in the snow stream. When the wave hit stone, he rode the upthrust — like a snowboarder in a half pipe, carrying the building free and twirling it for a moment in the air. He landed the building as it spun, and skated it across the wave to launch it skyward again at the next ridge wall.

With this technique he changed his speed relative to the wave. Every time he launched the building, more of the wave passed under them, and more of the trouble passed away from them, but his friends were still screaming. His friends were losing their handholds. Krork's feet shot out from under him, and he tumbled over to one of the central room's walls. Grace tumbled right along with him.

Krork landed upside down, his feet up near the ceiling. Grace landed upright, closed her eyes tightly, and screamed as centrifugal force pinned her and Krork to the wall. The building spun and whirled. Krork's eyes opened wide. He began to laugh.

Nonstop launched the building again up a ridge wall. The high, mid-air 360 showcased a changing panorama outside the windows where he could see the sky, and the snow, and the mountains, and then, for a jabbing instant, the chasm ahead of them.

A jabbing instant was enough. Nonstop saw the head of the avalanche slip over the mountain and out to a mind-boggling free fall. He gasped as the building descended, knowing he was stunned, and knowing he couldn't afford to be. His friends, who had seen the chasm as well, began to scream his name, began to scream warnings at him.

The building jolted as its bottom hit a rock outcropping Nonstop hadn't seen. Across the central room the display monitors flickered in and out of darkness.

"Keep those power levels up!" Brickyard yelled, "The kid needs power!"

Nonstop saw the moving snow. He visualized it pouring off the mountain like the spill-stream from an open box of sugar. His friends screamed more warnings to him. There were a few seconds to do something: maybe four.

He locked the gantry, slid without letting the gantry move, and then spun the big arm around the other way. The move was neat, like a basketball player back-spinning around a defender. And like the basketball move, it sent the initiator on a whole other trajectory.

The Outpost spun away from the drop-off, but continued slipping and spinning down the mountain, sending up fountains of loose snow as it sledded, facing backwards and speeding up.

"Nonstop. Dude," Wazzi called out. Nervous. Proud. Stunned, but growing more nervous.

The Outpost hit a snow bank head-on and somersaulted a complete inversion before landing at an angle in a snowdrift at the base of another mountain.

The teammates tumbled in the landing, and several wound up heaped and groaning against the Outpost's rear wall.

"Ohhh, are we dead?" Brickyard asked from a pyramid of laughing and moaning riders. She could see out one of the windows, where the air-buoyed snow was already settling.

Nonstop threw open his eyes. "Hey! Hey! That wasn't too b —" without warning, without power, and without ghosting, the Outpost vanished from the mountain.

* * *

The building tumbled in a dark channel of realmlines. The ringed vortex chamber in its roof drank from the pressing continuums around it, pulling power from them, shining brightly and pulsing strongly. Surges ran within the chamber's narrow band, colliding and flaring as they sped around the circumference of the building, making the Outpost look like a squat, bobsledding light-house as it rocketed along.

Inside the building, power levels remained low. No lights were on. The safety light did not spin. Only the small, multicolored lights of the consoles shone, offering twinkling and shifting dots of illumination as the building stopped tumbling and eased to a side-to-side swaying.

Light from the realmlines seeped into the room, coloring it with faint rim-light, strong in the ultra violet range, making all the objects in the room glow with an odd, neon light. Sometimes blue, sometimes green — most astonishing of all, the Bike Pilots floated weightlessly within the room, like astronauts, like tropical fish in an elaborate fish bowl, like glowing celebrants at the oddest rave ever.

"Did this ever happen before?" Slice asked, amused, launching himself backwards off a wall with a mere push of his fingers.

Norel, trying to right himself as his feet drifted above his head, managed to say "No, never," and "I don't know why it's happening now." Skyde floated near and gave his ankles a push.

Norel spun one loop, and as his shoulders rolled back to the upright position, Skyde held out a hand and stopped him.

"Anyone by a monitor?" Norel asked, noticing that the Bike Pilots liked the weightless environment and were exploring the art of moving in it as they tried to get back to their workstations. They pushed off one another. Some explored flying between the open gaps between the walls, and others explored flying through the open gaps over the work stations.

"Yeah. One second," Brickyard said as she pushed off a wall, and floated to the same workstation she had manned on the mountain top.

The main door's window offered a view of a light shining in the distance. The light grew brighter as the building drew nearer. Soon, white light filled the squared shapes of the building's front windows, painting squares of brightness on the faces of Dr. Norel and Skyde as they peered, studying the source of the light.

"What is that? Any idea?" Skyde asked, squinting.

"I've seen — Are we heading toward Earth?" Dr. Norel asked Brickyard.

"I can't really tell. I only got a blip before it locked out — but we could be near Earth, or headed that way," Brickyard said, studying the frozen monitor.

In the center of the light effect, a helix distortion revealed itself, intensifying as it pulled light pulses in from the surrounding realmlines.

Skyde peered at the spectacle. "That's — that might be a portal."

"That's the same distortion we've been seeing around Earth," Norel said, "If that is Earth, has the distortion always been this obvious?"

Skyde shook her head. "I've never seen anything like this before. Near Earth or not. I've seen that light quality before — in portals, but I've never seen the helix configuration anywhere."

"Those other lights, are they portals too, do you think?" Norel asked.

Skyde looked closer. "They look like they could be, same light quality. But they're being pulled into the larger portal. It looks like they're converging. What does that mean?"

"I don't know."

"Doctor, if that's a portal, it's the first one I've seen on this side of the realmlines, and I've *never* seen two portals together anywhere. What do you think? What could it mean?"

Skyde looked at Norel. Norel squinted, and continued to study the distortion. "I don't know," he said.

"What about us? Are we being pulled into the portal too? We are, aren't we."

Norel continued peering. "Yes," he said, nodding slowly, "I do think so."

* * *

**

On North Street in Exeter, small lights sparkled in the air, traveling like ghosts skimming over dunes. Following them, a pulsing disc of light formed near the brick wall above Kepler's Delicatessen, up where the brickwork of the deli joined the brickwork of the gray apartment building next to it.

A squirrel, crawling across a phone line, stopped and stood still as the disk of light grew. Then the animal turned, and fled from the glowing apparition.

Seconds later, four of the shop windows along North Street began vibrating. Seconds after that, the windows blew out into the street, filling the sidewalk with glass, and napkins, and lottery forms, and boxes of cordless drills.

* * *

An icy blue portal formed in the center of Lincoln Avenue, in front of a row of townhouses, above the sidewalk just in front of the ivied fences. Tendrils of blue light crackled out from the shimmering portal, and spread along the street, creating blooming frost patterns on the windows of the cars still parked at the curbs.

* * *

Jane and Hilda Brandt, two sisters who were both known to brag about their recently-earned driver's licenses, swerved their pickup truck alongside the un-manned warehouses of GregTim Road, their father on the seat between them, bleeding, and slipping in and out of consciousness.

Hilda drove, watching along the sidewalks for the blue signs that would direct them to the nearest hospital. The evacuation order didn't include Hospitals right? It couldn't include Hospitals. She'd just have to find one.

She studied the empty road, she examined the sidewalks. She saw a *No Parking* sign. She saw a *Bus Stop* sign. She searched the sidewalks high and low for more signs, and when a gigantic maggot-creature, as big as a crashing zeppelin, toppled out of the alley and slammed down onto the street, she drove straight into the dust cloud it created, screaming and grinding her foot against the brake — while her sister screamed as well, and grabbed the dashboard, and threw one hand to her father's chest as the truck threatened to overturn.

The girls screamed, and the truck bounced as it fishtailed around the head of the thrashing creature. Seeing a bit of clear road ahead of her, Hilda stomped the gas, and screamed every second it took them to pass the creature, and then screamed a good deal longer, even after the creature was far behind her speeding truck.

The driver's cab rocked as she continued racing down the street, gunning the engine, and searching for a hospital she and her sister would never find.

* * *

Though more would follow later, the last portal-manifestation of that first wave occurred on the west side of Exeter, where a patch of darkness churned above Pinewood Street. The Haas Mansion, a three story symphony of gables, cupolas and porch railings, stood near the center of that darkness, witch-light strobing in every black window.

Pulsing light punched its way through the windows at the front of the house, painting the building a shuddering violet every few seconds. The light ran along the exposed edges of the wood siding, all the way to the corner of the house, where the light changed slightly, adding a green-yellow tint to the flickering glow. The strobe effect continued down the east side of the house, past the shuttered parlor window, to the guest bedroom window, to the stone vestibule outside the kitchen door. The light varied its brightness, and in the instances where the flickering dimmed, the house was dark, despite the early morning hour.

No sparrow sang nearby. No sparrow flew. There was just the staccato light and its electric thrum, which filled the air and grew stronger toward the back of the house.

Behind the house lay more darkness. The great back lawn looked as if it were bathed in moonlight, a fact made more improbable when the back of the house itself was considered — because there *was* no back to the house. Merged in its place was a large and surging portal, three stories tall, bright as the sun, and yet illuminating only the inches of space directly ahead of it.

A land creature thundered from its brightness, huge and gray, with a long mouth full of curved brown teeth, and two rows of horns that ran from brow to shoulder, and two more that ran from shoulder to hip. Its eyes were set near the front of its head, at the tip of its snout. They glowed a neon red, and seemed to have no substance of their own.

The creature looked about the lawn, and when another of its kind came up behind it, the two galloped off, tearing up great clods of earth as they ran.

Above them, a steady stream of creatures soared out of the portal, dog-sized, with multiple legs and segmented bodies. Their coloring was a crab-like mottling of cream and pink. Frayed sheets of tattered webbing laced thickly between each set of their forelegs and served the creatures as wings, granting them swift flight into this unknown world.

As the web-winged creatures flew, a woman, an Inter-D being, with a hairless blue head and a great fanning neck frill, but a woman nonetheless, stumbled from the light, clutching an infant to her chest, hiding its eyes against her body. The woman moved her head, looking up at the sky, looking to the left and to the right, looking to the ground, and to the great lawn beyond, looking to the burning disk behind her, and to the square, dark, sinister thing that lay just behind it. The woman reeled and staggered, leaning back her head and wailing a great moan of unguarded misery. With nothing understandable, nothing familiar to her mind, she hid her baby's face against her chest, and wept.

* * *

Blue energy crackled over Varrage. The energy networks tracing through his body increased their output of light, moving from dimness to normal levels, and then beyond, and beyond again, to surging brilliance. His hands glowed fiercely; his boots dissolved at their seams and fell away from his glowing feet. The angles of his skin sharpened.

His eyes opened, his head rolled slowly in minute arcs upon his neck.

The lights within his eyes grew brighter, scintillating and cascading as he fixed his gaze outward, peering, seeing things unknowable.

* * *

**

Thunderstorms rolled across the sky of a faraway world, creating a light that seemed bruised as it seeped over a wind-eroded landscape the color of dead bone.

On a ledge within that landscape, a great beast, glistening with clotted putrescence, turned its knobby shoulder and peered out at the horizon. In the shelf of purple-black flesh that passed for its head, lights roiled within its row of small, glowing eyes.

Its knuckles pressed into the ground as it held itself upright on its long arms, its ribs hanging in shallow arcs from its spine, slack, like sails with no wind. Its four, sharp rear legs spread motionless under its bowl-like pelvis as it stood, and swayed, and peered.

Others of its kind crawled out from their holes and took up the same postures, peering beyond the horizon at some unseeable disturbance in the realmlines. They remained like that for a time, swaying slowly on the ridge line, upright, like headless, rotting apes, waiting for the right time to move.

* * *

The will to move came into Varrage, but not the ability, and with this announced disparity, his mind tried to form an idea, and could not.

He could raise his head. He could raise either foot, but his center resisted. Some ring beyond his center met the resistance more intimately and the firmness of sensation beckoned his mind inward from the enormous amorphority just beyond itself, and the answering of this beckoning formed his mind's picture of itself, and an idea gained the allowance needed to form.

Below his head.

He was held.

Whatever it was to be him; it was held.

He moved against the restraint, and the challenge to his effort ran in columns and defined for him his

Arms.

Tied

Lower

Near...floor.

Varrage lurched on the table and the table rocked and squeaked on its four metal legs. Varrage instantly lurched with his legs again, and this time his right foot grazed a shelving tower and he pushed against it powerfully. The top of the table moved faster than the bottom, and the legs collapsed with loud squeals and pops.

Varrage crashed to the floor with the table. The remnants commanded less space, and the tension in the cable loosened. With his arms free to move, Varrage sat up and absently freed his hands from his bindings.

In time, he rose, and stood unsteadily.

Boxes, light,

Under the door, thin, weak,

beam

—w do...I

feel? *I*

I ?

I

don't know.

Varrage raised his hand and gazed at it. Was it always so angular? The skin so sharp? The energy displayed between the rifts in the skin, was it always so bright? Was it always orange? Were there always thousands of pinpoint stars erupting within it?

Leave. Be out of here.

Varrage took a step forward, and was immediately buffeted with angular shears of light, roughly as tall as he was. He raised his arms in defense and stopped walking. The light shears passed him and vanished; no new shears followed them.

Keeping one arm raised above his face, he took another step, and the light shears returned, slamming into him, slamming through him. He took another step, and then another, enduring the shears, ignoring them.

Pressing forward, he struggled toward the door. As his steps became more fluid, the light shears thinned, becoming prismatic, revealing only portions of the spectrum and projecting them weakly, iridescently, like the surfaces of soap films.

Just before he reached the door, the shears subsided. Not precisely true: just before he reached the door, he had absorbed the light shears, whatever they were.

He felt acutely awake. A thin strip of light passed under the door, and by the time it filtered up to the level of his eyes it was very weak indeed.

But he could see the door. He could see its flat surface. He could see the fine, pebbled texture of its paint, and the long shadow of the doorknob as it reached for the ceiling. This door could not hold him. He could punch his way through it; he could kick his way through it. But there would be no need.

He placed his fingertips on the door, and it pixelated at his touch. His fingers swam through its surface, a gauze of atoms, a trillion curtains of atoms, nestled within trillions and trillions more.

He moved the curtains with his hand, and then with his arm, and then he stepped through the door without making a sound.

* * *

Rik Ty

**

The robot-man Dangler stood in the middle of the walkway near the top of the building's atrium, six floors above the research facility's little indoor park. He wasn't looking at the little trees, or the little benches, and while he could hear the water flowing over the stones in the decorative pond far below him, the sounds no longer registered with him.

He wasn't standing on the walkway for any of the atrium's pleasures. He was looking out through the tops of the atrium's windows, at the light show going on in Exeter. Every few seconds, bright flashes would spasm far beyond the nearby treetops, under what looked like a small isolated patch of thunderstorm clouds, a quiet light show far away, as beautiful as any carpet bombing he had ever seen.

The vision made him itchy for something to do.

The walkway he stood on spanned a wide, circular opening in the floor that provided a full view down into the atrium. There was a pathway along the window wall as well. Visitors could stroll along it and enjoy the view of the outside landscape as if they were walking in the air. Both the bridge-way and the window path featured short side walls made with gleaming glass and chromed safety rails, high enough to protect all visitors, but low enough to offer a thrill to those brave enough to rest their elbows and look down from the great height. Its design gave no thought to suicide, or to murder.

The hall leading up to the atrium was vaulted and vast: an open cathedral of sunlight, walled floor to ceiling with glass windows and tall glass doors that led onto a surrounding terrace; a place to throw parties and watch the sunset, or to throw parties and watch the sunrise, a place now annexed to warehouse row after row of white storage containers.

Dangler paid no attention to the room, or to the connecting corridors. He did not see Varrage leave the supply room, or the corridor that held the supply room. He did not see Varrage enter the wide, sunlit room where the walkway bridged the ring above the atrium. Nor did he see Varrage fix his eyes upon the pale robot-man standing *on* that walkway: the muscular man centered within arcs of spider-blade legs. He did not see Varrage take his first, purpose-filled steps *toward* that man, or see Varrage squeeze his hands into great and rocky fists as he moved.

He had no need to see these things.

Motion sensors within his spider-gun pets caught it all. The weapons whirled from their master's feet and sped to the edge of the walkway, instantly locking aim on the intruder and bombarding his chest with bullets and tracer fire. The gunfire roared within the large hall; echoing and *re*-echoing, louder than crazy.

Varrage struggled forward, the bullets screaming around him — each contact sending fresh waves of white impact diffusion sailing around his body — each flash, each step, awakening memory within his mind.

Bullets.

Bull...et-proof.

Eventually the bullets made Varrage stagger, and he took a step backward.

"Ah, nicccce," Dangler said, watching. "So, you're not dead after all. You have as much pulse as a rock." Dangler smiled and reached for the jamming-gun holstered below his hip. As he raised the gun, he willed his Lifer-unit into motion, spider-stepping down the walkway, adjusting his position via the same neuro-networks that once moved his own powerful legs.

He pointed the jamming-gun, and fired over the safety rail.

A wall of pain hit Varrage, attacking his synapses, relaying the immediate signal to his brain that his chest was being clubbed by iron and that his joints were being pierced by shards of glass — his nervous system screamed with the messages of pain, the intense and insistent warnings of pain, but something under his intellect challenged those messages, something commanded his body forward.

Actual damage to his body was slight: roaring pressure in his sinuses; rupture of his capillaries and the constant threat of overload, all forcing him to actively retain consciousness — and *that* struggle, inside the pain, was what he paid attention to: staying conscious, staying mobile, getting closer to the man with the gun.

/

Seeing Norel's agent step back from the beam, Dangler pressed forward, still firing, extending his arm as he pushed the gun, *willing* it to inflict more pain.

\

Varrage forced himself forward, regaining his lost step and claiming another.

THEY MUST NOT GET THE BI

He needed a weapon.

EVADE OR ATTACK. EVADE OR ATT —

— He forced his arm to reach behind his shoulder. The space was empty. His pipe was —

— THEY HAVE THE...

Varrage stopped, feigned right, and as the robot-rider swung the gun's beam to follow him, Varrage leapt the opposite way, diving out of sight behind the first row of storage containers.

/

Dangler covered the ground to the white containers in just a few steps, but by the time he could look past any of the boxes, Norel's agent was gone. As Dangler straightened and turned to look for signs of the escaped prisoner, a storage container to his right burst up from the floor, lifted by Norel's agent.

The prisoner charged.

Dangler laughed, and fired.

\

Running behind the container, Varrage felt pain attack him, most strongly at his exposed toes and ankles. He knew the sensations would increase the nearer he grew to their source, but he had to get close, only *close* could he inflict damage.

He rammed the container into the robot-rider and pushed. While the container had mass anchoring it, Varrage scrambled up its underside and leapt.

/

Dangler raised his weapon. Norel's agent appeared above him and Dangler fired. The wave caught the agent — an axe blow to the gut. Dangler followed it with an actual uppercut from his left arm, striking the agent's ribcage with his gauntleted forearm.

\

Varrage fell, thrusting out both hands as the robot-man slipped sideways. Varrage's hands hit the platform where the robot's legs rooted, and he pushed hard away from the complex structure.

/

Before the agent could reach the floor, Dangler struck out with his two right legs, burro-kicking the agent between the shoulder blades and at the base of the spine, sending the agent sailing over the floor.

\

Varrage hit the ground, speeding toward the safety railings. When he hit, the glass bowed outward for an instant and then shattered, spitting fragments out into the open air of the atrium. Varrage flew out with them and as the last portion of his body slid away from the floor's edge, he grabbed the safety railing and pulled himself back. He landed in a crouch, with his feet grinding glass.

/

The reverse move surprised Dangler. He expected Norel's agent to fall out to its death, instead, the man-thing was back on the floor, perched under the safety railing. Dangler's surprise faded quickly, and he fired the jamming gun at the black figure, keeping the trigger squeezed.

\

Varrage fought to ignore the pain from the beam, and worked to keep his actions true. Four inches to his right was a six-story drop. Twelve feet to his left was an adversary with the power to hurt him.

He lunged against the rail-posts he crouched between, throwing his shoulder against one and his foot against the other, in both cases near their tops, as far from their roots as possible. Both railings moved, instantly cracking the safety glass panels they connected to. The bent posts relaxed their holds on the crossbar at his shoulder, and he grabbed it.

/

The black figure stood at the edge of a death drop, framed within the broken section of safety wall, creating a target too delicious to resist. Dangler charged. On his third step, he pivoted, anchoring his body leftward as he swept with his right legs, supplying enough momentum to push Norel's agent over the ledge, but not so much as to be pulled over himself.

\

Varrage dove under the wall of sweeping legs and escaped with the crossbar. Clear, he slammed the bar into the floor, launching glass remnants out of its seams. He spun the bar around his chest.

It was heavy. It had saws of jagged glass at each end.

It would suffice.

He charged, targeting the bald head of the robot-rider, looking at the steel visor embedded in the traumatized flesh.

Did the rivets reach the bone?

Would the bone crack?

/

Dangler raised his arm and used his forearm gauntlet to block the pipe. The sound of metal striking metal echoed off the walls, repeating as the blows continued.

Varrage was fast and Dangler was talented. For a time, Dangler blocked each flurry of strikes, and Varrage smacked aside each aiming of the jamming gun. The combatants pushed; they struck; they counter-struck; close to each other finally, these once-men, the air thrumming electric with their flying elbows and fists, with their guns and their teeth and their lengths of cold steel; two men, gorging on battle, eager in the moment, free finally, to destroy without restraint.

\

Varrage, holding his pipe like a quarter-staff, attacked with both glassy ends.

/

Dangler blocked — using the gauntlets on each of his forearms, using the jamming gun, using the long sections of his multi-jointed legs, little by little allowing the prisoner to get close with his weapon and then reversing the battle on him — stabbing hard with the tips of each leg: blows striking high, striking low, forcing the prisoner to defend instead of attack. The agent's pipe whirled. Dangler's legs stitched and stitched faster, striking and jabbing, giving Dangler time to raise his gun up easy, giving him time to actually ai —

—Dangler didn't see the pivot, didn't see the pipe flash until just before impact. Then he moved — beautifully fast, and the pipe missed his head, coming down along his arm instead, drawing blood, and shifting the gun from its intended target.

\

The beam caught Varrage mid-thigh. Varrage winced, and moved to evade. He lunged with the pipe.

/

Dangler swung his entire Lifer-unit up and back with a wave-like shift of his robotic legs, fluidly clearing the strike. While high, he let loose with a stream of bullets from the machine-gun mounted under his leg platform — the bullets nothing more than a nuisance he knew, but enough of a nuisance to set up Norel's agent, to put his head right where it needed to be for Dangler to *slam* the agent's head with the wedge on his fore-arm gauntlet — an eight inch shark fin of welded murder — not once, bur twice, three times, right on the agent's temple.

\

Varrage slipped back, dodged, and the gun caught him on the left side of the chest with its pain beam.

Varrage rolled his shoulder with the beam, and swung up with the pipe, connecting with the gun, and knocking the beam away from his body.

Fast, he swung the pipe down. His adversary again swerved on his tall robotic legs and moved himself out of the way, taking a step backward.

Varrage lashed with the rail-pipe, looped it, and lashed again, making the robot-man take another step backwards.

The gun arced forward. The robot-man attempted to re-aim. Varrage smacked the gun away, then quickly thrust the pipe at the man's throat.

/

Dangler skittered backwards several steps. The floor —
— *Where was the hole in the railing?*
— Right behind him. Two steps away. Norel's agent continued its press. Dangler side-swept the pipe and deflected it outward, gaining the second he needed to leap sideways — *an uninterrupted shot* — He wanted a sustained shot at the black thing's yellow face — he wanted a chance to attack the skull itself, to see what delicious agonies he could cause within the strange creature's head.

Dangler sidestepped with a quick jump, then bent his legs deep, closer to the glass-strewn floor. Then he leapt for distance, back to the mouth of the skybridge — *get to the middle. Get to the high ground. Take as many shots as you want.*

\

Varrage saw his opponent heading for the bridge and ran to the broken safety wall, vaulting with the pipe at the floor's edge. As he sailed through the open air above the atrium, he let go of the pipe and it wind-milled through the flight with him. He caught the bridge's railing just as the robot-man passed him and the pipe clattered onto the bridge. Instantly, Varrage dropped, rebounded, and leapt to the walkway's other railing, even as the robot-man turned and fired at his first landing position.

Varrage jumped from the railing, seeking to kick the robot-rider's gun hand. The man pulled his hand back, and Varrage struck only the gun. It fired, and the beam hit the safety wall. Varrage snatched the rail-pipe from the floor, and one of the robot's legs hit him in the chest — a hard jab that drove him back. He turned from the blow, and two strikes hit him on the other side of his chest, driving him back. He angled his body, and as he raised his pipe, all of the robot-man pivoted. Both of the robot's left legs swept up Varrage's body, locking under his torso and lifting him to the edge of the bridge's safety wall.

/

Thrilled by victory, Dangler pushed further, willing his legs to push harder, to complete the act, to send the prisoner falling — to where he would land and break, to where impalement awaited upon the little trees so far below. The *pretty* little trees so far below.

\

Part of Varrage — the back of his lower thigh — slammed against the chrome safety railing, stopping him, stopping some of him. The rest pivoted; his shoulders sailed out into free space; his arms and the rail-pipe sailed out even further, his body moved downward —
— and the tops of his feet hooked tightly under the robot's rear leg, pulling it as Varrage fell. The rear leg hit the front leg, and both were pulled to the wall by Varrage's weight, pinned there by sheer —
— Varrage's lower back slammed into the outside of the walkway. He rebounded, sat up, and thrust himself back onto the bridge, pushing the robot's legs ahead of him. As Varrage pushed the legs further; he thrust his chest onto a middle segment and spun himself halfway over it. His feet rose, and —
PULL BACK.
— he kicked the robot-rider
PULL BACK.
in the face with the soles of both feet, as the shredded cuffs of his pants flew —
— *where were his boots?* —
— hold back — hold back —
— his mind stuck against visions of the robot-rider's head flying away from his shoulders — *Just hurt him; just stun him. Because* —
YOU NEED
Varrage righted himself, landing full on the walkway, pressing forward as the robot-rider staggered.

Varrage tried to — *what*? Breath and air. The pushing of an unformed — *idea* — from his mind. What?

He made a noise as he tried to speak, and the action made him remember what speech was, what it was for. He tried again as his opponent, near unconsciousness from the kick, slumped against the first joint of his front robotic leg.

"eRe..." Varrage said, and then, more forcefully,

"WheRe. . "

The visored face turned slightly to the voice.

"... iS My piPE?"

That was right. Those were words. He needed the pipe because his vortex bike was inside it. He needed the vortex bike because he was once... a...

He had a Mother.

Deidre. Townsend. She sang while she cooked.

/

Still dazed, Dangler raised the gun. Before he could fire, the black agent whirled the pipe and smacked the weapon from his hand.

\

Varrage was aware of the gun as it fell, and as it suddenly *stopped* falling. He looked: the gun was tethered to the robot-rider, rooted to —

— A wave of machine gun fire hit Varrage, coming from just below his waist. He looked down to see one of the spider-guns crawl out from under the robot-rider, firing as it advanced.

The robot-rider retreated out of the spider-gun's way, and leaned over the hand-rail to retrieve his own jamming gun. For that second, Varrage could see the other end of the walkway. He saw that his pipe was there, on the floor, next to his tap, and next to a lit tablet computer running a screen saver of a woman in a bikini, posing with a large machine gun.

Varrage stepped back, bullets attacking his chest, and caught the spider-gun with a swing of the pipe. Raising the weapon, he lifted the spider gun. The spider gun continued firing down at him. Varrage looked like a farmer, lifting a pitchfork full of live electric cables.

From the corner of his eye, Varrage saw the second spider-gun scurry up the walkway's entrance. Was it blocking his exit? Had the guns purposely surrounded him? Could they think?

Varrage whipped his pipe and hurled the spider-gun at the robot-rider. The weapon stopped firing the instant it pointed at its master — and at the same moment the robot-rider swung his arm reflexively, blocking the weapon's impact, but sending the legged cannon arcing over the side of the walkway, where it plummeted unimpeded down into the atrium. As it fell, the machine gun adjusted its aim, and fired at Varrage the whole way down.

The pain ray hit his shoulder — weaker. Varrage raised his shoulder to protect his neck, and stole a glance to learn why the second spider-gun wasn't firing — it was coming his way, clattering along the bridge's railing, and dipping behind the safety wall for the second it needed to pass Varrage. Once past, it dropped down, hooked its two front legs onto the inside of the walkway wall, and its two rear legs down the outside, clamping itself in place.

Varrage looked toward the robot-rider, still firing, and saw him gritting his teeth as he pressed the tether and the beam weapon together, both hands occupied.

The clamped spider-gun leaned backwards and swiveled. As soon as it cleared its master, it fired.

Bullets clawed at the right side of Varrage's head. He felt a fraction of each shot; he felt a fraction *more* of each shot as they piled on. The defense he relied upon was untestable, its limits unknown. It would only take one bullet getting through to kill him; he must move.

He stepped closer to the robot-rider. The bullets kept firing. Diffusion trails whirled around Varrage's head, blinding him as he moved. The robot-rider rammed two legs into Varrage's chest, stopping him, and continued firing his gun.

Varrage felt surges of pain, each building upon the last. He had to break contact. He was taking fire from two positions, he was blocked from going forward, there was nothing on either side of him but a six story drop — and stepping back just meant more of the same. Impact diffusion would let him survive the drop to the ground floor, but he'd lose the bike. The robot-rider would take it and run. How long before the spider-gun needed to reload?

Varrage staggered and lowered his arms, letting his weapon fall to the floor and swaying on his feet.

/

Dangler smiled as he fired, inching the sputtering jamming gun closer to the black agent's chest. The black agent leaned forward, slumping, the hail of bullets following him —

\

— Varrage grabbed the robot-rider's left foreleg with both hands and pulled hard, yanking the naked chest of the robot-rider directly at the machine-gun fire. In the move, Varrage dove under the robot-rider, trading places with him.

He heard two pings as bullets hit something metallic and then the bullets stopped. It didn't work. The spider gun stopped firing. Varrage was on the ground. Varrage was—

— he raised both legs, locked them under the robot-rider's leg platform and pushed hard, hoping to send the rider over the side of the walkway. The robot-rider left the ground and tumbled forward, legs thrusting every which way as he fought to regain equilibrium. The robot's left foreleg scraped along the handrail, and the spider-gun leapt to avoid it. The robot-rider's second left leg caught the pet in the air, and the spider-gun went sailing out into the atrium, down to the koi-pond, never once finding an approved target to fire upon as it fell.

/

Dangler recovered, turning in time to see Norel's agent roll near the computer, toward the spot where the agent's strange side arm lay in plain sight. Dangler didn't know what the device was, but he knew he didn't want Norel's agent shooting him with it. He charged.

As Norel's agent reached for the items at the far end of the walkway, Dangler rammed its shoulders. They both rolled. Norel's agent missed the weird gun, and had been forced to grab the pipe instead. That was fine. Dangler could deal with a pipe, even a heavy one. He jumped to the outer ring of walkway, off the bridge, away from Norel's agent, and raised his jamming gun to fire.

\

Varrage vaulted with his pipe, and rammed both feet into the robot-rider's chest, driving him back, causing the gun hand to raise high —

— Varrage landed, swinging the battle-pipe and catching the beam weapon with a direct hit. The weapon shattered into pieces. The pipe hit the Atrium's outside glass, creating a crack three stories tall. Varrage pressed the attack, swinging his pipe fast, up and over his shoulder, big and obvious. The robot-rider blocked the blow with his forearm gauntlet — allowing Varrage to pivot the bottom edge of the pipe against the muscular arm, and drive the tail-end into the visored face.

/

Dangler leaned back drastically, absorbing the blow, and struck out with a leg. The agent blocked it. Dangler struck out with two legs, the agent blocked both. Dangler backed down the walkway.

Norel's agent blocked his strikes no matter where they came from, so Dangler attempted to compensate with speed — jabbing and striking faster and faster. He tried jumping the unit, and striking while in the air, but it did no good, Norel's agent countered, having no trouble with two legs no matter where they attacked from.

They were reaching the end of the outside ring, returning to solid floor, across the gap from where the fight started.

Norel's agent had no trouble blocking two legs?

Dangler would give him three then.

He rose up on one solitary leg, extending it full, staying aloft by striking all three remaining legs violently against Norel's agent, ready to bring the entire gun platform down on him, lay him out, slice him open and fire the conventional gun inside of his chest if that's what it took. Dangler got started. He fired his underbody machine gun then and there, ignoring the threat of bounce-back, ignoring the fire's seeming futility, simply attacking, attacking, attacking.

\

Varrage countered the blows, absorbed the fire, and then allowed some of the spider-leg blows to land across his back. He braced. Each blow that landed kept the robot-rider in the air. He thrust the pipe and broke off the machine gun cannon. The blows still landed across his back and shoulders. What could he see under the platform?

Seams and rings and hints of hydraulics. What was inside? Fuel cells? Computers? Drive belts? Nothing was visible. He would simply have to strike blind.

He thrust his arm into the underbelly of the gun platform, puncturing its outer skin with brute force — but raw strength had not been enough to get him through the platform's interior frameworks. Passing through the steel's atomic structure was possible, he could tell, but no direct strike would do it, a direct strike against the material's field-curtains would stack them. He needed to ease them aside. He needed to concentrate to do it, and the robot-rider was moving: shifting, striking.

Varrage took the blows, but moved his arm between the sub-atomic curtains, moved until his hand felt the unit's interior workings; moved until his hand gripped some self-contained component, some component he could rip.

He tightened his hand around the blocky thing and pulled it free.

In the entertainments, the electronic games, the kung-fu films, the pulp-paper comic-books, this was where he ripped out the heart, and showed it, still beating, to the astonished villain.

He watched himself, oil dripping from the end of his hand, do just that. He watched as he lifted the junction hub, with its electric feed-lines dangling like so many arteries, and presented it to the robot-rider.

He was aware of himself as he watched the robot-rider's face, as he watched the wrinkling of the forehead's skin as the muscles under it contracted. *What? What was the robot-rider doing?*

The robot-rider looked a specific way. His forehead wrinkled, and his mouth hung open. He had no eyes to read. Varrage searched for the connection some part of him was trying to make: *worried*, the man looked *worried*. The man raised his shoulders, and thrust out his arms along his sides. The man sat in a bucket, connected by some girdered umbilicus to a ring cap atop a flattened spheroid of machinery, machinery which now teetered, and shook.

Balance.

The man-thing was trying to maintain balance. It would need to step backward. That meant, that to keep his viewpoint the same, Varrage would have to step... forward. He did.

The man in the bucket watched Varrage, and moved one of the robot's legs. The legs were on their own ring, under the main platform's ring cap. When the one leg moved, all the legs began to move.

Varrage stood still, and watched.

The robot platform failed spectacularly.

/

Dangler watched his unit's main platform go crazy. He twisted his torso, trying to gain some sense of what the platform was doing, trying to form a baseline from which to react. The platform was no longer listening to him. The legs were pistoning independently, driving the platform first one way, then another. He could only influence them by leaning, and even with that, the effect was minimal.

The legs found a pattern by maximizing thrust, each leg pushing against the floor at maximum power, each strike changing the angle of the legs until the entire platform became an insane, backward-whirling automaton, carrying Dangler along helplessly.

The platform headed toward the windows. Dangler leaned down and grabbed the safety rail with both hands. If he could keep his grip, he could at least anchor the leg platform and keep some measure of control while he figured out what to do. Where was Norel's agent?

Walking back to get that gun.

Pull the railing. Get into a fighting stance.

But the legs weren't obliging. He couldn't pull them, not enough. Norel's agent had the gun. Norel's agent —

—holstered it —

— and then turned to look at him, absently taking a few steps back down the outer ring walkway.

One of the robot legs hit the glass behind Dangler. He heard it. He felt it. Norel's agent stopped at the entrance of the walkway, sixteen feet from him, still watching. Dangler's leg dragged itself over the window, grinding its way back to open air, and then the next leg slammed into its place, repeating the process. Dangler pulled, and felt the safety railing shake under his effort, but the legs were still pulling him to the glass. The legs were still grinding and slamming into the glass.

The glass gave in. The glass shattered.

Dangler screamed. He heard himself scream. Nothing held the legs back now, and he felt his grip slipping from the railing as the legs rattled their way through the window frame. He repeated the word "No" again and again as his fingers slid from the chrome railing. The legs pinwheeled onto the terrace, and began dragging Dangler the last few steps to the small, outer wall. He reached for the window frame, but couldn't catch it. He looked frantically around the terrace. *Was there nothing to grab?*

Norel's agent — that black thing — stood unmoving. Watching. *Well*, Dangler asked himself, *What did you expect? Help?*

A reaction. He expected a reaction.

The edge of the wall drew closer. No question. The legs were going over. That meant *he* was going over.

"Help." He heard himself say, insanely.

He glanced at the edge. He could see treetops. No atrium this time. He flashed a look to Norel's agent, still standing there, not moving.

"Help!" he yelled as the first leg hit the wall with a thump, and the next leg hit it with another thump. "Help!"

He didn't care if yelling for help was crazy. It was; of course it was. He didn't care. He didn't want to fall off the building. He yelled, and yelled again.

"Help! Help!"

Thump.

Thump.

ThumpThumpThumpThumpThumpThump.

Two legs went over the side, and the gun platform raced along the roof wall's edge, moving suddenly, like a wheel on a track. Dangler slammed into the floor, again and again, and grabbed at its surface with a drowning man's desperation. It was what he wanted. It was solid. It was ground. By pressing his hands into the roof, he was able to stop the gun platform's rolling, but there was nothing to grab. "Help. Help," he heard himself repeating. His jamming gun remnants, tethered to the gun platform, lay abandoned at his side. The legs progressed over the balcony, and he was dragged quickly to the wall, slamming into it, banging into it, until he felt his bare belly scraping against its edge. His arms met the wall, and here he had a grip, here he had a chance. His arms were mighty. His arms were thunder wrapped in flesh.

But he could feel the robot moving along the wall below him, running back and forth and back and forth, swinging like a pendulum, and it was heavy. It was so heavy.

"Help me *PLEASE*," he said to the standing man, as his right arm was pulled down, and only its fingertips still gripped the balcony wall's edge.

The standing man moved. Dangler saw him raise his arm, and look at it.

*

Varrage watched as his own hand rose, reflexively, almost on its own, the first two fingers extending toward the horizon and then a little higher, his thumb extending too. Could his hand move on its own? Could that be so?

A promise.

The robot-rider about to fall.

Something

there.

Varrage strode to the edge of the roof, fighting to remember what had been promised, fighting to grasp what was calling for his attention, fighting to remember what was being lost.

He saw the man looking up at him, rocking at the shoulders on the wrong side of the roof. He heard the robot legs drumming along the wall.

"TaKe My hAnd," he said, in a voice like rolling gravel, reaching out for the fingertips that were discolored from the pressure on them, yellow-white at the nail, rimmed everywhere with pink.

Dangler reached up. As he let go of the ledge, his whole left shoulder swung down, and for an instant, it looked certain he would fall. Varrage lurched forward and Dangler's hand locked around his forearm. His second hand flew over and locked on the arm as well.

Blood slid instantly between Dangler's fingers at the touch of Varrage's sharp, black skin. The flesh of Dangler's hands sliced as the weight of the gun platform dragged him down, and his blood lubricated the descent. Could you pull yourself up by grabbing the sharpened edge of a sword?

Dangler, grafted to a robot, and with a visor in the place of his own lost eyes, looked up into Varrage's glowing face and asked "What are you?" as his bleeding hands slid further and further down Varrage's arm.

Varrage didn't answer. Varrage didn't know.

Varrage, with no countering imperative, merely held the man's hand as it slipped away, merely watched as the man fell, screaming shrilly, covering his head with his massive arms as his thrashing robotics dragged him down to crash against the cement six stories below, and then to lie still, bleeding from his hands, and then from his mouth.

Varrage watched.

With no countering imperative Varrage merely continued watching, while the energy that flowed beneath the visible plates of his skin surged and roiled. The energy seemed to roar silently, a sound only *felt* within his ears — was it blood? Did he even have blood anymore?

There was blood on his hand wasn't there? Did that count? Whether it did or it didn't, it would dry sticky if he let it remain. He wiped his hand absently against the dark, shredded cloth of his pants, with just enough pressure to avoid slicing the fabric.

Looking down at the robot-rider, he sheathed his pipe across his back.

He continued looking at the still figure. The soundless roaring continued in his ears, and his hand closed gently, a gesture he made without thinking, or realizing.

A flash on the horizon called his attention, a spasm of light in the dark twist of clouds beyond the trees, a spasm he felt as well as saw. What was it he was feeling? A shuddering? A pull? Could he find out by getting closer? He didn't know, couldn't even form the idea as a complete thought, but running to the flash seemed instantly right: to run, to leap, to inflict; and at least in traces, his mind saw investigating the flash as a countering imperative. At least the trace of a countering imperative.

It would suffice.

* * *

Rik Ty

**

Inside the portal, Outpost 14 bucked and swayed. Raw, electric light filled the windows, while the rooms inside remained dark. Those Bike Pilots who moved by the windows moved as silhouettes, and when the light outside spasmed, their shadows strobed on the air beside them.

Energy pulled the Outpost, on a current which could not be seen, but which carried the Outpost through the portal space, and which, beyond the portal's edge, sliced into the atmosphere of the world outside.

The portal's Earthward face commanded an entire sunlit field, which every few seconds darkened as the clouds above it shifted in intensity, one moment full and opaque, the next moment absent altogether, as if the sky had inhaled the strange clouds, as if the sky were breathing.

Within the first few feet of the portal's apron, the planet's air was pulled and torn and rejected, while electrical charges built and dispersed in riots of lightning. Something had entered the portal. That something must leave.

Outpost 14 blasted out from the huge glowing abrasion, careening across the field on a wave of charged air that threw forth long terrors of lightning and churned the soil in its path.

Sunlight flooded into the unlit rooms of Outpost 14, casting long, warm shadows that swung as the building moved. Skyde kept her arms wrapped tightly around a workstation and braced her foot against a side wall. Sunset clung to the console next to her. Everyone in the speeding building held on to something as the views outside the windows progressed from sky blue, to grass, to trees, to glimpses of houses and streets and street-lamps, and, if the eye could be believed, to other portals, smaller than the one they had just exited, but just as intensely bright, hanging in the air at different points along the field.

The rear of the building lifted as it rushed forward, almost tipping the Outpost onto its roof. Nonstop attacked his keyboard and swung the gantry arm up toward the sky. The building leveled and then dipped the other way. It crashed through the wooden back fence of a private home, then through the next fence, and more.

As the Outpost continued, Nonstop could see a steel water tower atop a slope of grass, shaking its way into view. He watched it. They had enough speed, they could definitely hit it. Slice, who was braced by the main door, saw the tower as well.

"Nonstop my man, you see that right? That aint no wooden fence."

"Yeah. I see it. I see it. I'll try to miss it."

"Try?"

"Sssh."

Nonstop shifted the gantry and the building shot suddenly off on a diagonal, picking up speed and tipping sideways. His friends, who had all gained secure positions, slammed into the walls anyway. Nonstop tightened his grip on his workstation as the building rode the slope upwards. Then he shifted the gantry arm again, causing the building to slow. The forward edge of the building lifted one last time, and then the Outpost stopped, gently, as if some piece of the building's apparatus had produced the landing instead of some spontaneous dispersal of some highly-unusual weather phenomenon.

The Outpost stopped on open ground, not far from a school, and not far from the mint-green water tower. After two hard years, a much anticipated event had occurred: Outpost 14 had returned to Earth.

No one gave voice to this idea. No one celebrated.

With the Outpost free from the realmlines, out of the portal, and released from the energy that carried it, its systems, including its computers, and the amber safety light in its main room, returned to activity, weakened as they were before. Norel ran to the workstation he had left, and returned to his analysis of the building's base systems.

He stood as the focus now, as the center of things. The center of the round room, in the round building, in the expanding circle of portals. His Bike Pilots watched him, and slowly gathered closer. Nonstop looked out the main door's window.

"Doc. This is Earth right? So aren't we supposed to be at Open Mind? You said the 'original positions' right?"

Norel watched the screen and nodded. "Yes. Adjusting for planetary travel, we should be within inches of the spot we left from — in the courtyard lab at Open Mind. However, the program is saying it can't verify these coordinates as the point of origin. It must be these portals. They're not supposed to be here, and they must be interfering."

"What about re-originating right here?" Skyde asked, "We're on Earth at least."

"Yes, maybe, but not yet. Not with the portals here. Once they're gone, they'll never be back, and the reality that makes up this origin point will never exist again — it will never be locatable. The baseline from which the system makes all comparisons, and all assumptions, and all star charting will disappear while in use."

Skyde nodded at this. Nonstop turned quickly from the window. His friends saw him perk up, and became agitated themselves, eager for inspiration as to what to do next.

"So we shut down the portals, re-originate here, and then we can just leave right?" Nonstop asked. Norel looked up, directly at the young man.

"You, get Grace to safety. Then you can worry about getting back here to help the team close the portals. But yes, that should be our idea."

"What about Bloch's men?" Skyde asked, running a hand through her hair, clearing loose strands from her eyes.

"Bloch's teams, right," Nonstop said, absently copying Skyde's move, pushing his hair away from his forehead.

"Where's Varrage?" he asked the group, "We can't fight Bloch's teams without Varrage. Where is he?"

Slice shrugged "Who knows? Gone on one of his things, right? I mean, isn't he?" At this, the group around him nodded and muttered comments of agreement.

"Varrage is already at Open Mind," Norel said, working briskly at his console, and not seeing the alarm his comment brought to Nonstop's face.

"He is? Does he know about the —" Nonstop turned quickly, looking around the room until he found Krork, who was already looking at him, and shaking his head "*no*". Nonstop leaned on Norel's monitor and spoke quietly.

"Look. Look, Bloch's teams have a weapon that works against us. I felt it!"

"What weapon?" Norel asked.

"Some kind of beam. It hurts. It keeps hurting."

Norel made a noise that was somewhere between a sigh and a grunt. "So none of us are safe now? Not even the four of you?" He rubbed his forehead. He addressed his teams: "All right, this has to be said. Everyone. Do everything you can against the portals now, work from cover, or work from moving bikes, but if Bloch's teams show up, or *when* Bloch's teams show up, leave. Get yourselves to safety."

"What about you?" Krork said.

"I'm going to get the power levels in the systems properly distributed. Maybe we can be gone before Bloch even knows we're here."

"You're going to stay here alone?" Krork took a step toward Norel. Norel looked at him and raised his first finger.

"I don't know how much time you have. Don't waste it," he said, holding Krork's gaze for a second and then returning to work.

Krork and his friends stalled and stood still. Slice slapped his hands together and bounded onto the balls of his feet.

"We'll need rides," he said and sprang toward the door to the bike lab.

Grace found Nonstop, and he absently led her away by the elbow. At the doorway to the bike lab they met Krork, and the three stole a last glance at Dr. Norel.

Norel sat, his head down, alone with his work, in a room that spun from dark to light and light to dark.

*

Where the Outpost had landed, the sky grew gray and heavy. A wind rode over the small hill and whipped the grass. Bike Pilots gathered behind the building, some on large rigs, some on machines the size of normal motorcycles, and once together, they dismounted to gather closer, clustering in a rough circle around Skyde as she took haze readings on her data-box.

"What can you see?" Krork asked, leaning toward her, speaking loudly enough to be heard above the rushing wind.

Skyde looked up at him, her hair thrashing across her forehead in the same staccato chop that whipped through the grass. "There's a lot. I — Hang on a second." She looked past Krork, to where Slice was trundling up on a red and white bike. She called out to him.

"We all set?" she asked.

"Yeah. The lab's all locked," he called back as he slowed his machine. He parked his bike and walked quickly over to the group, where the others made room for him. He worked his way close enough to hear Skyde and then asked her: "What's up? What do you see?"

She gave him a quick nod and then turned to the group, "Alright, there's haze everywhere," she said, addressing the team, several of whom were monitoring their own data boxes and nodding in agreement. "Lots of it," she continued, "I see a lot of dense spots with no migration patterns leading up to them. Those are portals — at least ninety-nine percent of the time those are portals."

"The big spot here," Tumbler asked, looking down at his own screen, "that's the portal we came through?"

"Yes. The big portal is the strong spot, but I see haze as far as ten miles from here. The strongest signal on that end comes from a major band running east to west."

"So what's the plan?" Wazzi asked.

"Fan out," Skyde said, "Drive west to the edge of the haze — wherever the edge is by that point. First priority is stopping the situation from getting worse. Close any portals you see on the way out, and then any portals you see on the way back. If you see soldiers — ghost."

"What about people?" Sunset asked.

"Keep them out of the way. Tell them to stay alert." "What do we tell them when they ask what's going on?"

"Tell them the truth — at least what we know — *the quick version*. Something's up though. I'm not hearing anything — cell phone service is not just bad, it's out altogether. And I don't hear any honking. I don't hear any screaming. Nothing."

"Do you think the portal did something? Killed the pe —"

"— No. God, I hope not. I think the Town's been prepped. Either they've evacuated, or they're keeping to their homes, and either scenario seems weird to me. Stay alert. We'll find out as we go."

"What about critters?" Wazzi asked.

"I imagine there are going to be some. If you encounter them, tap them. But don't chase any. We want to clear the way so the Outpost can leave — something has to get lowest priority, and the critters are it."

"Some of us can stay after the Outpost leaves," Slice said. "We can clean up the left over Inter-D then."

Skyde looked at him, but said nothing. Then she turned to the other Bike Pilots. They looked ready. "Okay," she said, "I'm going to fly over to the far point and see what's happening there. That will take me west, plus a little south. On my way back, I'll head north, and sweep back here. That will give us the whole overview."

"Can you fly in this?" Krork asked, gesturing toward the wind as he stood near the foot of his bike.

"Absolutely. Don't worry," she answered, nodding to Krork and setting her hands on her hips. Continuing her nod, she looked back at the group. "Okay people, let's go. A half hour is better than an hour."

*

Grace sat on the back of Rattletrap and braced herself as Nonstop gave the machine some power and drove it over toward Krork's bike, where three women were busy climbing into the bike's workbay: the girl in the blue, the girl in the yellow, and the old girl with the gray hair. Krork was talking to them and pointing toward the front of his bike. Grace looked beyond the machine and watched the girl in white rise into the sky on her electric surfboard. Skyde. The girl's name was Skyde. Well, no, it wasn't. Her fake name was Skyde. Well, anyway, the girl — Skyde, rose to about a hundred feet, then she changed the angle of her hips so that the bottom of her board cut into the wind, and then she flew across the sky sideways, as if she had grabbed the tail fin of some invisible airplane. Grace looked around her; no one else was even watching the flying girl.

She saw Krork, coming over to talk to Nonstop.

Krork. An alien. She knew an alien; one who was big enough to be terrifying, and yet one who no longer scared her in the least. She had hung onto his arm for safety, and now Nonstop was taking her out of here and she was never going to see him again. How long before he seemed like some dream she'd had?

"Where will I meet you?" she heard Nonstop call out to Krork.

Krork kept walking over, and as he answered, he pointed behind him with his thumb. "We're going to start on that monster portal we just came through. If we're done with that before you get back, just look for the biggest portal. You know — use the data-box, identify the most haze."

"I'll find you, smart guy," Nonstop said, chuckling as he raised his arm and offered the side of his fist. Krork gave it a good rap with the side of his own and smiled.

300

"Krork," Grace said, reaching out for his hand before she even realized what she was doing. He stopped and looked at her, offering her a fresh smile.

"Hey Grace," he said, and gently extended his arm, offering her the side of his fist, as well as the side of his giant forearm and his mongo elbow. His arm seemed like a ship to her, docking right at her eye level. She reached out to it.

"I'm sorry," she said.

"You're sorry?"

"I was scared of you."

"I know. But that makes sense."

"I'm sorry though."

"No insult. At all. Don't give it another thought," he said, and then he leaned toward her slightly, "And now you, have to get out of here Grace." He looked at her, smiled, and then tapped the side of her hand with his.

"Be careful," Grace said, tapping his fist back.

"Be safe," Krork said, nodding to both of them.

Grace smiled.

"Sure thing," Nonstop said.

Krork waved, and then strode back toward his bike.

"Biggest portal!" Nonstop yelled as he rode Rattletrap in a noisy circle, and then sped away from the Outpost's portico.

*

Nonstop dropped down the small hill, heading south. Grace felt the bike speed up, and was suddenly alarmed. Nonstop was going to find her a safe spot, and then what? Pick her up again? Just leave her on her own? The bike gained more speed, rolling easy on the grass. What was the right thing to do? The wind tossed her hair in quick jumps around her head. She was never going to be safe. She was never going to be all right. There was hard work to do before she'd ever be safe again. She raised up off the seat and leaned forward, speaking loudly near Nonstop's ear.

"Don't worry about getting me someplace safe," she said. "I have to upload."

"What?" Nonstop stole a look back at her.

"I have to upload. I have to broadcast. There *is* no safe place; not until I get the word out. Bloch is causing all this? Let's turn the tables on him."

"You want me to find a T.V. station?"

"No, but I need some stuff. Just get me to an electronics store. I'll take care of the rest."

A grin spread across Nonstop's face and he gave Rattletrap a little more speed. Beyond the grassy hill there was a road. Alongside the road, shaking back and forth in the wind, there was a metal highway sign which read:

EXETER
BUSINESS DISTRICT
3 MILES

"That sounds like us," Nonstop said, and they swept down the rest of the slope.

On the road, they turned at the sign, and driving west, the wind lessened. They sped up. Nonstop leaned over the control bar and grinned. "Okay. Dig it Little Chicken, whatd'ya need?"

"An electronics store. And don't call me "Little Chicken'"

"What?"

"You heard me Winky-boy. Don't call me 'Little Chicken."

"Winky-boy?"

The roadside greenery blurred as they drove; a low brick building came into view, and just as quickly vanished into the blurring.

"Winky-boy. Exactly," Grace said, waggling her fingers, "*Oooo, look at me' — winky—winky. 'I have pretty lights in my hair. Oooo. Winky, winky, winky.*"

Nonstop could hear the smile creeping into her voice, even without turning around. They passed a gas station and a tire store.

"So you *dig* the lights in my hair."

"What? No. Eui."

They passed a low brick building with a pair of smoke stacks.

"Nooo, I think you like them."

"That's stupid. Shut up. Be quiet."

They kept talking. They kept driving. They passed two drive-through restaurants and a tarot card reader and the blocks grew denser. They passed groups of buildings, built closer together, and with more floors to each building, and then with parking lots and parking meters, and then with street lamps and power lines. Soon they began specifically looking for an electronics store.

They approached an intersection with a traffic light. They went through. They kept moving.

"Where is everybody?" Grace asked.

"I don't know," Nonstop said. "I guess Skyde is right; they're gone. They evacuated."

* * *

Varrage stepped on the road outside the new wall around Open Mind and walked, vaguely in the direction of Exeter, vaguely in the direction of the disturbance that had pulled him into action. He felt the wind rise and wash up his chest and over his face. He became aware of something else around him. Everywhere he turned his attention, he felt a heaviness in the air. He felt a heaviness in his chest, nothing like a pain, and not a consistent feeling, but one he could find consistently, simply by turning to look for it. There was something peppered throughout the air that he could feel. He stepped toward one area of the feeling and immediately felt the heaviness shift to follow his new direction. With his next step, more heaviness appeared in the air, more density, and he stepped faster.

Whatever it was, it responded: following his steps as he moved and multiplying in accord, evident wherever he focused his attention. The air directly in front of him began to darken, creating a turbulent patch roughly his height and his width. He did not break stride. The turbulence actively moved closer in reaction to his speed. Within a few steps it overtook him, washing him in a buzzing arrhythmia.

He saw darkness. He saw darkness stretch. He saw the roadside trees, already gauzy and darkened by the surrounding atmosphere, stretch and lengthen and shimmer in the sun's brilliance.

He did not break stride. The sun dapplings became a shifting diamond-point mosaic and the air began to roar in his ears, pulsing in time with his every step.

The effect broke; suddenly and all at once. And when it did, he found himself walking near a small white maintenance building, a building that had been half a mile distant when the effect had started.

And he was off the road. He was on the grass.

He kept walking. With each new step the dark flecks approached from the edges of his vision.

* * *

Nonstop's tire kept constant contact with the road and its movement sent a steady vibration into the molecules of the asphalt. Usually, this disturbance dissipated instantly and without effect. But as Nonstop and Grace approached the intersection of Alighieri Plaza and Beatrice Street East, Rattletrap's tire on the ground became something like rain on a roof, or a breeze on a naked forearm: a warning, an announcement, a tug on a spider's web.

Nonstop and Grace blazed through the sunny intersection without disruption. But the second they passed its painted markings, a parked car on the far corner of Beatrice Street bounced on its shocks. A mound of asphalt slid out from between the car's wheels. It traveled until it hit the opposing curb and caused another parked car to bounce. The mound changed course, swelling toward the intersection, where it followed the vibrations announcing themselves in its domain.

* * *

Skyde grabbed some altitude, and immediately caught sight of a band of dark air running east to west on the streets below her. It looked like cloud shadow, though there were no clouds above it. The weather seemed different inside the band as well: turbulent. Skyde saw debris and newspapers tumbling just a few feet above the ground inside the band, heading west, like a river of ghosts.

There was big energy flowing west. The air above the Outpost had been rough; now the airflow was uniform and *massive*. Riding with it, Skyde soared with ease, but because of the speed it gave her, she caught only glimpses of the total Bleed Zone: she saw several portals outright; she saw the band of dark air; she saw a column of flying creatures as they looped over a building, but she passed too quickly to do more than note them. She couldn't truly observe them. All she could really do was ride the mammoth thermal westward – thermal was the right idea but the wrong word — she doubted temperature had anything to do with the surge she was riding, but it was strong and it was wide. She could skim it north or south and couldn't feel any diminishing of thrust. There'd be no good readings at the speed she was moving, and so she let go of the idea of taking any. She'd keep her eyes open, take the two minute ride to the outermost haze point, and then worry about how she was going to get back, if getting back meant flying into this same massive surge.

* * *

"I love these little fast bikes," Wazzi called out, as he and Slice hit the start of a long straight-away.

Ten damaged blocks ahead of them, something was pumping out large haze readings.

"Dude, this is serious."

"I am serious. I love these little fast bikes," Wazzi said, wheelie-ing down the open road for emphasis. Slice matched his speed and they pushed their engines. Something had damaged the tops of the buildings all along the avenue. There were brick piles in the street. There were dislodged window frames on the ground.

The two riders slalomed around debris in smooth serpentines. They drove onto sidewalks when needed, and over the hoods of low slung cars — they took any route that kept them moving fast and kept them on their mission: to close this haze-cluster, to look out for soldiers, and to move on to the next haze-cluster.

"Dude!" Slice said, pointing straight ahead of him, at a rolling wall of dust that was coming their way, still two blocks distant.

"That's it then," Wazzi said, reaching behind him for his helmet.

"Get your air-filter on."

"Yeah, I will. We're not near the center yet. This must be pretty big."

A loud thumping came from beyond the dust.

"Did you hear that?" Wazzi asked.

More thumping. Continual thumping.

"That's more than a portal, mate. Get your tap," Wazzi said as Slice secured his helmet. Then the two riders undocked their taps, entered the dust cloud...

...and drove right into an Inter-D free-for-all.

Huge, four-legged gray-beasts charged into creatures that looked like giant letter "M"s. "M"s with yellow skin striped with orange. The letter Ms were locking choke-holds around the necks of the gray-beasts. The gray-beasts were ramming the letter Ms into buildings. The fighting went on relentlessly, up and down the block, and the buildings were coming down.

Wazzi and Slice pulled close to a wall and watched the slamming warfare. Bricks and old mortar lay in the street, dust hung in the air, and dark silhouettes flashed by overhead.

Slice turned to Wazzi, smiling enormously, "Ready for some fun now?"

"What do we do?"

"Set up your tap. We send them home."

"Are you sure? Look at them."

"They can't stay here."

"They're not portals Jolly-O, technically, tech... well, they're not portals."

"You get the yellow ones, I'll get the gray ones."

"What if they charge?"

"If they charge, escape on your bike."

"But the ground's full of junk."

"If your bike hits junk, escape anyway."

"What if we get killed? Then the bikes are just laying around for Bloch to pick up."

"If you get killed, don't die."

"You know, there's no talking to you when you're like this."

"If there's no talking to me, don't listen."

Slice chuckled impishly and headed onto the street. Wazzi chuckled right behind him, and eventually the chuckling turned to cursing and the cursing turned to grunting and the grunting turned to yelling.

* * *

Grace spotted the store from across an intersection — *a boutique* — part of an old building, wrinkled everywhere with moldings and cornices and gleaming under fresh coats of white paint. The boutique took up the front corner of the building, offering large picture windows to each sidewalk, and each window showed Grace what she needed to see: beautiful displays of beautiful phones and wear-able electronics. Nestled between the two windows, she spotted a delicate set of glass and wooden doors. She pointed to them.

"There. There's an electronics store!"

"I see it."

Nonstop sped up, hit eighty eight, and ghosted into the building, ignoring the double doors altogether.

He had to swerve the bike sideways through shelves of merchandise before reaching an area open enough to materialize into. The space directly in front of the sales counter offered the best option, and he used it to phase them in, braking hard, less than two feet from the wall of the counter.

Grace swung off the bike.

"Wow. Look at this place," she said, gazing around, following her own advice. The interior sparkled wherever sunlight met it. Chromed pedestals dazzled under electronic pendants and broaches, flexbooks and tablets, black and white and chrome and purple. Grace looked over the small machines as she scouted for the items she'd need. She spotted some in the lit recesses of the back wall.

"What are we looking for?" Nonstop asked.

Grace hopped up onto the counter, spun her legs over it, and walked quickly to the back wall. "Here," she said, as she began rummaging through the items on the shelves, "We need something with some editing software on it. I need a cable that can link my old camera to whatever we find. That might be it, but who knows, we might even need an old satellite phone by the time we're done. It depends on what the Internet connection is like. I'll need a few minutes to get a rough cut together and a few more minutes to upload. We might have to shoot some new stuff too."

"What about a phone?"

"I don't have this on a phone, it's on a camera. And your friend Skyde said that the service around here is out."

"So shoot some new stuff with a phone and I'll drive you to where the cell phones work."

"Okay, if we need to. My phone needs a charge, and they might be monitoring my account — we can get a burner phone set up here, but that will need to be charged too. I want something we can just plug in. Do me a favor — Go over to where —"

A rumble came from the street. Nonstop turned to look and so did Grace. Outside the windows, in the full light of morning, a wave of asphalt ten feet high rode past them. White lane-markers slid along the mound's back as it moved. Sidewalks snapped and heaved, producing a roar like a passing avalanche as the mound plowed forward. It tossed parked cars. It tossed a parked SUV onto the sidewalk. The SUV crumpled a mailbox as it rolled and tumbled.

The road kept moving. Within a second, it was out of sight. Nonstop stood amazed, and then ran to the window to look further.

"Wow. Did you see that?" he said at the window, too late to view anything but more ripped sidewalk.

He looked a second longer, and then turned back to Grace.

"What was that?" Grace asked, stunned.

"Some kind of Inter-D. Right?" Nonstop said, "I mean it has to be. That couldn't be natural right? Like an earthquake or an underground explosion or anything?" Nonstop rejected his own ideas. "Nah, that's an Inter-D. Maybe some kind of side effect."

He heard tires screech, and the distant sound of a crash. Grace heard it too. Shocked, they both heard the muffled sounds of humans screaming. A tiny sound, blocks and blocks away. Nonstop looked at the window, looked at Grace, looked at Rattletrap, and looked at the window again.

"Go," Grace said.

Nonstop faced her, and once she caught his gaze, she continued: "Go. You can help them. Go get that thing before it breaks whatever internet connection we've got!"

"But, but — okay, but I'll be back."

"No. Fix the portal." Grace said, "Help Krork. I'll be safe once the story's out. If you can't come back, I'll find my own way home. Now... let me work."

"I... lock the door after me," Nonstop said, and after he paused one more second, he walked to Rattletrap.

Grace ran from behind the sales counter and met Nonstop at the door. A small white box stuck out from the wall near the entrance. It flashed a small red light.

"I think that's an alarm, right?" Grace asked.

"I don't know. I guess so," Nonstop said.

Grace reached for it. She pressed the large flat switch on the side of the box, and the red light shut off. Nonstop moved to open the door, and Grace waved him back.

"I've got it," she said as she reached for the top frame and flipped the brass lever at its edge. She did the same for the lever at the bottom of the old wooden door, and pulled both doors open.

"That's great. Thanks," Nonstop said, straddling the bike and duck-walking it the last few feet to the doorway. "I'll be back."

Grace looked at him, took a step forward and stopped herself. She pushed the back of his T-Shirt.

"Go help them."

He nodded as he drove off. She quickly re-closed the doors and locked them.

* * *

**

The situation in Exeter had more nightmares to reveal: levels and levels of nightmare, from different worlds, from different realmlines, and from sources on Earth as well.

Creativity, matched with the desire to maximize power, had resulted in wounded men, their minds usurped, their neuro-networks hijacked, being grafted into war machines. And at that moment, in the skies above Exeter, three of those men, grafted into those war machines, rode piggyback on drone aircraft, standing rearward on each set of wings, grasping each set of twinned tail fins in their devised, robotic hands, leaning back as they flew, soaring, like charioteers in some lunatic techno-pocalypse.

The lead Lifer gazed downward and saw a parking lot move. It continued watching as the paved surface rose, and spread, and receded rapidly, first along one edge of the lot, then another. It saw fissures open in the asphalt. It saw black tar split, concrete crumble, and the raw ground below open and become cavernous. The Lifer watched, impassive to what it was seeing. It saw a red pickup truck upturned onto its side at the lip of a new ravine. Then it caught motion in its peripheral vision and turned to investigate: an orange vehicle drove a straight road that would lead it right to the pickup truck. The vehicle matched imprinting. Impassivity turned to something more demanding in the Lifer's shackled mind. The situation achieved priority status, and the Lifer recognized the change.

The Lifer raised its wrist to its ruined mouth, where its remaining human teeth shone from under the shredding cables of its removed-tooth ports. A green L.E.D flashed on the com-link nodule near the Lifer's collar, and the Lifer spoke into it, its voice a slow croak, its words articulated through closed jaws.

"They're... here sir. Exeter. Heading west," it said as it flew.

* * *

Bloch moved in his office, the room lit by a small lamp on his desk, the drawers of the desk open. Bloch pulled a folder from the top center drawer and placed it into a black shoulder bag. A quiet tone sounded from his com-link.

He took the sleek handset from his pocket and used it to receive the Lifer's communication. He listened. He smiled. He spoke.

"Excellent," he said, and then slid his fingers over the faceplate of the handset, patching select Lifers into the communication, "Lifer 3, Continue flyover; identify the extent of Norel's positions." he said, and then, hitting another section of the handset's screen, he addressed the Lifers he had placed on standby. "Gentlemen, you will soon be receiving refined coordinates from Lifer 3's team. Identify the coordinates that fall within your sector. Move to an observation position based on the new coordinates and stop. When you have established the new perimeter, move toward its center. Engage targets. Force targets to a single cluster."

* * *

Nonstop saw a wide gap in the shrub-covered fencing that edged the parking lot — an entrance, and he drove toward it. He was surprised when he saw two women run out into the street. They didn't head in his direction; instead, they ran to the road that bordered the lot — until one of the women saw him, and then she *did* start running toward him.

"Ayuda!" she yelled and repeated, lacing the word with other words, Spanish words, words he didn't understand. "Ayuda!" she repeated, and then the older woman grabbed her arm and started dragging her up the next street, stopping only long enough to face Nonstop and point to the parking lot herself, adding her own "Ayuda" to the commands she yelled at the younger woman.

Nonstop nodded, pointed to the parking lot, and called out "Ayuda. Help. Si." as he drove in.

Only inside the fencing did Nonstop get a true idea of the lot's size. It seemed to go on for a mile in every direction; he had to turn his body to see it all. He could see the monster too; the hump in the road, still moving, calmly, far off. He watched as it slid from one edge of the parking lot to the other. What ever it was, it rebounded off the curbing below the lot's fencing. It kept a steady rhythm, and as he watched, Nonstop listened to the low, steady rumble its movements made: something like a wooden beam being dragged across a driveway. The movement seemed pensive, a temporary calm, like the pacing of a predator, waiting for wounded prey to weaken.

With that idea in mind, Nonstop moved. He could smell dirt. There was only one situation that needed dealing with as far as he could see: the red pickup knocked onto its side, super-close to the edge of this new hole in the ground — this new rip in the ground. *Deep though* — this new rip in the *Earth*. Nonstop jumped off his bike, grabbed the rescue rope from under Rattletrap's seat, and bounded over to the truck, which was so close to the edge, that the tip of its passenger window looked down into the drop. He heard moaning; he thought he heard low talking too. Someone left behind — *hurt* — had to be — but awake — saying something to himself.

"Hello! I'm here," Nonstop called, "I'm going to help — ayuda!"

Nonstop noted again how close to the edge the truck was. If enough dirt fell away beneath it, the paving might crack and the truck might fall in. A quick glance told Nonstop that that was a very real worry. All along the walls of the fissure, he could see crumbling stripes of dirt and rubble falling into the rift.

He got to the truck — he'd tie the rope to the door handle, tie the other end to Rattletrap, pull the truck back onto its tires and then get the guy out.

— No.

No good.

Close up, he could see that the truck didn't have handles — not the kind he could use as cleats. Instead, he found a number keypad and a latch, a metal flap you could stick your fingers behind and pull, but nothing he could tie a rope to — Where was the monster? — he turned to look. The asphalt wall was still sliding, but he witnessed as it reversed direction, nowhere near the far edge of the parking lot. Its pacing route was now shorter. What should he tie the rope to? The side mirror? No. Shorter pacing? The monster's run was shorter — what did that mean? — Side mirror — If he tried to use the side mirror to tip the truck, he would just pop the mirror off, or worse, he might get the truck halfway righted and *then* pop the mirror off. That could send the truck rocking — maybe rolling right into the ravine. He saw no side rails on the truck bed. Any roof rack? How hurt was the guy inside?

To see, Nonstop would have to climb onto the truck, would have to add his jumping weight to the truck. And what would his added weight do to the truck's balance? Maybe he didn't need to jump; or, at least not jump heavy, like a bear or anything. He could staircase — tire, tranny, tire, then a cat jump, maybe, light, to the cab behind the door — staying as far from the roof as he could manage.

The monster. Where was it? At the far fence, rebounding. Nonstop glanced at his tap — holstered at his thigh. His hands were full of rope and he had to climb. He tossed the rope onto the door and its landing made soft clattering noises, like a volley of hail. The man inside the truck yelled "Help! Help!"

"Yeah, I got you brother; I got you," Nonstop called back, loudly, as he started climbing, doubting the man could understand him, but knowing that the sounds of his voice were needed.

The truck rocked under Nonstop. The guy in the cab must be moving, risking everything now that help was so close. "Stay still! Stop moving!" Nonstop yelled, and as the truck jostled, he reacted without thinking, finding himself on top of the truck cab — near the door - and a little surprised to be there, his staircasing hadn't registered with his mind. He could see the ravine from his new position; out of the corner of his eye. It dropped away into a great darkness beyond the red rim of the truck bed, and he didn't dare turn to look further. He opened the truck door, and looked in the cab instead.

He saw the man, in a white T-shirt, sweating, looking right back up at him, with eyes that seemed huge and white. The man kneeled on the passenger door, leaning his chest into the seat padding, holding his left leg with one hand and reaching to Nonstop with the other. At the sight of Nonstop, the man began speaking, Spanish, a language Nonstop knew only little of.

"I gotcha," Nonstop said to the man, and then Nonstop looked away, getting back to work. He could tie the rope around the open door. He — no. The steering wheel was closer. He tied a quick hitch knot to that, and spoke to the man in the truck, repeating "I'm gonna get you out." The man jabbered language back at him, neither man understanding the other. Nonstop lifted the tag end of the rope: "You pull this," he said. The man nodded. Nonstop turned to check the monster — moving, turning away from the far fence as if it were steering to miss it, picking up speed. Nonstop glanced down at the man as he got the door's window open enough to feed the rope through. He gave a quick thumbs up, closed the door, and hopped off the truck.

He hit the ground running, feeding out rope behind him. What was his next move? Get the guy out — get him away from the breaking street-monster — then a hospital? — ghost him to the next state maybe? — ghost him five blocks from here? — take him back to the electronics store? — Nonstop didn't know. He watched the Monster as he ran.

Maybe it was his pounding footsteps, but the monster stopped its sliding movement and gathered into one concentrated spot, growing into a large hill, no longer sliding in either direction.

Nonstop worked the rope, and had the second hitch knot half tied by the time he reached Rattletrap and threw the rope around Rattletrap's control bar. He got the knot completed, but before he started the bike, he thought he ought to —

— the mound started moving, slowly, closer, not fast. Not yet. But soon, probably soon.

Nonstop undocked his tap, cocked it open, and rapped the ground with it. He started the bike. It rolled forward and the rope pulled taut. The monster moved faster. The truck behind him didn't move, and then the monster charged.

Nonstop saw the surging asphalt and fired directly at it, a sustained blast, but the mound didn't vanish; there was no blue glow.

It retreated though. The mound retreated from the tap.

Then the asphalt wall glided to his left, coming nearer. Nonstop fired his tap at the mound's leading edge, the left side, and the mound moved right.

Nonstop kept the bike driving; the rope pulled tight, and the pickup began to tilt. His tire slipped against the blacktop and kept on slipping against the blacktop. Too light. The bike was too light and the truck was too heavy. The monster turned its retreating curve into an advancing wave. Nonstop swung his tap to the monster's far right and kept firing. The mound moved left, but got closer. Nonstop was in danger of the truck pulling him back. He worked Rattletrap's claws, but they couldn't find purchase in the asphalt. He rolled a thumbwheel on the control bar and the multi-tire went smooth, like a dragster's fat slick.

The new surface gave him great contact with the dry asphalt and his traction improved. Rattletrap pulled. The rope shook. The bike shimmied sideways. Nonstop watched his wheel as he continued firing with his tap, trying to keep the monster at a distance if he couldn't send it home outright.

The bike lurched forward as the truck thumped and squeaked behind him, bouncing as it righted itself onto its four wheels, and at this, the wall of asphalt charged.

Nonstop fired. The asphalt shrank at the point where his beam touched it, but grew and advanced on either side of the beam, coming anyway.

Nonstop heard the man cry out behind him, and then heard the truck start. He stole a quick look back and saw as the driver struggled behind the wheel — in pain, but determined — not to be rescued, but to drive.

Nonstop yelled for the driver to release the top end of the rope, to pull the tag end out of its loop, but all the driver did was shove the rope aside on the wheel, look at Nonstop long enough to wave a trembling thank you, and slap the truck into gear. The truck started backing up.

Nonstop yelled to the driver, then turned to fire at the asphalt again. It had regrouped into a single shape and his shot hit the mound dead on, stopping it. Then his shot flew wide as Rattletrap was yanked sideways.

The truck was leaving, rope or not.

Rattletrap slid backwards.

"Pull the top rope!" Nonstop cried as the truck dragged him. He looked back at the monster; moving again. He tugged the tag end on his own part of the rope and tried to feed it free, but the bike was being pulled, and the rope yanked tight every time he got it loose. Rattletrap continued moving, turning and shifting to places Nonstop wasn't asking it to go, and by the time he got the rope fully loosened, he was blind to the position of the monster.

The rope raced suddenly away, free, and lost forever as it followed the truck's bouncing, backward ride toward the street, leaving Nonstop pointed at the ravine.

A low wave of asphalt passed beneath him, rocking the ground in a single, sea-sick motion. As it did, Nonstop turned to gauge the creature's position, looking up in time to see a towering wave of asphalt rush toward his left side. With the ravine straight ahead of him, he shot Rattletrap backwards.

The asphalt wall moved past him and instantly collapsed. Its base continued surging forward — widening and spreading as its top sank in on itself. Then the entire length of the wave's side wall began to swing toward Nonstop, sweeping like the second hand of a clock — like the advance line on a radar screen.

Nonstop saw the attack coming, even as he saw a flash of the red truck through the far-off fencing, racing up the same street the woman had escaped to. He pointed his tap at the outer edge of the oncoming wave, at the sweep — at the absolute *hammer-blow* flying his way. His beam hit, and the asphalt mound, hammer-blow and all, shrunk back. Only a series of ripples in the ground plane reached Nonstop, passing underneath him, as harmless as spent eddies on a shoreline.

And then calm.

He looked around. The parking lot stood quiet and still. The sky to his right shone with a greenish tint, as if thunderstorms were coming. A row of strange creatures flew out of the darkened air, black in silhouette, and then almost cream-colored against the blue sky when they hit direct sun.

What should he do? Could his team leave with this weird asphalt Inter-D here? Or those flying bugs? His team could come back for the Inter-Ds. Once the Outpost was gone, and the others were safe, the *"Thrill Kings"* could come back and take care of this road puddle and whatever else was keeping it company. Right? That was the plan, Right?

He drove forward, on a diagonal that would avoid the ravine and follow the pickup truck out of the lot.

A saw blade of asphalt rose and sank in the path ahead of him. He shifted course, and another appeared. He stopped the bike and looked. All around him, in a perfect circle, dark saw blades of asphalt rose and fell, rose and fell, trapping him, circling him like a ring of sharks, waiting for the right moment to attack.

The darkness in the sky crept closer. Creatures flew in it. A wind hit Nonstop's face.

* * *

Krork stood by Sunset in front of the large white portal, both braced against the wind that swirled through the field. The light near the portal made the yellow of Sunset's jumpsuit and the yellow of Krork's skin stand out from the colors around them. It had the same effect on Diamondsong's blue riding uniform and Brickyard's teeth, making them all actively iridescent.

Together, the four Bike Pilots fired their taps into the large white portal. They fired high at the edges and low along the sides, and then from the edges to the center, and from the center to the edges, but they achieved no results. The portal stood as it had before.

"Do you think it's too big?" Brickyard called to Krork.

"Maybe," Krork said loudly, holding up his hand to block his face from the flying dirt, "but taps get stronger when the fields they're fighting get stronger, and mine feels like it's doing nothing."

"Yeah? What do you think that means?" Brickyard called back, and Krork shook his head.

"It's absorbing the tap? Ignoring it? I don't know," he said.

"What if we all hit the same spot instead of sweeping the edges?" Diamondsong said, looking from one teammate to another.

"Sounds good," Sunset said, aiming her tap at the lower edge of the portal. "Let's try the 7:30 position."

As they fired, the air around the portal grew dark and violet. The wind roared around them, sweeping the grass into great spirals that raced across the length of the field, and that changed direction whenever the wind shifted its angle of attack.

Three smaller disks of light fed out from the large portal and sailed away on the air currents. The main portal remained unchanged. The last portal to emerge curved away and doubled back along the tree line. When it stopped, it elongated, then reversed, passing through itself.

Sunset lowered her tap, eyeing the last portal. "That little one doesn't seem very stable. Let's see if we can get rid of it — try and get rid of one portal at least," she said, already stepping toward the glowing disk with her teammates following her.

It was hard to assess the small portal. It looked like it was spinning in place, while at the same time it seemed to be shifting its edges, growing wider, then taller, like two versions of itself overlapping, trying to align.

The team fanned into positions across the portal's face, and agreed to fire together at the middle of the top edge. They aimed, they fired, and at first, nothing happened.

"How long do we do this?" Diamondsong asked, leaning forward against the scouring wind. As she fired, she spotted something in the distance over Krork's shoulder, and pointed to it.

"Look, quick!" she said.

Her friends stopped firing and looked. In the distance, a small portal, hanging low in the air, actively sparkled as it slowly faded from view.

"We hit this one, and that one shuts down? Are they linked? Entangled?" Brickyard asked, raising her hand to shield herself from a salting of flying grit.

"Could be, I guess," Krork said, using his forearm to shield his eyes from the same flying dirt.

Diamondsong's helmet provided eye protection, but she raised a hand against the wind anyway. "So this big monster's not going to close until all the little portals are taken care of?"

"I don't know," Krork said, "Let's close the ones we can, and see if that changes anything."

* * *

Rik Ty

**

Violet light spread over Hedberg Avenue, an east-west road in the middle of Exeter. Every house on the street stood deserted. No dog barked. No resident peeked out from behind pulled curtains.

The eclipse light intensified. Street lamps came on. The only movement came from a drifting portal, which rolled down the blacktop like a slow motion tumbleweed, spreading and stretching as it moved, expanding and compressing as it inched along.

237th Street crossed Hedberg Avenue at the end of the block, and from it, a second portal, wavering similarly, came into view.

Each portal drifted toward the center of the street, gunfighters in this new west. They continued, slowly approaching each other.

Both portals teetered and swayed as they moved, the pulsing of their edges becoming more syncronized the nearer they grew to each other.

Finally their edges touched. White light burst up and down the street, strobing as the portals sank into each other; as they stretched into new shapes, as they tangled and pulled apart and crashed together — with the sounds of tearing electric fields accompanying every passing of every wayward edge.

New portals drifted onto each corner of the street. A third portal floated harmlessly through a small house. All three portals drifted toward the writhing, glowing portal in the middle of the violet road.

The portal that had passed through the house joined with the merged portal, and white light spasmed down the street again. Bursts of light continued spasming as the joined portals writhed and twisted into new shapes.

Both flanking portals drifted down the blacktop and merged with the spasming portal from opposite sides simultaneously.

The edges of the portals fought within each other, churning, engulfing, sometimes rhythmically, sometimes arrhythmically, until the portal became a glowing, erratic sphere. Portals crashed and fought within the shape, increasing speed until the sphere stabilized and the portal edges locked into an undulating rhythm.

The glowing light around the sphere slowly withdrew *into* the sphere, absorbed into the intensifying light of the sweeping portal edges, revealing in the gaps, glimpses into other worlds, worlds that changed with each overlapping pass of the illuminated borders, first a world of lush greenery; then a stratified world of floating mesas; then a dark mushroom city, with a billion bioluminescent lanterns glowing; a new world with every pass.

No longer harmless, the churning portal sphere began to drift. It made contact with a lamppost, slicing clean through it, sending sparks flying as the lamppost's interior cables severed and its steel cap fell to the street.

A new portal appeared at the far end of the next block, near a spot on the sidewalk where the sunlight made a bright border with the darkened eclipse light.

The portal sphere drifted slowly toward the new portal. The new portal drifted slowly toward it.

* * *

Skyde dropped below the surge at the ten mile mark. The air was calmer, but as she looked back, that seemed temporary. A trident of dark weather fronts approached from the east. It didn't look like things were getting better. She checked her data-box. The haze spot was still a bit south of her, but it hadn't changed in intensity. It was still weak.

She passed a deserted highway, and then flew over a field. She saw vast spills of fresh earth, dark, richly colored. She saw pillars of exposed rock. She saw debris and charred grass. Then she saw the wreckage of an Army copter — a black Chinook, and then she saw a second, mangled Chinook, half twisted into the ground. How does a helicopter wind up half buried in the ground? Taken together, the sights made a great semi-circle of displaced earth and exposed rock formations that jutted out of the ground like giant dinosaur teeth, though if this were a dinosaur, it would be the size of a County.

There were no soldiers on the site, no rescue teams. There was haze, but it was weak.

She flew a loop around the area. The ground displacements, what was it about them? What did they remind her of besides dinosaur teeth? What was tugging at the back of her mind? She looped a little higher, looking down on the area with a wide...

A den. The semi-circle looked like a den. An underground animal of some kind? — very, very large? Was the haze signal weak because it was only residual? Or because something gigantic was still underground and the earth was shielding it? How big would it have to be? How far underground did it have to be to register so weakly? How big a problem was this?

Portal or not, she thought she should have a ready answer to that question, that question at least — though getting it would be terrifying.

She'd have to ghost. Not easy with an un-wheeled vehicle. She'd have to ghost, and she'd have to sustain the ghost underground, flying through solid earth. If she faltered, she'd materialize underground. She'd be as buried as the helicopter.

Was she going to do this?
Yes.
So get on with it.

She looped high, standing upside down on her board at the apex of her run. She activated a shoulder-light on her gear harness in case the displaced stone and earth indicated a cavity underground — even if it did, she mustn't stop. If the cavity proved small, she might not be able to reach eighty eight again. No. One loop in. One look around, then north to the upper edge of the Bleed Zone.

She looped downward toward the earth. Thirty feet above the ground she began to ghost. Green light enveloped her and she slipped into the ground.

The ghost light colored some distance in front of her eyes, but it was less than an inch. A steady cascade of pebbles and soil played out in her sight line, along with occasional fields of rock.

Don't blink; don't turn your head, just ride out the loop, see what happens.

The space opened instantly around her. A cavity. Yes. She thought she'd see an animal warren, instead, for the second she arced through the open space, the glow from her ghosting shed its light onto two Army trucks, both leaning nose-first into a pool of vapor. She saw the tires on the front of the trucks — what was left of the tires, floating on the mist, like oil on water, being pulled by mild currents. And she saw soldiers, dozens of them, lying on rock, and lying across the trucks that were sinking down into the vapor.

And the soldiers saw her. Several reached up weakly as she passed. And then she hit solid earth again. Rock and dirt flying past her eyes in a rapid progression. Those soldiers were alive — *don't move, don't blink*. Is that vapor poisonous? *Don't blink. Ride it out.* Are they using up their air? What will that vapor do to them if it's dissolving truck tires?

And then she was out in the wide air. Free to breathe, free to blink.

How could she help? Were there any explosives in the helicopters? Would she just cause a cave in? Would Norel have any equipment in the basement that could free those men?

She turned back down and flew inches above the ground, looking for gaps in the land displacements. Looking for any idea. She saw a crease between two boulders. A small black gap, it looked like it offered an airway down into the cavity, but it was shouldering a small pile of stones and debris. She stopped her skyboard and stepped onto the ground. She reached into the gap, but her arms weren't long enough to clear everything. She tried her leg, which was much longer, but it wouldn't fit. She'd have to find something. She took off again, flying over the field of debris, looking for an idea. Radios, guns — could she shoot the debris free?

She saw a length of rotor blade and swooped down for it. When she picked it up, it was lighter than she expected — some type of fiberglass, but sturdy. It would work.

She flew back to the crevice and fit the rotor section between the stones. She worked frantically. She couldn't stay. She dug at the blockage until the stones moved aside or fell into the cavity. The small hole might vent the vapor, or give the men some air. She hoped so. She wished she could talk to Varrage. If a grenade or a bullet could open up an airway, he would know.

Was there more she could do? Was there? She didn't know, couldn't think of anything — if there was someone nearby to speak to — to tell — but the place was deserted — the town itself was deserted. She could mark the site — leave — a note? A sign? — so that if someone passed by they could know what she had just seen underground? She had nothing to write with — no pen, no marker, no cardboard — she had the latest digital methods of communication, but nothing practical — let alone spray-paint or road flares.

Could she spell a message out in rocks?

Just one. Just one rock. That's all she needed. She looked down at the ground, at the newly turned soil — dozens of rocks — hundreds — she picked a gray one, rough and cratered, long and slender and flecked with bits of black. She stooped to one knee with the rotor still in hand and started scrubbing back and forth on its surface with the rock, leaving thin white scratch lines from her efforts. Excellent. She worked faster. A moment later the words

NEED HELP

stood out on the black rotor, and she added a thin arrow to the bottom of the message, pointing down.

She stuck the rotor in the ground near the vent she had widened. Narrow and tall, it grabbed attention. It looked like a grave marker - she hoped it wouldn't turn out to be one.

It felt pathetic. Nowhere near adequate. But it was all she could do at the moment, and it was done. She had to move on.

* * *

Outside, in the courtyard of Open Mind, the sun dappled through the tall trees. Bloch walked briskly to his black command vehicle, got in, and started the rover himself. His handset buzzed against his thigh. He pulled it from his pocket and answered it as he pulled away.

"Seventeen, what's the status on the perimeter?" he asked, and Lifer Seventeen's voice came over the handset, grated, slow, and deliberate.

"Perim-eter set, sir. Sev-eral a-reas of portal active-ity. Norel's teams. Creatures."

"Head in. Conventional ordnance. Break up the streets so that Norel's teams can't reach escape velocity, but use the jamming rays to clear the bikes. We don't want the machines damaged."

* * *

In a northern sector of the perimeter, Lifer 17 stood in the back of an army truck modified to act as its personal transport. The truck idled quietly. The Lifer stood, inactive for a second as its pulse light flashed over its right eye. Then it ratcheted its right forearm into a bazooka-like shell-launcher. That done, it answered its colonel.

"Com—ply-ing," it said.

* * *

**

Nonstop could not let his gaze lie still. There was no place he could afford not to be looking, except maybe the sky overhead. The ground under his bike was swirling. The center of the parking lot had taken on a bowl-like shape, huge and inexplicably moving, as if its entire acreage spun upon some giant potter's wheel, one that was abandoned, owner-less, and yet still running.

Nonstop had his tap at the ready. As the swirling ground carried him, he countered, never allowing himself to be too predictable a target: he drove forward, then backward, he'd hold still, he'd change course, all the while studying the swirling walls of asphalt, looking for a way out.

Timing-wise, the next attack seemed just about due. He decided to lure it. He bounced his bike in one spot over the moving ground, broadcasting his position with every thump of his wheel, and he watched, tap ready, reflexes set to dodge.

The attack came: a jagged mound of asphalt; fifteen feet high, eight feet thick, twenty feet long; rolling, and grinding into the spot where he had just been thumping. Nonstop had scooted a few feet to the side, and from the new position, he fired tap at the leading edge of the attacking mound and then spun backwards out of the way as a second, smaller attack wave launched from a different direction. He raced for the wall's upper edge, trying to escape, but the bowl-shape tilted to stop him.

"Not tired yet huh? Okay brother-man, but I'm getting your number," Nonstop said, suddenly leaning, and driving across the middle of the bowl. The bowl rose to counter him, keeping whichever portion of itself that faced Nonstop higher than Nonstop could drive. Nonstop tried a few attempts to get over the edge, but with the same result. Then he tried it a few more times as a stall, while he searched the ground for another idea. He looked to see if he could spot the direction of the asphalt's movement. He thought he could feel it through resistance on the bike, but he hoped to verify what he was feeling with what he could see. He let the ground pass under him, snapping his head in all directions — bird-like — watching for any sign of attack. Nothing new happened. The pavement remained occupied with its game of cat and mouse, and when Nonstop thought the ground had completed a full turn, he fired his tap into the asphalt and threw Rattletrap into reverse, pacing the lot, trying to keep the tap hitting a single spot.

And the ground changed direction. It was sudden, and it spun Nonstop and Rattletrap a good two turns before Nonstop could get them righted, just in time to dodge a succession of incoming strikes, crashing pseudopods of arcing asphalt. Nonstop backed up out of a cloverleaf of jagged strikes, and discovered the parking lot rim was very high, the bowl shape much smaller, and tilting to keep him in. *Must look like a volcano*, Nonstop thought. Nonstop was thinking that if he could breach the rim, he might be able to ride the slope all the way out of the parking lot before the Inter-D could counter, and maybe lose it somehow in the streets, ride on the sidewalks or something, but then a second thought hit him. *If the rim keeps getting higher, it will be able to close above me, and then a quick collapse will bury me.* He raced for the upper edge of ground as the moving asphalt tried just that.

Nonstop rose and the asphalt spired skyward to keep pace with him, higher and higher, the road thinning, the wheel touching less, until some limit was reached, and the spire collapsed. Nonstop rode it to the ground, where the parking lot leveled again: a great, wide, turning pan.

They were starting all over again.

Nonstop let out a slow breath. There was a line of shops at the back of the lot, starting with a king-sized supermarket. Maybe he could steer the asphalt towards it, use the surge as a ramp, and then confuse the Inter-D by driving onto the roof, fake it out.

That's when the first explosion hit. North of them. A low concussion, followed by another.

"Bloch's teams," Nonstop said out loud, possibly talking to the Inter-D hiding somewhere inside the ground. And just like that, the parking lot stopped swirling, and sank back to normal, flat and solid. The jolt surprised Nonstop and he nearly fell off his bike. He righted himself, and could see the Inter-D rippling to the edge of the parking lot and out onto the road, insanely fast, a wave under the asphalt, heading north.

"So, there's something you hate more than me huh? Good to know." Nonstop said as he started the bike up again, gave it some throttle, and jolted forward, instantly tossed from his seat. He slid over Rattletrap's air scoop and hit the ground, rolling with his shoulder. Rattletrap's arms saved its robot torso from slamming onto the parking lot's surface. Nonstop got to his feet, and looked at the bike. Tail high, torso low, with the bottom two inches of its wheel somehow embedded in the solid asphalt. *It trapped me. The Inter-D trapped me.*

"I don't believe this," he said out loud.

It wants me here until it can come back.

No way. Absolutely no way.

Nonstop ran a hand through his hair. Axe-hammer, what else? He hit a button on his control bar and a tool kit flipped out from the gear array under the vortex chamber. He selected a pry bar and a Phillips screwdriver and sat down on the asphalt. Placing the screwdriver point onto the ground next to the tire, he hit the screwdriver handle with the back of the axe-hammer. Thusly, he began chipping out his bike, grumbling and grousing with every strike.

* * *

Sunlight hit the shoulders of the two Lifers on Morgan Street as their forearms chugged and their launchers reloaded. Standing calmly, they aimed their arms at opposite ends of the street and fired a second volley of shells into the ground. Explosions followed, immediate and deafening. Glass rained from the nearby office windows and black smoke raced into the wind.

The Lifers fired more shells, furrowing the streets further, turning them into jumbles of undriveable asphalt. Lifer 4 fired a volley eastward. The shot hit a gas main and the explosion ruptured the remaining street instantly, knocking both Lifers off their feet. The burning gas gave rise to an enormous fireball that unspooled and expanded as it climbed beyond the buildings and rode up into the sky.

* * *

Even from the far end of town, Skyde could see the plume of rolling fire rise into the air, so small, she could have blocked it from her sight with her thumb. She had a pretty good idea what the sudden explosions meant: probably soldiers. Probably Bloch's men. Like most people, her instinctual reaction to violence was fear, but her reactions quickly narrowed to anger. Clearing the portals was going to be hard enough, and now it was going to be violent too. She went high for an overview.

As she flew, she studied quick glimpses of the conditions playing out on the streets below her. She saw coffee cups and napkins rolling in the wind. She saw a glowing portal standing near a snapped tree, the tree's wooden core bone-white against the darkness of its bark. She saw two waddling creatures, bristling like wet raccoons, dart behind the corner of a bank. She saw rooftops and power-lines. She saw a large flat section of cardboard pressed against the metal of a rooftop venting system, held there by the strength of the wind, and her mind intruded with an unwelcome irrelevance: "*That used to be a box*" she thought as she flew.

In the middle of one road she saw a car suspended three feet in the air, and had just enough time to notice that it wasn't moving, and that the shadow under it was soft and very dark. She saw a portal glowing in front of a jewelry store, so still and so out in the open, it might as well have been standing guard.

She flew along a street, and then immediately over its rooftops, and then down the length of the next street. She saw two moving portals, each heading north at about the same speed. She looked toward the horizon to see if she could determine their destination, and saw a third portal, moving across a fenced in construction site, traveling at an angle, but headed on an intersecting trajectory with the two other portals: all moving toward a dark band of cloud cover a few blocks up. Perhaps the dark band was fog, or mist, or some other type of atmospheric trick, something that glazed the land under it in strokes of twilight.

She accelerated toward the band.

As the rooftops swung under her, she caught a quick glimpse of something, partially blocked by a building at an intersection: a flash of flat army green, something large, perhaps a truck, perhaps a tank.

All the more reason to hurry.

* * *

It was the hardest thing they had ever done, and they were laughing. Slice leaned back against a building that was still standing and let his shoulders touch the brick. He took off his helmet and tapped Wazzi on the arm with it. "I don't believe it, a whole block of rampaging monsters and two guys took care of it. We should be on Bleed Zone duty all..." Slice heard a hydraulic whine that was distinctly *not* a monster. It sounded like a garbage truck.

Wazzi heard it too and was searching for the source, tap ready in case it was an Inter-D he could send home.

"Bikes." Slice said, "Get to your bike."

They ran. Wazzi's com-link was closed, but he heard Skyde's voice come out of Slice's data-box, halting, fighting against wind shear, "Everybody, Bloch's men are here. Be careful," she said, and then the com-link fell silent. Wazzi stole a look behind him and saw the barrel of a gun — *a cannon* — slide into view at the corner where the alley met the building.

Their bikes were moving by the time the Lifer stood fully in the street. *Just get away,* Wazzi's mind repeated as he wondered what he was seeing, what kind of new toy the Army was playing with. He saw instantly that it was a man, somehow, a man in green slabs of Army equipment. He saw it raise its arm. He saw the flashing light over its right eye. He saw its ruined face, and saw that it wasn't really looking at him — and he thought there wasn't enough time to turn the bike around, to get onto another street. No, not enough time. He was about to be shot.

Instead, the machinery of the Army toy's forearm started changing around. Slicing. Weapons? The bike turned, and he could no longer see the Army-thing. Now he wouldn't even know what killed him.

An Army truck drove into view two blocks ahead of them. Another one of the Army toys stood in the back of it, working levers that poked out of the cab's roof, and this time Wazzi felt that the Army-toy *was* looking at him — right at him. He sped to the next intersection, not shot yet. "This way!" he yelled, and he and Slice blazed onto the side street before either Army-toy fired a shot. Before either Army-toy even made an attempt to shoot.

They took the turn much too fast, especially with shattered brick all over the road. Both bikes shuddered along the curve as the riders turned. Their shoulders dropped close to the ground and then rose as they straightened their trajectories and found escape along the next road. And while the next road proved much better to drive on, neither rider felt safe. They both felt it. They both knew.

They were being corralled.

* * *

The Portal-Sphere stopped drifting west. It began revolving around a single point in the ground, cutting into the asphalt as it turned. It began to travel, cutting a curved furrow into the ground that, as the sphere continued traveling, expanded into a spiral.

The sphere began moving east, thrumming as its internal edges surged through each other.

Its path pointed it toward a two story home with a peaked roof: a small building, gleaming whitely in the thunderstorm light.

The portal-sphere advanced slowly. It reached a parked car and simply ate through it. The car didn't move, didn't bounce on its shocks, and even after it had been cut through, its remaining sections didn't fall until the portal had broken contact fully.

The portal traveled neatly through the sidewalk and across the lawn until it sank into the house and the house swelled — and then exploded in a burst of splintered lumber.

The portal-sphere continued eastward.

* * *

For the hundredth time, maybe the thousandth time, Varrage took a step in the dark turbulence and found it sweeping away from him, found the air around him clearing, and found the location around him transformed, but this time, when the turbulence dissipated and his new location became apparent, Varrage stopped moving.

Something churned in the street ahead of him, a bright portal, a sphere of portals. He stopped to see it fully, and to feel it.

He stepped again, and with his movement his knees bent and his arms spread wide. Each impact of his foot upon the ground caused an energy surge somewhere in his body, like lightning within clouds. Across his back, broad sheets of energy pulsed in and out of existence, matching the rhythm of the surges around the portal-sphere, seemingly linked to the sphere's raw power. Varrage continued advancing in this way, fingers tensed, and spread like claws, hunting prey somewhere beyond sight.

*

Overhead, Skyde studied the streets, and was in the right place at the right time to see Varrage step out into the open and walk toward the portal-sphere. He didn't look right at all. There were hard-edged sheets of something that looked like translucent light jumping all over his back, disappearing and reappearing instant to instant. And his posture was wrong: he looked like he was stalking the portal configuration, not moving to examine it. She saw also, that his tap was still clipped in its holster.

She swooped toward him, yelling to him, "Varrage! Get away from there!"

Varrage reached the threshold of the churning sphere, where he stopped, and turned to look up at Skyde.

"They'Re cOmINg," he said, and then he stepped into the portal, in between swipes of its glowing edges.

Skyde dove, and flew in after him.

*

She entered a realm-world where the hills looked like giant plant spores, like round islands pressed together, with curving spires that reached into the air, and with burrowing holes at the base of each spire. She turned left and saw glowing edges closing around an aperture to another world, a world with a moonlit hill. Varrage was walking on that hill, and she flew toward him. The sparkling line of the portal edge rode down the sky, and she crouched on her board to slip through.

"Varrage! Wait!" she called.

If he heard her cry, he gave no reaction. He simply kept walking up the hill, without breaking stride or slowing down.

When he reached the top of the hill, he looked out over the horizon. The energy around his chest beat erratically, leaping and receding. He sank to a crouch in a slow, smooth motion.

Skyde landed a few feet from him, stepped off her board and crouched too. She looked at Varrage, alarmed at the jumping energy signatures his body was producing.

"What's going on with you? Are you all right? Who's coming?"

He turned his head slowly toward her, and then slowly back to the horizon. This was Varrage, but this wasn't Varrage.

It pointed.

Far, far in the distance, between slicing bands of portal edge, Skyde could see an alien city in twilight, its buildings scaffolded with walkways that linked ornately bordered terraces.

And then she gasped, seeing the black, putrescent creatures that walked those terraces, shambling on long forearms and clawing on rear crab-like legs; creatures who had no more place on those terraces than she did. She stumbled from her crouch, and her hand braced her as she landed in the grass.

"Voracitors," she said.

She got back up. She unzipped the collar of her flight suit and pulled a pair of necklaces out from under it. The necklaces held small, white, triangular pendants, carved from Voracitor bone and hung from fine, braided cords. Skyde enclosed them in her fist, then turned to Varrage and spoke loudly:

"If they make a kill, Earth will become a hunting ground. We can't let that happen."

Varrage made no acknowledgment. He continued watching the horizon.

"There are soldiers who need our help," Skyde continued. "And Doctor Norel needs our help. Bloch's teams are blowing up the streets. There are - just lots of portals to close. The guys are closing them now, but they're closing them unprotected. Varrage, we need your help."

Varrage looked at the horizon. Skyde looked too.

An arc of portal edge swept the horizon, replacing the alien city with a landscape of moss covered boulders. Skyde would not allow herself to gasp again at what she witnessed, but she had to suppress the urge to do just that. The Voracitors walked in the new landscape too, continuing their approach step for step, as if nothing had changed.

"Varrage, we have to come up with some kind of plan. We have to get Doc out of here. Varrage?"

Varrage stood, the energy in him wild. He slowly opened his arms, his fingers spread apart and tensed, the energy at their tips bouncing white hot, like small acetylene torches, sharp as talons.

He looked at Skyde once more.

"BloOD," he said in a long, extended grate.

And then he leapt the crest of the hill and sped toward the horizon. Toward battle.

Skyde stepped on her board.

And went the opposite way.

* * *

The bikes that hadn't been hit roared down Berber Street, much too close to each other, frantic for a route of escape, frantic for the road space to hit eighty eight and ghost.

Lifer 9 strode in from the east, walking the double yellow line dividing the four driving lanes. It blasted the ground in front of the escaping drivers, and when they were out of range, it simply turned, and fired at other targets, leaving the escapees to its partners hiding in the cross streets to the west.

The walking machine blasted and fired, blasted and fired, and smoke drifted everywhere. Five blocks west, Lifer 6 was firing shells as well, closing in from the opposite direction.

Bike Pilots lay in the street. Despite the portals they had closed already, the job remained undone. Portals hung in the air up and down the avenue, indifferent to the explosions and the smoke and the screaming engines.

Threading a weave around the shattered road sections, four Bike Pilots raced to hit eighty eight. Two of them, Flashpoint and Swerve succeeded, ghosting out amid glowing fantails of swirling energy.

Lifer 24 stepped out from an alley and fired jamming rays into the third rider, Jumper.

The wall of pain hit his body and he let go of his machine, causing the bike to tumble and bounce and slam into his friend Toxic, sending his bike tumbling as well.

Toxic came to rest near the corner of the block, and a Lifer with a white 25 painted on its chest stepped into the street. It raised its jamming ray and fired, leaving Toxic to gasp and bleed with the other Bike Pilots on the road.

Lifer 25 activated its shoulder camera and scanned the street, capturing the broken roads, the rising dust plumes, the grounded vortex bikes, and the grounded vortex riders.

Lifer 25's camera also captured two Bike Pilots on the far end of Berber Street as they bent to pull two of their comrades from the road. The man inside Lifer 25 saw the Bike Pilots, but they meant nothing to him. The scrambling figures had not touched the bikes.

Lifer 25 contacted the Colonel, and sent him the video feed.

* * *

Skyde turned around on the moon-lit hill and saw nothing but the grassy landscape, no portal, no aperture to another world, no pathway that would take her home. She guided her board back in the direction she had entered from, and kept her eyes open.

She became aware of movement high over her shoulder. She caught the shimmer of a portal edge as it swept down the sky toward her. It would bring with it access to another world. What would she do if it weren't hers?

She studied the landscape before her. The hillside was dark, the grass shone silver in the moonlight. She spotted a faint dark patch in the air ahead of her, just about where Varrage might have come in.

She decided to test it.

* * *

Bloch pulled the rover to the side of the road. He did it without thinking; he was within sight of Exeter and he had the road to himself. He could have parked on the double yellow line if he had wanted to, instead, he followed habit.

He looked at the feed on his handset and grinned. Berber Street looked like a war zone, but it had many spots that were open and sufficiently wide. On the ground, as the camera panned, Bloch saw bike after bike after bike. His grin broadened.

He acknowledged reception of Lifer 25's video, and contacted the surviving Chinook's flight team.

"Chopper One. Southwest along Berber. We've got a whole road of downed bikes. Come and harvest."

* * *

As Skyde hoped, the dark air pixelated upon contact. It wasn't an open portal, but it was roughly where she might have entered this world. Though what did that mean? There might have been dark spots all over the portal-sphere. She didn't know anything about how portal-spheres worked. The thought flashed in her mind that this might even be the first portal-sphere that had ever existed — *ever*.

As she moved, she hoped to see Earth on the other side. And in the same instant, she hoped to help the soldiers, and hoped to help Doctor Norel, and hoped to warn her teammates about the Voractitors, and she hoped to somehow help Varrage.

One of the things she did remember her father saying, one of the intangible things she had absorbed into herself, was the idea that you should never hope more than you work. She'd test this residual spot, and then she'd do what she could.

She leaned the rest of the way forward and slipped through the darkling air.

She emerged into the violet eclipse-light of the Bleed Zone street on Earth, and continued flying to fully escape the portal sphere, not wanting to test its crackling edges to see if they would slice through her as neatly as they were carving through the surface of the road.

The buildings around her looked dark. Rows of street lights blazed.

She arced her view across all the sky she could see beyond the tops of the darkened buildings. Dark flecks of debris drifted in the air like armies of war-refugees. She found that the clouds still looked bright despite the dark glaze the air laid over them. How far did this twilight go?

As if in answer, the sun peeked out from behind the cloud she was watching. It had to be the sun. But what she looked at, looked nothing like the sun. Her sun, her mighty sun, now looked like an x-ray, a black circle with a jumping, silver corona pulsing around its edges. It was nothing she wanted to see.

She banked across the street in a long, sliding move, and then coasted into a gentle curve upward. As she glided, she turned to look at the portal-sphere.

It was heading east.

She would head east herself. She'd grab sky, and learn the extent of this band of darkness.

* * *

Lifer 3 flew in the rear position, behind its teammates. Its free eye was called toward movement above the rooftops to its right and it turned to look. In the distance, it saw a white figure on a white board, flying just above the buildings and picking up speed.

It watched for a second, and then another, and then its croaking voice spoke one word aloud.

"Matches," it said, and then it veered in pursuit.

*

Skyde, gladdened to see clear sky beyond the stripe of twilight, heard the screaming engine of the drone jet as it approached her. She turned to investigate, and her first thought upon seeing the thing that was rushing toward her was that she was facing an Inter-D, some monstrous creature the portals had pulled into this world. Then she saw the Army Insignia painted on the nightmare shrieking her way, and she dove her body forward.

Her board accelerated, and Skyde streaked back down below rooftop level, mindful of the street lamps and the overhead power cables, secure in the belief that no jet would follow her down below the roof line.

Lifer 3 reached the avenue Skyde escaped into and banked below the roof-line without hesitating. The Lifer wasn't actually on a jet. Its rig was much smaller. But it was easily as fast as Skyde's board, and perhaps much faster.

Lifer 3 raised its left arm and ratcheted its fore-most assembler into a jamming beam emitter. It re-gripped the left-tail fin, then turned its right fore-arm assembler into a rocket-launcher.

Skyde heard the screaming engine coming behind her — jet noise below the roofline, approaching from the middle of the road.

She veered left and flew over the sidewalk.

Lifer 3 drew closer, raising its left arm and aiming its beam-emitter... needing one more second...

Skyde cut speed — and veered out from the sidewalk — back over the street, banking to a lower position.

Instantly, the drone jet flashed over her head, and she rose, deliberately side-slipping the jet to avoid its exhaust blast. Rising, she sped up, aiming the bottom of her board at the shoulders of the man-machine — who was in the process of turning his shoulders — aiming a weapon her way.

Her board hit the rider and pushed its jet off course, but she never felt it; at the moment of contact, she was hit with a wall of pain so intense it momentarily froze every muscle directly under her skin.

The drone-jet bucked and spun, and the beam broke contact with Skyde. Her overwhelmed muscles would not let her scream. She tried to — she tried every second that her board pin-wheeled behind the jet. She had to stabilize — she spun — she saw the Lifer's jet smash through two wooden telephone poles ahead of her; she saw the transformer on the second pole explode — she saw waves of blue-white voltage leap over the man-machine as it let go of its jet. She saw blasts of yellow flame erupt from its right fore-arm. She saw the sparking end of an electric cable fall toward the street.

And then her tumbling arc showed her sky and clouds and the buildings behind her — she'd have to stabilize, or she'd —

crash.

She heard the enormous sound of impact as the jet smashed into the building — *a truly enormous sound* — so close she could feel it on her skin as well as hear it in her ears. She was rocketing toward the same point herself — she tried to swing her feet, but the cramping muscles in her legs fought her intent. She managed only to twist her board, and then forced herself to twist it again, trying to steer it — *anyplace* — anyplace other than directly into the rising fireball of vaporized jet fuel — which she saw, and felt, and at the last second, somersaulted over, clearing only by feet, less than the length of her board.

She hadn't noticed the secondary explosions. She was surprised when a length of brick wall leaned into her flight path. Impact diffusion re-routed ninety nine point nine percent of the blow when she hit, but the falling wall obliterated her flight line, and sent her careening along the roof beyond the falling brick. With the impact, her boots broke field contact with her board and she went tumbling across the rooftop alone, slamming her body, her head, her hips, her ankles, into the hard and hot paving of the roof, over and over again, impact diffusion having less and less effect, until she finally came to a stop and lay in a jumble on the roof's surface, unable to move.

The building shuddered under her. Dust rose. From far below she could hear the rumble and roar of collapsing bricks. The roof moved, and as the upper corner of the building leaned and toppled, she could do nothing more than ride the structure down to the ground.

* * *

Once a video hit the social networks it became legitimate news. The video didn't even have to be true. It just had to be true that it had been seen somewhere. Any network that wanted to, could report the fact that the video was making the rounds on the internet. If, after repeated viewings, the viewer began to accept the video as truth, coming from the networks that proposed to *tell* them the truth, that would be judged as the viewer's fault.

Grace's sensational material would get on the air, but she had trouble believing that would protect her. Bloch could kill her, and deny her charges as mere camera tricks. The story might go away. If she never showed up to dispute Bloch, it might be claimed that she was hiding, and that that was proof of her guilt. Someone would have to demand proof that she was safe. She needed the weight of the people to protect her, and to get that, she'd have to live through the day on her own.

She had the beginnings of some credentials. More importantly, she had peer contacts. Contacts interested in news, in documentaries, in truth, and in public disseminations of truth. Each contact offered their own network of contacts, which spread out until they overlapped.

As she'd hoped, Grace's postings spread like wildfire, mostly because the few people who knew her, believed her.

Grace had powered up the banks of display televisions in the store, including those that faced street-side in the picture windows. Most of the televisions showed the news channels, and soon, most of the news channels showed Grace's footage.

CNN showed Nonstop's face as he spoke by a campfire on a bluff in Hawaii. FOX showed a pan of the bike. The BBC showed Krork, close up and smiling, an alien, looking bemused at being on camera, speaking in English, and leaving, because he had better things to do. K.A.L. re-aired a story of a missing Grandmother.

The News Channels also showed Grace's latest footage. On some screens the shot showed a shaky run to the electronics store's door, then Grace's hand opening the door, then a change in light level as Grace stepped out onto the broken sidewalk and aimed the shaking camera over the small buildings. At that point the camera showed two machine-men riding piggyback on two miniature F-15s. And then the camera zoomed, shakily, in on the flying machine men, showing the rippling air of the heat exhaust, and showing the white letters on the green steel that read: U.S. ARMY. MC-8.

* * *

The remote to the TV was in Colonel Wyatt's desk, in the middle drawer. The small television set stood across the office, on a sideboard of wooden cabinets. Wyatt stood in front of it with his arms folded. His aid Henderson stood watching the television as well, feeling astounded, betrayed, and decidedly uneasy.

"What is that thing? Do you think it's real?" Henderson asked.

"I don't know. It looks real," The Colonel answered absently, "'MC-8' is a number that would fall within Bloch's unit." The Colonel strode to his desk and reached for the phone receiver. "The President is going to want answers. The Generals are going to want answers. See if you can raise Bloch on the phone. I doubt it, but try. Then alert Tesson that we may need every chopper he's got."

The phone under his hand started ringing.

* * *

Lieutenant Camille viewed a large monitor at her desk. The screen showed three things: a video feed of a docked cargo ship, a video feed of Grace's broadcasts, and a basic computer folder entitled

"HAIRSTYLES". She dragged Grace's broadcast to the folder, and spoke into the black handset she held to her ear.

"Sir, I am feeding you a signal now. A woman is broadcasting in Exeter."

In the rover, Bloch looked at his handset and said, "Broadcasting? Now? You mean live?" and as the video began on his handset, the lieutenant's voice came through as well.

"Current at least," she said, "And there could be other cell phone cameras in the area."

"There probably are, but we have the local cell towers shut down. We control the airspace over the three towns, and we have all passing satellites requisitioned to us. We just have to worry about getting the bikes and getting out."

"Sir, we have to assume Command is seeing these broadcasts as well."

"Don't worry about Command Lieutenant. We've got the bikes. We'll be telling Command what to do."

"We're leaving a large footprint sir. We're tearing up that town. You've got three Lifers down already, do you know that? Lifers 3, 4, and 28."

"4 and 28, that's the gas main that blew? The explosion took them out?"

"Not immediately. The explosion was on Morgan Street. They're down three blocks north-east of the gas main explosion, alive, but non-functioning. The same with Lifer 3. His Raptor is down, crashed. He is alive but non-functioning. Sir, the ship is ready. Can we continue this operation from the ship?"

"Lieutenant, there's a bit of street sign in this video you sent me. Work it until you can read it. Then triangulate the broadcast site, and send it to the nearest Lifer team."

"Sir, can't we just go now?"

"The copter hasn't even landed yet. Don't go weak on me Lieutenant."

"I'll have the position in a few seconds, Sir."

"We're going to write the rules Lieutenant."

Bloch frowned. He looked through his windshield at the Exeter skyline, low as it was, and slid his hands along his steering wheel. Lieutenant Camille spoke through the handset again.

"The corner is Clinton Place and Davidson Avenue. Shadows indicate that the woman is broadcasting east of Clinton and Davidson."

"Patch it through," the Colonel tapped an area on the handset screen, and spoke. "Gentlemen, you are being fed a target area, east of the intersection of Clinton Place and Davidson Avenue. A woman is broadcasting there. Shut down all activity. Top priority."

Bloch broke the connections and quietly asked himself where Chopper One was.

* * *

Lieutenant Camille looked around her, reached under a manila folder on her desk, and ran her fingertips over the two damaged lenses she had hidden there. She pulled the red lens out first, casually, and placed it on her lap, hiding it with her back. She looked down at the lens. As she moved, the light played across its faceted surfaces, shining dully in the indirect light. She moved the lens out of her shadow, and its appearance changed as the light played over its many planes, making some dark, some dull, and some brilliant.

She looked around her, not sure where to turn her back, not sure where the cameras, *if there were any cameras*, might be hidden. Finally, she succumbed to temptation, and lifted the lens to take a better look. She shifted it slowly in her hand, and the light danced across it in all the expected ways, but within its translucent facets, she saw what looked like other layers of facets, one deep inside the other. If so, the lens wasn't cut. *Was it glass?* Was it made in layers? Was it grown? Was its depth simply an illusion?

No. While its top surface was perfect, whole groups of its inside facets were damaged, their sharply edged planes filled with tiny black pinholes, each edged with cloudy, abraded rings. Taken together, the pin-holed facets made parts of the lens itself seem cloudy, but in truth, the cloudy appearance was caused by these facets within the lens that had — *what*? - melted? exploded? *tunneled?*

Lieutenant Camille put the lens down and reached into a shoulder bag by her feet. She pulled out two tan colored T-shirts, wrapped the lens she was holding in one of them, and put the T-shirt back in the bag. Then she pulled out the blue lens, and did the same thing to it.

She took one more look at the ship on her monitor; the ship bound for the port city of Callao, and closed the program on her computer. She hit a key combination on her keyboard, and a white rectangle expanded on the screen, presenting the words AUTO-

SCRUB in the title space above a thermometer bar that was just beginning to advance.

The lab suddenly looked too small, the cabinets too tall. It seemed as if, with a single decision, she had changed the physical world.

She grabbed a few papers from her desk, added them to the shoulder bag, and then left, the sound of her heels filling the room as she departed.

She walked toward the stairs, her mind working, alert for — the small picture frame would do. Inside the frame was a warning to take the stairs instead of the elevators in the case of fire. Yes. Fire would be another good reason to avoid elevators; the first being that "people" could cut the power to elevators and you could wind up trapped. "People" could lock the stairwells too for that matter.

Lieutenant Camille lifted the plastic frame from the wall, and placed it between the door and its frame as she entered the stairwell. She'd at least be able to get back in if the door at the bottom of the stairwell were locked.

She took the stairs quickly, turning smoothly at each landing; it was only on the last few steps that her knees trembled. She saw the final door of the stairwell. If there had been a camera on her in her office, and the Colonel had seen what she had done, or if there were some type of tripwire system that had alerted the Colonel of her melting hard drive, the door would now be locked.

She had changed her whole world. Now she would learn if she had ended it too.

She raised her hand, felt the ridges on the door's aluminum bar as she touched it with her palm, and pushed.

The door opened and nothing else happened. Was it possible she was free? She walked briskly through the hangar to the courtyard entrance.

Dangler lay in the workbay of a small crane buggy, still wrapped in the hoist straps that had lifted him from the ground outside the Atrium. His gun pets stood at his side, looking up at him like worried dogs. There was a good chance he'd live. If not, the sea could have him. She had her own muscle strapped to her thigh, and even more in the shoulder bag.

"Go ahead, get in," she said to the spider-guns, gesturing toward the buggy's workbay. The guns pointed at her, as if considering, and only then, when she was looking directly down the black barrel-holes of the weapons, did she fully realize she was not talking to someone's pets.

The guns obeyed her. They turned, and spider-stepped around the buggy and into the workbay. One gun had a bent leg, but that was the only damage visible from the recent falls both guns had taken.

The lieutenant got behind the wheel of the buggy. She drove it out to the van she had selected. She parked the buggy and then worked to get the wounded Lifer into the back of the van. She disconnected the pulley system from the crane and threw the loose ends down next to the Lifer unit's legs. When she was done, the spider-guns crawled in next to their master. She closed the rear door and locked it; then she walked around the van and got into the driver's seat.

And then she drove; and as the wheels turned, Alicia Camille, the young Lieutenant, left Open Mind, left the Colonel, and left the Army, forever.

* * *

The pilot of Chopper One wore his helmet with the visor down and his bio-light activated. He flew the bird with full confidence, secure in the knowledge that he was protecting his brain from lasting damage.

He landed on Berber Street with no problem. The four open lanes, plus the two unused parking lanes, provided more than enough room, and with his visor down, that's all he paid attention to. The state of the town as he flew in never fully registered with him: not the broken streets, not the drifting smoke; not the walking tanks, not even the flying monsters. He saw them. He avoided them. But they didn't register.

He, his co-pilot, and his engineer, concentrated on their mission: landing safely, getting the rear door open, taking on field cargo, and awaiting further orders. These were the things they did. And when the huge robot-soldiers started pushing bike after bike into the rear of the copter, it didn't seem odd to them at all.

* * *

Lifer 13 and Lifer 8 flew eastward toward the large portal. At one hundred feet they pushed against a strong headwind. At three hundred feet, flying was easier, but visibility to the ground was obscured by the strange air effects. Lifer 13, flying lead, never saw the portal, and overshot the eastern border of the mission zone by five miles. Lifer 8 followed right behind, and overshot the portal position as well. The two Lifers doubled back at one hundred and fifty feet, and restarted the westward sweep of their reconnaissance.

At one hundred and fifty feet they were still above the turbulence, and it was easy to see the ground below them. They approached the field and noticed the large, glowing white disk set within it. The disk stood in the center of a two mile circle of violent ground turbulence which extended well beyond the local field. There were smaller disks of glowing light in the air around the large light disk. There were damaged fences behind several of the homes bordering the field. The Lifers saw all this, but did not react: the situation warranted only low priority status.

The Lifers saw Norel's agents in the field near the large portal, on foot, banded closely together, and this was also granted low priority status. Only the large yellow vortex bike in the field was tagged as high priority. Lifer 13 called its position in to the Colonel.

Upon passing the large portal, the Lifers separated, Lifer 13 flying the northern half of the field and Lifer 8 flying the southern.

It was Lifer 8 that spotted Outpost 14 near the water tower.

"Matches," it said aloud. Then it banked south to curve around for a second look. On the next pass, it shot video, and patched the video through to the Colonel.

Flying westward, back over the afflicted streets, it spoke into its com-link.

"Spotted... Building... Sir. Matches... Video... Records.

* * *

Inside Outpost 14 Norel worked hastily, orchestrating which aspects of which systems received which degree of the available power. He no longer heard the wind howling outside — it had stopped registering with him a while back. Then the wind made a second sound — maybe — and he stopped to listen to it. Yes, maybe, a second sound, but already fading.

Less than a minute later, the sound came again, and this time he paid attention to it immediately. It was faint, and it was brief, but he knew it — *jet engines*. Bloch was here. The Outpost had been spotted.

He turned to a second console and powered it up. The console became active and he typed a few commands into it. Several control panels lit up in the consoles around him. He kept working, watching the console's monitor.

*

Outside, the vortex ring surrounding the Outpost's roof sputtered to life, glowing first in one spot, then another; these light pulses slid back and forth inside the ringed chamber until their strength stabilized. At that point, the light pulses began racing around the roof until the entire ring blazed with bright green light, and then the entire building became enveloped in the same green light.

*

The monitor in front of Norel flashed the warning:

INSUFFICIENT POWER
DISENGAGE REALM-JUMP

Dr. Norel read the warning, let out his breath, and nodded. Then, without doing anything further, he turned back to his original workstation, and continued prepping the building for re-activation.

* * *

Bloch leaned forward in his seat when he saw the video of Norel's building on his handset — Norel's building was here. Norel *himself* was most likely here, and that meant, if he was right in his thinking, that the documentation of the technology was here — in its entirety — the blueprints, the testing data, the underlying theories — all the elements he'd have to manage in order to move forward. All the elements he'd need to parcel out in order for the project to be realized — not in five to ten years, but in five to ten months. After two years of blind hunting, he had forced the pacifist to return, and now, with so many rewards from the day already, there were suddenly so many opportunities for more.

So easy.

So fantastically easy.

He tapped the handset.

"Lieutenant, Norel is here! We'll have the bikes *and* the plans. We have... Lieutenant?"

He heard nothing. He jabbed the handset again, and still heard nothing. Camille was not answering. Not answering? In trouble?

Deserted?

Really? Yes, and likely. Lieutenant Camille may indeed have deserted her post.

He looked at the town of Exeter a few miles distant. He saw smoke, and light flashes, and long, dark tendrils of what looked like glowing darkness, negative light maybe?

Alright then.

He'd deal with the Lieutenant soon, but first he'd finish dealing with Norel.

He put the rover in drive, raised the handset to his lips, and headed into Exeter.

* * *

**

Something hit the street outside the electronics store and exploded. Grace screamed. Something *else* hit the street outside the electronics store and exploded, and then something hit the flipped-over SUV on the sidewalk and it exploded too, bursting into a bright ball of flame and blowing the store's picture window to bits. Grace covered her head as the window pieces flew into the store and broke further against the toppling computers and cell phones. A small slice of glass grazed Grace's left cheek, and she felt a tiny stream of blood well up on her skin.

She snatched her small camera up from the collection of hardware she was working with and yanked its connecting cords from their ports. She looked across the rest of the counter. *What would make a good weapon?*

There was nothing. The closest thing was a long outlet strip. She grabbed it, and ran with it and her camera to the back of the store, away from whatever was coming toward her.

*

Two Lifers, one marked 7 and one marked 22, lumbered on the adjoining street a half block away, not yet able to face the store directly.

*

Grace reached a door, which led deeper into the building. She passed through it, and entered a dark corridor, which was lit only by a ring of windows down at its far end, where the corridor linked with other corridors.

The hallway's condition shocked her — the showroom had been bright and clean, but the corridor was dark and full of empty cardboard boxes. The paint on the walls was blistered and peeling. The walls themselves were scraped and marred with patches of exposed plaster and shadowed gouges. She touched her cheek. Her finger came away wet. No glass, but she could already feel the rough surface of her blood drying, already knitting her its small layer of protection. She ran toward the windows. She was on the ground floor; if the windows led to an alley, she could escape.

She reached the windows and noticed a cluster of tall weeds outside them, bright green in the sunlight. She didn't see an alley, but there still might be one. Attached to the window's bottom slat she found two metal clasps, hooked and flat, lumpy from too many coats of paint. She put the power strip on the window ledge and reached for the clasps. Her camera, its cord looped around her wrist, clanked against the short section of wall below the window. She paused long enough to jam the camera back in her tool belt. Then she reached for the clasps again.

They were filthy, caked with dust, and she cringed when she touched them. She pulled, but the window moved only slightly. She looked up at the top of the frame: the twist lock looked open, but sealed in paint, or at least coated to the point where it wouldn't open easily. She tried moving the latch, and cringed again as she touched its grimy surface.

The latch, open or not, wouldn't move. The window wouldn't move. She banged its frame around the lock with her fists, and then gripped the painted frame around the lock, pushing up with her palms. As dirty as the clasps were, the frame near the twist lock was even worse. A natural shelf, it had proven a worthy resting place for years, *maybe decades*, of falling dust and dying flies, and as her fingertips — as *all* of her fingertips — touched its surface, she had to turn away and gag.

But she pushed, and the window moved a little more. And she banged, and the dust flew in clouds she could see against the sunlight, and she held her breath and she pushed harder, and to her satisfaction, the window opened a little more. Still just a crack, still just three inches, but even if the window never opened fully, she'd still be able to crawl out with a few more pushe —

— BAM — *Something blocked the light, slamming against the glass — filling it with —*

350

— guts — and wet cartilage, — and raw chicken-cutlet stuff with moving stick legs busy slipping against the glass — a creature — a monster trying to get in. Grace screamed loudly, took a step back and then grabbed for the powerstrip on the window's ledge. As she touched it, one of the creature's pale, jointed legs found the opening of the window and reached in. The leg was thin but much too substantial, much too real. It was from another world, another *dimension*, and now it was right next to her hand. Right next to her skin. She was alone, in a filthy hallway, with explosions going off in the streets, and now, little by little, a monster was getting into the building with her.

She pushed down on the window frame. The window wouldn't move. A second leg tip entered the window opening. Grace backed away screaming, the powerstrip clutched to her chest, her mind in paralysis, overwhelmed with revulsion and fear.

She ran. Not back to the showroom. Not to any other window. She reversed, and ran down the corridor facing the window.

Another explosion rocked the street outside.

She reached an old door with a slim, curving handle, grabbed it, and pressed the leaf-shaped thumb-latch right above it. The door opened and she rushed through. She couldn't bolt the door on the other side — *but, that still might be okay, right? The bug couldn't open a door latch right? —*

She dragged a dusty cardboard box full of water damaged envelopes away from the wall and pushed it up against the door, under the handle spot, where she wished there was a lock.

The corridor beyond the door seemed in better shape. Its lights, weak fluorescents, flickered in the dropped ceiling. The walls, she saw, had at least been painted within the last century — a horrible, muted green. *Who would want a paint that color? Nobody. That's why it's on sale, and winds up in places like this, places nobody sees — maybe they mix their leftover paints together, and that's what makes this dead dull green. God. God. Get moving.*

Grace raised her power strip and started walking, side-stepping around shabby boxes and old furniture, running when the floor and the dim light allowed it.

* * *

351

Outside the small round Outpost, Lifer 19 fired. A shell launched from its wrist, arced through the air, and descended; passing directly through the glowing building and disappearing into the ground below it. As the shell exploded, the ground under the Outpost bulged, changed shape, and spit out a burst of sprayed earth, but the real force of the detonation shunted down some unseen conduit, and erupted at the back of a nearby home, throwing up great portions of ground and grass, and blowing the back wall of the house to bits.

More Lifers fired shells at the Outpost and into the strange energy field surrounding it. Redirected explosions destroyed the ground, and the structures around the ground: the back lots and the private homes.

*

Inside the Outpost, Norel turned his back on his work, and watched the console that monitored the Outpost's prolonged ghost-attempt. He studied it for any fluctuation that would signal that an adjustment was needed. He felt the rocking concussion of each detonation. He was afraid to leave the console that monitored the ghost-attempt, but he'd have to. Whether it failed now, or six hours from now, didn't make any real difference. It would fail eventually. It would drain all the power the generator had loaded into the systems, and if he didn't get back to the line by line system prep, if he stayed in place and worried about the realm-jump monitor, the power would drain away pointlessly, and then the building would be taken.

He knew that. He sensed that. But that didn't make it any easier to turn away from his only protection.

* * *

When Bloch stopped his rover a second time, he just eased on the brakes in the middle of the road, and never thought about the shoulder. The views on his handset demanded his full attention. The four Lifers surrounding Norel's building were each sending him live feed. Each view was different, though very similar: one showed the glowing building with a background of ruined homes, one showed a tilting water tower, the other two showed debris and smoke. All the ordnance was passing right through the building. The building was in the process of jumping dimensions. And yet the building was still here.

Bloch spoke calmly into the handset, mindful to speak clearly and deliberately.

"Lifers 10 and 19, keep firing. 2 and 5, fire your jamming beams into the building. I'm two minutes away."

* * *

At the white portal, Krork heard the explosions, and tried to pinpoint their locations. They had to be close to where the Outpost was. Brickyard ran over to him.

"Krork, we have to get these kids away from here. If we stay out in the open we're going to be easy pickin's for Bloch's men. I think we should go."

"Brick, I have to go help Doc."

More explosions thumped beyond the hill.

"That's by the Outpost?" she asked, her voice raised to be heard above the wind. She looked to where the sounds had come from. "What do we do?"

"You take the bike and get the team out of here."

"And you'll do what?"

"I'll be okay. Start code is 431. To ghost you —"

"I know how to ghost. We're staying anyway. We're not quitting. I just want to get the kids out of this field. If things get bad, and we have to leave, I'll —"

"— Brick. It's better if I don't know," Krork said, raising a hand and turning away.

"Wait Krork."

Brickyard pulled a looped cord out of her pants pocket, and used it to twirl the metal knife handle it was attached to. The handle slapped against her palm and a sharp blade leapt out from it, gleaming. She offered the knife to Krork. "Here. You might need this."

"I'm not cooking anything. You keep it."

He touched the back of her hand, and she shifted the blade out of his way. They nodded to each other as she closed the knife. The wind rushed past their ankles and over their shoulders and they each turned to their tasks. Krork looked outward, and ran toward the explosions, up beyond the long, sloping hill.

* * *

A large explosion on the street rocked the walls around Grace, and the pressure wave seemed to jump right into the hall with her. The noise was enormous and terrifying. It pressed at the inside of her ear and actually hurt. She winced and cried out, but she kept running. Above her, the fluorescents in the ceiling panels flickered and died. Around her, dust and plaster fell from a thousand untended cracks and seams. She wanted to move by the walls, to get out of the middle of the hallway, but the debris showers were heaviest near the walls, and so she just continued forward.

With the lights out, the corridor slipped to a natural dimness, not completely dark, just dark gray. Sunlight filtered in from somewhere — and sunlight was what Grace wanted.

Around the next turn in the hall, she saw the source of the light — a narrow strip of windows up by the ceiling, a white bar in the gloom — a transom, built high in the wall at a time when tall ceilings and high windows were the best defense against the California heat.

The ceiling panels ended right before the window and then picked up again on the other side of it. Both sides rose to meet the actual ceiling with slanted panels, creating a skylight look around the window. Grace passed the skylight area in a few steps. She didn't have a ladder — on this side of the window or the other, and she didn't think she'd be able to squeeze through the window even if she were able to reach it. She might, or a kid might, but she doubted it.

She kept moving — away from the explosions, away from the monsters, running every few steps when she could see that the way ahead of her was clear.

She headed into a shadowed portion of corridor, moving further and further from the sources of light. She slowed as her surroundings grew darker. As the light failed her, she relied on her ears. The hall was silent. She was breathing hard, searching for any warning she might pull from the sensory void around her.

In the silence, her ears detected something: a rapid tapping coming from the ceiling far behind her, advancing her way — *not the ceiling*, she reminded herself, *the ceiling tiles* — a cardboard highway

— probably asbestos coated and ready to crumble — but an absolutely perfect highway for any rats that were running from the explosions.

Rats were bad, she thought as she forced her tension levels down, but rats weren't monsters — *bad,* but not *monsters*. She was running from the explosions herself, right? The rats might even show her the way out.

That's if they are rats.

Who said the creatures making those sounds *weren't* monsters? Weren't there windows above the cardboard? Windows just like the one in the hall? windows blocked from view by the tiles? Probably. Were they locked? Were they *broken*?

She ran then, darkness or not, arms out, as the sounds from the ceiling multiplied and spread out behind her. And suddenly she was sure — it *was* them — those creatures, with their jointed legs and their disgusting underbellies — they were *here, now,* right above her, and the next explosion might dump them through the ceiling and right on top of her.

She crashed into a pile of boxes that were only waist high, and they fell around her feet as she powered forward. She almost fell too — as her feet maneuvered among the tumbled cartons and their spilled contents, but her hand hit another tower of boxes and she righted herself. She needed a room - any room - any wall that went up to the ceiling — any wall that would block the monsters.

Another explosion rocked the hall. Ahead of her, a jumble of ceiling tiles fell. Enough light leaked in from the new hole to show the dust swirls created by the falling tiles. It sounded like they fell behind her too, but she didn't turn to look. The tiles were still in place where she was running and that was all she could bring herself to think about. As she ran, the light from the exposed ceiling changed what she could see — enough to show her through the floating dust that there was a closed door at the end of the hall, black and old, with a glass panel in its top half, and a transom of its own in the top of its frame.

She heard the creatures in the ceiling behind her — and the thought pressed in on her that there was no ceiling directly ahead of her — no ceiling *tiles*. She either beat the creatures to the door or they'd get her easily. They'd land in her hair and on her shoulders. They'd trip her, and — what if the door was locked? *She'd be trapped* — they'd be in the hall with her. They'd get her. The monsters would get her.

She steeled herself as she ran under the exposed ceiling. No insect legs reached her skin; no insect legs tangled in her hair; no insect jaws bit into her body.

The door was far, but she reached it and it opened easily. She ran in, and as she turned to close the door behind her, she saw that she had been right: the creatures were spilling out of the ceiling, one after the other. Some had already hit the floor and were leaping her way — jumbles of jointed legs and cobwebbed legs and small, hard, black-holed mouths.

She'd have to be quicker; she'd have to close the door even quicker...

A creature hit the door just as Grace was getting it closed. The impact shuddered the wood against her palms and pushed her back. Another creature hit the door and the door slammed back against her hands again and its glass panel cracked. Grace took notice of the thin wire honeycomb embedded in the glass, and sent her hopes to it, willing it to be strong, willing it to be strong enough to help her. She pushed at the door as another creature thudded against the glass. A white line tore up the window's center. Another monster hit the door low, and another hit the door higher, and still the door wasn't fully closed; whatever lock connection there was, it wasn't made yet.

No screwdriver. No pen. No weapon.

Grace pushed the door even as another creature slammed into it, and another. She screamed as the glass began to bulge, and as the door's wooden frame shook against her palms again and again.

She got the door closed. She heard it click, but the slamming continued. More cracks ran along the glass. She looked at the wire in the glass — *how long would it hold?*

Grace flipped the latch by the doorknob and backed into the room. The thumping stopped, but she could hear the creatures walking on the wall beyond the door. There was light behind her, and a constant crumbling sound — the sounds of small bits falling — of rock, or plaster — or bricks. She turned.

A jagged seam ran across the top of the wall that led to the outside of the building. She could see sky, too high to reach — but hopeful. It was hopeful to see the sky — despite the fact that she was seeing it through a hole in a brick wall that wasn't supposed to have a hole in it. She wasn't supposed to be inside a broken room that had the weight of a whole building pressing down on it. She wasn't supposed to cross all that hard distance, suffer through explosions, and broken glass, and creatures from other worlds just to end up in a trap anyway — either the building was going to come down, or the monsters were going to get in — and they could get in all sorts of ways: from the gap in the bricks that showed the sky, or from the broken glass in the door. Right that very second she could hear the creatures crawling across the wall, the door, and the glass transom.

Her mind wanted to fly away. She couldn't let it. She had to think.

* * *

The Inter-D stayed under the tree. The tree didn't move. The tree was fragrant. The tree tasted terrible.

The yellow thing ran in the field. The yellow thing ran in the field alone. The yellow thing ran and got closer. The yellow thing didn't stop running.

The Inter-D snorted loudly.

The yellow thing ran in the field. The yellow thing ran and got closer. The yellow-thing didn't stop running.

The Inter-D charged.

* * *

Krork heard the explosions beyond the wrecked houses. He heard one volley after another, coming faster and faster. Then he heard a heavy gallop, coming from the trees right behind him, coming fast. He turned, saw the dark gray gargantuan charging at him from the tree line, and reached behind his shoulder for his tap.

Too late. The creature was too fast. Krork had his tap in his hand, but the creature was on him before he could tap it on the ground and aim it.

The creature's knobby head caught Krork in the ribs and lifted him off his feet. The creature continued galloping, carrying Krork, perhaps looking for a tree to smash him against.

Krork struggled against the creature's horns until he could feel the ground with his feet. He tried to dig his toes in the soil to brace himself against the creature's charge, but the ground was too tender, and his feet only plowed strips of sod as the creature ran. It was a long half-minute before the creature slowed down.

Krork's face pressed against the creature's forehead, and as the creature tired, Krork pulled away. All he could see for a second was the creature's massive shoulders and its wrinkled skin, dark gray, and cracked. Within the cracks, the creature's skin was black.

When the creature slowed to a forceful walk, Krork succeeded in striking his tap against the ground. But as he raised it to fire, he felt the knobs on the creature's head press against his ribs, and actually squeeze to grip him. The creature twisted its neck suddenly, and Krork went tumbling to the grass, his giant tap somersaulting away from his hand.

The creature adjusted and charged again. Krork rolled in the grass and rose to meet the running monster, grabbing the protrusions on its long head to keep the creature from capturing him again.

The creature rushed forward, tossed Krork with a twist of its neck, and then watched Krork's descent. When Krork landed, the creature was right there to do toss him again. Each time, Krork was pushed or thrown further from his tap. Already, he only had a vague idea of where it was.

* * *

Finally, Rattletrap was on the road again. There was a slight bump to the tire — Nonstop was aware of it, but he'd either get used to it, or it would wear away. He didn't pay it any mind.

There were explosions all over the town, some close, some not. Any one of them might signal someone who needed help. And what about Doc? Portals or not, maybe it was time to pull the plug. Maybe it was time to get him out of his building. To get him somewhere safe. Nonstop caught sight of the water tower moving in the distance. As he watched it, it leaned, and fell over in silence. *Yeah, you bet it's time to get Doc out of his building,* he thought, and as the sound of the falling tower reached him, he sped up.

In the distance to his left, there was an explosion, followed by another.

That's close, he thought. *Grace is close. Those explosions were right near Grace.*

He stopped the bike.

Which one? Which way?

Like a fool, he turned his gaze back and forth between the two problem areas.

She's alone. I brought her here.

He turned the bike, and drove toward the recent explosions.

* * *

Grace looked for anything that would burn easily. So far, she had a very old push broom and a dusty strip of cardboard. She had tissue in her zipper pouch, a crumpled wad Nick had left her, along with a small, powerful lamp that ran hot. She was pretty sure she could get a fire started, but she needed something that would keep burning after she did. She wanted paper bags, a shirt, an old newspaper, the fabled oil-soaked rags — anything she could wrap around the short, squashed bristles of the broom and use to burn the creatures from a distance.

Bricks were falling from the gap in the wall, one at a time and in clusters, but more and more of them. Maybe she could climb somehow — and just deal with the fall on the other side. Could she move any of the stored furniture to climb up to the gap? Stack the old cabinets? She started ripping strips of cardboard and wedging them in the bent bristles of broom, making a torch that might burn for thirty seconds. What else? What else would burn? She looked deep into the corners of the room.

* * *

Even approaching from two blocks away Nonstop could see the destruction along the street in front of the electronics store. The asphalt was a sea of jutting black slabs — concrete capped with tar, and the machines that had produced the destruction were like nothing he had ever seen before — *robot-men* — not drawings in a comic book — right here in front of him, army green, ten to twelve feet tall, every bit as dangerous as tanks. *Look at the street.* Maybe more dangerous.

The two robot-things faced the electronics store. The closer robot raised its arm, which was thick and heavy and loaded with weapons.

A streak of white vapor shot from its forearm with a loud *pffft* sound. Whatever it shot went into the building and exploded. Dust and smoke and debris shot back out of the broken picture window at the same moment the boom hit his ears. *They're going to kill her.*

Nonstop leaned on the control bar and switched the bike out of whisper mode. The engine roared. *Let them see me.*

The rear robot turned to look at him. It had a big white 22 painted on the left side of its chest, and Nonstop could see that it had a face. *A human face* — twisted like a zombie cartoon, but human, with its head leaning back, and one eye staring into a flashing light.

It raised its arm and aimed it at Nonstop. The components on its forearm were magically shifting, changing into some new piece of machinery. Then Nonstop saw a piece he recognized — a magenta-colored light panel, narrow and slim, rising upright from the robot's arm.

Nonstop swerved, even as the other robot turned, and raised its weapon arm at him.

* * *

Grace looked around her as an explosion shook the building — *was it bigger than the last one? Closer?* Was it inside the building? Would the door hold? Would the ceiling fall in?

She looked to the left and to the right, and a whole row of hanging bricks on the outside wall let go, falling on the wall of standing bricks below them, knocking a large section of bricks to the alley floor.

She could leave. The gap was big enough. It was almost low enough.

She'd just have to pass through a collapsing brick wall.

That would only be a few steps.

She pushed the wall that still blocked her from the alley. It held fast. She grabbed its top and pulled herself up, the edges of the brick sharp against her fingers. She had to kick and push and struggle, and with each effort, she imagined the rest of the wall falling on her. *That* part was easy at least. It was easy to imagine the bricks raining down, landing on her back and ribs in thumps, maybe on her head, and that pain would be sharp. That pain wouldn't thump. That pain would ring. She hurried and she fought, and she managed to pull herself over the top and roll off, dropping to the alley floor, hands and knees landing on jumbled bricks, her ankles fighting for purchase on the shifting pile — sharp pain against her palms, pain in her wrists, and a pain in her knee caps that she immediately wanted to walk off. She stumbled to her feet, ready to run, but as soon as she did she felt daylight on her face — and its touch made her forget about her knees. Its touch made her greedy for more. She wanted to rush to where there was direct sun, to where she could raise her face and feel warmth on the skin around her eyes and on the skin around her mouth. But that wasn't the smart thing to do. She should do the smart thing. What was the smart thing?

The wind in the alley strengthened, then flared harshly, bringing with it the reminder that big guns, or something like them, lurked somewhere beyond the alley's edge. Monsters too. Guns and monsters and falling walls. How did this day get here?

Alleys have two ends, and if there was a gun at one end, then her decision was already made for her: she'd have to escape through the other. She turned, and saw only another brick wall, big, and solid where she didn't need it to be, with a dumpster at its base and a series of closed doors and windows across its surface. She processed the new information, the new trap: three brick walls and an alley wide enough to drive a truck into. What —

She heard Nonstop's bike suddenly roaring out on the street.

* * *

The rear robot-man fired. Nonstop didn't even have to dodge — the shot never reached him. It hit the ground in front of him and roared under the asphalt.

Immediately, the road underneath him swelled and spread. He rode its new shape, an expanding hump, and crested it forward, just that much faster than he had already been traveling. As the hump started to break apart, the front robot fired at him, the light panel on its arm flashing in quick magenta pulses.

Nonstop saw a clear lane hiding within the slabs of broken road, and sped along it to avoid the weapon of the front robot.

A second rocket blasted the ground in front of him, lifting the road. The moving road carried Nonstop backwards, where the pain-ray hit him, and a bolt of sensation tore through his shoulders. His hands let go of the control bar. He crossed his forearms around it and spotted a slab of road just as his eyes were squeezing shut. Blind, he steered, and felt the bike rise as it rode the slab like a ramp.

The ray hit him again, and he sailed into the building, tumbling over its broken front wall.

*

Grace saw less than a second of it. Looking down the alley, she saw the broken wall she had just left; she saw the ragged, saw-blade gash the hole created between the bricks; she saw that the gash ran almost the entire length of the building; she saw the undamaged wall of the building across the alley, and then, near the street, beyond the bright gap between the two buildings, she saw her friend Nonstop fly by in the air. She saw him twist as if shot; she saw him let go of his bike; and she saw as both he and the machine sailed toward the front of the building.

She heard crashing sounds — a great deal of them — but couldn't decipher what story they told. — at least not beyond the obvious. She'd have to see what happened. She'd have to sneak closer. She crouched down and sped along the alley wall to a low pile of bricks near the front of the building. Using her hands as well as her legs, she scrambled over the pile and made her way back inside, where the floor was so littered with debris it threatened to twist her ankles out from under her. Ahead of her, the explosions had blasted hunks away from the walls and she could see the next room through the exposed timbers and floating dust. She waded to the wall for a better look.

"Nonstop," she called out cautiously, peering through the wall at what was left of the showroom. With no lights on, the room became a shallow cave, lit only by the openings to the street. Plaster dust covered everything; it hung in the air. It coated the shelves and the merchandise that lay jumbled across the floor. A broken beam hung from the ceiling with a slab of plaster suspended from it. The plaster blocked most of the light from the picture window, and most of the view, but Grace could still see bits of the outside street. Outside, she saw the sunlight and the swirling dust and the middle-sections of two green machines that bobbed up and down as if they were walking.

The flying things — or things like them.

The machines moved slowly. They were approaching the building. They were approaching Nonstop. The room gave Grace cover, but she didn't have time.

Across the floor, she could see Rattletrap's vortex chamber poking out from behind the sales counter. She high-stepped her way through the junk on the floor and rushed behind the counter.

Nonstop lay on the floor near the bike, trying to get up, and she ran to him. "Oh my God," she heard herself say.

He was bleeding. Blood ran from his nose and striped both sides of his mouth. The middle cut on his arm was bleeding freely. She pulled the sleeve of her shirt up over her palm. The material was thin. It wouldn't absorb much. She knelt beside Nonstop and wiped his face clean.

"Are you hurt bad?" she asked him. He blinked.

He saw her. He seemed dazed, but he saw her. He reached his hand up, and ran the back of his finger over the tiny scab on her cheek.

"Forget that. Are you hurt bad?" she said.

He blinked some more. He moved his head.

"Nonstop, are you hur —"

"— No. I'm sorry I left you."

"Let's just get out of here."

"Not — easy," Nonstop said. Then he took in a hitching breath, and looked down his legs at his feet. "They have a pain-ray I can't do anything about."

"Let's do that ghosting thing"

"The street's all busted. We won't reach eighty eight. Not here. Not without getting shot by that new thing."

The sounds of booming footsteps came from the street and Grace turned to look. Shadows and light shifted around the rim of the plaster slab attached to the hanging beam. One of those robot-things was right outside the building.

"Oh God," she said, "let's get you behind the counter before it sees us." Crouching, she moved behind him and grabbed him by the armpits.

"I'm good," he said, waving her off, "It's fading."

He tried to move on his hands and toes, but his arms wouldn't hold him and his face hit the dust-filled floor. Grace pulled his harness straps; he pushed against the floor with his toes and his forearms, and together, they got him behind the counter.

"It's good," he said, "It's getting better."

"Shhh."

SLAM

The room shook. The shelves gave way near the sales counter. The boxes on them tumbled — *did the robot just punch the building?*

There was another slam, and the beam with the hanging plaster fell to the floor. Light flooded into the room through the fog of dust, instantly brightening the plastic window-sheets of the packages that had fallen from the shelves, each offering a steady reflection of the scene outside the building. Grace could see repeated images of the robot-thing's torso, standing just outside the broken picture window. The robot-thing twisted at its waist.

Loud clattering noises came from the area up by the ceiling. She couldn't see the robot's arms.

A tumble of bricks fell to the street — a dull sound — so minor — a cascade of thudding stones. The robot stopped twisting.

Thump

on the ceiling.

Thump

on the ceiling again, and then the whine of hydraulics and then a great cracking sound and then a rain of debris from the floor above them.

"It's going to tear down the whole building!" Grace said, "We can get to the alley — I was just there." she said, as she grabbed his shoulder straps and started pulling. He tapped her hand and got up freely, grabbing the top of the counter to stand, and then using it as a support to walk to the bike.

"An alley? Can we drive out?"

"I don't think so. It's all the backs of buildings. There are doors."

Above them, they heard the muffled pfft sound of something being fired high into the building.

Nonstop righted Rattletrap and started pushing it to the cracked far wall.

The explosion roared. The building shook, and shook again as above them, piece after piece of the upper floors began to fall.

Nonstop and Grace pushed the bike to the cracked wall and to the sunlight beyond.

"Stay low," Nonstop said, "Out of sight, below the broken stuff."

* * *

Bloch arrived at the Outpost and stopped the Rover. Hands on the steering wheel, he reached down to shut off the engine and made no further move. For the moment, he simply watched the strange scene through the windshield.

Outside his car, specially recruited soldiers, outfitted in mobile-armor-suits that stood ten feet high, fired ordnance into a glowing round building that was and wasn't there.

As he looked, he noted that the rover's windshield was all that stood between him and the situation he had set in motion, between him and the prize he had been chasing so intensely.

He sat behind that final barrier, and studied the activity beyond it.

He observed the Lifers on the perimeter of the blast-field, their complex metal arms, chiseled with shadows under the bright sun, repeatedly fired charges at the building, each blast adding to the overturned earth that blackened the ground, each blast happening away from the building, somehow re-directed to spend its energy elsewhere in the field. Long bands of dust and smoke traveled the air over the field, periodically obscuring the surrounding wall of destroyed American homes, causing them to fade in and out of view, like accusing ghosts.

While the explosions jostled Norel's building, Bloch saw none of the white streaks usually evident when Norel's agents received fire. Was this shielding different?

Why wasn't the building gone?

A Trojan horse of some type?

Yes, perhaps. Though hadn't he himself created this field of portals? Wouldn't it have been hard for Norel to plan a trap that spontaneously?

Actually, how spontaneously? Didn't the portal field only get created *after* Norel's agent delivered the lenses into his lap? Was this triumph, or trickery?

He removed his key from the ignition. Whatever trick Norel might intend didn't matter now; he was here, and triumph would be the only outcome permitted.

He surveyed the activity outside the windshield and allowed his mind to attend the immediate problem and only the immediate problem.

He watched the shells reach their target, pass through the building and detonate. He watched the blast streams. He watched the glowing field around Norel's building. He watched for what there was to see.

Shots fired through the building, hit the ground below it, but detonated beyond it, providing great noise and useless damage. Most of the ground immediately under the building held, as if the building were sending the explosive force away from itself, but even so, some material was being lost. He could see that the ground beneath the building did slope a bit. The glowing building itself sloped a little too, and was no longer resting fully on the ground — he had to lean his head sideways and down to see it, but the building was floating.

He watched the gap between the bottom of the building and the ground.

Each detonation caused the building to wobble slightly, and while the ground underneath it continued diminishing, the results were nowhere near proportionate to the force of the blasts. Bloch saw one particular detonation cause an arc of electricity to jump from the ground to the bottom of Norel's building.

He nodded.

There was a link of some type between the building and the ground. Definitely. He needed to see more. He needed to see everything. He opened the car door, breaking its gasketed seal, and climbed out, cracking the last shell that separated him from the world. Immediately, he felt the sun on his head.

He spoke into his handset.

"10 and 16, direct all fire to the ground below the building. 2, switch to classic ordnance and join them. Lifer 5, keep the jamming beam on the building. If Norel is in there, I want him incapacitated."

The Lifers did as ordered. Bloch retained his grip on the handset as he put his hands on his hips and watched, studying every impact and weighing every result.

* * *

Lifer 22 lumbered toward the alley to the side of the electronics store. The slabs of asphalt in the road were too difficult to maneuver on, and so it was forced to use the sidewalk across the street, which was also broken, but did not teeter under the Lifer's immense weight.

The road slabs, and the brick piles on top of them, roughly hid the first four feet of the ground around the target. The Lifer had a clear shot at everything above that.

From where it stood, it could not see Grace or Nonstop, nor hear them as they whispered.

*

"So we can't drive on this," Grace said, lying on her belly, looking past the pile of shattered bricks near her shoulder and out into the ruined street beyond.

"No," Nonstop said softly, shaking his head as he too, studied the road.

"So what are we doing? How are we getting out of here?" Grace turned and looked at Nonstop. Nonstop turned to look behind him at the alleyway.

"Are any of the doors unlocked?" he asked.

"I don't know. I came out through a crack in the wall and ran to get you. I never checked."

"Maybe we could push that dumpster under a window and get in that way. Rattletrap would have to jump it. We might get shot."

"We could go back in the crack — there are monsters, but you could get rid of them right? You can send them home, like you said?"

Nonstop nodded, "All right, let's do that. But let's just wait until this guy here clomps someplace else, because if he shoots us with that ray we'll probably let go of the bike, you might let go of me..."

"And they'll shoot us."

"Yeah."

"And I'm not bullet proof."

"Yeah. Look, maybe we can cause a distraction. Get it to go back down to the other side of the building or something, and then go back in through the crack like you said."

They heard the loud pfffft of a weapon's launch come from the street. Grace grabbed Nonstop's arm and pulled herself to him as a vapor trail sailed through the patch of blue sky above their heads.

The launched shell hit the electronics store's building, smashing through a third floor window with a dull thud accompanied by the tiny sounds of breaking glass. A second later an explosion blew hunks of the roof into the air, and the third floor's remaining windows burst out into the alley.

The top of the building sagged. Grace watched as the crack she had escaped from closed like a brick stage curtain. Dust rolled into the alley and spread into the breeze.

"What do we do now?" she asked, her voice rising.

"I don't know. We have to get that army-thing busy somewhere else."

"A diversion."

"Yeah, any ideas?"

"I don't know, throw the bricks? What about the road? Could we crawl under the pieces? How far do they go?"

"Under the road," Nonstop said, out loud, but absently. "That's not a bad idea. We could..."

"What? Crawl under the road pieces?"

"What? No. We can't crawl under the road pieces. Maybe a snake, but not us, and not Rattletrap."

He unclipped his tap, and hit it against the ground. Grace watched him.

"What then?" she asked him.

He started crawling away from her. "You know that bulge in the road we saw before I went to help the truck?" he said, just shy of the end of the rubble pile.

"The tru...? Well, yeah?"

Nonstop lowered his arm into a hole by a road slab. Then he squeezed the activator on the tap and fired, looking around for any reaction, any falling stones, any clomping robot-men. There was nothing.

"Nonstop, what about it? What about that thing in the road?"

"It's an Inter-D," He said, looking back at her.

Grace crawled closer to him, and he continued, whispering: "I don't know exactly what it is, but it didn't like me, and it didn't like my tap. It left — it stopped fighting me when the explosions started." Nonstop rechecked the street and kept talking. "Now the explosions are all over town. Maybe it will pay attention to the explosions going on *here* if I add my tap to them."

"What do you mean pay attention? You mean come here?"

"Yeah."

"No. No, no, no, We have enough trouble. We have more than enough trouble."

"We can't win this as it is. We have to shake it up. Change it."

"No. That's crazy."

"We need a diversion — let the road monster and the robot guys deal with each other."

"No. Stop. Don't bring any monsters here."

"A distraction, like you said."

"I didn't say anything like that; this is stupid; I don't thi..."

* * *

"Stay on it," Bloch commanded as the Lifer's shells blasted the crater under the Outpost, expanding the size of the hole, first deep, then wide, then deep again — with each detonation causing a stronger reaction in the glowing field under, and around the building. Attacking the building was useless. Attacking the ground under it might not be.

Bloch watched Lifers 10 and 16 re-shape their arms in order to reload. Their systems worked remarkably well, a tribute to the lieutenant's good work. Perhaps when he tracked her down, he could find an excuse to let her live.

In the crater, the ground below the building began to slide, spilling new soil down into the small lake of broken earth.

Bloch smiled, a slim line between curving lips; everything was forever in the process of changing, and there were often rewards for steering that change.

"Cease fire," he commanded, and the Lifers obeyed.

In the sudden stillness, Bloch and his Lifers watched as the back half of the Outpost began to sink, and its front half began to rise. With the angle of the building becoming steeper, the energy around it grew erratic: the air around the Outpost, the air directly in contact with the field of glowing ghost-light, began to fold and distort. Flares of green energy whipped free of the building, streaking the air with brief pixelation effects. The flares from the building intensified, launching with greater frequency, doubling back, reaching higher and higher orbits — burning brightest and thickest at the furthest points of their arcs before returning to the field around the Outpost and then launching again.

As the Outpost settled, the flares from its dying ghost-light rose taller than any building in Exeter.

*

Grace saw them first. "Nonstop, what is that?"

Nonstop had to raise himself up off the ground to see what she was talking about. He saw the flares in the sky grow and die, one after the other. He knew at least one light that was that color. He knew roughly where the light was coming from.

"That's the Outpost," he said, staring.

He closed his eyes and blew air from his lips. He lowered himself fully again, and stuck his arm even deeper into the hole in the broken road's edge.

"Come on. Come on," he said through clenched teeth.

* * *

There was a final second. A final second where the building glowed green, and its uncommitted state protected it. Then the ghost-light around the Outpost sputtered, and then it vanished. The effect ended. The Outpost fell to the ground: a drop of less than two feet, but sudden, and somehow very heavy.

"Jamming beams only! Steady fire! Doors and windows, keep those beams on the weak spots!" Bloch pointed and paced. The building started to slide.

* * *

As the room tilted, Norel hooked his arms over his workstation and dug his shoe tips into the floor grating. He was only a few steps from the swing chair, and if he could reach it, he had no doubts that its anchorage was strong enough to hold him and keep him from falling to the other workstations — the ones that were now below him as well as behind him. He slid his left arm a few inches across the console and started moving toward the chair.

He listened intently. He had heard someone yell outside. He had heard the sound, but couldn't make out the words. Now all he heard were the structures of the building, groaning and creaking.

He didn't feel well. Yes, he *really* didn't feel well.

He felt queasy. Then the nausea in his stomach crystallized, and turned to pain. The pain spread, and ran riot. He struggled to breathe. He struggled not to scream. He forbade it. The scream rose anyway. It escaped from his throat, and he fell. His body struck the work station below him, spun, and landed on the back wall.

But the pain didn't stop. The pain hammered at him, from above and from below. His muscles jumped and trembled, each firing warnings to his brain. He didn't feel the building slip the last few feet down the incline. He didn't feel it level out, and when gravity recalled him and he fell forward to the floor, he didn't notice. His conscious movements were slow, like petals closing, and with that speed, he curled his legs around his organs, and he curled his arms around his head. His wrist felt something wet.

His eyes were bleeding.

* * *

Nonstop saw it coming, far on the horizon.

"Get to the bike. Stay low."

"What? What do you see?" Grace said, moving toward Nonstop instead of the bike, then laying next to him, then advancing further, sliding to his back, her shoulders near his shoulders, her cheek against his cheek, straining to see what he was seeing.

"Oh my God," she said.

Far down the road, many blocks away, a parked car flipped and spun in the air. Then another car flipped end over end, and another. Something was coming; there was no difference in the color of the street, there was little difference in the light, but there was no mistaking what they were seeing. Down the road, a tidal wave of asphalt was headed their way

"M-mountain," Grace whispered, and then said, "Mountain right? Mountain."

"Yeaaaah... *mov-ing* mountain," Nonstop pointed behind his shoulder with his thumb. "Get to the bike, go ahead."

371

Grace crawled away from his shoulders, mindful to stay low until she reached the higher rubble piles. Nearer the bike she was able to crouch. When she reached it, she patted the cowling near the seat.

Escape.

She turned to examine the doors on the back wall of the alley — to see if they looked open —

— She screamed into her palms.

Bug-monsters scrambled out from the broken windows at the top of the building, pouring over each other in a wave.

* * *

At the Outpost, Lifer 10's mechanical hand hit the main door. It worked its fingers into its seams, and got a grip against the interior steel structures. The Lifer braced its foot against the door frame.

The Lifer pulled, and slowly, the door opened.

Bloch side-stepped down the loose dirt of the crater. He checked his footing as he went, observing the small waves of dirt as they slid over the toes of his well-polished shoes.

He stopped when he reached the Outpost, and for a second, he simply stood still, looking at Norel's mysterious building, finally, finally, open before him.

Two steps led up to the open door. Two steps worth savoring. The first lay deep and wide, rising with a mild slant. Perhaps Norel, the sentimentalist, intended the space for a welcome mat.

Bloch tapped his right shoe hard against the white riser under the second step. Dirt rolled off the toes of his shoes. He wondered if there was dirt stuck within the spaces around any of the stitches, and made a mental note to inspect his shoes when this was over.

He cleared his left shoe the same way, kicking Norel's building with slow, loud strikes.

Tap.

Tap.

Tap.

He stepped onto the second stair slowly, with no effort to muffle the sound of his footstep. He matched the move with his second foot and paused in the doorway, framing himself, offering himself as a target, sneering with the knowledge that his offer would not be taken.

After a second, he crossed the threshold and entered the building.

*

Norel moved with outstretched hands. The pain that had crippled him had eased, but he still couldn't see well, and he still couldn't move far without needing to rest. His ears had been hurt. He heard only pieces of sounds: incomplete scrapings and poundings — metal sounds, sounds that would stop abruptly and then reappear, sounds that seemed to shift location, and tone, and volume. Logic told him that someone must be forcing the main door open. He attempted to verify that hypothesis, and found that he could barely lift his head to face the front of the building. When he turned his gaze to where he knew the door to be, all he saw was a spreading rectangle of white haze, surrounded by the darkness of the room. Then the spreading of the white haze stopped, and it held its rectangular shape.

Shadows moved within the white haze occasionally. He stared, watching for what those shadows might do, his body too weak to do anything else.

A shadow grew within the haze. Norel could detect that there were sounds being made, but he couldn't catch them consistently.

The shadow in the white haze grew larger, until its darkness split the white haze in half, and in that moment, Norel's logic left him. The entirety of his vision filled with the indistinct split between light and darkness.

Again, here at the end, the symbol.

He caught his breath and held it. His heart began to hammer.

The dark haze began to spread. Involuntarily, Norel attempted to back away. His shoulder rose as his torso spun. He pushed again, and his shoulder blade hit the tri-ladder behind him. Even with his body stopped by the ladder, he kept pushing, kept trying to get away. Was it here? Underneath this reality, was the symbol actually here? Could such a thing be? Was there something under the concept, some actuality, that could enter a room and visit him? — *claim* him at the moment of his death? — or had his mind formed this perception to punish him *at the moment of his death? Had* something entered the room to visit him, or were his perceptions discovering something that was here all along, or were they busy discovering something that wasn't here at all? Oh God, what was real?

And then, to his utter horror, his mis-functioning ears heard the symbol speak. In distorted tones, its sounds said:

"It'S oVer for you noW NoReL."

And then the dark haze came closer, becoming blacker as the white haze vanished, and Norel pushed away, and tried to move back, and as he did, his throat released a tiny moan of soul-lost fear.

* * *

Maybe the roaring winds carried it, or maybe dimensional flux created a proximity that physical space itself would not allow, but Krork heard that sound; he heard it, and recognized it for what it was. Upon hearing it, he threw his shoulders back and roared with uncharacteristic fury.

The Inter-D faltered mid-charge, two of the steps of its gallop landing out of rhythm — but the creature didn't stop; having already committed to the charge, it completed the action.

Krork met the charge with none of the caution he had been using with the animal. He stopped trying to steer it back to the tap. He stopped trying to send the creature home peacefully. He stopped trying to send the creature home at all. When the creature was within reach, Krork ignored its horns and grabbed it by the neck instead. He added a powerful twist to the force of the creature's gallop, and sent the creature crashing to the ground.

Then he ran. He ran up the incline of the field as fast as he could, listening all the while for what the creature might do, or what the forces acting against the Doctor might do.

The stunned Inter-D rose to its feet and turned to face its opponent. Its opponent was running away.

It let it.

*

The first house Krork reached was only partially damaged. Half its back deck had been obliterated, and the remaining half hung off the building at an unstable slant. Krork ran past the house, and over the remains of its back fence.

After that, the amount of debris in the grass increased, until Krork was running on entire sections of houses, on what was left of them. On smashed wood. On flattened roofs. On shingles. On furniture. On beautiful scrapbooks.

He saw the crater. He saw the Outpost in the crater. He saw the man-machines lining the crater's rim. Had he been thinking, he might have doubled back and gone around the hill to sneak up on them, letting the hill keep him out of sight. As it was, he wasn't thinking.

He was bullet-proof. He was strong. He was desperate. He simply charged.

Two man-machines by the crater raised their arms at him. They did it calmly, as if they had all the time in the world.

Krork ducked whatever they were firing, and leapt at the closest man-machine, slamming into it and knocking it backwards. The second machine bent toward Krork. Krork grabbed its arm and swung mightily, snapping the massive arm clean off. The rest of the machine tumbled into the crater, rolling and bouncing like a car wreck. Deep in the hole of the machine-man's shoulder joint, Krork saw a hand, opened and outstretched, each finger dripping with fine, thin cables.

Krork ran for the front door of the Outpost.

The first jamming beam caught him right between his shoulder blades. He had a bare instant where he remembered Nonstop's warnings about the new weapons — a bare instant of anger at the intrusion, and the insistence, and the barbarity of Bloch and his forces, a bare instant before the jamming beam caught him full — before the pain caught him full.

It took him four strides to fall.

A machine stepped out from the other side of the Outpost, and then another. They added their beams to the one hitting Krork, delivering wave after wave of sensation to Krork's nervous system — sending him the message that he was being crushed and sliced and burned.

He roared again as he fought to get up.

*

Norel grabbed the rungs of the ladder behind him and pulled himself off the floor. As he rose, his leg slid out from under him. He didn't know which of his muscles worked. He didn't know if his body was ruined permanently, or only momentarily.

He did know some things though. Some things that propelled him. This was Bloch in the room with him. Bloch or some minion of Bloch's. And whatever they had done to his body, they were now doing to Krork's.

He staggered to his feet and crashed onto a workstation, hitting it with his chest and his mid-section. Supported, he began pulling himself across the workstation with his arms, heading toward the front door. "No" he said to himself, and he continued saying the word as he fought his way toward the end of the workstation.

He reached the end a moment later. He'd have to cross open space before finding a wall. He gasped Krork's name for the strength it gave him, stretched out his arms, and plunged forward.

"Not so fast there Doctor," Bloch said, extending one well-polished shoe outward, connecting with Norel's shin, and watching with amusement as Dr. Norel crashed to the floor.

With no strength in his arms to absorb the fall, Norel hit the grating hard. He turned his head in time to protect his teeth, but his face took the brunt of the impact. It was just more pain. It was just pain on top of pain. Krork was outside. Krork was being hurt. Krork was being hurt because of him.

He started to crawl.

* * *

When the first monster-bug flew away from the wall of the electronics store, Lifer 22 fired at it with the same ordnance he had been using on the building. The shell missed the creature and sailed to the brick wall at the end of the alley.

The explosion flashed white at its center and launched a dark outer skin of dust and broken bricks. Its noise more than covered the sound of Grace's screams. She hid under Rattletrap, and its vortex chamber blocked most of the debris from the blast, but bouncing chunks of brick and wood found their way to her, slamming into her legs and ankles. She winced, but refused to yell out. She felt herself start to cry.

The web-wings leapt from their perches, colliding in a tangle of erratic flight paths, screeching warnings to each other as they tried to clear the confined air space between the buildings.

"Shoot them! Shoot them!" Grace called to Nonstop as she shrank back further against the rubble wall.

"I have to keep firing here," Nonstop said, "I don't know what the road-monster will do if I stop."

Grace pointed skyward. "*There* are the monsters. Shoot *them!*" She yelled.

The creatures began settling back along the rooftops, clustering at the front corners, crawling along the sun-lit brick, hiding among the alley's shadows. Grace felt a sharp corner of rock press against her back — *monsters in the road* — *monsters on the roofs* — *monsters in the Army robots* — she felt surrounded. Pale jointed legs. A thousand clicking footsteps. Trapped. Trapped. Trapped.

"I was so stupid," She said, whipping her face toward Nonstop, who was switching his attention between the roof-lines and the road. "You had me believing you. You, with the lights in your damned hair. This is your fault! *This* is what your precious technology does! *This* is what your precious Dr. Norel does!"

"Take it easy," Nonstop said, angling his neck to look back at her.

"I won't take it easy. You want to tell me that you should control this technology, but you can't control it. You want to tell me that Dr. Norel should be in charge of it, but look what happens!"

"Doc didn't do this."

"Yes he did! He invented this stuff."

"No. This isn't his fault."

"You can insist all you want, but that doesn't make it true."

"Look, we're going to get out of here, just..."

The creatures began moving along the wall. Those that brushed against each other moved to find clear space. Some ventured downward.

One of the descending creatures spotted Grace, and jumped in her direction. A second creature, higher up, followed it. Grace screamed.

Nonstop fired at the first creature. A blue glow enveloped the web-wing, as machine gun fire burst from the street; passing through the creature and then strafing upward along the building and into the air.

The creature faded from the world. Grace scrambled to Nonstop as he fired at the second creature. She grabbed hold of his ankle, cringing as the gunfire erupted again.

The ground began to shake, loosened bricks fell from the electronics store, and the web-wings abandoned their perches again. At their launching, the Lifer sprayed them with machine gun fire. Those hit, twitched in the air, and fell to the ground like wet laundry. Those hit, died, their bodies ruined by bullets, by objects their minds had no spaces for, killed on a world not of their birth, by a creature who barely knew they were there. Killed, because they moved.

Nonstop looked out at the road once more, and grabbed hold of Grace's wrist as the gunfire stopped.

"Get on the bike — now!"

Nonstop turned to the bike, mindful to keep his shoulders below the rubble line. He kept contact with Grace's wrist, and matched her moves as she crouched closer to the bike's seat.

"Okay, put your hands in my straps — don't let go of me no matter what."

Crouching, Nonstop started Rattletrap from the ground.

RRRRAAAARRRRRR! The stupid jungle cat sound.

The noise drew fire from the Lifer as Nonstop flipped Rattletrap back into whisper-mode. Then he slid his chest onto the bike as more bullets flew, keeping his body low to avoid letting it rise above the rubble. He got fully onto the rolling bike and looked back at Grace. "We're going," he said.

Grace tensed. They were moving closer to live machine-gun fire, to where a skin of brick and rubble might or might not block the bullets. Nonstop expected her to fully trust that it would be all right because he was magically bullet-proof. But she was too, right? When she held onto him?

She tensed in her back, trembling in her knees and ankles, almost closing her eyes, just wanting to get it over with - to be gone already. Staying low on the bike still put her body high, inches - *inches* — from the top of the rubble line. She didn't see how it could work, but she wanted to go. She really, really, wanted to go. With the machine gun firing, anything was better than staying. She tightened her grip around the harness at Nonstop's shoulders, and buried her face in his back as the bike rolled — *forward* — not to the rear of the alley as she expected, but towards the low section of the rubble wall — toward the street.

"Where are you going?" she screamed, forcing her voice to its loudest level so that it might be heard above the wind, and the machine gun fire, and the weird vibrato screeching the web creatures were making.

Nonstop heard her question, but his mind was filled with moving things: moving spaces, broken lengths of sidewalk, distances from the moving sources of gunfire, an approaching wall of asphalt with its own rate of speed. He couldn't form any words to answer her. He made the barest attempt, uttering an extended grunt, and then he swerved the bike onto the ruined sidewalk and sat up fluidly: a movement so correct it caused Grace to sit up as well, and she found herself perfectly positioned behind him on the bike, screaming all the while, momentarily distracted by a thousand things, and slowly coming to the realization that the thumping she was feeling was in fact, the impact of bullets attacking her body.

The asphalt wall, *the road-monster,* the abstract thought accepted when diminished by distance, or by the motion of departure, filled her vision when she looked at the end of the block, and alarmed her mind to the point of surrender. *Look at that — it's real.*

It rolled forward, stretching the road up past the second story windows, sending painted road lines streaking up and back along its advancing, raging surface, grabbing its full portion of sunlight as if it had every right to be where it was, barreling forward, tossing aside rubble and cars and the contents of trashcans.

Machine gun fire bounced along its surface, and there was only time for Grace to see that the bullets had no effect on the road at all — did not slow it down, or advance its speed. The road simply roared forward from the corner to the exact spot that the bike was — *driving to.*

Nonstop slipped up the back of the road mound with a move as easy as the wave of a hand. Amazed, Grace stopped screaming and clutched tighter around Nonstop's belly.

Nonstop kept the bike back at first, allowing the front of the wave to block them from view. The road surface grew irregular under the bike, jagged, as the wave shuffled the broken street and re-aligned its slabs. Nonstop aimed his tap at the road and forced himself to pause. *Leave it alone. Tap it now, and all these broken pieces might go flying. Stay where you are; retreat and you might wipe out on this, you'll be exposed when the wave sinks back in — maybe. Ride it out. No. Ramp it up.* He grimaced, and as the ground beneath them smoothed, he slid the bike up to the top of the wave.

He caught sight as the road overtook the Robot-thing with the 22 on its chest, tossing the robot backward off its feet. The robot-thing landed on the broken sidewalk and bounced out of sight as the asphalt advanced.

Nonstop saw the second Robot-guy, the one with the 7 painted on its chest, retreat against the wall of the electronics store on the left side of the street. The front of Robot-guy's arm was already open, and as he raised it to aim at the wave, its components were refolding into new shapes.

Nonstop fired a quick burst of tap on the right side of the road. The road wave suddenly veered left, smashing into the building and into the Robot-guy. The corner of the electronics store burst at the impact, showering chipped bricks and mortar down to the street in soft arcs Nonstop would never see the completion of, left behind as the road wave sped forward.

Nonstop cut off the tap, switched it to the left side of the road, and fired again, turning the whole mass rightward, smoothly completing the curve onto Throckmorten Road, where there were no robot-men and no creatures, only wind, and a band of darkness at the horizon. He fired into the road-wave again, and neatly took the left at the corner.

One more right, and they'd be headed for the Outpost. One more right atop this crazy steed, and they could help Dr. Norel.

* * *

Norel braced himself near the door, the white brilliance of the sun assaulting his eyes as he forced them to stay open. Somewhere in the haze, Krork was in trouble. Somewhere in the haze, hydraulic systems were moving. Somewhere in the haze, his friend was roaring, at least trying to, over and over, trying to contend with the pain he was enduring.

"Stop hurting him. I'll give you what you want. Just call this off," Norel said to the intruder — the intruder he still hadn't seen, but whom he had heard step closer.

"All right," the intruder said, calmly, with a practiced compassion so false, it was itself a form of mockery. The voice was deep, Norel heard it without distortion, from a point above his ear. Would Bloch work with anyone taller than himself? Not likely. Was this Bloch? He couldn't tell. Perhaps his ears were still as overwhelmed as his eyes, perhaps the twenty years that had passed were too long to hold the memory of a stranger's voice, even an enemy's. He could not say for certain whether this was Bloch or not.

"Give yourself a moment to recover, then take me to the plans," the intruder said.

It is Bloch. Who else would it be. Apparently, his wounds were not severe. Perhaps no more than burst blood vessels, and his eyes would clear soon, and when they did, he could look at this man, and be certain.

"Call off your soldiers."

"When I have the plans."

"Stop hurting him. I yielded. Surely you can too."

"I don't have to yield Doctor. I won."

Norel heard the rustle of cloth, and then the intruder directed his voice toward the haze outside the door. The haze quality was changing, no longer solidly bright, it fluttered between dark and light, as if fast clouds were passing overhead. A warm, dirty breeze pushed against Norel's chest. The intruder continued speaking, clearly, and calmly.

"10, 12, 2, and 5, cease fire on the current combatant. Don't shoot him unless he moves. 26, 14, 20, and 23, I have you in the area, I'm feeding you full updates now. Fall in. Form a perimeter around this building. Let no one enter until I come back out."

A pause, a few tapping noises, and then the voice reached Norel directly again. "Anytime you're ready," was the simple message it conveyed.

* * *

Skyde heard someone crying: a baby, and she rolled over in the street. There was dust on her skin, as well as grit and shards of brick. She moved her hands through her hair and across her face to clear what debris she could. Rising onto her palms and elbows, she looked around her. Covering the street, broken hunks of building jutted into the afternoon sunlight. She couldn't see the ground. She couldn't see her board.

She reached into a pouch on her belt and placed her finger on a flat button. She pressed it. From somewhere past her feet she heard the *pap-pap-pap* sounds of grit falling, and then she saw her board rise into the air, tilted at an angle, spilling building-debris to the ground.

The board glided toward her. When it reached her arms, she held onto it and used it for support as she stood. The board rose steadily, keeping up with her progress.

The falling building had crushed a car, and had sprayed debris up and down the street, including deep into the curving entrance of an underground parking garage. Beyond the entrance, she saw the backs of tall buildings, modern looking, with windows that rose from the ground to the roof in slim glass columns. She saw glass walkways, and concrete walls tinted a variety of soft browns.

The garage must be for the workers, Skyde thought, a little fuzzily. *The crying is coming from their parking garage.* She staggered closer to the entrance, her board following her. The crying grew louder, amplified by the funnel shape of the entrance. She heard a second sound: someone trying to calm the baby.

"Hello?" she called at the mouth of the entrance. "Hello?" she called again as she took a step downward. Another step and she got on her board. Then she glided down to investigate.

Under the overhang, the warm light of the sun gave way to the weak fluorescents of the parking garage and her eyes were slow in adjusting. Underground, the garage seemed little more than a cave with a phosphorous ceiling. The baby cried again, and again someone tried to quiet its wails.

Skyde followed the sound and saw a shape near the base of a wall, a few feet above the floor. She saw a pair of terrified eyes, brilliant gold in the gray and black surroundings. Everything else took a second to make sense of, but those eyes communicated instantly. A blue woman with a crying baby, sat with her back against the wall. As Skyde approached, the blue woman stood up and ran.

"Wait," Skyde called out, without any real hope of being understood. She followed the woman, slowing down on the ramp to keep the woman from panicking. Panicking, the woman might fall with the baby. The woman's hair looked like two folded arms, like she was holding the top of her head, with the elbows of the folded things bent at about shoulder level. Only the things weren't her arms, and they weren't her hair, they were some other part of her body. They seemed to be what she had instead of a neck. They seemed to be what held her head attached to the rest of her. She had arms and legs as well, and they seemed to fall within standard bi-pedal definitions. Her eyes were large and reflective, like a reptile's. If she weren't so upset, she would actually be beautiful.

On the flat portion of the next parking level, Skyde flew in front of the woman, blocking her. The woman took one step back. Bent legged, and bent-waisted, protecting her child. The woman let out a cry of defiance. It sounded like an animal noise, like a sheep, or a goat, only prolonged, and anguished. Skyde raised both hands.

"I won't hurt you." *Where was Krork? Where was Krork to open a dialogue with this woman, where was Krork to ease this woman's mind?*

The woman looked behind her, saw the ramps leading upward, saw how hopeless it would be to run, and then turned to look at Skyde.

"I won't hurt you." Skyde un-clipped her tap. How could she do this? How could she make the device not look like a weapon? She gripped it and pulled it free.

"This is going to make some noise, but it's all right. It will be a little scary, but..." Skyde tugged and the tap snapped open. The woman ran.

Skyde struck the tap against the ground and flew in front of the woman. The woman cried, and screamed, and stomped her foot at Skyde.

"No, no, here. Watch." Skyde lit the tap and passed her arm all through its main channel. The arm was brightly lit, but nothing harmful happened. Skyde brought the tap to her chin and place her own face into the beam, to no harmful effect. The woman calmed, but watched intently, ready to run. Skyde opened her hand, palm up, slowly, and obviously, so the woman could see. Then she flapped her hand away like a bird flying. The woman had to know this was not her world. She and the woman were not so different that there was no hope of being understood. And what did it matter? One action would send Mother and child home, would give them their most heartfelt wish, so why delay?

Because the woman was afraid. Because she had not given her consent.

Skyde surrendered the idea altogether, raised the tap and fired. The woman cried out and shielded her baby as the tap wave enveloped her and made her and her baby glow. Skyde hoped the woman might open her eyes before fading away, that Skyde might see her recognize aspects of her home-world, that Skyde might see her understand. But the woman kept her eyes closed, and never looked at Skyde again.

And then she was gone.

Skyde deactivated the tap, and the only glow she saw came from the overhead lights.

Skyde looked around her, but there was nothing beautiful to see, just dark brick in weak, ugly light.

She turned the board. She had work to get back to, and she didn't know how long she had been unconscious, or for that matter, how long she might have stayed in the rubble pile if the baby's cries hadn't awakened her.

She flew back to the ramp, saw sunlight coming down the entrance and flew to it. She enjoyed speeding up the curved enclosure of the ramp, and by the time she hit open air, the speed and the sun had renewed her.

* * *

This was a new kind of freedom, and Grace was surprised to have the moment to reflect on it. There was no one shooting at her, no one charging at her; she and Nonstop were moving swift and steady, twelve feet up in the air at least. They were twelve feet up in the air on top of a road that moved like a wave, and that ruined the sidewalks behind it as if it were un-zipping a dress — a very *long* dress.

She felt Nonstop shift as he moved to fire his gun-thing into the wave, sometimes on the right, sometimes on the left, sometimes near the wheel, and sometimes anyplace else along the road. She couldn't make sense of what he was doing, but it seemed to be working. He kept the ride going. It didn't seem to panic him.

"You haven't done this before have you?"

"What? No. What do you think though? Aces right?"

"Right. Aces. What is this thing?"

"The monster? Some kind of Inter-D."

"How come your machine doesn't send it home?"

"I don't think the road is the monster. The road belongs here. I think the Inter-D is hiding *in* the road, using it as a shield maybe. I don't know. Something like that."

"So, what? it likes that thing?" she patted the skin near his right elbow, the arm that held the tap. *Keep your eyes on the road.*

"The tap? No, it doesn't like it. I'm pretty sure I'm annoying it."

"But... "

"Outside the road this is an annoyance. Under the road, it's a threat. This thing doesn't like threats. It's useful though — we can —"

"What about behind us — on this thing? There's a lot of open road. Could we do the ghosting?"

"No. Not now. We have to use this to even the sides for Doc, after that, we'll send it home... somehow. Then we can ghost anyw —"

"— Even the sides for Doc? What? — What does *that* mean?"

* * *

From its perch on the lead drone, Lifer 13 saw the road-wave as it crossed Jointer Avenue along Susan Mears Road, heading toward the east end of Exeter. Norel's agents were on the wave. New orders instructed that Norel's agents should be blocked from the eastern end of town.

The new orders allowed the full use of weapons.

Lifer 13 banked the drone high. Sunlight caught the full weapon array on the drone's underbelly and flashed on the metal I.D. bands around the R-7 missiles.

Lifer 8 made the turn and took the lead position, heading for direct intercept. Lifer 13 banked high, and followed.

* * *

Rik Ty

**

The targets rode steadily on the top half of the road distortion. Training the machine gun cannons on Norel's agents was a simple matter of looking at them directly. Firing the weapon was a simple matter of moving a finger. Lifer 8 touched the trigger on the over-ride panel, and fired.

There were no warning bursts on the road as the Lifer found its aim. It already had its aim. The bullets hit Grace square in her back.

Grace screamed as the thumping found her, and she watched with sudden horror as white diffusion streaks flew instantly around her, and around Nonstop, and around the bike.

Nonstop slid the bike left, and the bullets took a moment to find them again. He fired his tap in a sequence that flattened the road's surface, and he watched for the next intersection. Not far. He took the corner left and they headed North.

Lifer 8 overshot the corner and had to bank its jet high to turn. Lifer 13 turned early, and retook the lead position above the fleeing riders.

The Lifer worked a panel on the drone's right tail fin. Warning lights on the small console announced that the missiles under the jet's wings had gone live. Very small lights on the missiles themselves, made the same announcement.

The same systems that allowed the Lifer's brain to drive its suit, allowed it to direct the jet. The Lifer made its missile selection, and ordered the jet to fire.

The left wing's outer-most R-7 missile began to tremble as its core ignited, and less than a second later, it launched, trailing a streak of white vapor behind it.

The missile screamed above rooftops that were built long before the invention of the jet-engine, let alone the strange, undesignated aircraft that flew above them now.

Nonstop heard the missile in the last seconds of its approach, and turned to look.

"HANG ON!" he yelled to Grace as he forced his back to unlock, and sped the bike forward.

The missile hit the wave low, exploding somewhere beneath Nonstop and Grace, detonating with a concussion so loud they could *feel* the sound as it spiked at their eardrums. They felt themselves lifting with the bike. The road swelled for a full second before its expanded edges slammed into the passing light poles, and its sides ejected shears of pale smoke and brilliant light.

There was no controlling the Inter-D at that point. The forward edge of the wave shot left, and sank low as if falling. It knocked away street lights, and only changed direction after grinding against the buildings for a moment, leaving white gouges and black streaks above the window lintels where the monster's asphalt and concrete dragged along the brickwork. The road-wave plowed through a parked truck and then bounced along the open road before crossing over to the right side of the street. *Was it dying?*

It hit the buildings on the right side only long enough to touch them, and then it started to rise. *No,* the creature was not dying.

The road sped up, and Nonstop had to fight to stay on its back.

It continued increasing speed, surging upward. It lifted Nonstop and Grace above the second floor windows, and then charged for the third floor. Nonstop heard a massive ripping sound below them, near the street. The monstrosity shook and spasmed, and swayed as it rose.

And as it continued rising.

The road dropped huge chunks of concrete back to the street — *shed huge chunks of concrete back to the street* — as it powered its way forward. Buildings shook, and sidewalks shattered as it passed; slabs of concrete exploded under pressure, bursting like dropped bags of plaster-dust as the road-monster tore itself free of its bed, and rose like a great, impossible sea-serpent. And now that the ground couldn't hold it, it would not be held. Black with asphalt, gray with concrete, it surged forward with none of the steadiness of the wave. It shifted left and right and up and down, constantly adjusting position, constantly recalculating, and constantly rising: passing the surrounding windows, passing the walls and the brickwork until it crested above the rooftops themselves.

Grace held tight to Nonstop. Nonstop held tight to the control bar. The road-monster surged on, and Nonstop fought just to stay in contact with it. He didn't think of trying the tap — he didn't dare — but they were rising above the roof line, where they would be easy targets, and he knew they couldn't stay where they were. Immediately, he heard the jets to his right. He turned and saw them, banking into firing position. He cut speed to sink lower on the road-monster, and as he did, he saw a missile leave from under each jet, he saw the white vapor trails that were just beginning behind each missile, and then he saw only the roof line and the brick walls as he worked lower onto the road-monster's back and prepared for the shock that was coming when the missiles hit, and their payloads blew the monster's head off.

But the missiles didn't hit — the road-monster lowered its position too. It followed Nonstop below the roof-line, then matched his speed exactly.

As the missiles shot past, and continued flying without hitting their targets, a smile began to form on Nonstop's lips. The smile grew bigger as Nonstop rode the serpent another three seconds and the missiles exploded. There was a corner coming. *Now was the time to try it.*

He switched the tap to his left hand, waited a beat, and then fired a quick burst into the road. The road switched onto the next avenue, sped up, and thrummed smoothly, surging forward like a jet-boat on calm water. Nonstop's grin stretched his lips wide and then wider still.

Smile of the Lupine.

"Come on baby!" Nonstop practically sang as he braced himself up off the seat a bit, knees bent, up on his toes. He would have stood full, but there was a terrified person hanging onto his back.

They charged along the next block, and then the towering monster lurched down a side street.

"Hey!" Nonstop said.

"What?" Grace said, looking at Nonstop, then turning to look at the speeding road.

"I didn't tell it to go down this block," Nonstop said, shifting his position on the bike and ramming his tap down at the monster, squeezing the tap's activation bar.

"Well then shoot it," Grace said, growing wide-eyed.

"I am. I am. It's going anyway —"

Slam

The roadway crashed its left edge into the side buildings, causing Rattletrap to skip toward the end of the roadway. Nonstop lunged right to keep the bike on the monster and —

Slam — Into the next group of buildings, and then the next, and then across to slam into the buildings on the other side of the street. Nonstop kept lunging on the control bar, leaning way out past it, forcing the bike to stay on the road — but he was no longer firing; he was no longer even aiming.

"Nonstop!" Grace yelled.

"This is no good," Nonstop yelled back, adjusting the bike with every slam into the buildings, and working the crook of his elbow around the control bar, freeing at least his forearm to aim the tap. "This is the wrong way!" he yelled, firing. "This is heading us west — deeper into town — Doc is east! — the other way!" He fired his tap again and again, as steadily as he could manage, but the monster surged west-ward with even greater speed.

"Wait. There!" Grace pointed to the end of the block, where the street was noticeably brighter.

Nonstop looked where Grace pointed and saw the brightness, saw the suggestion of a wide open space: Berber Street, by the sign he could see on the corner.

The creature surged into the new area, and the new area was huge, three lanes in each direction, plus a parking lane on each side. The monster turned fully onto Berber Street, still surging, still heading the wrong way.

"This must be it, this big street must be what it wants," Nonstop said, driving up to the crest of the monster's back - aiming his tap to the right, hoping to turn the creature left with his next shot - and then keep it turning left until it turned around.

"What? What do you mean?" Grace asked. "Do you think it wants more road?"

"I think its trying to get back in - I think it's trying to ditch us"

"Good! Let it! Let's get off this thing!"

"No. We need it!" Nonstop said, leaning close to the creature's roadway back, and firing.

The monster spasmed noticeably, but pulled the last of its staggering length onto the new street, continuing in the same direction, rising sharp and fast.

"Hang..." Nonstop started to say, but didn't finish. The road monster slammed itself down onto Berber street, its two lanes grinding on top of Berber's eight, the force of its motion aiming downward as well as forward, as if it *was* trying to find its way back into the road network, with the grinding of its attempt roaring like the battle-cry of some prehistoric giant, *more* — like the sound of a thousand, stampeding, screaming megamonsters bent on forward motion at any cost.

And then it didn't. And then there was no grinding sound at all, and instead of being six feet off the ground, they were four. Nonstop felt panic. He drove up to the head of the creature. He saw ripples forming on the surface of the Berber roadway. The road he was riding was acting like some kind of giant alligator, half submerged in some swampy river and swimming for the tall reeds.

Nonstop fired at the front of the road, at what passed for the top of the monster's head. He kept his beam focused on a single spot as the road thrashed, and surged, and shifted positions.

It worked. The Monster rose up. As the bike slid down its back, the monster twisted, trying to smash the creatures riding it with the battering ram of its forward edge — except, no — its forward edge did not have a battering ram shape. Its forward edge had jagged blocks of concrete hanging immediately below its top surface, then a dark undershelf below that, and then another shelf of jagged concrete slabs. *Its front edge was split.* The creature had formed some kind of a mouth, some jagged, rock and cave imitation of a mouth, but a mouth imitation that was functioning, and trying very hard to bite Nonstop and Grace.

"Oh my G— It has a mouth!" Grace screamed. "How can a road have a mouth?"

Nonstop dodged with the bike, watching his adversary, watching the parameters of his little patch of moving blacktop. "It may have a mouth," Nonstop said, "but it aint got no throat — at least none I can see."

The bike fell back as the creature lunged, then Nonstop sped up again — slipping under the creature's head as it lunged again.

"Let it go back — Stop pretending you know! — Let it leave. It's going to eat us!" Grace screamed, hugging Nonstop tighter, and catching glimpses of the lunatic blue sky.

"Nah, it aint never gonna catch us — but we gotta turn it around — we gotta get control of it. We gotta help Doc."

The whine of the jets reached Nonstop's ears. *Where?* Behind him. Left side. Nonstop wanted height, but he was riding near the head already. He leaned far back to the right side, leaving his seat, surprising Grace by practically laying across her thigh, and stuck his arm behind Rattletrap's wheel, firing the tap full blast.

The writhing monster rose swiftly beyond the bike, still trying to shake Nonstop and Grace from its back. It stretched forward, leaving the ground far behind, and Nonstop stayed on, not a bronco rider — a pilot fish, a tick bird. The creature rose higher still...

And then it twisted — so that its blacktop faced the earth below — upside down and still moving. Nonstop felt the alarming pull of gravity. Nothing would keep them in contact with the road except massive forward momentum. Nonstop gave the bike full acceleration, and for a second it worked; the wheel dug in; the bike moved forward.

But the creature merely continued rising, and the inevitable happened: Nonstop fell away, seeing the brilliant sky emerge on either side of the black road as his bike slid downward in the air and the surface of the road shrank away.

As they fell, the creature kept moving, and one of its coils came into view. Holding the control bar, Nonstop threw his weight outward, twisting the bike, and influencing its descent.

They hit the road and bounced, impacting against the blacktop with the bike's side. White streaks flared around them as they tumbled on the asphalt only to strike it and bounce off it again — but it was a thousand times better than falling, a *million* times better — *an infinite amount of times better*. Falling might have meant death. Falling would have meant an unprecedented test of his impact diffusion, but landing badly on the road was landing. They could recover. They plummeted in a series of skidding hops, with Grace screaming as they rocketed downward, her hair flying in tangles above her head, but they did keep contact with the road. They did recover.

Detecting the return of its antagonists, the road-monster curved back, coiling around its entire upper third to strike at them with its make-shift mouth.

The creature dove at Nonstop and Nonstop dodged, only to have the creature strike at him again, and again have to dodge. While attacking Nonstop, the entire tangle of twisting, hi-jacked blacktop descended westward along Berber Street, colliding and crashing against cars and walls and power-lines, but no switch of trajectory, no altering of velocity, would allow the creature to catch Nonstop.

So it changed strategy. The creature humped up a fold in its rear section, and sent a wall of asphalt up its back to trap the riders and push them to a select striking point. Grace looked behind her in time to see the wall rushing toward them. Nonstop felt her turn, and looked where she was looking even as she screamed.

"Nonstop! A wall! Look out!"

"I see it!"

Nonstop sped up the creature's back, looping around a coil that started at the second story level. He looked to end his advance at the roof-line, but rose even higher as the monster stretched in reaction to the creatures on its back.

The giant head came for Nonstop from the side, its rocky maw opening to shadowed blackness, its jagged concrete escarpments ready to grind and crush.

It was hard for Nonstop to judge the monster as a landscape. He didn't know how long it was. He didn't know any of the rules for how much asphalt it could pick up or discard, or at what rate it could do it. So he couldn't keep track of the head unless he could see it. The creature's strike surprised him, and the best he could do was vault when his peripheral vision caught sight of the massive head swinging his way.

He slapped Rattletrap's arms down on the asphalt, cart-wheeling the bike to the edge of the moving road, and grabbing the road's edge to swing under it.

To Grace the action was a blur, the Monster's head came rushing at her; the bike jerked; she saw sky; she felt the inertial swing in her whole body as her shoulders looped around and she inverted, suddenly not on the seat anymore, suddenly hanging on to straps and whatever her feet could catch onto, as the ground looked up at her from seventy feet below — and as she found out that she wasn't done moving yet. Rattletrap's rear section swung under the ripped and fissured concrete of the monster's underbelly. The monster's head came shooting past the road section they hung onto, and the entire road twisted suddenly upward. The twist forced their section of road to invert, and the concrete side-edge suddenly raced toward the sky. Nonstop took advantage of the twist, catching its momentum, and then simply made the bike let go.

The bike was airborne for a second, touching nothing from its top, its bottom, or its sides. Even the outward-stretching ends of Grace's hair touched nothing.

And then gravity called them back as the road untwisted and corrected itself. Two seconds later, they landed — perfectly centered on the white line of the moving blacktop — *an explosion rocked the creature from below*, thundering loudly, and sending a smoke cloud rolling upward. The creature sped forward.

Lifer 13 and Lifer 8 banked in, swooping down for another shot at the creature and the riders on its back.

The creature uncoiled and lunged at the jets, using its length to gain height. Nonstop skidded down its back, the bike hopping as it skimmed backwards and then sideways. Grace saw the rooftops change angles, then saw their stairwell doors, their air vents, their fire escapes. The view dipped and she saw broken concrete and black asphalt again.

The creature's lunge missed the jets. They circled to aim at Nonstop again.

The road folded tightly near its head and shot backward, sailing past Nonstop to re-address the flying threats. Nonstop, driving forward, was suddenly faced with a road that was disappearing in front of him while at the same time speeding alongside him and traveling on behind him.

Nonstop stood up on the bike and bounced it on its tire. The bike hopped, and he did it again, higher. As the end of the road curved nearer, he bounced the bike higher still, and at an angle, and twisted it in the air. This allowed him to land the bike on the other section of road, facing the other way, where there was plenty of monster to speed forward on.

Nonstop grinned again — a second dose of smile of the lupine — and shot the bike forward, toward the head.

Then he saw a move from the creature he wasn't prepared to see: one of the flying jets sped toward the creature — Nonstop could see both of them without turning his head — he didn't have a word for it, but he could see what was coming, and it happened fast — the head of the road-monster swung to the right, curving to strike with the flat, blacktop surface of its head. Its head caught the robot with the 8 painted on it. It caught it under the wing and fuselage of the jet. The road-monster pushed the machine off course for an instant before snapping it downward and sideways and sending it crashing wing over wing along the rooftops — where the jet broke into pieces as it gouged along the tar and skylights, until finally, it erupted into a fire-ball somewhere over the streets.

Nonstop heard the next missile coming. The sound of its approach was sharper, right on top of them. He slapped the ground with Rattletrap's claws and swung the vortex chamber in a crazy break-dancer move, extending all the arms on the rear gear-array, while standing the bike up on is vortex chamber. The missile detonated an instant before it hit the road — and impact diffusion raced over the bike as the explosion sent it tumbling. Hunks of the road surface split apart like fingers opening, only to be pulled back and fused into place by whatever field animated the asphalt tonnage.

Rattletrap tumbled to the brink of the road's edge, and then over it. Nonstop managed to lash out with the bike's claws and hang on to the last bit of blacktop as the bike's vortex chamber sailed out into open air. Grace locked her arms around Nonstop's waist and the monster coiled tightly in reaction to the explosion.

Suddenly the road offered Nonstop a range of choices — surrounding him with several ways to get back onto its surface — providing he moved before the creature uncoiled. He made the bike let go of the road, and Rattletrap simply slipped to a coil beneath it.

To Grace it looked like they were driving on a rope that was tightening into a knot. Coils of road moved all around her, she saw white lines moving up, and she saw white lines moving down. Every section of curve had white lines moving, and they all moved at the same speed, but she could tell by the rushing buildings, and the rushing feeling in her stomach, that the whole collection of road coils was moving — *moving really fast.*

Nonstop was driving simply to stay on the road, and what he was accomplishing was a miracle. As the coils thrashed, he skidded or vaulted — flipping and slipping, sliding and gliding — but staying in prime position. The road launched in high arcs and banking rolls; the streets below flew into view, soon replaced by views of brick walls, then views of sky — some with tranquil white clouds, some with streams of debris silhouetted against the open blue — a new view with every twist of the undulating behemoth.

There was no air left in her. She felt the constant shifts of the roller-coaster dips, and she felt her stomach churn. She could throw up... she might... but her head... was so heavy...

Nonstop turned, and looped his arm around her just as she slumped. He held the control bar in his left hand. He held Grace and his tap in his right.

"Grace! Grace! Are you okay?" he yelled as he watched her, and watched the crazy, curving road, which finally was beginning to open. The slight stabilization of the road improved Grace's blood-flow, and her eyelids fluttered open. She made a sound that wasn't a word.

"Grace!" Nonstop yelled, seeing the improvement in her condition, "Can you grab the straps? Can you wrap them around your wrists?"

Nonstop watched the road as he felt Grace try to sit up. He never got the chance to see her do it, but he felt her shift in his grip, felt her move to stroke her forehead. Before he could look at her, another missile hit the road — somewhere on the coils below them. Nonstop didn't see the direction the missile came from, but it rocked the road, and it delivered another deafening roundhouse of sound.

The road monster lurched. And as he careened along with the bike, Nonstop felt Grace go limp, and slide down against his ribs. He had a loose grip on her, but only with his finger tips. He was holding the tap, and his palm was trapped against the activation bar. He used his forearm to pin Grace in place as she fell against his thigh. She was twisted like a rag-doll, and her ribs pressed against his leg, right above the knee. His fingertips strained as he fought to keep her from falling further. A few more inches, and she would fall away. *No. Hold her. It's a hundred feet, maybe three hundred feet to the ground and you're moving. Hold her. Hold her or she dies.*

Grace's eyes came open full, her body went rigid, her hair whipped about her face and she felt her sneaker slipping across the curved cover of the vortex chamber. She screamed and she thrust out her arms — her left hand smacking the top of the motorcycle, her right hand finding purchase around Nonstop's knee.

"NONSTOP HELP ME!" She screamed.

He worked his thumb free of the tap, which released the device to loop around his wrist like a cinder-block bracelet. His thumb wrapped around Grace's upper arm and his grip improved.

Her foot slipped from the vortex chamber. Her weight shifted. Her hips turned. One foot folded under her and pressed against the bike's foot deck. Her other foot, free in the air, fell, and bounced against the moving road.

White flashes spasmed up her leg as diffusion protected her from the impact, but the jolt that ran up her body still hurt, and she shifted against Nonstop's thigh, slipping down another inch.

"Oh God," he said as she fought to get her leg back onto the vortex chamber, shifting with every move. He couldn't let her go. He couldn't. He couldn't. But oh God, he couldn't hold her.

He let go of the control bar and grabbed her left arm. The bike veered toward the far edge of road. He pulled Grace higher on his thigh; her position improved and he threw his hand to the control bar — yanking it to keep the bike from sailing over the road-edge. Then he returned his hand to Grace, and raised her to the point where she could grab the control bar — much, much better. Nonstop yanked the bike into position again as Grace felt her weight come off her pressed foot. If she could get her foot flat on the deck, she could use it to...

The road coil shifted. Swinging upwards and sideways, so that the bike was riding a sidewall, the insane, choppy border between the monster's blacktop and its concrete. Grace's feet came away from the bike and she hung out over the edge — *screaming* — sliding lower again on Nonstop's thigh.

Nonstop leaned and twisted to throw both his arms around Grace, while he hooked his left foot under the control bar. Grace screamed, watching the changing, distant ground framed by shifting, moving coils of roadway. Nonstop pushed the control bar with the sole of his shoe, dipping the bike back onto the blacktop as he shifted his hands and brought Grace up to his chest, keeping the bike steady on the curve.

Grace kicked her feet until they found the deck's foot rail. She hooked her left foot onto it and pushed. She rose up steadily. Nonstop smiled and pulled. He grabbed Grace around the waist with his right hand, caught the control bar with his left, and sank his left leg back down to the foot rail. He pulled, she pushed, and just like that, the beautiful girl was sitting in his lap with her arms around his neck. Alive.

Where was the jet? Where were they? He looked around as best he could through the gaps in the road. He caught sight of the wide street below them and of a huge black helicopter parked on it in the distance. More to worry about.

Where was the jet? A dot in the sky, over his right shoulder. Where was the head? Up? Down? At the wound where the missile hit?

He looked up and saw the head of the monster, eclipsing the sun, causing bright, stabbing flares of solar light with its moving edge. *No good.* He still needed the monster — down closer — where he could control it. He sped up along the coil. His motion caused the coils to shift. He watched the head. He watched the coils. He watched the jet.

"Get back on the bike behind me!"

"No. No," Grace's muffled voice said gently against his chest.

"Wrap your hands in the straps at least. This isn't over. Sorry."

She reached weakly over his shoulders, and groaned as she secured her hands in the straps of his gear harness. She trembled.

"I'm sorry Grace," he said.

He sped up, holding out his tap with his right hand.

Closer to the head, he fired the tap behind him, seeking to get the creature running. It would straighten out. It would abandon the chaotic tangled posture that would only rob it of striking power. How could he lure the jet? Varrage would know. Where was Varrage?

He kept the creature running, and it did straighten out. It sped up and began trying to throw Nonstop off.

That was an Army copter up ahead. Nonstop saw its markings. Its rotors were turning slowly. It had been parked awhile. Nonstop saw vortex bikes lying in the street near it, clustered, almost in a pile. He saw one of the robot-men back out of the copter. Even stooped, it filled the whole rear hatchway.

He didn't have to worry about luring the jet. The jet was there to *find him*. He heard it shrieking nearer. He stopped firing the tap and slid down the road. The road stopped surging, slowed, and then coiled back to contend with Nonstop.

Nonstop watched the roadway's bobbing head as he slid down its back, and listened to the approaching jet. Could the monster hear the jet? Could the monster sense it in some other way? Nonstop watched the head, and saw it freeze, and then turn toward the sound — *Yes it could sense the jet.*

The head of the beast locked in on the position of the flying machine and froze, but its coils continued moving. They flowed in the air, from a long halo-shape, to a tight "S" position, so fluidly, that it looked like magic.

The jet fired a missile at Nonstop. The road-monster flipped out of the way, slamming broadside against a townhouse. Inside, the lamps shook and the walls cracked.

The missile hit a parked truck. The fuel tank burst and a fire-ball blossomed riotously up from the street. Nonstop saw the monster's head move then lost sight of it within the passing orange and black cloud.

He saw the road-monster's head emerge from the other side of the flame-cloud, and witnessed as its jaws grabbed the entire drone-jet and its pilot, lightning-quick, and pushed them backwards in the sky, raising them, fighting them until the jet engines stalled and their resistance quit.

And then the head and neck of the road-monster rocketed downward, until it slammed the plane, pilot and all, decisively into the ground.

As the monster hovered over the ruined jet — examining its kill — Nonstop rode up its back. The monster turned, as if unsure of where to place its attention. Nonstop rode nearer to its head and fired his tap into the creature's back.

"Can't let you go just yet," Nonstop said, and steered the road-monster toward the helicopter.

Grace turned her head, "What are we doing?"

"You feeling a little better?"

Nonstop slowed, and pulled Grace to his chest.

"Lift your feet."

Grace, already surprised by the close hug, was also surprised by the command. Nonstop felt the movements in her back that told him her legs were rising, and as Grace voiced her confusion about what he was up to, he dipped her head down, still hugging her close, and raised her hips high with his leg. Her legs lifted higher.

"This will work a lot better if I can see," he said, and holding her close to his chest, mindful not to hit her head on the control bar, he swung her around to the back of the bike.

It was clumsy. Her legs hit the vortex chamber, but her left leg slid over to the other side. Her hips slipped around him, and she was seated back on the bike behind him.

If he had remembered the straps, it would have worked perfectly.

"GAAAAAHHHHH," he cried as her arms tangled around his head, and then slid down to clamp onto his neck.

"Hold on. Hold on," he said, as he slipped his head out from under her crossed arms.

"My wrists are still tangled! I can't get them out! Stop the bike!"

"Can't! They've seen us. They're gonna start shooting."

"Who is? The planes?"

"No. Them." Nonstop motioned with his head as he steered the bike back into position, and found the sweet spot again with his tap. Grace looked where he indicated, and saw more of the robot-men, lining up outside a long black helicopter with two sets of whirly-blades. She saw a row of Dr. Norel's bikes lying on the street in front of the robot-men. *They're stealing the bikes. All this trouble everywhere and they're stealing the bikes? All this just to steal the bikes?*

Grace turned her wrists. How? How to get them out? She looked back at the robot-men. They were holding out their arms, flipping them into new shapes. More explosions. More violence. More pain ray.

She was rising. Nonstop was rising. The road was rising, and Nonstop was driving them higher on the road. She couldn't see Nonstop's eyes. She didn't know what he was thinking or where he was taking her. They were passing the second stories of the buildings, then the third. They were also speeding up.

They were charging.

She had to get free. She had to let Nonstop work. Her fingers were red. They were swelling. She lifted her forearms — *get the weight off them.* She rolled her right wrist. It simply spun in the strap.

Machine gun fire. *Why?* She pulled both her elbows away from each other, bringing the wrists closer together. She felt a thump hit her ribs and ignored it. Impervious to flying steel, she was trapped by a strip of sewn leather. She hooked the first finger from her left hand up into the tight, twisted strip around her right wrist, and pulled. When she rolled her hand this time, it moved. It was a fight, but she squeezed it through the loop. She shook her hand and flexed it, looking over her shoulder as she began to free her other hand.

A light started flashing on the arm of one of the machine-men, from a long flat bar standing off its forearm. Nonstop swung his gun-thing, firing into the left side of the road-monster. The road-monster lurched right. Grace shook on the bike and actually had to re-grab the straps to steady herself.

They rose higher, the pain rays couldn't reach them, the bullets didn't stop them, they were...

Something hit the monster dead center in the roadway, right where they drove. The blast came from the under-side, pushing slabs of the road apart and sending surges of light flooding between the broken chunks of asphalt — and then the field within the monster brought the slabs back into alignment, sealing them tightly, but not so tightly that Grace couldn't still see the seams between the pieces.

Nonstop swerved the bike, sped it forward, and then she couldn't see the seams any more.

* * *

From his hiding spot within a stand of trees not far from the highway entrance, Slice witnessed the monster work its way down Berber Street. He wasn't alone. The wooded area was full of Bike Pilots tending to fallen riders. He was helping Tumbler, who had been shot off his bike by the tank-suit zombies, and who was only now coming around. On each side of Slice, friends of his were struggling back to consciousness. Some were moaning. Some were sitting up. He heard someone crying; it wasn't Scorcher, though Slice had heard that Scorcher's arm was broken, and so far, that seemed the worst of it: bruises and lacerations; no one was actually shot; no one was dead. But the dream was dying. They had lost at least a dozen bikes — delivered them into the hands — of what? What were those things?

Wazzi trundled his bike over. He hadn't gotten blasted. He was ferrying riders to the other side of the highway underpass, away from direct lines of fire. He stopped his rig near Slice.

"I just dropped Bronco off a couple of streets from here, and he tells me he's feeling good enough to steal a truck and come back here for everybody."

"I wouldn't put it past him," Slice said, "He'll probably come back with a bus."

"Or a bulldozer. How's Tumbler? Can he sit up on a bike?"

"He's coming around. Just a minute. Do you see what they're shooting at?" Slice asked, gesturing down Berber Street.

"No, What — dag... What is that? Is that a road?"

"Either a road or a big bag of snakes. The Army things are shooting at it hot and heavy."

"Think we can steal back the bikes while they're busy?"

"They're still right on top of the bikes. And that's live ammo they're using now. If we charge for the bikes, I think they'll kill us."

"Still. It's the best chance we're likely to get. What if I cripple the copter? Do a kamikaze into one of the rotor shafts."

Slice looked at him. "No man. Come on. Don't talk like that."

"We could make some gasoline bombs. Stall them."

"Yeah. We could do that. But they'll start shooting for sure. We have to get these people out first."

"Maybe, but if we don't want that copter to leave, we probably don't have much time to do something about it."

"They're still loading bikes, and that thing has bought us some time too. What is it?"

"What's that on its back? That little orange dot?"

"What dot?" Slice asked as the road-monster drew closer. He squinted, straining to see.

"Holy — Oh my God — That's crazy-boy!"

"What?"

"Yeah, that's his bike. That's him!"

"We've got to make some gas bombs. Give me your water extractor. You got anything else that will hold gasoline? Give me tumbler's extractor." Wazzi twirled a screwdriver up from his belt. "I'll pop a tank on the nearest parked car."

"No, hold up. Look. He's charging," Slice stood up full — "Crazy-boy is charging."

He looked down the sun-lined street, and saw the road-monster stretch high, then fold back, then thrust forward, dipping low and speeding up. Yes, that was Nonstop on the road's back. He could see him now — and the girl. The girl was still here too, still in the game, hanging on as Nonstop bent low and pumped tap into the road. And the stupid army zombies kept shooting, even as the passing road upswept under all of them, sending them tumbling and cart-wheeling, crushing their weapons-systems, *mangling* their weapon systems, and not stopping there, not stopping the sweeping destruction until it crunched through the copter too, lifting its frame, rolling it, tearing it, smashing it — until it split — until the colorful bikes it held spilled out into the street like candy from some dragged and ruined pinata.

An un-suppressible cheer went up through the Bike Pilots. It wasn't planned, and it wasn't smart, but they couldn't help it. The copter's fuel tank ruptured and some spark ignited it. The broiling flames and rising smoke offered cover, and those Bike Pilots that could, ran back onto Berber Street to snatch back their lost machines.

Then Slick watched as Nonstop turned that crazy, towering road like a cowboy in the movies, rearing it up until it nosed the sky, spent its momentum, and then turned back eastward as it descended. Slick saw Nonstop look down at the Bike Pilots in the street as they began taking back their rigs, and Slice watched as Nonstop stood, raised his tap high in the air, and swung it in a greeting as he sped by, and the road-snake-thing plowed the unmoving tank-zombies further down Berber Street.

And Nonstop had said something as he drove past his friends. Slice couldn't hear it, couldn't make out what it was, but it looked like a war-whoop.

* * *

Norel staggered along the catwalk in the Outpost's basement, his eyes clearing, his body weary. Colonel Bloch followed a few feet behind him, cautiously stealing glances at the strange space around him. Beyond the catwalk the room seemed impossibly big. The ceiling stood at least four stories tall, which, judging from the door they entered through, would put it higher than the outside ramp on the top of Norel's building. Also, parts of the room were moving. He'd see a corner or a column, then he'd take a step and it would seem to be gone. He looked at open doorways, moving up and down, moving cross-wise, sliding on the walls. Some of the doors slid over the walls and the rooms inside them stayed perfectly aligned and visible. Some doorways slid, and the rooms inside their door frames changed. When he saw two open doors slide through each other, and the overlapping space between them revealed a third room, he had to look away. It wouldn't do to get too puzzled. He had to watch Norel. Pacifist or not, there was no reason Norel couldn't whirl with a knife, or a gun, or attack him with some hand-held thing every bit as crazy as this room. He had to stay focused. In this shifting cave, a sniper could be anywhere. One bullet could ruin everything. He ran his thumb along the handgrip of his 45, sliding his skin along the seam between the steel and the walnut grip plate. A fine weapon. No doubt.

He watched Norel.

* * *

Krork's eyes opened partially and then closed again. There was dirt on his tongue; he could taste it. He couldn't lift his head, and as memory returned to him he realized that was a good thing. Lifting his head would have been a bad idea. He was in the dirt. He was near the Outpost. The things that had shot him no longer stood over him, but as he moved his eye to glance around, he could see that the things were still close by, and that there were more of them.

He needed his data-box. He worked slowly to get it. One arm to his chest and one arm to his waist — make no sound — make no sudden shifts in visual pattern — stop occasionally. Every scrape of his arm against every grain of dirt seemed loud to him, seemed sure to announce his movements. Every inch he moved seemed too daring, too risky. Doctor Norel was alone with Bloch. Doc's dream was dying; Doc's dreams were ending. Doc's nightmares were coming true.

Krork was laying face down in the dirt, in a wide open space. He might be able to manufacture one move, but that would be all. He couldn't stand. Not now. Not quickly. By the time he got up, they'd cut him down again. Doc needed help. Doc needed help right this second.

Krork worked his hand down to the data-box on his belt, and when his fingers felt its contours, he pulled it free. Slowly, he transferred it to his chest, where his second hand took it. Half a minute later it was by his jaw. He worked the controls, glancing down to verify that it was in com-link mode. He brought it to his lips. He heard the wind around him — varied — at times distant, at times shrieking. How loudly should he speak? How loud could he get away with? How many Bleed Zones were here? Certainly more than one. How many chances would he get? Not even one. Not a full one anyway. He opened the continuum band, not sure what the multiple Bleed Zones would do to the signal, not sure if his words would go out over one of them, or all of them, or get hopelessly mixed between them. He didn't know, but he could only do what he could do, and so he spoke quietly into the data-box, taking what chance there was to take.

"Somebody...Doc needs help..."

He saw the nearest soldier-machine turn toward him, raising its arm. He saw the others follow its lead. He spoke louder, forcing the words through a body that could hardly take a breath: "The Outpost... Bloch has him... Hel. . "

The Lifers fired. One beam upon another. Krork screamed. His scream became a choking noise and he convulsed as if electrified. His body, too pained to rise, rose nonetheless. His muscles, overloaded with command, forced his vast body up on its fingertips and its toenails. He shook in involuntary spasms until his head dropped, and merely bounced from the movements of his shoulders.

The Lifers cut the beams.

And Krork's body fell.

Lifer 23 approached and bent to grab the back of Krork's shirt. The Lifer raised Krork's body and dragged it toward the nearest slope in the ground, trampling Krork's dropped data-box as it walked, breaking the device into so many ground-up pieces in a township now reduced to ground-up pieces.

Without hesitating, Lifer 23 threw Krork's body down the hill. It crashed into a damaged wall, and the wall crumbled, covering Krork, burying him, hiding him from the light of the tormented sky.

* * *

The end of town neared. Nonstop kept the ride surging toward it, wrangling the monster as steadily as he could. He stared straight ahead, watching the path in front of the road-monster, trying to allow himself to do only that, trying to push aside all the other things he was seeing, all the other things that were screaming for his attention and firing his impulse to act. Dark streaks jumped in the sky above him, and he tried to block them from his mind at the same time he tried to block his thoughts about the creatures he kept seeing as he traveled: the slab-men stumbling in the dirt-filled wind, the centipede-things crawling into the Law Firm's broken window, the white stilt-puppets clinging to the ledges of the office building; all the crazy things that were screaming for his attention, screaming for him to stop what he was doing and deal with them, all the things he had to ignore because there was something more important to take care of: *Doc.* Doc was in trouble, and without Doc, everything was going to fall. Until Doc was safe, nothing else mattered.

So he ducked his head and he pushed on. He pushed the road-monster toward the end of town and he tried to look at nothing except the clearest route out of the business district. Behind him, Grace seemed okay; he could feel her pulling on the straps at his shoulders. He could feel her weight in the way the bike moved. He could feel her forehead touching his back and thought she was probably looking down at the bike — if her eyes were open at all.

"You okay?" he asked her.

"I'm scared. I think —"

They entered an intersection - easily — but were hit without warning by a freight train of turbulence — their conversation aborting into screaming as their bike tumbled — *as the whole road-monster tumbled, pulled by the churning wind.*

* * *

Bloch descended behind Norel along a rampway, surrounded on every side by a vast, open space, enclosed by far walls of twinkling technology. All the lights seemed to be in small panels alongside doors. Were they access screens?

Perhaps.

The rampway led to a terrace with a walkway and a wall of wide open rooms framed with heavy bulkhead doorways — like a row of storefronts in an abandoned shopping mall.

The lights were on in one of the rooms, and that was where Norel appeared to be heading. The area seemed stable. Nothing was moving. Bloch felt himself relax, and noted that he hadn't been aware he had been feeling any tension.

Norel walked into the room. As he did, Bloch took note of a luminescent touchpad recessed in the wide door frame. Norel never touched it. Did that mean anything?

The room inside was lit from the entire ceiling. There were no light fixtures that Bloch could see. The space seemed clean and simple: a long gray table, some rolling chairs, and a dark wall of open cabinetry showcasing — what? Thin components, vertical, spaced tightly. It looked like a giant book shelf filled with tall magazines. Norel stopped in the center of the room.

Bloch stopped, and watched Norel's back.

Norel bowed his head, and then looked at the rear wall.

The wall was blank. Gray.

Painted?

Don't quit on me now old man.

"I'm glad you're finally seeing reason Doctor."

That did it. That did something. Norel turned. He stopped when he faced the cabinetry, but then turned his head to face Bloch. He looked disgusted. That was fine.

Norel turned back to the cabinetry, and without hesitation, raised his arm to a file, and pressed it with one finger. The file popped forward, emerging about eight inches from its neighbors. It looked to Bloch like a panel of sheet metal.

Norel pulled it out from the wall, revealing it to be at least four feet long. It seemed to have some weight; The Doctor had to work to carry it. But he didn't strain. Bloch thought he understood. Norel was carrying one of the panels he himself had taken from the strange rider back at Open Mind, and if Bloch was right, the panel was going to grow when opened. If it opened up to plans, fine. If it opened up to a weapon, he'd end this right here and bring a team down to open every one of these insane cases... *No. He wouldn't.* There were no teams left to order. The world outside this building would be growing hostile. His bureaucratic restrictions would be growing less and less effective. Soon the Army would be coming, F.E.M.A. would be coming, local police and fire would be returning. He had to get this right — right now.

He took a step further into the room.

* * *

Nonstop and Grace fought to stay on the bike and fought to stay on the road. The tornado-like wind tore over them; grit scoured against their arms and their faces. They screamed. They screamed again — as the wind roared past their ears, they screamed; as the road-monster thrashed and banged, they screamed.

Nonstop made the bike grab the road with its claws, trying to use the road's underbelly to block the wind — firing his tap to influence the road's position — but it proved hopeless, the road moved too erratically to be used for protection. "Get us out of here!" Grace screamed, turning her head so that her mouth stayed clear of the flying dirt.

"Just hang on!" Nonstop yelled as the wind pushed and pulled against the bike, swinging it every which way along the moving road. Nonstop looked in every direction he could, and everywhere, things were crashing against the road-monster –- window awnings, café lanterns, garbage cans — a thousand little things, a thousand little bits of the town, a thousand little testaments to the daintiness allowed by civilization, all too weak to stay rooted, all now lost to the raging air.

"It's going to be all right," Nonstop called over his shoulder as he pushed the road-monster toward a street corner, a direction the monster seemed to be moving to on its own. Grace said something, but he didn't hear it.

At the corner, the front length of the road-monster turned onto the new street easily. The bike moved with it. Grace looked left and Nonstop looked right and as they did, the road-monster's middle length slammed into the bank on the corner, producing an enormous noise, a bang, a shuddering crash — the sound of two buildings smacking together.

"The wind still has it!" Nonstop screamed, as both he and Grace looked behind them in time to see the tail end of the road-monster crash its way past the intersection, still pulled crazily by the turbulence. The road under them dragged backward, back toward the corner.

"Get it to go! Get it to go!" Grace yelled. And then the monster started moving forward on its own, grinding its midsection against the corner of the bank, crumbling the brickwork as it chewed its way forward, out of the storm.

* * *

Bloch stopped as Norel placed the long panel on the table. Norel reached for a rectangular device clipped to his jumpsuit and placed it on the middle of the table near the case. The device had a screen. What was it? A bomb? A taser? A gas canister?

"What is that? A phone?"

"Data-Box," Norel said, as if that explained everything, or, more truthfully, as if that was all he were willing to say. Fine. Name, rank, and serial number. Fine. *Fine.* Bloch had an idea.

"This building, it can go anywhere? Paris? South America?"

"Anywhere compatible with human life."

Norel stepped to the case and opened it. As Bloch expected, the walls of the case rose as the lid opened, and the items inside were taller than the case had been when it was closed. *Don't think about it. Don't get puzzled.*

Norel reached into the case and pulled out a stack of ledgers and portfolios. He placed the items on the table before Bloch. Then he gestured with his hands, and took a step back.

"Here are the plans for the Alignment Drives, and the first generation Vortex Bikes," he said.

"Very good. Very good. Now, I'd like to take this building to South America. Someplace isolated. Near the border between Peru and Columbia."

Norel turned away, and then sat in the chair at the end of the table.

"I will not aid you. You wanted to control my technology, control my technology." Norel gestured to the files with another wave of his hands. "I give you to God."

Bloch stared at Norel. "You'll do what I tell you — or I'll kill your men," he said.

"My teams are beyond your reach. As are yours."

Norel met Bloch's gaze calmly. Other than that, he didn't move.

Bloch reached into his pocket and pulled out his handset. He hit button after button with no result. Finally, he hit the buttons in a sequence, and a green line appeared on the black screen. It moved steady and flat until it reached the left side of the screen, and then it started over again on the right. Bloch turned the screen to its default mode and slipped the handset back into his pocket. He looked at Norel.

"I'll kill you," he said.

"I'm sure you will kill us both. We will be entombed, along with crucial aspects of my work. That may buy humanity some time."

Bloch studied Norel for a moment, sitting in the chair, fully resigned, it seemed, to sit there forever.

"I didn't realize you were crazy."

Bloch took a step further into the room. Norel didn't look at him. Bloch ran a finger along the metal file stacks, looking at them, and then looked at Norel. Norel still hadn't moved. Bloch got behind Norel. He touched a slim pouch attached to his belt, and opened it. The snap made a small noise in the quiet room. Bloch raised his pistol.

"Do you remember the bullets you were so weepy about Norel? The ones with the expanding prongs that ripped such huge holes in people? I enjoyed making them. They won me a promotion. Of course, they're illegal, and the Army won't use them, but I've got a clip of them right here. Pistol caliber. Made special."

He exchanged magazines in his pistol and walked closer to Norel.

"How about we turn your leg into hamburger? Or maybe make you a candidate for your Spinal Bypass inventions?"

Bloch stepped around Norel and leaned on the table, just far enough away that he could avoid any sudden pounce from the Doctor. He placed the butt of the gun on the long table. It made a loud clack. He lowered his head until he was eye to eye with Norel.

"Doctor, I can make it hurt, believe me."

He stood back, relaxing his posture, "And I won't wait forever. Keep that in mind while you play your games." Then he sat in the chair that faced the doctor.

The Doctor stared into space.

"This building Doctor, this basement, tell me about it. What does it do?"

Norel said nothing. But he did turn his head.

"Is it interdimensional? Are we still on Earth?"

"Yes," The Doctor said slowly, "We are still on Earth."
And once Bloch got an answer, he asked more questions.

* * *

The road monster, free of the roaring storm, began moving again. Nonstop tugged the bike in several short surges to keep the bike from getting tossed, and once stabilized, he found himself suddenly speeding along a new street, quickly looking from direction to direction to get a sense of his new path, his new options. He spotted a pizza shop, some small thrashing trees, and then a red and white fire station. Nothing unusual. Grace twisted on the seat behind him.

"Oh G —! What is that?" she said, and he could feel her pointing to a spot above his left shoulder. He looked over the rooftops and saw a long blade of jumping violet light tear at the sky. The light headed eastward, seemingly on a collision course with their bike. As the light-band jabbed at the air around it, it made the air look *squashed*. Nonstop could see visible folds in the sky: rings and streaks, as if the air currents were casting shadows. The air swirled into tighter and tighter coils, and he could see dark slivers of clouds as they suddenly flowered into existence, and then just as suddenly disappeared back into the coils of air. He turned away to look back where he was driving.

"What is that Nonstop? That's this Realm-dimension stuff?" Grace asked, still watching the air.

"Yeah. Probably. I —"

"— Nonstop, that's the sky!" She screamed, turning quickly to look at him, and seeing only the back of his head. "This stuff changes the sky?"

"No. Usually it's just things, creatures —"

"From other *realmlines — from other realities!*" She looked back at the moving, violet sky.

"Right. Yea —"

"— How can skies mix Nonstop? Oh God, *how can realities mix? What's going to happen to us? What's going to happen to Earth?*"

Nonstop felt Grace yank her head away from the sight, and could practically feel her squeeze her eyes shut. He heard her voice then, much quieter.

"Please, please tell me we can reverse this," Grace said.

"Doc can."

Grace's eagerness to believe Nonstop's answer bothered her. She sat up, and as she tried to pin down what she was thinking, she saw something else strange, beyond Nonstop's shoulder: a simple fenced-in lot, full of trees, approaching fast, but going smeary, as if the rows of leaves on the trees were zig-zagging against each other. Her eyes widened — and then the world turned white, and the electric roar of lightning filled her ears.

The next second they were driving at the beginning of the street again, re-approaching the pizza shop and the fire station as if she had hit the rewind button on her editing deck.

She screamed, looked to the sky, and kept screaming.

As they passed the fenced-in trees she yelled: "Get this fixed! Get this fixed!"

"Yeah. We're going to! We have to help Doc. That green light we saw in the sky back at the electronics store, that was ghost light, and it was coming from where we left the Outpost — but ghost light doesn't jump and flare. Something is wrong."

"I know, I know, but —"

"— Doc is probably in the same kind of trouble you were just in —"

"Guns?"

"Yeah probably,"

"More robot men?"

"Yeah, prob —"

"— But what about the sky? We can't j—"

"— The teams will have to fix the portals."

"But the bikes are in the streets!"

"We have to help —"

"— What if he's gone? What if that green light was the building disappearing again?"

"We... Uh...maybe, but we have to at least see. If he's gone, then you're right. If he's gone, then we'll have to try and close —"

They neared the end of the business district, and as they passed the last of the town's tall buildings, Nonstop looked into the wider vault of sky. He tensed, and Grace felt his muscles tighten through the layered membranes of their shirts.

"What?" she looked up, squinting as she peered, her eyes mostly closed, as if reserving her right not to see if what she looked upon proved too horrible.

She could see the violet light — from its rooftop height to its crazy rooting along the ground. It was some kind of storm, some kind of mini-storm, jagging its way eastward. At its center, on the ground, a giant ball of light churned upon itself, standing at least three stories tall, with blazing edge-lines that swept continually over each other, like a knot, trying to make itself tighter.

Nonstop slowed down as he watched it, and the road-monster rose higher.

Off in the distance, he could see the white portal the Outpost had come through earlier, still standing in the field, burning with the same white light as the ball within the rolling storm.

He had the tap he held in his hand. That was all. It seemed small against the power he was looking at. *Get close. Tap the rim, work inward* — No. Where was the Outpost? He should see it. If he could see the white portal, he should already see Outpost 14.

He thrust his tap down by his left foot, blasted the road full power, and caused the road-monster to swing right as it climbed higher. Where was Doc?

The monster charged ahead and Grace saw the toppled water tower — and the ring of demolished homes.

"Oh my God Nonstop! Look at what they did."

With the height of the road-monster's upswing, Grace could see more. She saw a wide hole in the ground: a crater, and she saw the Outpost resting within it. In the same instant, she saw the ring of soldier-robots surrounding the crater.

"There they are," she said, tensing.

"I see them."

She pulled closer to his back. She hid her face between her forearms. He could feel her tremble.

"Do you want to find a place to hide?" he asked her.

"Yes — no! Something will find me - or I'll disappear, or I'll get shot — or God, something will *eat me*."

"Okay. Grace, I'm going to hit them low. I'm going to hit them really, really hard. This might not be bad at all."

She started to answer his statement, but then just tried to crawl into his shoulder-blades instead.

He fired his tap. They picked up speed.

Nonstop steered for the blast-crater. There in front of him, was a whole collection of Doctor Norel's personal nightmares in the process of coming true, in the process of actually happening: Bloch was attacking, coming for the bikes, and at the same time, something really weird was happening to the Earth. To worry further, when Bloch had the bikes, what else would come true? Slaughter for the leaders of the world? Some new Junta with the power to enslave every man and woman on the Earth? Or to force us all into one way of living? Or to kill us for pleasure? Or *who knows* for what reason. Nonstop would like to say that was silly. But it was happening.

He dipped his head, raised his shoulders, and pushed the monster further. "Hang tight," he said, "The harder we get hit, the more protection the impact diffusion will give us."

He powered the road-monster through destroyed homes, scattering more wreckage into the air as the serpent raced.

He saw the Lifers from above, and saw them as they reacted to the approaching road-monster, raising their arms to fire. He got two seconds closer before the Lifers launched a wall of rockets at the asphalt monstrosity he rode.

The creature shifted, and the shells erupted behind it, throwing fountains of dirt in the air as the creature sped closer.

Nonstop saw two Robot-things shifting the equipment on their arms, and decided that he didn't want any more of whatever they had in mind. He curved the road-monster fast and high. It streaked upwards toward the darkening clouds, and then Nonstop banked it down sharply — a sideways baton-strike — how many tons? How much animated concrete and roadway?

In the last second, the monster's head blocked Nonstop's view. He didn't see if he hit the robots high or low. He just saw obliterated equipment fly away in all directions. He had to look back to catch a glimpse of what had happened, and when he did, he saw men on the ground, wrapped in cages of ruined machinery. The men didn't move.

Nothing is important until Doc is safe.

They blinked. He saw them blink. Right?

The white portal lay ahead down the grassy slope. He snaked the road back as shells exploded around him. At least one hit the road dead on, close behind Rattletrap, causing another rupture in the moving roadway — a rupture that spread directly under the moving bike — and then re-gathered, imperfect, but whole. Grace screamed as the road did this magic trick under her feet again, and she kept on screaming as the road swung and her view filled with the sight of the rolling portal storm.

The portal-sphere churned forward, surrounded by a wide ring of night in the middle of the day, advancing on tendrils of erratic lightning as it cut a steady path across the field.

413

Nonstop could feel its energy on his forearms, and in the gums around his bottom front teeth. The three slashes on his arm began to bleed. A long flare of realm-light rooster-tailed from his hair, followed by two more. Grace recoiled from them and shrank away. Nonstop never saw them.

Every few seconds, shells exploded near the road-monster, but the creature was doing a good job of avoiding the blasts on its own. It moved away from shells Nonstop didn't even know were coming.

Nonstop noticed two robots shooting jamming beams his way. He streaked the monster past them, so fast and low over the ground that even sideways, he was able to drive the bike without feeling gravity's pull, and with the move, he was able to turn the monster's belly and use it to block the jamming beams coming from the robot-men.

Once past the pain rays, he leveled the monster, turned to face the road behind him, and fired his tap at a section of the road monster a long way off – toward its tail end. The creature stopped its advance at that section, effectively pinned to the spot. Nonstop quickly slipped the bike to the right side of the road-monster as he kept his tap firing at the back, and the whole massive creature swung left — *like a gate*, knocking four of the robot-men to the ground. Explosion upon explosion filled the air as the monster's underbelly lit with a pop-corn eruption of bursting shells. The creature kept moving, absorbing and compensating for the explosions while it swept the robot-men into the crater.

The road-monster slipped into the crater as well, and instantly convulsed within the loosely piled earth. The bike bounced on the creature's back as the creature coiled and bucked — its aversion to the soft landscape even stronger than its aversion to Nonstop's tap. The ground swirled. The Outpost sank.

* * *

Bloch jumped to his feet as the floor swayed under his chair. He looked up in time to see the lights flicker: blackness, light. *An attack? Norel - escaping?*

No.

When he looked, he could see that Norel was still seated, calm as ever, staring at whatever lay beyond the doorway.

What was at the doorway?

Block raised his pistol, squaring his back to the wall. He took a step away from the Doctor.

Now? Was Norel set to pounce?

No. Bloch glanced back. Norel was still sitting — but *far away.* The room seemed to have stretched in the instant his head was turned. The table had stretched. The files had stretched. The paper had stretched. The Doctor had not. *Drugs?*

Bloch whipped to face the doorway, raising his pistol to the firing position. But his hand didn't finish the move. Instead, Bloch just stared.

The rooms outside were turning — The vast space itself turning — like a giant Ferris wheel — like concentric Ferris wheels - stacked within each other, ringed like a target, each band grinding opposite it neighbor, no edges distinct — wait, yes. Yes, some very distinct. Some razor sharp.

* * *

Nonstop rode toward the tail, as the road-monster twisted in the dirt, tossing the Lifers it had just pushed, thrashing everything it came into contact with. It struck the Outpost, passed it, and then returned to it, slamming the Outpost until the Outpost moved — *pushing the building* — *trying to mount the one solid object in the soft earth* — until the Outpost's bottom edge rammed up against the ground at the crater's rim and the monster could scramble and slap its way over the little building and get back out onto solid ground. As the monster surged forward, Nonstop glanced back at the Outpost and saw it sticking out of the crater with its front door tilting skyward.

* * *

**

The basement calmed. Bloch watched as it stopped swirling. "Rooms within rooms," the Doctor had agreed to, and then had explained his basement with a series of questions: how many rooms could you fit in one storeroom if each storeroom became a photograph of itself? How many of those storerooms could you flatten, and then fit in a basement? This was merely a new technology, Norel had said, one used too early, out of necessity. And Bloch could believe it. He had only to look around him. He could also believe that no attack was coming from the Doctor, since none had come during such opportune moments. And he could therefore also believe the crazy thing the Doctor seemed to be relying on.

They weren't getting out of this place.

But that was impossible. He would get out. And he would claim this technology as well. Replace the notion of rooms within rooms with war-machines within delivery vans.

But first — he'd have to deal with the here and now. What had just happened? Was it an earthquake? A malfunction? A ploy? What? The power loss had moved like a wave, or like a series of waves, across the strange network of rooms. Even as he looked, Bloch could still see far off areas twisting and going momentarily dark.

And things were still moving. The Ferris wheeling had stopped, but in the area close to the doorway where he stood, walls were still sliding slowly. Some were rising, some were moving laterally, but no matter where he looked, if he looked long enough, he would see movement.

One particular terrace, or balcony, if that's what you'd call it, required no study for the detection of its movements. It was convulsing: blatantly and rhythmically. It would be normal one moment, then blur in a rapid see-saw motion, and then be normal again. It repeated this cycle over and over and showed no signs of stopping. Bloch didn't like that terrace. Not at all. He took one last look around, breathed, and then turned back into the room.

"Enough tricks Norel," he said.

The doctor, close again, stared as before.

*

Norel sat, dis-mindful of the Colonel, with his thoughts a million miles away, finally, a million miles away. So many things undone. So many mistakes.

His hands, from the physical systems deep under his skin, began to tremble.

*

The lights across the basement spasmed again. Bloch noted them, and re-entered the room. There was blackness in that light-flicker. Blackness darker than any night, or any tomb. He had just seen it — just for an instant, true, but long enough for the blackness to register.

"Enough tricks Norel," Bloch said, striding. "We're going to play this *my* way."

He raised his pistol, aimed at Norel's knee, and fired.

The muzzle flash sheared out sideways along an angled plane that crossed the entire room. The flash began at normal speed but slowed as it traveled the plane, and as the flash within the plane reached the walls, the surfaces of the walls began to boil kaleidoscopically.

Confused, Bloch pulled back the gun — *but the gun wouldn't move.* He was sure in that instant that if he released his grip on the handle, the gun would simply hang in mid air. He didn't try. He didn't dare.

The bullet crawled free of the muzzle, spinning. The air around it broke into gelatin-like cubes. Slowly, the cubes forced open seams along the bullet's tip, and the bullet grew fangs, one point opening into five, four seams curving into blades. The bullet became a spinning turbine that would blossom into shrapnel as it sawed into flesh. It spun, on a course with Norel's knee.

Bloch watched Norel. Could Norel Move? If he could, he didn't, and it raised the question: *If the bullet was slowed in this space, what of the target?*

A second plane flared, the color and texture of the bullet. The bullet widened and narrowed to fill the plane. Even the highlight that marked the cylindrical nature of the bullet widened and flattened. Somewhere, someway, the bullet was traveling normally.

As the bullet traversed the air, a seam formed in the floor and pushed its way toward the ceiling. Bloch felt himself tilt with it, and saw Norel tilt away on the other side of the floor. He saw the ceiling take on an angle, one corner rising with the floor at one speed, one at another, and he saw the slow trajectory of the bullet rise to stay parallel to the floor. Then suddenly all evidence of the trajectory was gone: the plane of the muzzle flash, the plane of the bullet, the paths of cubed air, all gone, all vanished from existence, or at least from sight.

And then the lights in the basement shut off, or perhaps they followed the bullet in its beyonding. In any case, Bloch was still moving backwards when the space around him blackened.

* * *

Nonstop got the monster stable. As it lurched in one direction, he'd get it to swerve in the opposite, again and again, and as the robot-men fired, he managed to dodge. All the while keeping his eye on the Outpost - fighting to keep it in his sight.

Would it sink back into the dirt?

Should he drive the monster into the crater again and push the building all the way out? He pointed his tap at the road mons—

— a beam from the Lifers caught him in the chest. He seized. Grace's hands flew back before she could even think. Her contact with Nonstop let some of the beam jump into her, and she felt the pain as if it were live current. Her mind flashed to her Uncle's abandoned garage, to the round, twisty light switch that was bolted to the wall. One rainy day, when she had snuck into the garage to marvel at its leaning walls and ruined woodwork, she turned the knobby light switch and a jolt of current ran up her arm. That's what the pain jumping off Nonstop reminded her of — but back at her Uncle's garage she could pull away and run from the light-switch. Here, she was on the back of a motorcycle, up in the air, on the spine of some outer-space road-serpent, and there was no place for her to escape to.

Nonstop was no longer firing.

Nonstop was no longer moving.

The monster ran free, speeding away from the crater, grinding just its middle section along the cherished solid ground, and keeping each of its thrashing ends moving freely in the air.

It raised its tail and swung it without being forced to.

*

The Lifer who shot Nonstop saw a moving wall of concrete swing his way, faster almost than his taxed brain could process. The wall and the dirt hit him. He saw the sky, and then for a time, he saw nothing at all, not even the compelling light that pulsed over his right eye.

*

"Nonstop steer!" Grace screamed as Nonstop slumped forward and the bike drifted toward the edge of the road. She shot her arm past his ribs and slammed the control bar. The bike shifted back toward the center of the road, but rolled past it and headed toward the other edge. Grace reached for the control bar, but her fingers couldn't wrap around it; they stretched and waggled in open air.

"Nonstop!"

She shoved his back, and her fingers reached the bar. She gripped it, and pulled the bike back to the midpoint of the road. She managed to keep it there, though she could tell the bike was sliding down the creature's back. She had no idea how to accelerate the crazy machine.

"Nonstop. Come on! Wake up! Drive!"

She tested spots on the control bar as the creature raced for the open field, and found a section that revved the bike when she twisted her wrist. She played with it — trying only to keep the bike right where it was. She tried tugging on the control bar to stabilize the bike, and for the moment, it seemed to be working.

The road-monster moved on its own, and she thought it wise to let it. The creature pulled them back into the wide field where the Outpost had come through the portal, and again, there was that weird, electric feel to the air, and again, here too, the sky was discoloring in bands.

The creature bounced over something on the ground. The bike moved and threatened to drive over the edge of the roadway. Grace yanked the control bar, the bike twisted, and she yanked it again the other way.

"Nonstop! Wake up!"

He did. A bit.

Nonstop looked at the road and moved his left hand, fumbling over the control bar. Rattletrap's left arm moved, swinging lethargically as if it had felt the pain-ray too. Nonstop leaned on the bike, and made Rattletrap's left arm grab the edge of the road. Then the claws of the bike's right hand gripped the rough edge as well, and for the moment, they stopped moving on the monster, safer merely being carried by it.

"You okay Nonstop?"

"Y-h-h. Yesss."

It was true. The overload to his system was easing, at least the pain overload was. As Nonstop sat, weakly panting, the sight he saw in the field filled his mind, and his brain sent out a signal of panic his body could not respond to. He could only watch. Grace saw it too, and was speechless, even the road-monster paused, swaying in the field as if it didn't know which way to turn.

Grace wanted to scream, tried to think instead, and could only manage a series of sharp gasps.

The portal sphere, grinding, and arcing with wild lightning, pushed itself into the edge of the white portal and fed its crackling energy to the white portal's rim. Thick branches of lightning shot from the white portal up to the lowest-lying clouds, and then across the grassy field. Light eruptions from the portal sphere shuddered across the sky. Dark flashes and loud thunderclaps erupted from within the brilliance of the white portal — some of the dark flashes lasted only an eye-blink before vanishing, but others remained stuttering in the air, and some slipped around the portal's edge, shining like dark beacons, running riot along its rim, doubling and tripling as they ran through each other, as their beams crossed and re-crossed, creating gaps that occasionally offered glimpses of the pure blue sky beyond the storm. Grace looked away from the bright portals, and instead followed the black striations as they vaulted to the top of the sky.

"Oh my God," Grace said, "look at the sun."

Nonstop did, and it didn't help him at all. He didn't want it. The sight made his joints feel like water. The sight made him feel like a kindergartner repeating a nonsense phrase: "My poor little planet. My poor little planet."

The sun was black. It wasn't even black; the sun was an absence, a hole in the sky, the same way the pupil of the human eye is really a hole. And it wasn't just a hole. It wasn't just an absence, or an aperture to permit the passage of light – it was an *insane* absence – it was a big, black, circular shape, connected to a smaller circular shape, which itself was connected to a tiny circular shape, like a dark snowman, and all along the rims of these holes, were smaller versions of the same patterns of holes, and all the edges of these patterns were moving, bleeding with smaller versions of themselves. Beyond them, in the darkness, grew tendrils of slow-motion lightning, tendrils whose paths stayed etched beyond the sky, spreading like some great network of capillaries, illuminated again and again as fresh flashes blazed around them. The sight made Nonstop feel sick in his mind. What sky could show the sun like this? Not his.

An electric roar, like amplifier crackle, pealed across the field. At the sound, Grace threw her arms around Nonstop's chest and squeezed. The road shuddered. Rings of light, like waves upon a shore, began rippling across the sky, radar green where the sky was dark, smoky white where the sky was blue.

And then the white portal split. No, to Nonstop that didn't seem true. The portal sphere was involved though; he had seen a portal separate from the churning sphere and lift into the white portal. Only after that, did the new portal slide into the field and take its position next to the white portal.

As Nonstop found his breath freeing, the portal transference happened again and again. Portals peeled from the sphere, were pulled into the white portal, and passed through to become part of a growing wall of huge white portals.

Nonstop took a deep breath. Grace saw glowing aurora waves stretching in the vast, puzzle-fit sky, and wanted to bury her head again.

"Is this as bad as it looks?" she asked, forcing herself to move beyond panic.

"I don't think it's good. It doesn't *feel* good."

"What do we do?"

"We get Doc. We go around the crater, if any of those guys are left, we hit them where they're not looking."

"Back to that? What about all this?"

"We get past those guys. Doc will have the best idea of how to deal with all this. Right now those guys will have to split up to watch all the angles, so getting past them will be easy."

"Back to that? Easy? Really? You're already planning?"

Faster than Nonstop could answer, an image of Varrage's strange face popped into his mind, and with it, under the image, came an image of Jaquon's real face. Unhappy. Had he ever seen Jaquon any other way? The image of Varrage regained dominance in his mind as the smirk died on his lips. He answered.

"One by one, the Army guys will be easier to take out."

"Kill?"

"I don't think so. The two guys we hit were still alive outside of those suits, still blinking anyway. But, I don't care. I'm not worried about it. I'm not."

The road spasmed. Its top half started to rise.

"What – what's happening?" Grace asked.

"I don't know," Nonstop said, craning his neck to see what the top of the road was doing.

It was far above them. The sky's radar-light rode down the road-monster's towering length, defining its shape in moving rings of green light.

The asphalt edge Rattletrap held onto started to crumble beneath its claws. Nonstop moved them to a new spot, but that began crumbling too.

The next spot he grabbed held, and they hung there, nearly completely vertical. There was no way to ride at this point. He could only drive down, and even that would be more like falling. Could he hit eighty eight before they hit the ground? How much would his impact-diffusion spare them?

"What do we do?" Grace asked.

"There will be better hand holds on the other side, the concrete is rough. We can —"

A roaring peal of lightning shocked him silent – the sound loud and extended and sharp – like a pool cue slamming onto a wooden tabletop mixed with the buzz of electric ripping. Nonstop and Grace looked up again, to the road-monster's head-section, where sizzling lightning discharges were jumping back and forth and connecting it steadily with the radar-light weather front. A full lightning strike blasted into the road-monster itself, and traveled down the inside of its body, making it glow with green light from the inside out, showing every one of the asphalt's cracks, revealing to Nonstop and Grace just how damaged the road surface was. The light rode through the creature down to its tail end, where it bled out onto the ground in a perfect circle, a green light-ring that spread quickly, and then weakened until it faded from view.

The creature's midsection coiled in reaction, pulling its rear lengths closer while its head remained high and vertical, swaying gently, as if it were hypnotized by the green clouds around it.

"Now. We get lower now," Nonstop said as he made the bike let go, and started driving it down the coiled road. The creature's lower half reacted to his movements, running counter to everything Nonstop did. Any section of road he drove down, the monster would raise. If he tried slowing down, the monster would angle. Nonstop tried driving with Rattletrap's arms thrown in — jumping and crossing to new sections of road, but the creature was hard to confuse: it reacted the same way every time Nonstop jumped, not seeming to realize that Nonstop was trying to leave it. Nonstop slowed, and then coasted as the road tilted. Now descending at a predictable rate, he waited to see what the road would do. In the distance, past the hill, past the ruined houses, up where the sky was a swirl of dark green ink, he saw Skyde flying his way, and a small part of his heart lightened.

"Look, here comes..." he started to say.

"No! No! You look!" Grace said, pointing below her to a slab of road that fell away from the creature, and then to another slab that leaned out from the road's surface, jutting up like a tooth.

Thunder cracked again, loud, and the sky flashed with jagged spears of light as the white portal absorbed the last bit of the portal-sphere.

The creature's thrashing began again as electric charge flooded the air; it pulled its head free of the weather front and began moving across the field.

Nonstop kept descending, but the cracks in the road were now evident. He could see them plainly, even in the odd eclipse-light, and more importantly, he could *feel* them as he drove. Suddenly, the bike seemed much too high to him. They were a hundred feet in the air. He had to get them lower, had to get the *creature* lower. He fired his tap at a section of road above him, hoping to make the monster sink. It trembled instead, and three sections of road fell away along the middle of the creature, in the section between the bike and the ground.

Watching the falling pieces, Nonstop saw a black claw sweep out from under the road-monster, from a spot near where the road's underbelly touched the grass. The claw was large and thin, and part of his mind wanted to believe he hadn't seen it, that it was a crack, or a tree shadow. The same part of his mind wanted instant verification of those nice ideas and told him to turn around, to make sure that what he had seen had only been a trick of the foul light.

He spun the bike and drove higher along the road-monster.

"What? What's wrong?" Grace asked.

Nonstop looked over the edge and went rigid. He spun the bike again and returned to descending.

"What? What?"

"Here, take this." Nonstop handed Grace the tap.

"You want me to steer the monster? I — what?"

Nonstop didn't answer. He pulled his sword from its sheath.

"What? Oh no," Grace said, and turned to see for herself. The road thrashed, her sight-line shifted – she twisted her head, rejecting views of the road and the sky and the portals before she got a look at the ground, before she saw her new friend's worst nightmare.

Elephant-sized creatures that looked like walking jumbles of tar-covered bones, strode out from the glowing portal wall.

Grace whipped her head to see more. The monsters were spreading out across the field, splitting away from each other. Three walked close to the road-monster but were already moving toward the top of the slope, toward the Outpost. Grace glimpsed a fourth monster, saw fire, and then the bike lurched and lurched again. They were no longer rolling. The road was no longer smooth. Nonstop had the bike hopping on its arms as well as driving on its wheel, moving across a conveyor belt of broken road sections as if leaping from stone to stone in a stream. Grace turned to look behind her and see what was causing the change in the road, and found herself looking through the road instead. The surface was broken, and the segments that remained were barely touching each other, suspended in a strange field of turbulence that pulled a green tint from the air around it. The energy field rippled as it moved, distorting Grace's view as she searched for the creatures on the ground through the prism of the disintegrating creature in the air. How much further to the ground? What would they do when they reached it?

Nonstop halted the bike by grabbing an up-turned outcropping and letting the tire spin. — the wheel turned furiously as the bike churned in small ovals. White smoke drifted out from under the tire.

Nonstop ignored the smoke and watched the suspended pieces of road around them, searching for the right move. Grace strained to see where the monsters were on the ground. She spotted them, and noticed that the fire she had seen on the one creature was really a man – a man-shaped version of the monsters. Translucent energy flares danced on the man's back and neck. His skin was black and split in dozens of places, revealing thin orange and yellow lines of light. He rode on the back of one monster, continually raising his right arm high and slashing ferociously at the creature. Grace witnessed as the creature tossed the slashing-man with a twist of its shoulders and in the same instant she saw that the man-shaped monster wore pants – shredded to the knee in long strips – but pants nonetheless. What kind of monster wore pants? What kind of man looked like black ice cracked above a molten sea of fire? The question felt like a puzzle, one she should know the answer to. Was he on the Outpost? Was he on the world they visited first? She hadn't seen him. She would not have forgotten some —

The road twisted violently. The small slab they clung to tilted, but stayed in position as the creature moved, as if the slab were a knife blade stuck in the creature's side.

Nonstop launched the bike as the slab fell free from the creature. He hit a new section of road, adjusted as they bounced, only to find that the new section of road had gone inert as well, useful only as a last-second ramp back to live road – *if there was any live road.* Nonstop tensed as they launched again into the air. Grace held her breath.

Nonstop landed them on a long section of supple roadway and continued the drive downward. Grace breathed.

She looked above her. *Realm-wind* her mind said, not noticing that she had named something. The road-monster extended high above where they were driving, its head framed by the darkest of clouds. Waves of glowing green wind washed over it.

And tore chunks of asphalt from it.

Through dust and distortion and refracted light, Grace thought she could see the creature itself as its asphalt skin fell away. Its true body wavered in form, as if fighting to stay together outside the asphalt. It did seem serpent-like. A majestic river-snake made from cyclone, vanishing in and out of sight. Blameless, she understood. She thought she was probably watching it die.

She held the tap. Could she send it home – could she? How high were they? What would happen to the road without the creature?

What would happen to the road if the creature died – or got swept away by the realm-wind?

She raised the tap, but couldn't bring herself to fire it, didn't even know for sure *how* to fire it. She looked again toward the monster's head, where her sympathies –

"Nonstop! Look out!" she yelled as several chunks of road fell straight at them.

Nonstop, who was so good at reading landscapes and their subtle shiftings, had become expert at reading the landscape of Grace. He could already tell by the increased pressure of her thigh against his; by the touch of her forearm low against his ribs; and by the weight of her hand in the strap at his shoulder, that she had been frightened by something. He knew she was aiming the tap. He knew she had looked up. He knew from her tensing that she was going to scream, and when she yelled out, he was already moving. Only one of the concrete chunks hit the road, and by then they were long gone.

"Go ahead! Shoot it! If you've got a shot, take it. We're on the tail half. I can get us down." He looked over his shoulder to see what he had encouraged her to do, and was amazed at the sight of the creature – the true creature, body-less but snake-like, a field of energy trying to hold together without the jacket of the road, spreading and shearing and then blinking into shape again.

Grace found the trigger ahead of the handle and the tap fired. The distortion wave hit the exposed creature and it whipped left and right to get out of the way.

"Keep the beam on it," Nonstop said.

Grace shot it again and the creature thrashed, lowering its midsection to the ground and raising its tail up quickly.

Suddenly they were back in the air. Suddenly there was no path to the ground.

"Stop! Stop firing!" Nonstop nearly shrieked.

Grace moved the beam. Nonstop drove toward the end of the tail section, and then the creature whipped its tail toward the ground, the descent so fast Grace felt her stomach rise.

Nonstop nosed the bike and they stayed on. Then the very end of the roadway slapped against the grass, and the roadway shattered.

Nonstop skimmed across two slabs of road before the bike slammed into the ground and white diffusion streaks ripped around them wildly, blinding them.

With only the slightest warning — *a crackling thrum they could hear and feel*, the energy-wall of the creature's tail hit them, and sent the bike tumbling across the grass.

More diffusion streaks raced around Grace, and Nonstop, and the bike as they rolled. They separated, and then the white streaks raced only over Nonstop. From that point, Grace felt every bounce and smash, and Nonstop heard every cry, even above the howling wind.

Grace came to a stop in the grass, looking small and somehow deflated. She struggled to raise her arm, pawing feebly at the air. Then she gave up the effort and let her arm drop back to the ground. No thoughts remained of the tap she had just held, the tap that had flown from her grip the second she had hit the ground and that had tumbled to land just a few feet from her motionless hands.

The gigantic, un-housed monster convulsed in the grass nearby, seeming to take up the entire field with its coils of thrashing energy — any inch of its body as dangerous as a runaway truck or a live electric cable.

Nonstop ran for the tap. The tail of the creature rode the ground like an errant column of lightning, moving in no predictable way, rushing toward Grace, rushing away from her, rushing back. Nonstop watched it as he ran closer, knowing he would need luck as well as speed to get past the creature.

The tail moved in a left-ward sweep, retreating a few yards from Grace, and Nonstop sped toward her, never raising his eyes above the level of his own head, never taking his eyes off the creature's last point of contact with the ground, never daring to look up and see what writhing tornado-shape the creature made in the sky — though he wanted to — but in the second it took him to look, the creature could move. It could sweep beyond him, and if it did, it would find Grace unprotected.

In the end, he ran right past the tap on the ground. He took the extra stride to reach Grace, and when he did, he fell to the ground and threw an arm around her shoulders.

"Are you all right?" he asked, glancing at Grace before glancing back at the creature, and then glancing at the tap, just a body-length away.

"ahhh — uth — ehh," Grace managed to say, as Nonstop looked at her. He nodded, and then lunged for the tap.

Once he had it in his grip, he fired it at the creature. When the beam hit, he swept it upward; and then he did see the rest of the creature: a cyclone made of dust and realm-light that offered only hints and glimpses of the serpent at its core.

Nonstop kept the beam steady on the thrashing creature as it tried to escape. The creature dove to reenter the ground, but the storm, or the tap beam, prevented it from entering completely. It merely tore at the ground with every strike until the topsoil became too loose for the monster to work with. It tried over and over again, dirt blasting away at every point of contact, failing and re-trying until the creature's head began reversing course before the rest of its body could even complete a move, doubling back, creating something like a figure eight formation, and then continuing to double back, twisting and turning like a living knot, huge, and almost invisible in the middle of the field.

The tap started to take effect, the creature glowed blue and stopped resisting. At the last second, as it faded inside the blue glow, Nonstop saw the creature uncoil and run, like a mouse let out of a box.

"Grace, can you make it back to the bike?"

"Yeahhh...h."

Nonstop shook his head and sat up, keeping one hand on Grace's upper arm, a soft fit in his open hand.

With the wall of portals at his back, he took a look across the open field. Dark skies, sickly green, coated with radar light, and interrupted only with tiny patches of blue. He saw lines of light moving in the sky as well, adding to the radar-light impression, in some places wide and wavering like the lights over the North Pole, in other places thin and fast like visible radio waves. Near the horizon, past even the parking lot where he helped the people in the truck, he could see the lines in the sky, moving fast, and occasionally jolting violently.

Within the tree line across the field to his right, he saw the silhouette of a three-taloned claw open and close amid the vertical slash-lines of the tree-trunks.

Voracitors. Where was his sword?

He let go of Grace's arm. Where? The field looked big suddenly, like fifty million sword-sized pieces. Standing up in the grass would attract the Voracitors, would bring them right to Grace. How could you build a sword, carry it around for two years, and then lose it the minute you needed it – the minute someone else would pay the price for your foul up. If that didn't prove you were stupid, he didn't know what would.

Think.

Think.

Stop freaking out. Think.

The wipe out. When the creature hit them. He was holding the sword. He probably dropped it on one of the bounces. It would be around Rattletrap, maybe in front of the bike, maybe under it.

"Grace, stay low please. Don't get up."

"I can get up...in a minute," she said fuzzily.

"No. Don't get up Grace. Don't get up."

He pounced onto his hands and feet, looking around him as he moved, looking for charging monsters, looking for monsters materializing in thin air, looking for a slice of monster bone wrapped in a motorcycle handle. He found that he wanted to pray, though if there was a God in this insane field, that god was angry.

But as Nonstop's head scanned from side to side, and as his eyes moved even faster, he found himself praying anyway. Little child's prayers, over and over: "Dear God, please let me find the sword. Dear God, please let this all work out." Over and over again.

Nonstop.

By the time he reached Rattletrap there was already a Voracitor crossing the field toward him. Should he get on the bike? Draw them away from her? Maybe. But her head would clear soon. She'd stand up. She'd feel abandoned. If someone let you stand up when there were Voracitors nearby – you were as good as abandoned. What difference did anything else make?

He could throw her on the bike and ghost out. Take her to Phoenix, take her to Montana. Get her safe like he promised Doc he would. Okay.

He saw a bar of white under loose dirt. *It could be.* He ran over and scooped it up. It rose, and he could tell instantly by its weight that it was the sword. Soil poured from it. He swung it, and the dirt on its blade launched away.

He was thanking God when he saw two Voracitors materialize in the field to his left, keeping pace with the one charging to his right.

He ran closer to them, away from Grace, and then spread his feet and bent his knees, holding the sword out away from him, ready to go.

When they got close, he popped onto the balls of his feet. A fraze of realm-light shot back from under his hair and rooster-tailed for several feet behind his head. He scowled at the creatures. He grinned. He felt the jazz ride up his back — *smile of the lupine.*

The field-crosser extended a great taloned claw and swung it down. Nonstop's instincts screamed for him to dodge — he forced himself to stand, and met the creature's wrist with the sword.

First test. If the hunter was right, the Voracitor would feel it. Voracitors were Omni-dimensional — invulnerable to the weapons of any particular realmline, which meant pain was a rare feeling for them. If something managed to make a Voracitor feel pain, it would forget all ideas of prey. It would leave. Only Voracitors could hurt Voracitors; pain was a warning about territory, or a means of fighting for position within the hierarchy.

The monster didn't leave, but it did recoil. It seemed to feel the wound. Nonstop checked with a glance; his blade tip was dark.

He'd just have to deliver more pain. He jabbed and jabbed, and prodded and ducked. The other two Voracitors got behind him.

Grace.

He worried, until he saw that the monsters weren't going after Grace; they were turning to face him — and he could hurt them. More would come, attracted to the circling of prey, but that was good too: they'd leave Grace alone. And if more wanted to come and fight, they were welcome to; he felt like he could fight forever.

The two behind him stepped closer, and the one in front of him slashed out with its great taloned arm — so big it looked like a crane boom swinging. Nonstop waited until the last instant, and then dodged the strike. The dodge had him leaning right, and he brought his left hand over to join his grip, and then drove left with his legs and his arms, a serious strike aimed at the ribs. *Grip the sword. Don't let it get pulled out of your hands – it will do you no good hanging out of a Voracitor's rib cage.*

The strike never touched bone. It sank easily into the creature, deeper than even the worst talon strike. A talon strike that deep would be followed by massive ripping and tearing. Nonstop simply slipped the blade back out of the flesh. Voltage of some sort ran up the blade to his arms as the monster vanished, blinking out of existence in a sinking of blackness — a flash, like void-light.

Nonstop felt pain. Suddenly. Not in his arm, but in his cuts. It felt like his arm was turning sideways in each slash, turning sideways three separate times like window blinds.

But, pain or not, his strike had worked.

He had driven a Voracitor away — *He won.*

He whirled to face the other two — they were cautious, studying him, and a new Voracitor appeared to the side of them, very close and very fast. Nonstop hopped back to face it. As he coiled to strike, he saw a streak of flame rise up from behind the creature's shoulders. Astonished, he watched the flame rise higher, then quickly shifted his eyes to spot the creature's claws, only one was pulling back to strike, the other was rising straight up, as if reaching for the — *rising light* — *not fire at all* — *jumping shears of light* — rising, and then, under them, *Varrage.*

It shocked Nonstop to see his teammate, shocked him because Varrage seemed to come from nowhere, and shocked him because Varrage *looked* shocking. He seemed flooded with energy. It swept over him and rippled waves of distortion above his skin, rushing from his chest and sweeping out behind him. Shirtless, Varrage's chest sections looked like a stencil drawing of a dragon — not a random formation, but like an actual piece of artwork — a piece of art made out of *him.*

It struck Nonstop as peculiar, but he had no time to think about it. He did know however, that he was having a *new* feeling.

He was happy to see Varrage.

Varrage raised his arm and slashed it down on the Voracitor's back. Nonstop jabbed with his blade, jumped to a new spot and jabbed again; and the creature swung, its arm fully extended to reach Nonstop, its taloned hand sweeping through the air like a wrecking ball, big, and easy to dodge. Nonstop ducked under the blow, and gave the arm two quick jabs before ducking the arm again on the return swing.

The creature's underbelly stood unguarded. Nonstop spotted the exposure and forced himself not to attack it. The creature *had* no underbelly, just a big, ribcage mouth that Nonstop wanted no part of.

Nonstop stabbed at the other parts of the creature while it rose above him. He stabbed its armpit, its elbow, its rib, and the creature, hurt, simply disappeared, simply vanished from the world.

Something fell — *Varrage* — landing on the balls of his feet, ready to touch the ground if stabilization proved necessary.

"Varrage man, I am so ha..."

Varrage leapt at the nearest of the two Voracitors — his hands extended, his fingers like glowing yellow claws. He charged. He slashed. When the creature's big arm swung for him, he slipped under it. The creature's shoulders were large, and capped with curves of silver horns, or silver bone spurs — something — whatever they were, Nonstop had never seen anything like them before. The creature's arm swung back and Varrage leapt onto it, puncturing its skin with his claws as he scrambled up past the sharp shoulder-horns to the creature's back, where Nonstop saw Varrage's foot grab purchase on the emerging skull of some long-dead Inter-D.

Nonstop caught a glimpse of something on Varrage's own back, under the pulsing energy field: his pipe-thing — so Varrage wasn't exactly shirtless. He still had his gear harness. *If he had the spiked pipe, why was he fighting with his bare hands?*

Nonstop ran to the creature's rib-side, and readied his sword for another deep thrust. The second Voracitor came out from behind the first and stepped forward. Nonstop saw Varrage swing an arm across a row of the first creature's eyes. He saw the flesh split away, and saw Varrage's glowing hand come up dark and wet.

Now between both monsters, Nonstop jumped towards the advancing creature, stabbed its ribs, and saw the creature vanish instantly. Without pause, Nonstop rebounded to the first creature and drove his sword into the creature's rib sail, deep, almost up to the hilt. He stopped the blade before the hilt could get tangled, and was pulling it free, fully expecting the creature to disappear, when the creature pivoted, and one of its arms came swinging back for him. He got the blade free, but the back of the creature's claw caught him in the ribs and sent him flying.

No impact diffusion. None. Nonstop felt everything. His shirt was ripped along his ribs, and he could feel the wound in his skin. Not deep, not a puncture. The creature was opening its claw at the time of the strike — Nonstop was on the ground — vulnerable. If he had been alone, the monster would have finished him.

But he wasn't alone, Varrage was on the creature's back, slashing at it, and the creature was slashing back at Varrage. Varrage had learned the spots on the creature's body that the creature couldn't reach, and he worked to stay in those spots.

The creature lurched. Varrage shifted to regain balance and one of the creature's arms smacked him to the ground. The creature thrust down with its talons. Varrage rolled, and the creature gored only dirt. Varrage slipped under the creature, and —

Nonstop felt a sudden pain in his ears. He heard a strange sound, like a headache attached to a gasoline generator — a sound that made the inside of his skull feel pulled and stretched.

Skyde flew in, and continued flying, circling the creature and swinging something in each hand — really whirling the things, whatever they were. Nonstop couldn't get a good look at them. They weren't big, just two little white triangle things on the ends of strings, but they were making the noise, as far as he could tell.

The Voracitor clearly didn't like what Skyde was doing. It staggered from the sound, taking tentative strikes at Skyde as she whirled around it. Skyde dipped her board and lashed the Voracitor's back as she passed, first with one triangle, then tilting on her board and striking with the other, slashing the monster doubly before sailing out of reach.

The Voracitor *still* didn't disappear. Skyde made another pass, whirling her sound-blades above her head. She swept in close to the creature and lashed the blades ferociously into its back, exposing the forehead of a partially surfaced skull, which jarred her in the split second she saw it. Its empty eyes seemed to be pleading.

Varrage leapt into position and attacked the same spot, cracking his way through the network of digested bone remnants, hitting the pile again and again, searching for the living tissue beneath, the tissue he could bring pain to, the tissue he could punish.

Nonstop picked up his sword, took a wide path around the creature's arms, and stabbed the creature everywhere he could. The creature turned, swinging at Varrage. Skyde flew in, drawing the creature's attention, causing it to abandon its attack on Varrage and lunge at her. As the creature moved, Nonstop saw its rear legs shift, and saw its knees — jointed like a crab's — and quickly stabbed at the unshielded sections of the joints. The creature staggered, its torso upended; as it fell, it vanished, stabbing the air with a flash of black light.

"Skyde!" Nonstop called, pumping his sword in the air as Varrage's feet hit the grass and Skyde banked a curve in.

Varrage stood up straight and scanned the horizon.

Skyde glided to a stop near Nonstop and followed Varrage's gaze for a second, but, seeing nothing, quickly turned back to Nonstop. "We have to help Krork," she said. "He said Norel is in trouble."

"Yeah, the Outpost has *been* in trouble. We're trying to reach it." Nonstop looked up the slope, expecting to see the robot-soldiers, or to see Voracitors, but instead saw only a glowing, riotous pocket of turbulence in the air beyond the silhouetted shells of ruined homes.

"Looks like the Outpost is *still* in trouble," Nonstop said, pointing.

"Krork could be in there,"

"Yeah, or someplace close by.

Skyde turned. "Varrage, we're..."

But Varrage wasn't listening to them. Varrage wasn't looking at them. Varrage was peering toward the trees, stepping, changing position, and then peering again.

"What's wrong? Do you see Voracitors?" Skyde asked.

He did not look at her. But he did answer.

"NhhhhhhoT in cHanneL. Nhot in worLD. CLosssse. ClosE." And with that, he walked quickly out into the field, and away from them.

"Channel?" Skyde asked herself, and then asked Varrage, though he was leaving, and if he heard her, he did not acknowledge her. Skyde watched him as he walked. "Look for Krork!" she called to his back, as his feet pounded, and his stride slashed through the grass. The air darkened directly in front of him. Skyde saw it, and her mouth fell open. She watched as the air around Varrage distorted and chopped. She watched as he stepped into the distortion and vanished.

Stunned, she saw him reappear an instant later in a different part of the field, where he walked across a grounded piece of rooftop and leapt to the remnants of its peak. She watched Varrage as he stood on the wreckage, moving his head in quick snaps, looking at the trees, into them, beyond them.

"Look for Krork!" she yelled, and then cried "Varrage!" but he wasn't listening. He was moving again, into the trees, vanishing as the air around him darkened.

"People can't do that," Skyde said to herself, but within earshot of Nonstop.

"I don't know a thing about it," he said, stunned himself.

"I have to help Grace," he said, looking up at Skyde, and as Skyde turned to look back at him, he was already moving, taking his first few strides sideways, and beginning his run back down the field.

"That girl is still here?" Skyde asked, banking her board and following Nonstop's movement. She paced him for a second, and then sailed past him toward Grace.

She stopped near Rattletrap and hovered, Nonstop somewhere behind her. She arrived as Grace pushed at the bike and stood it up off the ground.

"Grace are you all right?" Nonstop called out as he ran closer.

"Great," Grace said, straining to keep the bike from falling to the ground again, and then, once it was set, adding, "I'm okay."

"You are? You're okay?" Skyde asked, grim faced as she looked Grace over for blood or broken bones.

"You're Skyde right?" Grace looked up, smiling, with her hair a mess and her clothes filthy, "That was awesome. The way you swooped in and saved those two guys — just amazing."

"You shouldn't be here. This is dangerous," Skyde said, as Nonstop reached the bike and helped stabilize it.

"I want to help," Grace said, "I'm an extra brain, an extra set of hands."

Skyde rode her board higher and looked at Nonstop. "There's no time for this," she said, "Keep her away from the Voracitors," and with that, she flew off toward the hilltop.

"You hurt?" Nonstop asked Grace, as he moved to sheath his sword, and found that he couldn't bring himself to do it. He watched the horizon.

"Yeah, but not bad," Grace said, "Look, this is big. I want to help —- but I don't want to slow you down or anything. I fully give you permission not to rescue me if that's what it comes down to." She held his tap out for him to take.

"Thank you," he said as he accepted it, and as he lowered his arm to holster the device, Grace gasped.

"Nonstop, look at the cuts on your arm."

He did, and he saw what had shocked her: the scabs on his arm were raised and jagged; not only that, they were clear, with only a wine colored tint around their edges. It looked like there were glass saw blades stuck in his arm. "Yuck. Must be all this Realm-stuff," he said, turning his arm to examine the strange surfacing.

"Does it hurt?"

"I didn't even know it was there. No, it doesn't hurt. But let's talk about it later."

He threw his leg over the bike and looked back at her, "You ready for round two?"

She slipped onto the seat behind him, "Actually, this is more like round one-hundred-and-seventy-six."

* * *

Bloch advanced carefully in the darkness. He found that he could walk in slow steps and only occasionally be surprised by shifts in the floor's orientation. Often, changes in the light heralded accompanying surprises in the room structures around him. The basement lighting would stutter on and off, and when it stabilized, he would find that the room he stood in had changed around him: growing vast, or growing narrow, perhaps changing all together, shifting location independent of the distance he might have walked. But he kept moving. He was looking for the Doctor. He was looking for steadier light.

He thought he could see some in the distance, maybe blocked by a corner, maybe not there at all, maybe simply an after effect burned onto his retinas.

As he advanced, the light grew stronger. He came to the corner that blocked the light, and when he did, he turned past it and stepped into a small walkway with a larger room beyond it. What he saw in the ceiling of that room stopped him for a moment: a line of pale blue light ran around the ceiling's perimeter. Below it, a similar line marked the floor. As Bloch watched, the two lines began moving: the glowing ceiling traveled down, and the floor traveled up. Bloch continued watching as the two surfaces passed through each other, and the room turned inside out. When the surfaces stopped moving, the new room kept the faint blue light, but spread it evenly across its entire area. The new room seemed solid. The new room seemed normal. Bloch tested its floor with his foot, and when the floor didn't move, he walked across it toward the next doorway, toward the room beyond, where the light, finally, seemed steadier. Light would help him. He might find the Doctor — if the Doctor were also moving toward the light. If he didn't find the Doctor, he might at least find a clue on how to exit this insane construction.

The next room appeared to be a row of open walled storage bays, lit from the inside as well as the outside. At the end of the row, there was a larger room. As Bloch walked toward it, he took note of the contents on display within the bays. He saw something like a spacesuit in one, something like an elongated archery target in another, and then he passed one whose contents threatened to stop him fully. Just a glance, just three steps, but enough to register. Centered within the room, he saw a large glass dome, capping a turntable of thin robotic arms, all terminating in shapes something like windshield wiper blades, or maybe violin bows. In any case, shallow arches holding taut strands. More guitar strings? The base of the dome was ringed with keyboard stations, so more likely piano wires, but what type of item was it? The second half to what he had already seen and dismissed back at the research facility. Was it a musical instrument? Just a musical instrument? What had he missed?

Nothing. He was here. He was the force in the moment. Gaps overstepped were inconsequential. Find the Doctor. That was the task.

"Norel," he called as he walked toward the larger room, his footsteps echoing in the deserted hall.

* * *

Here, at the end, Dr. Edmond Norel was surprised to find that there was something he wanted. And he was surprised to find that he would have to struggle to get it.

He needed his data box. He needed to avoid Bloch's pistol for a few minutes more. He reached for handholds in the darkness. The floor below him felt slanted. Where was his weight? *Was* the floor slanted? The basement? The building? Was the programming malfunctioning to create slants? Was his continuum different than the floor's? Where was his weight? Was he still in the file room? Where was the table? Would the data box still be on its top? Would it have slid down over the table's edge? Was it on the floor behind him?

Norel turned, and thought he saw a hint of light - was it blue? Yes?

He made his way toward the faint light, getting strange clues from his body as to where the floor was - one motion told him he was seated, the next put gravity against the side of his calf, the next against his heel. He got closer to the foggy glow, and reached a wall. He turned his head, and saw the data box - saw three data boxes - superimposed near each other - from different angles - one on the floor, one on the floor slightly higher, and one on the floor to the left. Three. He reached for the device and saw two silhouettes of his hand - each moving perfectly with his instructions, but also from different angles. Three realities overlain? Then why two hands? His damaged eyes? Then why the different perspectives?

He moved his fingers and found that he could accept both versions as long as they obeyed him. He thought them offset — from the same center point? But what was the center point? Him? His mind? His brain? The chemicals between his synapses? The *results* of the chemicals between his synapses? Where was the center point of himself? It felt like everywhere. Behind everything. Above everything.

But the third data-box? Where was his hand in the third version of things? If he seized upon the device, would his third hand sink up from the floor to grasp the data box? Inanimate matter - in a field — behaving differently than living matter? Romantic notions in tangible form. If so, if so *unprecedented* a circumstance — what of it? What is the force called into being by the animation of matter? What fountain, pouring continually into the universe? — why would he be different than the machine? He would assume he was not. Yet here he appeared to be. The machine — emanating three realities. Himself, two. Yes? What emanated what? Did three realities hold Data-boxes? Did the Data-box emanate three realities? Did his mind, searching, locate three realities, or create three realities?

Both versions of his hand reached the data box, and upon contact, there was only one. Whatever insight the third hand might divulge, it would never be divulged to him.

The room he had been sitting in had capsized. A seam had formed in the middle of the floor, and the fold-line had risen straight up to the ceiling, spilling him one way and Bloch the other. He had not seen Bloch since that happened. He could occasionally hear him, but he didn't know if that meant Bloch was close or not. He had to be, didn't he? Just around any corner. Norel supposed he was, though he also supposed that closeness was a moment by moment condition in the basement currently. He listened, and tried to learn the basement's acoustics. He held the data-box to his lips. He blocked the light from the data-box and re-created the darkness, and in the darkness, he willed his mind serenity so that he might think of what to say. Here, in the center of his last chance.

* * *

Near the highway, in a rubble pile of broken homes, Varrage emerged from the realm-tunneling he walked in. The tunneling hadn't drained away this time, as he was already used to; it had been blasted away, ripped from him.

He was now walking across debris, near trees. He heard gunfire, which compelled him to greater speed in the here and now. Darkened flecks of air appeared in his peripheral vision, but stayed in place, vanishing and returning, no longer gathering. He kept moving, fast: deftly traveling over a sea of household wreckage, step after step over broken strollers, sullied photographs, collapsed ceilings, listening intently as he moved, pushing against a turbulence he could now feel hitting him in waves.

The sounds of machine gun fire ended, and the sounds of high explosives began.

Useless.

He could see the combatants down on the entrance ramp to the highway: walking tanks backing away from puppet-stick-tar-pits.

Varrage ran toward the grouping, and saw the end-game begin. The Voracitors allowed two of the man-tanks to back away as they surrounded the remaining one. The man-tank fired its arsenal at the creatures, but the Voracitors kept advancing. As they got closer, they extended their arms and flared their ribs.

Varrage moved, willing the dark air to gather, but it did not. He felt the steady pulse in the air, working against him, perhaps sweeping away any cohesion possibilities the dark air might operate within.

Varrage urged more speed from his legs. It was possible to be too late. Despite desire, despite urgency, it was possible to be too late.

The left-flanking creature hit the man-tank, swatting it towards the right-flanking creatures. Varrage heard the driver scream as the machine-suit cart-wheeled along the entrance ramp, losing pieces as it crashed along.

Everywhere the suit landed, the Voracitors took turns slashing at it, and with each strike, Varrage saw more of the man-tank's armor fly away.

After several blows, the tank's driver landed on his back, with just the framework of his armor left. He was tangled within it, within its coils of machinery. Despite the damage to the suit, the flashing light that had been clamped to the driver's eyelid was still pulsing, but it had been torn free, and now hung down by the driver's ear.

On the ground, the driver screamed.

"*No. No. Stay away. Oh God, Stay away,*" he said, as the monsters drew closer.

Varrage spotted the glowing lights beginning within the open ribcage of the right-most Voracitor. He was a few strides closer when he saw the Voracitor reach down and pick up the screaming human/soldier — *man* — and lift him into the swirling lights, and then he saw the creature's ribs begin to close.

Varrage leapt atop the nearest Voracitor's back, crossing it in three strides and leaping. He landed in front of the right-most Voracitor and slashed it before it could react.

"YoU aRe NOT... DoiNg iT... to Him!"

Varrage ducked low and slipped under the creature. He sank his talons into the monster's ribcage and tried to pull it open while the man inside the ribcage screamed. The creature tore away from Varrage's grip and stepped back to slash at him, black blood gurgling from its wounds. Varrage side-stepped the creature's strike, and then dodged its next series of strikes, always one step ahead of the creature, slashing at its arms every time it set to deliver another blow.

The monster's ribcage, laden with prey, swung as it moved, then slipped open a bit. The screaming man's arm slipped through the opening, then his shoulder slipped through, then his head.

The man screamed. The pulsing light, now down by his ear, could offer none of its comforts, none of its lies, none of its illusions. Now, at the moment of his devourment, the man's mind offered him only the sparkling clarity of the moment, only the truth that the innocent body he could no longer feel, was undergoing yet another intolerable defilement — and that he could do nothing to prevent it. He screamed, and in the shadow of the beast, he wept.

Varrage slashed the staggering creature until his yellow hands dripped black. Buckling, the creature hissed: a rusted, grating sound — like a vapored curse escaping a tomb.

The curse, if any, slipped around Varrage, who stood defiantly as the creature released the screaming soldier, dropping him to the ground like a birthed calf.

Varrage leapt to stand beside the man as the Voracitor took another weakened step backward and leapt from the world, flashing the surrounding air with darkness during the instant of its departure, as if its leaving created a vacuum that sucked the very light from an exposed ring of existence. The beast gone, the air normal, Varrage spun to face the other two Voracitors, his claws glowing like two suns.

The soldier on the ground looked up at him, bewildered.

"Sarge. Sarge," the soldier said, illusion, or some fatigue-induced cousin, finding him again.

Varrage stepped toward the black monsters. The black monsters retreated, and then faded — vanishing from the ground they stood on — from the Earth — from the Human continuum all together.

"Sarge. Sarge."

Varrage heard the man at his feet. He scanned the area and saw no Voracitors — *felt no Voracitors*. He looked down at his hands and saw no glow, and no black liquid.

And saw no skin. Saw only islands of black glass atop a tiny, boiling sea.

The man below him continued calling. Varrage took a final look around the area. He sighted the other walking tank men, far down the highway, lumbering with weapons raised as if patrolling, seemingly following orders, locked into programming, awaiting the arrival of some countering imperative.

Varrage looked at the air above them and followed a huge, seeping darkness as it swept the sky.

"Sarge. Sarge," the man below him called, looking at Varrage, but seeing someone else.

Varrage turned to the man, lowered his shoulders to look at him more fully, and then, finally, knelt by the gasping man's side.

"You're going to be all right Soldier. At ease. Be at ease."

The soldier lay motionless on the embankment, grafted within tangles of broken machinery.

"Sarge," The soldier said, closing his eyes as exhaustion carried him, perhaps to dreams.

Varrage looked at the man's face, and then straightened the man's arms, and then untwisted the man's left leg. He pulled a tangle of cables from the ground, and when he saw no way to detach them from the soldier, merely laid them neatly on the ground between the man's arm and his ribs. There was an open panel on the man's chest, and Varrage pressed it closed.

Varrage looked at the man. What would he wake to? What *could* he wake to?

"Be at ease Soldier," Varrage said again, patting the panel on the soldier's chest.

Varrage stood, and as he did, he saw something astonishing: a bright streak of red blood on the chest panel he had just touched.

It wasn't there before he touched the panel. Where did it come from?

Could I be bleeding?

Could he? Varrage lifted his hand and slowly brought it up to his eyes.

He looked. He looked carefully.

Yes.

A small cut ran along the palm of his right hand. He pressed it with his left. The wound glistened, and a small swell of blood ran down his palm. Then it dripped from his hand's edge and fell. Below, it made a red starburst on the pavement.

"I can bleed," Varrage said, stroking the wound slowly with his fingertips. He closed his eyes and bowed his head, taking two short breaths before filling his lungs, wherever they were, with one long one.

He let his hands fall away and opened his eyes. The man lay at his feet; the grassland lay beyond the embankment. Up on the slope, the trees rose from the ground and leaned in the wind, above them, black debris rode through the bands of dark air.

The sky held strata, layers of sliding grays and greens that seeped to black. Within them, like a rend in their fabric, like an open defiance, shone a long streak of blue sky.

And that blue sky looked deep. That blue sky, just outside the turmoil, looked like it went on forever. Varrage found that he loved that blue sky, and that he was thankful for it.

"KRORK," he yelled, and then he ran back toward the Outpost.

* * *

Norel sat in the dark, with his back to a wall, listening for Bloch, and somehow not knowing how to begin. Light spasmed in some corner of the shifting basement, a cold light, electric. Could it lead to fire? How would the basement treat its own burning? Could you trap a fire in two dimensions? Would it still burn upon reopening? Could incandescence be made inert, or only extinguished? More seconds gone. More ideas dancing in his head.

"Dawn," he said. He said the name aloud. He said the name as an incantation — to stop the ideas in his head, to cast off the fear in his back, and now that he had spoken, he realized he had presented himself as an auditory target. He could perhaps speak in a quieter voice; but he had to keep speaking. If they were going to find his body in some future year, made inert by Bloch or by his own inventions, there were things he had to at least try to say. Even if they helped Bloch find him.

"Sweetheart, This is Daddy. I... I. Hello... Hello Sweetheart... Years may pass before you hear this — you might even be a sweet old lady when you do. You might be a young woman. I don't know. I hope you hear this when it might still do you some good. But...

Hmmm.

I wasn't a good son. Or a good husband. I was not attentive — but, strangely enough, loving you has taught me something about being a son. I love you fully. All I want is for you to be happy in the world. To make your way, and be happy. And because I feel that way about you, I can believe my parents felt that way about me, and it makes all my wrong turns seem forgivable. I would forgive you anything.

Let's see, I should give you some advice shouldn't I? Advice from Dad. Hmm... Effort conquers all. Failure is necessary. Nothing is what we think it will be, and mistakes are course corrections toward how things actually are. Change the word. Failures are *revelations* — for the select few brave enough to make them. Make your mistakes and make sure you keep going. Brag about your mistakes to your friends as if they were fishing stories; be greedy for them. Never be afraid of them... At least... At least... At least when it comes to work. Our private mistakes are much harder to talk about. Little Love, I remember when you learned to crawl, when you taught yourself to walk... God, it was so cute. It was so inspiring... Dawn, I'm sorry... I'm sorry for so much. I never mea — I...

You are the treasure of my heart. You always have been. If your love for me makes this hurt, please don't be sad long. I would hate that. Any parent would hate that. I realize I am speaking retroactively, but love is magic, and magic can *be* retroactive.

Love can fix the past.

Please be happy. Grab the world and be happy. You do that, and I promise, my spirit... wherever it winds up being... will soar — is that okay? Do we have a deal? Be happy sweetheart. I love you. Let's make this easy and just say goodnight, okay? For a little time anyway.

Sweet dreams.

Sweet dreams little love.

Good night."

Norel hit a panel on the screen and stopped recording. As last words went, these seemed feeble. Should he take his own advice and try again? No. They were at least honest, and he would let them be. He closed his eyes and tried to think of what to do next.

* * *

"Cover your nose," Nonstop said as he pulled his T-shirt collar over his own. Ahead of the bike, the Outpost's upended tip pointed out of the crater. The air around it swirled, picking up sheets of dirt which curved in the turbulence like swarms of insects. Green radar-light sizzled and flashed behind the little building, back-lighting it as it sat with its main door ten feet off the ground, seemingly center-point to some other-worldly tornado that was threatening to be born. Grace pressed her mouth against Nonstop's back and covered it with her hands.

Nonstop saw Skyde far along a swirl of air, still outside the Outpost. He saw her weave through the gusts and head for the Outpost's main door. The closer she got, the more she had to fight to move forward. Realm-shear seemed to be pushing out from the building's main door as well as thrashing around the edges of it.

Skyde tried again, and again she was buffeted as she flew nearer to the door. Finally, the realm-shear tumbled her back to calmer sky where she paused to study the air patterns around the entrance. If they didn't shift or travel on, she'd have to find another way into the building.

"Our turn," Nonstop said, sheathing his sword and banking the bike low to the ground, chopping through the loose soil at the edge of the crater. The bike accelerated, and Grace felt apprehension grip her stomach. It was getting so that any increase in speed made her anticipate horrors.

The bike sped toward the Outpost. Nonstop waited for the right second, and made Rattletrap push forcefully off the ground. Nonstop launched out of his seat and onto his toes, adding his own efforts to the vault. Grace, her wrists strapped to Nonstop's shoulders, lunged forward as the jump yanked her off her seat.

Shocked, and frightened, she...

They hit the side wall of the Outpost and the accompanying clanking noise made some of Grace's curse-on-curse invective hard to hear — and the *continued* clanking of Rattletrap's metal arms on the side of the building *continued* to make Grace's curse-on-curse invective hard to hear. Still, it was a tribute to her resolve and perseverance that as Rattletrap battled its way up the support column, she was able, through continuous vocal expression and swift punches upon Nonstop's defenseless shoulders, to effectively communicate her extreme dissatisfaction.

"GAAKK! All right! All right! What did I do?" Nonstop said as the bike climbed up to the roof's gear ring and grabbed hold of it. "Grace, you gotta quit hitting me," he said, turning to look back at Grace.

"And YOU have to quit flinging me around back here. I can hit a lot harder than that you know —"

Nonstop scrunched his neck into his shoulders.

"— You could kill me. One second I'm riding; the next..."

Nonstop squinted and looked around him. He noticed the Outpost's doorway. Dirt and debris scoured the air around the entrance, making the turbulence that much easier to see.

"Okay, sorry, sorry. Huddle up," Nonstop said.

"... put up with a lot back here, and I don't even — What?"

"Huddle up Angry-girl. We're about to get rough again; get close and stay low — *and no punching.* I'm going to try and slip us in past the corner of the door frame."

"How are we going to get in? — it just pushed Skyde like crazy."

"Yeah, but her board is built to catch air, Rattletrap isn't, so that might help us. But we'll still need to have as small a front surface as possible."

Grace looked at the doorframe.

"Okay. Okay. Sorry," she said, and she let out a breath.

Grace crossed her arms around Nonstop's waist, her hands flat against his hard belly. She pressed her cheek against the middle of his back — as huddled up as she could imagine being.

* * *

Moments after Norel had finished his message to his daughter, Bloch called from somewhere in the gloom.

"— orel. Get me out of here Norel! Where are you?

Norel looked up quickly, listened to the sounds, and nodded.

Good.

Record more.

Let her hear the truth of this as well.

Norel stood, glancing through the darkness around him, trying to place the voice's position. The room shifted around his feet and he fought to stay oriented. He steadied himself, took a deep breath, and reactivated the recorder. Holding the data box out at arm's length, he spoke loudly out into the room: "How could you do it Bloch? How could you jeopardize so much so thoughtlessly?"

Norel stepped forward, arm extended, holding the data-box tightly in his fingertips.

*

Bloch, unseen but drawing nearer, mirrored Norel's posture step for step, walking with his gun in his hand and his arm extended outward. Both men listened. Both men moved in the darkness. Sound was the rope by which they pulled each other closer.

"Me, Norel? I just used what you made. You're the one who left the lens." Bloch said as he stepped.

Norel stepped as well. He could make out a hard edge in the darkness ahead of him: a wall, a door, something — with a light somewhere behind it. He stepped toward it as Bloch continued talking.

"You're the one who activated the building that made the lens glow," Bloch said. "We never would have suspected its properties if *you* hadn't demonstrated the connection."

Norel stepped beyond the dark edged corner, still recording. He entered a dark room with a doorway on its far wall. Beyond the door, he saw more darkness, but also many, many, small points of light.

"So, congratulations Norel," Bloch's voice continued, from somewhere unseen, "*You* are responsible for all of this."

Norel strode toward the next room, where the active safety lights would offer better visibility, and he would be closer, he hoped, to the Colonel.

"You abused what I made," Norel said, looking around him as he walked into the larger room. Four enclosed rooms stood within it like wide support columns. Most of the space seemed terraced, rimmed with a half wall that offered a vast view of other rooms, far off and dark, like a city in its sleeping hours, lit by thousands of tiny safety lights, pale blue and twinkling — a landscape of captured stars.

"Norel..." the Colonel's voice said.

Standing in the open, Norel heard the voice and spun toward it, but saw no trace of the man. There was just the voice in the empty air. It continued.

"I push Norel. I push everything I find. I push technologies. I push lesser men. I get what I want."

"No. Not today," Norel said, holding out the data-box to catch the reply. "Not today Bloch. Not anymore."

*

Bloch stepped toward the Doctor's voice, continuing past rooms and corridors, some rising, some sinking, trying not to allow himself to become confused.

* * *

Nonstop drove the bike hand over hand along the gear-ring, and then dropped the bike down to the main entrance. He checked his timing as he and Grace braced against the wind, and then he slipped the bike over the door's frame like a salmon escaping a fishing boat.

Realm-shear hit them hard. It pushed them firmly — not outward, but *against* the entryway's wall. They strained against the shear and it stalled them several times before they broke through to reach the interior of the building.

The inside floor sloped. It offered no place for the bike to stop. The bike slipped sideways and began grinding slowly down the floor gratings. Nonstop looked around quickly. Where was Doc? Where was anybody? Quickly, he turned his attention back to his control bar and slammed Rattletrap's claws into the floor grating. The bike stopped sliding at least.

The wind screamed through the dark building. The few active consoles painted the walls with weak, blinking light and jumping shadows. Nonstop spotted only one monitor on, down to the right, near the back wall. He couldn't make out what it displayed and he never got the chance to look closer.

He felt Grace tense, and then she yelled: "Nonstop! What is that?"

Grace pointed down at the open basement door, where impossibly, the rooms on the other side were continually changing — like shutter clicks on a camera. In quick succession, the doorway showed an open hallway, a room with a chair, a hall of tires, and then more rooms and more rooms, changing almost faster than the mind could make sense of.

Nonstop could only shake his head. "I don't know; the basement is crazy," he yelled.

*

Skyde, followed Nonstop's lead, landing by the door and slipping her board over its frame. She held her board in front of her as the wind pushed her tight against the inside wall. She pushed back, and slowly fought her way through the entry space.

The winds inside the building were easier to manage, but not by much. The air rocked her, thrumming against her board as she gripped it. She climbed on, crouching, and then slipped the board into the air.

The turbulence pushed her upwards, where she had to raise her arms to keep some distance between her head and the ceiling. She started hand-walking along its surface, fighting to keep steady in the violent air.

*

Nonstop saw Skyde come in, saw her move up to the ceiling and saw her adjust to the wind in the room. He saw her look down and study her board. As soon as she was free to look at him, he called out to her: "Skyde." He lifted one arm and pointed. "There's a monitor on in the back. Can you get there?"

She nodded, and started to make her way across the ceiling toward the monitor.

Nonstop craned his neck to watch her. Grace followed his lead and leaned out to see her as well.

The bike tipped, and the floor grating lifted out of its frame.

They fell.

Screaming, they plummeted toward the shutter-clicking basement. The floor grating clanged loudly against the doorframe, and when it bounced away, they were gone.

* * *

Rik Ty

**

They hit the floor driving — *fast* — and there was no safe place to stop. The first room they drove across was swinging from side to side in long arcs. Nonstop had worked a summer at an amusement park when he was sixteen, and was instantly reminded of a ride they had called the Viking Ship that moved the way the room was moving. Once the ride got started, it would keep swinging higher and higher, and before long, its riders would be screaming like crazy. Nonstop hoped not to be in the room long enough to get to that point.

The door to the next room was sinking slowly along the surface of its wall, on a path that would take it past the rocking floor of the room they were in. Nonstop sped up to reach it. There was still enough doorway to drive the bike through, but with the next swing, the floor would rise up, and if the doorway kept to its current path, the floor would cover it. *Then what would happen?* Maybe they'd drive up the wall. Maybe their room would disappear. Maybe another door would open; maybe the *floor* would open.

Nonstop barreled forward, and the bike slipped through the doorway.

The second room was very long, and it felt perfectly level, though its walls were jittering. The entire room was pixelating. Every spot in it was moving in some way; every surface seemed to be oscillating energetically, with some portions bouncing up, while their neighboring portions bounced down. Nonstop could feel the room's atmosphere in his fingers. It hurt. The cuts on his arm hurt down to the bone. The atmosphere hurt his eyes — it hurt to receive the light from the room. It hurt to breathe the air from the room. It hurt Grace's teeth, and she said so, and when she did, the sounds of her voice chopped and oscillated too, garbled and gargled as if they were torn. She pulled tight on Nonstop's harness straps, and brought her forearms close together to shield her face.

New pain ripped into Nonstop's forearms. He glanced down: fissures split his strange scar tissue. Light poured out from deep within the seams. *He had seen this before* — Varrage. Varrage had —

the light surged and the scar tissue burst from his arm, vaporizing in a flash of warm light. He looked to where he was driving and then glanced down at his arm again — *Varrage, this is what happened to Varr*—. The wounds on Nonstop's arm glowed red and then dulled. The pain subsided. Scar — a new — a door appeared in the wall. It caught Nonstop's eye and he shot the bike through it.

The next room offered another long hall. Nonstop and Grace sped into it and found its floor dropped at an angle. The sudden shift tugged at their stomachs and alarmed both of them; but it was a *natural* feeling at least, and an absolute relief when compared to the doomed feeling of the last room, where it felt to both of them like they were being dissolved, like they were being chewed. Nonstop's arm felt normal. There were three jagged scars on his forearm - but so what? They weren't glowing. They looked normal. He still looked like a normal person. At least he hoped he did.

The wall on the far end of the hall started turning counter-clockwise, twisting its side-walls. The surfaces on Nonstop and Grace's end of the room remained unchanged. The room seemed like it was wringing itself out of existence. Nonstop sped up and raced through the shrinking door. The next room seemed vast; its ground plane appeared level, but its walls were shifting. Halfway through the room, another room rushed through it — from the back wall to the right wall, and out of that room, another room swung out to the left, and out of that, another room swung out to the right, and so on, room after room, threshing with a machine-like rhythm — like a set of grinding blades running in reverse.

The whooshing doors the bike would have to drive through offered their own dangers: each one sank into the wall it bisected, and each one seemed insanely solid. Riding through the shifting doors would be like riding through guillotines. Nonstop, eyes wide and moving, entered the puzzle through a door on his right, and then spun and slalomed through door after door, hunting for any sign of stability.

Grace didn't know where to look, everywhere around her, rooms were shuffling into each other with crazy speed. She could never have driven in this. She didn't see how Nonstop could be driving in it either, except he was. And as the rooms flowed in and out of each other, she wondered if she had lost her mind.

* * *

Skyde made her way to the back monitor. The winds had lessened, and she found that she could lower her hands from the ceiling; the realm-shear was either dying down, or moving on. She lowered her board and braced it against the work station's support post, making herself a level platform to stand on against the tilted floor.

There was text on the monitor. Before she could read it, her eyes were attracted to the basement doorway, where the rooms beyond the doorframe changed every second — impossibilities, happening right before her eyes. She forced herself to turn away and look back at the screen. The words on it read:

STABILIZING CODE: 2865

She looked for an active com-link anywhere on the console, or on the nearby banks of equipment. She saw none. She took the data-box from her gear belt and called on it, hoping Nonstop would feel the buzz on his data-box, and know how to answer it. Or that he had the com-link open already. Or that it was even possible for her message to reach him.

"Nonstop, are you okay? Can you hear me?"

She repeated the message several times before a faint, crackling voice answered:

"Barely. Go ahead."

Skyde's rigid posture collapsed as the tension in her shoulders quit. She spoke quickly and loudly: "You have to find a code-box and re-enter the stabilizing code! It's 2865! You may have to find more than one."

"What? No. I can't do that! I can't work a code-box! I don't know h —"

"I can't do it here. I'd have to close the basement up and start over. You have to do it. The basement is paradoxing. It will kill Doctor Norel. If you get trapped, it will kill you too. The code boxes have red and black cov—"

"I know. I know what they look like."

*

The sweeping rooms they drove through slowed down.

Swoosh.

Swoosh.

The rooms had become darker too, lit primarily by safety panels that arced in streaks as the walls moved, providing just enough light to suggest the bike might be driving through a dance club, or a subway tunnel.

Nonstop threw glances to the walls, seeing recesses and panels and crevices.

"How am I supposed to find a code-box in this? And when we find one, how are we supposed to stop to use it?"

Grace didn't answer him, but she did start hunting for red and black code boxes. She saw windows on the passing walls and looked into them. She saw rows of vortex bikes in one room. In another, she saw a yellow vortex truck with three sets of knobby tires and a large roll-bar. In the next, she saw a room filled with something like deep sea diver-suits, some with big robot arms, some with skinny robot arms, and some just with armored sleeves — and she also saw walls full of boxes and hoses and cables. Everything she saw seemed impressively complex. Nonstop was right: finding a code-box in these crazy rooms was going to be hard.

* * *

Bloch reached the corner he thought the Doctor's voice had come from, and turned, entering a wide room that opened to a terraced space with four wide rooms at its center. His triangulations were verified. Norel was at the far end of the terrace, his back freely visible. Norel didn't move as Bloch approached, and didn't seem to see him, even peripherally.

"Oh, that's right," Bloch tested. Norel still didn't move. Bloch stepped closer. "You're so much smarter than I am: the vaunted, insurmountable intelligence, the mind to eclipse all others. Well, this simple-minded man can teach *you* something Doctor." Still no response. Bloch stepped closer.

"I can teach you just how persuasive pain can be."

Bloch raised the pistol — Norel's hand. That thing he's holding. Obliterate them both. Erase the man ounce by ounce. If this room reacted strangely to the bullet, fire another. Fire a thousand. Win through attrition. He had enough ammo to experiment; perhaps the next few bullets would absorb any of the basement's effect, and a following bullet could get through smoothly. Damned well time to find out.

Bloch fired.

The muzzle flash kaleidoscoped at the end of the gun and the effect fanned out and faded, similar to the last shot he fired, but not the same. Norel moved away from the sound, toward a side door to another room.

Bloch swung his arm to keep aim on Norel. Bloch fired two bullets and neither one kaleidoscoped. Both sheared to the walls. The first bullet caused a streak that ran parallel to the floor; the next ran at an angle to it. A steady flow of bullets might have created a circle.

The floor did not rise, and there was no kaleidoscoping at the point where the shear met the wall; but there was an effect.

The shear touched a raised panel box on the wall, and the panel box slipped back into the wall's surface, no longer three dimensional, suddenly two dimensional. The effect spread like a stain: jacketed cables slipped back into the wall, panel boxes, docking ports, junction hubs, all slid back as well. The effect spread on and on, clacking like a wave of castanets.

Bloch looked at the strangely shriveling wall, and thought it was a very good time to leave — a very good time to get very tough with the scientist — a very good time to get back to where things made sense.

He raised his gun, and took long strides after the Doctor.

* * *

While Grace remained watchful for red and black boxes, Nonstop sped the bike through the rapidly sliding rooms. Each room swung them in its own direction. Each room demanded that Nonstop spot an exit within its shifting space; each room demanded he get through its confines before its walls or its doors crushed him and his bike and his passenger.

It took all his concentration. Continually escaping the rooms demanded that he pay attention only to the situation in front of him. He no longer had any idea where they were in the basement. And he wouldn't, not until they could spot a code-box and get the basement stabilized.

They entered a long and complex room, its walls faceted by intersecting portions of other rooms. Pale, weak light seeped in through many open doorways, and together, painted the room in a blue twilight. Nonstop noticed that everything shared the blue tint: his hands, Rattletrap, the floors, everything he looked at. He stopped the bike.

"What? Why did we stop?"

"The room, Grace. It's not moving."

"Oh... wow..." Grace said, and then stopped talking, to marvel at a room that wasn't moving, and to laugh at herself for doing so.

Nonstop looked at the space. It was big and complicated and full of wrong angles, but he didn't see why there wouldn't be a code-box nestled somewhere along its walls. He began looking section by section for any sign of a red and black box when his eyes were pulled back to one of the doorways.

"...We could look for a code-box here," Grace said.

Nonstop peered at the doorway. He saw a telescoping length of open rooms, each ending in an open doorway leading to another room. A light source came from the rear, from the most distant rooms, and whether the light came from the last room, or the last fifty rooms, Nonstop couldn't yet say, but the light was coming closer.

The connected rooms began to undulate, as if they were boats docked at a marina and the water had become rough, or as if they were railroad cars, with all their end-doors open, riding a stretch of track that had become — *okay winky-boy, why are you watching this? What's wrong?*

Grace watched along with him. As the bright end came closer, detail in front of it became easier to see. Grace craned her neck forward and squinted.

"What's happening? It looks like things are flattening out."

Nonstop jabbed his thumb back at the straps on his shoulder. "Are you hanging on? Hang on," he said, and then he restarted the bike and drove for one of the doorways not aligned with the oncoming train of rooms.

"What? I'm right? The rooms are flattening?"

They left the room. They left the next room. They left the room after that.

"Nonstop, talk to me. The rooms? Are they flattening out"

"Yeah, I think so. It looks like it."

They drove through room after room, and only stopped running when Nonstop spotted a code-box, eye-level in a room off a corridor, highly visible in a pool of light.

"There," he said, and pointed.

They drove up to the little panel-box and stopped; then Nonstop stole a glance behind him. He could see the bulkhead back to the corridor, and through it he could see a bit of the corridor wall and a bit of the floor. They both looked fine so far. The floor was a simple grid of square tiles and the wall was the same shadow-box tapestry of panels and tubes it had been when they drove past it. Nonstop locked the sight in his mind, and turned back to the box on the wall.

"Red and black, this looks like a code-box right?" he asked, as he pulled open the device's little metal cover.

"How would I know?" Grace looked over his shoulder and then looked back to check the doorway. The corridor beyond it seemed fine. She looked it up and down and then craned her neck to look around the crazy room they were parked in. It was another collection of slanted room bits, another case of crazy-basement freeze tag.

Nonstop watched the screen activate inside the code-box and peered closer when a dialogue box appeared. Grace heard a buzzing sound - a lot of faint clacking, and looked back at the doorway. She saw a patch of warm light creep into view along the floor of the corridor.

"Hurry!" Grace said as she whipped her head back to look at the code-box. Nonstop was reading the screen, dragging his finger under the text. "Nonstop, what's taking you so long?" Grace said.

"What? What? I'm reading the instructions like you said." He jabbed a button on the screen.

"Are you crazy? Don't you even know your own equipment?"

"Hey! I'm taking lessons with Krork," he said as he studied the screen. "Starting tomorrow," he added, tapping his finger on the digital buttons, "If we live."

The entry pad lit on the screen. "Okay, I got it. I think." His fingers flew over the keypad image. Where was the enter button?

Grace turned to look at the corridor. Warm light filled it; brightening the floor; coming in from the side; rimming the edges of the panel boxes, and casting their shadows long and dark. Bit by bit the elements on the wall began to flatten like dominoes falling — with a steady clacking noise that sounded to Grace like a thousand skeletal fingers drumming in dry boxes. Grace heard the sound grow louder, and then louder still.

"Nonstoooooooooop."

"2865. I already sent it. I'm sending it ag..."

The 2-D wave swept past the bulkhead doorway, entered their room, and spread outward along the wall.

The effect stopped in one sudden pause, and then the wall rocketed to twice its height, three times its height, four times — pulling its portion of the ceiling with it, creating a long slant in the roof above their heads. Then the wall stopped, and the room fell silent.

And stayed silent.

Grace's breath shuddered out from her lips. Nonstop felt her ribs shake softly. Then she threw her arms around his neck and they both started cheering.

Skyde's voice came over the data-box, and she joined the cheer. "That's great!" she said, and then added, "You're off-course though. Doc's original position is... sixteen rooms to your left — with gaps. Everything around the original position is off the system — black. Thin ice Nonstop. Thin ice."

"I'll be careful, thanks. With a little luck, maybe Krork will be with Doc."

* * *

Dr. Norel surprised himself again; he didn't want to be shot. Absolutely not. He could accept dying if it would stop Bloch; that was absolutely true; but he could not accept being killed by the Colonel. Was this a competition of some sort? Why did that need to be a question? Wouldn't he know if that were the case? *Shouldn't* he know if that were the case?

He had heard the shots behind him, and took to the shadows immediately; but it wasn't fear that drove him. It was caution. He had heard several shots, but felt none. Colonel Bloch must have been shooting at him; wouldn't that be the case? It would be an odd suicide to use so many shots before the final one. Odd, but not impossible. Could Bloch have been shooting at the basement itself? Also possible, but the most likely target was Norel himself. But if the Colonel had been shooting at him, why hadn't he been hit?

Norel had no good answers, and no good ideas. He would wait this out. This next phase anyway.

* * *

Skyde checked the screen in front of her. The wind in the central room had lost most of its strength, but it still sent her hair flapping around her head. The image sections on the screen that weren't simply black were starting to move again. In two instances, complex room shapes changed down to simple rectangles. Then this effect spread to the rooms nearest their upper edges, turning those rooms into simple rectangles too. This process repeated and repeated, looking like a chain-reaction, looking like two giant snake trails slithering through the animated map of the basement.

"Nonstop. Go back! Enter the code again! It's starting all over." Skyde said into the data-box. And when she heard no response, she held the device away from her and looked at it. Nothing. Silent. "Enter the code again! Nonstop? Nonstop, can you hear me?"

She looked at the workstation's monitor. Thin yellow lines appeared next to empty fields of black. The black fields revealed no information. No width. No length. No depth.

They could be in the black fields. They could get killed in the black fields.

She looked at the screen and realized that Nonstop and the girl might succeed in getting Doc, only to find that they had no way to get back out. What coul —

The screen went white. Black text read:

UNEXPECTED ERROR: RE-INITIATE STABILIZING CODE

She closed her eyes. Her mind tried to conjure a picture of Nonstop driving, and she found she couldn't do it. She could put him on the bike, but she couldn't put the bike anywhere. She thought of the code-box. She didn't know what the rooms looked like, but she knew the shape of the path that led there. *She* could do it. She closed her eyes. *And how long would that fix last? As long as this one? Find the code-box. Enter the number. Shuttle back and forth if you have to, but don't let the basement kill them; because he might just do it. Crazy-boy might just get Doc out.*

Buy him some time.

She looked around the room, taking an inventory of what she had to work with. All the central room's loose materials lay heaped along the back wall. She saw papers, and wrenches, and ropes. She saw Diamondsong's blast-boots. Further along the wall, she saw her own. She looked back along the wall, and when her eyes reached the basement door, she had trouble looking away. The rooms inside it were moving again. She saw a stasis crate pantry with a grill-wagon in the middle of the floor. She saw a bike-lab that was dimly-lit, and then a room with a wide metal staircase.

Then she looked away and punched the stabilizing code into the monitor's keypad. The screen blinked, but flashed the error message again. She tried twice more, and then looked back to the shutter-clicking rooms beyond the basement's doorway.

She'd have to do something.

She stepped onto the workstation's support arm and lifted her skyboard. Holding it, she ran down the slanted floor to the basement door, and once there, paused, rocked her knees to catch her timing, and slammed the board into the doorway while it was open, wedging it. The room on the other side stopped moving, and merely wavered in place, brightly lit.

Did that work? She clambered back to the workstation and tried punching in the code again. Nothing. No change. She tried calling Nonstop on the data-box as she ran down to her blast-boots, but she didn't reach him. She continued trying to contact him as she slipped into the boots, but continued getting no answer. She docked her data-box on her belt, and powered up her boots.

Their thrust lifted her eight inches above the point where the back wall and the slanted floor met; she leaned in, and the boots shot her forward.

At the basement door, she rode the boots along the doorframe, to a point just above her wedged skyboard, and then dove into the doorway like a paratrooper.

She fell for a bit, until she caught up with the slanted floor, and then she fed the boots power and blazed across the first room, bouncing its wavering floor under the pulse of her boots until the room shimmied like a houseboat in a hurricane. Then she shot into the next room, where she hit solid footing, and was able to feed the boots more power. Surging on thrust, she raced through the twisting strings of rooms, banking high on the walls as she turned, searching the surfaces of each new room for red and black code-boxes.

* * *

Nonstop drove — slowly. All the rooms around him had stopped moving, but they looked exactly like what they were: rooms that had been flash-frozen in the act of swirling through each other. There were crazy angles everywhere: corners of rooms poked out of ceilings; doors sank into floors; windows had been caught sliding through other windows; rooms with narrow, zig-zagging floors, led to wide, expansive halls; tall rooms fed into short rooms, short rooms curved into rooms lying sideways — all lit in blue diffusion. It was strange, but kind of beautiful as well.

As for what sixteen rooms to his left meant in a space like this, Nonstop didn't know. But as he drove toward his left, the spaces grew continually more expansive, and he found that encouraging.

Finally, the bike came to the rim of something.

* * *

Norel heard Bloch every few moments. Taunting. Sometimes close, sometimes not, but always near, always with the promise of suddenly appearing and ending the separation between them. Norel actively listened: for footsteps, for breathing, for gunfire; and while he was listening for these things, he heard something else instead, far off — maybe — a quiet engine. Was someone coming? Who? Where? And what would Bloch do when they arrived?

* * *

Nonstop slowed near the edge of something gigantic and strange: an enormous hollow space, so big it was dark on its far side, with a dome-like roof, and a crater-like floor. It was bigger than a football stadium. It seemed gigantically bigger than the crater that the Outpost itself had slipped into. Nonstop didn't see how that could be, but he didn't question it much. He just looked at the room. He looked at the other passages that led to it. He looked at the structures he could see down in its center: a jumble of freestanding rooms and partial walls. Those rooms were the most modern structures that man had ever built, and from this distance, they looked like a collection of ancient ruins. The whole place looked like an ancient ruin, like that place in Rome, where the gladiators fought.

But he thought it was the place Skyde had sent him to. He could believe they had traveled sixteen rooms, and there didn't seem to be anything to the left of the crater. Not for a long way in any case. He'd go down to the freestanding rooms next, and if there were only ruins there, and more ghostly ideas of gladiators, so be it. He thought of Varrage — *because of Gladiators?* No.

Because of the floor.

The floor of the crater-thing was long and sloped. He could see features in it. It seemed like a 2-D version of a complex 3-D structure, only extremely stretched. Whether the 2-D surface had once been made of walls or floors or ceilings, Nonstop couldn't say, but something about the long expanse brought Varrage to mind. Varrage. Varrage who had rescued him, who had been devoured by voracitors and freed, who had lain in a cavern, cocooning in the same jagged scar tissue that had just ripped from his own arm, who had burst into light the second they had brought his body back into the realmlines — that man — who hadn't healed normally — who hadn't gotten a chance to fit back in with people — who had felt what Nonstop had just felt, though not on a slice of skin, but all over his body — inside every organ and bone, every space and every fraction of skin — *that man* — *Varrage*, Jaquon.

Nonstop searched for his original thought — invited it to return to him — *had* Varrage ever said anything about football-field sized, inside-out ceilings? No? Well then, what? What was he feeling? What was he worried about?

"DOCTOR NOREL? ARE YOU DOWN THERE?" Grace called, and Nonstop turned to look at her. He had sort-of forgotten she was there.

"What?" she asked.

"SSSSh, I don't know. I was just trying to think, that's all. Quit yelling"

"Well, we're here to find Doctor Norel right? How else are we going to do it?"

"We're about to cross open ground, you can't just yell out because you feel the impul..."

Nonstop's face froze for a second, and he got a faraway look in his eyes that Grace did not understand. She heard him say "Ohhh," but she wasn't sure if it was a word or just a sound. She looked directly into his eyes, and he came back to look at her.

"Sorry," he said, "just, just keep it down. You're vulnerable when you cross open ground. Don't call attention to yourself unless you're sure you want to be seen."

"Well don't we? Aren't we here to find Doctor Norel?"

"Yeah, but, I don't know, keep it down for now."

Grace felt the impulse to tell him off, or to roll her eyes and say something dismissive, but she'd been shot at. She'd spent the day being shot at, and she saw the sense of what he said. She punched his back gently with the side of her fist, and then tapped him with it again. "Okay, sorry," she said.

Nonstop pulled the bike back to get out of sight from the rooms at the bottom of the basin. He trundled along the rim and found a different spot to ride down.

"Seriously, I don't even know what I'm worried about," he said. "Don't be scared."

He went a quarter of the way around the large rim, and then banked over the edge.

* * *

Rik Ty

**

Norel caught a glimpse of movement out at the edge of the light. A shadow, out where the basement had stretched so drastically. The shadow dipped onto the distorted floor and he saw the patterned light of a vortex chamber; someone was driving closer.

"Don't come down! Go back!" Norel yelled — in one direction and then another, unsure of the course his voice would take.

Now that he'd yelled, Bloch would know where he was. At least most likely. The Colonel could charge from behind any corner, waving his gun, or firing it.

And maybe that would be better, Norel thought as he looked around the maze of shadowed walls. Maybe a gunshot would carry better than his voice did. Maybe a gunshot would make a better warning.

But Bloch did not shoot. And Bloch did not find Norel.

Norel found Bloch.

Norel saw the Colonel from the back, standing between the shadows of two walls, his bald head very evident, his pistol held high and aimed with both hands.

Beyond the Colonel, Norel saw more of the rider. It was the boy — Nonstop — the tinkerer — the young artist with the crazy vortex bike. He was coming with his young friend seated on the bike behind him, here because of him, both heading quickly toward the man in the shadows with the gun.

Norel rushed toward Bloch.

As he ran, the image of Bloch moved ahead of him. He got no closer. He ran harder, and the image moved faster. *Impact diffusion — would it protect the boy from that damnable bullet? Would it protect the girl?*

He stopped pursuing the image of Bloch and turned frantically to look around him. A blank wall immediately to his left. He pounded it with the side of his fist and turned again. Would the boy's diffusion properties even exist in the strange fields of the basement? Was he about to see the boy's face blasted into a ragged hole? That too? The

465

desecration of the innocent, was that too, part of the price he must pay?

He turned again, and saw Bloch's back again. He ran toward it. With the very first step, Bloch's back grew closer; Norel took two longs strides and then leapt.

He didn't know what rules time followed in the basement. He had time to see Bloch's finger tighten on the trigger, and to worry about it, and to wonder what to do next.

Norel hit Bloch a micro-second before the gun discharged. With the pistol's report, the air around them... *faceted*. Everything visible became fragmented. The fragments that described the room and the two men fighting in it floated and orbited like motes of dust in a column of sunlight, like seeds suspended in slowly swirling oils.

Bloch became an aggregate of floating images mixed among shifting sights of cabinets, and tubes, and latches. One floating patch displayed his ear, another displayed his ankle, another displayed his ear from a different angle, and all flowed within a sea of floating patches. Norel saw fragments of what looked like the back of his own head, and fragments of hands that might be his, and he saw fragments of moving folds of fabric behind a knee that might also have been his.

Across the images, he saw Bloch snarl, one eye six feet from the other eye, both pupils moving together as they looked about them, both a yard in front of the fragment displaying Bloch's compressing lips, squeezing so tightly around his clenched teeth, that Norel could see the blood drain from them, could see the little white streaks as they emerged around the perimeter of each lip. Every aspect of Bloch, the back of his head, the top of his head, his collar, his wrist, floated disjointedly about, but the images within the collected fragments moved in unison, and focused on Norel — wherever he himself was — with a glaring hatred that promised instantaneous and savage violence.

Norel closed his hands into fists, into clubs, and saw the motion orchestrate upon a thousand fat snowflakes. He swung, even as the pistol's flash released a million starpoints.

Where wsa time? oCuld they eb eesn? eHer wehre the lghit bolied oragne and eyllow and bleu, and all htat creatde relatiy was the wlil to destroy?

Pour toujours la violance dans nos coeurs. Horse. ?A d'onde se ponemos? Silk. Stone. Veil and Ring and Summers Gone. Bloch brought down... Abrade... his fist... Where... Where can we lock you away? To walk is to grind the dust, woe upon insects unswift or unseen.

Drenj suii o tttt float hhheoo blank mdom. eiohnev,k upon your ji 22 mind. olgw what can i give VVV forsaken .emit ni hcir era uoy .gnirahs peeK .gnivol peeK .gnirevocsid peeK .yaw siht evaheb stsilihin nevE .meht htiw yrevocsid ruoy erahs ot dna ,erom neve evol uoy esoht evol ot eslupmi eht leef ot si tra yb dehcuot eb oT vvv swung... hIS boDy, its silhOuetTtte vioLET, the roOm sWirlinG oranGE... jsae... The next blow landed. The knuckles of Bloch's left hand, so little skin hiding the bone, connected with Norel's jaw. sopj Oejj . aPin dna defiance. Norel squeezed his eyes shut against the enormous and sudden pain. He pushed back against the bigger man's chest... renewed through Bloch's veins. He knew how to rain his fists down upon the cowering... fist... to the back of Norel's skull, above and behind his left ear. The bone... hard, and Bloch felt the impact up his forearm. Norel staggered, not cowering yettttt jihroi rgfj , but it must be close. Norel threw his right fist against Bloch's face. Bloch smiled, and delivered his fist again, two — three times on the same spot above Norel's ear. Norel's face squeezed, a thousand lines radiated from his clenched eyelids. But he did not let go of Bloch, still he did not cower, still he moved to strike out with his own fists.

This was so delightfully easy. Bloch could batter Norel until his own fists were bloody and sore, and he needn't stop there. He could batter this weakling beyond breath. He pushed an open palm against the side of Norel's head, smearing blood. And then he cleaned his hand against Norel's white forehead. Norel glared and threw a punch at Bloch's ribs, another at his jaw, another at his jaw from the other side. Bloch stepped back. *All right Maggot. You want a beating? You're going to damned well get one.* Bloch filled his lungs with air and raised his fist high above his head...

... And touched the wall with his bleeding knuckles. And touched the source of the dimensional kaleidoscoping with his bleeding knuckles. And touched his death with his bleeding knuckles.

When seen from one angle, Bloch was whole. When seen from another, he was a swarm of swirling particles lost within a sea of swirling particles, and when seen from another angle, he was a cloud of fragmented images, soft-edged flags of moving aspects of eyes and teeth, of blood and knuckles, of shoes and belt loops. And the second he touched the wall, it was this version of him that was treated as real. His scream, lusty and full, folded, and garbled down to two dimensions and then to silence. His body, in the time it stood between fragmentation and cohesion, between two, and three, and some unknown tally of dimensions, delivered to his brain all the feelings associated with his body's new condition. And for the instant before oblivion, he felt he had been de-boned alive.

Then his body became inert. Without life, it became gray. Without cohesion it became dust. As dust, it fell upon the ground.

Norel suddenly had only one view of everything: a conventional view of an unconventional space. He saw the gray powder on the floor, and was still looking at it a split second later when Nonstop and Grace turned around at his sudden appearance.

"Doc! You disappeared. Then the wall disappeared," Nonstop said, bending to lift the Doctor from under his arms, gently, but with insistence.

"It's happening again," Nonstop said, "We have to get you on the bike." Around them, above the rim, they could hear the steady, ratcheting sound of things falling. It sounded to Nonstop like thousands of High School auditorium seats being lifted back to their upright positions. The sounds seemed far off, but they weren't receding.

Grace helped pull the Doctor to Rattletrap.

"You take the seat," Grace gestured to Norel.

"No, no miss, you take the seat. I'll be fine."

"He will," Nonstop said to Grace. "You want to drive?" he asked the professor.

"Not on your life."

Grace sat down, Nonstop sat down, and Norel crouched on the foot deck, gripping the sides of the control bar.

They reached the top of the rim and saw just how bad the situation was: rooms were flattening and reopening everywhere they looked.

"Daaaag," Nonstop said.

* * *

Skyde hovered at the code-box, feeding the stabilizing code into the touch pad over and over. There was no longer any lag time between when the green light announced the acceptance of the stabilizing code, and when the red light announced the need to reenter it. She was re-entering code as fast as she could type. Unless the breakdown of the basement ended on its own, it wasn't going to end.

She watched the tiny monitor, and saw that steadily, fewer and fewer rooms were re-opening, and understood that the crisis wouldn't end by the basement's spontaneous stabilizing, but by the closing of each and every one of its rooms, including the one she was standing in, including whichever one held Doc, including whichever one held Nonstop and his friend.

She watched the shifting graphic as she punched in the code over and over again, chains and chains of rooms, some that kept their length cycle after cycle, and others that grew continually smaller, creeping closer and closer to the position she held. Closer from every side. Fewer and fewer options.

Which meant fewer and fewer options to drive, and which meant that all routes would lead Nonstop closer and closer to the active code-box where Skyde hovered.

She heard his bike first. *He's alive. Someone's alive.* Then she saw him, far-off in a chain of rooms, whipping the bike through collapsing walls and ceilings. She saw his face, and then he saw her. And he smiled.

And he had Dr. Norel.

He did it.

Crazy boy did it.

Skyde's chest lifted. She wanted to live and there was a chance after all.

"HURRY," she yelled, typing as fast as she could. She rode her boots to the side of the code-box, and kept typing; when Nonstop passed, she was going to speed after him.

But Nonstop didn't keep going when he passed her. He turned, deftly, his wheel drifting as he spun the bike in a small circle that placed him right behind Skyde, where he made the bike reach gently around her arms and grab the control bars of her boots. Then the bike closed the circle and shot forward and Skyde fell back against Rattletrap, suddenly part of a hyper-strange caravan, the lead car in a runaway roller-coaster. She felt giddy. She felt euphoric. She turned, and saw the rooms collapsing right behind them like the crunching jaws of some summer-movie dinosaur, and even as terrified as she was, she started to laugh, loud and strong.

"Go. Go. Go!" she yelled, and Nonstop grinned with her. No way. No way collapsing rooms were going to get them. Mindful of Doc's arms, and Grace's arms, Nonstop rose in his seat, and then leaned, letting his weight bank the bike, letting the tire chew, reaching for every advantage that might buy them an instant or two's lead time against the collapsing rooms. They saw the doorway to the central room. They saw Skyde's board wedging it open. They had one room to go. Maybe three seconds. Just as they approached, Skyde lifted her boots and knocked the skyboard free of the doorframe. In the instant they were out of the basement, the basement door slammed shut behind them — a gigantic sound: a *THWUMP* that seemed to push them further into the central room and that made all their heads ring.

And then they cheered. And they hopped off the bike, and they slipped out of their blast-boots, and they jumped and yelled and danced like fools.

The central room was no longer the cave it had been. Sunlight poured in from the main door and created a stripe of warm light that ran all the way to the back wall and that softened the shadows of the round room. The angle of the floor had improved as well, and while the group walked on it, the building lurched.

Surprised, they followed each other toward the main door — which was across an incline still, but not a climb. As they got near the door, they slowed. Anything could be beyond it. Surviving one catastrophe was no protection against the next.

Skyde moved to stand out of sight alongside the doorframe. She unclipped her data-box and crouched to the floor with it, watching its screen as she used it to peek outside the entrance.

When she saw the image on its screen, she pulled back the data-box, sprang to her feet, and ran out of the main door, jumping the four feet the doorway still occupied above the ground while she yelled "Krork! Krork!" over and over again.

Nonstop smiled at Norel and Grace, and ran out too. Grace and Norel walked to the door.

Grace looked out into the sunlight and was stunned. She looked at Norel. He looked out of the doorway as well, squinting and puzzled. It looked like he wanted to smile, but he kept his lips pressed together instead.

The robot-men were standing outside the Outpost — *calmly, peacefully,* in two neat lines, pulling at thick, braided electric cables that reached up to the Outpost. The cables were collections of dead power lines, twisted together, still cluttered with dangling slats of wood and swinging ceramic disks — but functioning well in their new role of improvised rescue devices.

Krork had stepped into the open space between the two rows of soldiers, and Skyde and Nonstop were hanging all over him, Skyde hugging, and Nonstop headlocking; both of them laughing, and Krork laughing along with them.

Grace saw that there were no longer flashing lights beating above the soldiers' eyes. She saw dried blood on some of the men where the light systems had been ripped away. Norel looked at the young men in their strange battle armor, and then looked at the floor as the Outpost lurched forward a yard, and settled onto the ground.

"Soldiers?" Norel asked Grace.

"U.S. Army; I'm pretty sure," Grace said, and then she leaned out of the doorframe, and stepped out into the day.

"They're helping us?" she asked Krork as she walked toward him.

"Yeah," Krork said, peeling Nonstop off his back and holding him above the ground so that he could look eye to eye with him. "They have a language," he said, and then deposited Nonstop next to Grace. "I just had to find a way to make them hear it."

Skyde hugged Krork again. "I'm so glad to see you. Did Varrage find you? Have you seen him?"

"Varrage is down at the portals with the others."

Grace and Nonstop both looked down the field. Varrage, and several teams of Bike Pilots had the Portals down to four. Nonstop spotted a fresh team arrive as they pulled up to the portal wall and dismounted from their bikes.

"Is the Bleed Zone done?" he asked no one in particular. He turned to Skyde, "What's the haze like?" Skyde turned and looked at him. He kept talking. "Would you mind checking?" he said, shrugging his shoulders and smiling meekly.

"Haze levels are great," Krork said, counting on his fingers while Skyde checked, "Diamondsong told me. Tumbler told me..."

"Unbelievable," Skyde said as she looked at the little screen, "Yes. The haze is almost gone, a couple of small pockets, but most of it is down in the field." She looked at Krork. "Really? All that activity is cleaned up already?"

Krork smiled and raised his hands. "Over twenty Bike Pilots on vortex bikes, no more opposition..."

Skyde looked around her, beaming. She rubbed a hand through her hair and looked at Nonstop and at Grace, and at the sun and the grass, and at her friends — who were nearby and alive — and then down to the portals, where she could see more of her friends, working, fixing a problem with ease. She blinked, and her eyes sparkled with the bright kiss of tears. "It feels like Christmas," she said to herself, laughing softly.

Norel approached the middle soldier in the right hand line. Looking at the machinery encasing the young man, he nodded grimly. He turned to the person inside the armor, the person inside the damaged face, the person that did not try to meet his gaze.

"What's your name son?"

"Nick Marlane. Private Nick Marlane," the young man said with difficulty.

"Mr. Marlane, thank you." Norel turned to the other young men in the battle suits. "Thank you to all of you. Thank you very much," and then he added: "These suits are abominations. Smaller, humane versions can be devised. I will... I will give the information over so that a team can get started." Norel lowered his head and rubbed his temples. He said thank you again, and turned as Krork approached him.

"They told me something you'd be interested in sir: Bloch had them activate lenses that were found at Open Mind, and that's what has been causing the Bleed Zones. It's a misuse. It's not anything inherent in the technology."

Grace looked happily at Nonstop. Nonstop just happily watched Krork. Norel nodded his head.

"Bloch admitted as much, boasted, in fact."

"Bloch is here?" Krork tensed. Then his shoulders dropped. "No. He's not."

"Bloch is dead. He died in the basement, caught in a malfunction. Nonstop," Doctor Norel paused to look directly at the young man. "Why isn't Grace home?"

Nonstop looked surprised, worked his jaw to speak, and Grace spoke instead. As she scratched her elbow, she muttered: "I...I want..."

The sounds of approaching helicopter blades interrupted her. More than one helicopter. Many more than one.

* * *

Colonel Wyatt moved to the edge of his seat in the lead copter and removed his sunglasses.

"What in the world am I looking at?"

He peered down at the field, at a row of three disks, each fifty feet tall, each glowing as if a bright light were shining on it — or more truthfully: each glowing as if it were *made* out of bright light. As he watched, the disk furthest on his left faded from view. Behind it were a bunch of kids in colorful motorcycle get-ups, running around with pronged guitars, or laser-guns, or who knew what. Wyatt saw the motorcycles as well, sleek and polished. What were fancy machines like that doing in a field? Wyatt turned to his pilot: "Circle the town. Let's get the whole picture."

* * *

Brickyard brought Krork's bike to a stop close to the Outpost. Diamondsong and a small band of Bike Pilots climbed down from the workbay, every one of them watching the line of passing helicopters.

Norel's gaze followed the helicopters' west-ward path, and he was surprised to see that the sun was already low in the sky. He heard a cheer rise from down in the field, and glanced back in time to witness the white portal closing. The Bike Pilots in the field jumped and celebrated, and he found that he could not muster their exuberance. He went back to watching the helicopters. Skyde stood nearby, and he spoke to her without turning.

"Cynthia, please begin the new Origin Point procedures — start the prep work."

"Those are Army copters?" Skyde asked.

"I imagine so, yes."

"I have something I absolutely have to tell them."

Brickyard stepped in. "I can start the procedures," she tapped Skyde's arm, but looked at Norel. He watched the copters and nodded, a move so subtle it might have been mistaken for blinking. Brickyard waved to Diamondsong. "Come on," she said, and Diamondsong and Sunset followed her as she walked toward the Outpost's entrance.

Norel watched the chain of copters turn and head back, not rushing, just continuing on a long, graceful curve around the area that would lead them back where they started.

Bike Pilots arrived from the field, some walking, some pushing bikes, some driving slowly. Some Pilots, upon cresting the hill, looked up at the sky and discussed the approaching copters. Norel stood in the open, awaiting the Army, and the Bike Pilots followed his lead, forming a half-circle behind him.

Norel turned his head toward the young people around him, but kept his chest facing the copters. He didn't smile. "If you have a bike, please get it into the building."

Panhead was the first to move, trundling his fat-tired vortex-trike toward the back of the building. "I'll get the bike lab open," he called back as he picked up speed, and the rest of the riders began following him.

Varrage walked his way through the crowd of slow moving bikes, and continued past the backs of the standing Bike Pilots. He neared the Outpost, and then walked freely.

He passed Dr. Norel unnoticed, and slipped into the Outpost's main door. Inside, he found a shadowed perch, where he could watch the Doctor and not be seen.

* * *

Colonel Wyatt's copter took a front and center position, hovering above the field as its subordinate copters fell into formation behind it. Flanking copters veered off to secure landing positions over other clear spots on the ground. Three of the copters headed for the highway.

Norel watched the machines flow around each other, dividing the sky. He watched their blades as they chopped in perfect circles: dark, light; dark, light; dark, light. He saw the patterns the blades made. Afraid, he watched the copters touch gently to the ground.

He had no model for this. He had never considered being surrounded by helicopters. He had no idea what to expect. He thought his mind was open to anything, but he was surprised when the lead helicopter activated a loudspeaker and someone inside began to speak.

"COLONEL BLOCH," the voice on the loudspeaker said. "YOUR ORDERS ARE TO STAND DOWN. I REPEAT: STAND DOWN."

And then whoever was on the other side of the microphone spoke directly to him: "Doctor Norel? Are you hurt? Are you all right?"

Norel nodded and lifted a hand. He looked around him. Was Krork still there?

Krork was standing right beside him.

"Can you tell anything from his voice? Why is he here?" Norel asked.

"Seems straight. It's hard to tell from a broadcasted voice. Microphone-type reproductions are almost worthless."

Norel nodded and looked back at the lead copter. Its blades were slowing. A man exited from the front of the vehicle, from what Norel assumed to be a passenger seat. The man had some age, and his uniform held many decorations. Norel could not tell his rank over the distance and let it go at that. Pin-pointing the officer's place in the Military's pecking order was not a priority of his at the moment; this was the man he would be dealing with immediately, and he didn't really need to know more than that. He would listen to what the man had to say.

It would still be a minute or so before the man walked up the field. If the Outpost were ready, they could simply run again, but the Outpost was not ready. Even if all went perfectly with the origination procedure, it would still be a few minutes before they could leave.

Norel would walk to meet the Officer then.

He started.

The short walk, with no tasks except reducing distance, left him free to notice the area around him. Down at the highway he caught glimpses of people — *civilians* — running to Army helicopters. He saw soldiers step out to meet the people, to speak with them. He saw no weapons held or drawn. As he turned away, he saw a pair of young women half-carrying a staggering man toward the copters.

Norel's steps met debris, and he watched his feet.

Those people at the highway had all been subjected to this Bleed Zone. All of them had been yanked from their lives and forced to hide from the Bleed Zone's terrors. He walked across a piece of wall with a medicine cabinet still attached to it. The people's terrors were easing now. Their soldiers had arrived.

Norel's feet hit a tangled rug peppered with fragments of wood. His next steps brought him to a slide of dinner plates and timbers. He watched his steps. People's homes. What was his part in this? Was it all Bloch's fault? As his steps alternated amid the wreckage, his mind matched their rhythm with half-formed ideas:

Bloch's fault,
my fault,
Bloch's fault,
my fault, simple phrases, continuing in his mind as if he were pulling petals from one of the field's flowers. He thought he might be

able to find a balance between the ideas of his guilt and Bloch's guilt. As long as no civilians had died in the Bleed Zone.

Please don't let there be any bodies. Don't let anyone have died here.

A step. *Because of Bloch.*

A step.

Because of me.

A step.

Because of the things we wanted.

Norel walked, and there were no bodies in the rubble, or under the rubble, or around the rubble, just broken things. Things he had ample holdings to help rebuild, better than before, if that would be any consolation.

Norel stepped beyond the worst of the debris and walked toward the Officer as the Officer walked toward him.

He noticed Krork was just a few steps behind him, Skyde was walking down too, her Skyboard under her arm, and behind her, Nonstop side-stepped through the rubble.

The Officer stopped walking. They were still a few paces apart, but Norel stopped too. Krork and the others stood near Norel, immediately behind him.

The Officer removed his sunglasses, tilting his head downward as the glasses caught on his nose. Then he looked directly at the doctor.

"Doctor Norel? I am Colonel Montgomery C. Wyatt of the United States Army. The President has asked me to extend you every courtesy. He will be here as soon as the area is secure."

Norel felt no urge to smile, and so did not.

"I take it every courtesy means you will not stop us from leaving?"

"We'll do this any way you'd like. Doctor, we're just learning what you've been through. The President wants you comfortable. Now, first thing. I need you to tell me what the dangers are here."

Krork turned to Norel, smiled, and nodded.

"The dimensional bleed problems appear solved," Norel said, "There is extensive property damage..."

Skyde stepped forward. "Sir, if you don't mind, may I please interrupt you?" Skyde said, addressing Norel, and then, immediately after Norel nodded a surprised yes, turned to address the colonel.

"Colonel, you were just in the air, so you've seen the gas main fire and the property damage — all from Army missiles and explosives I might add. But Colonel, right now, most importantly, you have men who need help. You've got soldiers trapped underground. Getting to them without causing a cave-in is going to be very tricky. Can I show your teams where they are?"

Wyatt nodded, "Yes, we could do that." He pulled a handset from his pocket, and kept talking to Skyde. "Go down to the helicopter I just came out of. The pilot will take you to the site."

Skyde stepped onto her board and lifted off from the ground. When she paused a second later, her board was already level with the colonel's chest. "Just tell him to follow me," she said, and flew off.

The Colonel, a little wide eyed, raised his handset. Then he gave the order for three choppers to follow Skyde. He signed off and looked at Norel.

"Is Colonel Bloch underground with those soldiers?"

Norel met the colonel's eyes. "No. The Colonel is dead. It happened in the basement just a few minutes ago."

"Colonel Bloch is dead?"

"Yes. An accident, if that helps any."

"No, that certainly does not help any. This complicates things Doctor."

"I imagine it does." Norel pulled a pen, one of many, from a line of pockets on his chest sewn just for that purpose. He undocked his data-box, and dipped the pen tip into a port on its side. "I have a recording of the last half hour. It will show you everything that happened. There was a basement malfunction and the malfunction killed the Colonel. At the time, the Colonel was hunting me with a Colt 45."

Colonel Wyatt looked at Norel. "You have a recording." He put his hands on his hips. "I'm sorry to say this Doctor, but the idea I get when I hear that you had the Colonel in your building, and that the next thing that happens is that he dies in an accident, well, that sounds to me like the accident was intentional, like you set a trap."

"On the contrary. All this," Norel swept a hand to indicate the field, and the homes, and by connection, the whole of Exeter, "All that happened here today is a result of the Colonel setting a trap for us."

"Hmmm, and you just happen to have a tape ready to excuse you from charges."

"I do expect the tape to excuse me from charges. I didn't expect to live. I wanted some record of the truth of what happened here. I only escaped the basement because this young man," he gestured to Nonstop, "was skilled enough to drive in and get me — though I suspect that's a simplification." He turned to look at the other Bike

Pilots who had followed him down the hill, and then turned back to the Colonel.

"Colonel, I'm very glad this tape exists, because it makes it possible for us to move forward. You say the President wants us comfortable. Well, you will not keep us here unless you shoot us, and even then, you will not shoot all of us. I have prepared additional files that give an overview of the technology and a look at some of the discoveries we've already made. No design secrets of course, but Colonel, when people demand answers from you, these files give you something you can show them. The president will consider it progress, and he will see for himself, Bloch's abysmal behavior. If it helps, you can say that I lied, and told you that I didn't know where Bloch was."

"That would make me a liar. Where is the body?"

"There is no body."

Norel softened, and briefly lifted the pen and the data-box. "The body turned to particulate. You'll see on the tape. I'm not sure of more than that. I'm not even sure if we can collect the particles. We'll try. And we'll return what we can for the next of kin."

Norel looked down at the data-box. "It also appears you have some men here who have been outfitted in perversions of a Spinal Bypass system we were developing. I'm including files that will help you to help them." Norel undocked the pen, and offered it to the Colonel. The Colonel pulled out his wallet, and removed a business card. Suddenly holding too many things, he put his sunglasses back on. He accepted Norel's pen, and offered the card.

"My numbers are on this card Doctor. Call me when you feel safe. Call me soon."

Norel accepted the card, and smiled at the Colonel. As he did, he saw something that took the feelings behind his smile and curdled them to dread. He tried to disguise his apprehension, and so did not rush to look away.

The Colonel's mirrored glasses reflected the landscape. In their warped surfaces, Norel saw dual reflections of the Outpost, and in the reflections, dual ghosts of the Chinese symbol, with a returning helicopter taking the role of the black dot, and his own face, contrasting against the silhouette of the Outpost, taking the role of the white dot.

He felt reality swerve, mindful of how his work, and the day's events, had made that complaint preposterous. Nevertheless, he had to force himself not to react. Instead, he spoke.

"Colonel, the Bleed Zone events that occurred here today may have years of aftershocks. What of that? If we return to close them, will we be hunted?"

"No Doctor. We are eager to help. We need you to tell us how."

"Of course. Colonel, I will be in touch. Please excuse me."

Norel turned. He pressed his lips. He could feel Krork looking at him, wanting to speak, but he moved his gaze to the clouds as he walked, and did not acknowledge his friend. Skyde approached beyond the Outpost. A few more minutes and they'd be gone. A few more minutes and he could breathe. He turned once more and waved to the Colonel, smiling. Then he walked quickly, his Bike Pilots following him.

* * *

The Colonel watched the Doctor go, then called in a series of orders that allowed the roads to be reopened, and that allowed emergency services to come in and help deal with the gas main fire, and to come help with whatever that flying girl had been talking about. What would they need there? A crane?

* * *

Norel shepherded the Bike Pilots into the Outpost, including Skyde, who landed in what could be called the dooryard, and then stepped off her board and bounded, smiling, into the Outpost.

Norel entered the building and stood in the threshold as the door closed. Then he turned to look back out the window and watch the world as the Outpost powered up. He saw the perfect grass, with its late afternoon's long shadows, marred with slats of white wood, lying amid the blades like unburied dead. He looked away. He looked up. His eyes moved to the sun. Yes. The sun, a fine way to say goodbye to the Earth for a time.

The sun itself, sat orange in the sky. Some atmospheric event, some disturbance in the flow of air, made its image waver. The black smoke from the gas main fire, pulled by that same disturbance, rose through the sky slowly, as if ascending the steps to a stage. Norel watched, already suspicious of the message this particular speaker would give. With no flair or subterfuge, the smoke column moved within his line of sight with the sun, rose to cover half the image of the burning disk, and then rose no further, casually coiling its way southward as if it had no message to impart, as if it were merely rolling innocently along, particulate suspended in a continuum influenced by temperature.

Norel looked away. He didn't hear the chatter of the Bike Pilots discussing what this moment meant. He didn't hear the whine of the Outpost as its systems powered up and thrummed steadily. He looked at the moving tips of the tree line, where the newest portions of branches, unblocked by mature leaves, foremost and alone as they stretched into the new medium of the sky, met the most disturbance. He wanted to see treetops swaying. He loved to see treetops swaying. He would keep looking until that was what he saw.

*

*   *

*

June
18th

8:18
P.M.

EPILOGUE

Rik Ty

**

It was a noisy reunion. The Outpost ghosted back to the base camp, an inch to the left of its original position. The ghost light around the building painted the ground a twitchy electric green and threw long shadows behind the pebbles and the trees.

Tents, previously folded and fastened, sat atop lockers, which sat by bikes, which sat around a large, multi-wheeled, multi-robot-armed rig with a cargo hold full of stasis crates.

Loading the gear into the crates, and the crates into the rig, could have been the last human acts on this unnamed world. That had been the official plan. Instead, earlier, Krork had returned for the generator, and had informed the Bike Pilots that the Outpost had not crashed, or become lost, and that there was good reason to hope for its return. In the hours since then, the pilots had sat around a large fire, had slept, had told stories, had made agreements, had waited, had worried, and had hoped. They agreed that even if the Outpost took weeks to return, or never returned, they would not disband until forced to. They would foray back to Earth, find out what they could, steal what they'd have to, but they would not disband voluntarily.

And now the ghost-light was here, and they jumped to their feet — and they saw the Outpost, sitting within the green light, and they cheered — and before the green light could fade, they ran to the main door.

The Bike Pilots within the Outpost heard the cheer and cheered back. Varrage stood, his back to a central room wall, and moved his head from Bike Pilot to Bike Pilot. No one met his gaze, or even paid attention to him.

Someone outside pounded on the door, and Varrage stiffened, looking straight ahead, appalled at the lack of caution and its encouragement.

And then the door opened, and Bike Pilots spilled in, and Bike Pilots spilled out.

The central room emptied. Branches were added to the fire.

Norel walked to the fire and filled the Bike Pilots in on what had happened with Colonel Bloch, and what had happened with Colonel Wyatt, and what he thought it meant. Something old had ended, which meant something new had started. Wazzi found the wine, passed the bottles out, and opened the bottle he held. Getting more from the basement seemed like a bad idea for the time being, but if they needed more, they agreed, Paris was only a ten minute drive.

It was a long reunion. It would be longer still. There was much to tell: people had battled monsters, had escaped explosions, had contended with military robots, and had seen reality swerve and twist. They had seen a road come to life, had seen the dreaded Voracitors, and had seen their teammate Varrage slap the monsters around; it would, in fact, be a long night. They had to re-establish base-camp. They would need more wine, and at least this once, Norel would offer no reprimand on the dangers of sneaking back to Earth.

Norel felt duty pull him, and left the youth to their fun. He stepped further from the fire's light, and walked back to the Outpost's main door.

*

The Outpost, empty, had switched to power-conservation mode, and the interior loomed, dim and crossed with shadow.

The Doctor walked the circular corridor to his office. He'd have to examine all the system information from the last twenty hours, and see if any energy readings had been taken, see how they compared to the distortion readings, start the safety checks of the basement, build fresh fire-walls, see if...

Norel opened the door to his office and was shocked by what he saw, though that reaction immediately seemed stupid. Of course this had happened, anyone should have expected it.

The entire floor of his office lay buried ankle deep in loose items. Every paper, every trinket, every carton, lay spilled and jumbled along the floor.

Norel held the door frame for a second, and then waded in, his feet lifting platforms of loose paper with every push into the room, shuffling the papers further.

He stooped to reach for a carton, and then knelt — so many hand-written notes, accompanied by drawings, accompanied by equations, "funnel wave up through emanation", "increase speed of polarity cascade", "mirror, enfold, select".

Kneeling, and with no energy at all, he started one pile for pages with equations, one pile for pages with drawings, and then another pile for pages with both, and then another pile for pages dealing with amplification, and another pile for pages dealing with identification of energy samplings. He put the pages down. He wanted to scoop them up and burn them. Start over clean; put them in a stasis crate and lock them away. But they were current — most of them. He needed them, or might. If he packed them away, he'd forget them, and then he might as well burn them.

He stayed where he was. Kneeling became sitting, and sitting became leaning on the counter behind him. Hundreds and hundreds of pages. Thousands of pages. His thoughts drifted. Solutions seemed to hover on the horizon. Which to choose? which problem to solve? As soon as he focused on one, another would jostle into its place and demand his attention. He looked back at the pages.

"God, I can't." He looked at the papers and picked one up. A drawing. He placed it down on the pile for drawings. He thought of the broken homes, the displaced families. He thought of the burning gas main. The next two pages went on the drawing pile as well. He thought about Bloch. Bloch had tortured Krork. He thought about Krork. He thought about the new Colonel, the one who was offended by lying. He thought about the helicopters, and the men in the helicopters, and the men in the armored bypass suits. He thought of the newscasters, and the rival technology giants, and the politicians. He picked up the next page and couldn't even look at it.

"God, I can't. I can't control this. I can't control every drop of rain. I can't control the hearts of men."

"Please."

"Please help me."

He closed his eyes in the empty room, breathed, and opened his eyes in the empty room.

The page he held belonged on the equation pile. So did the next, and the next, and the next. He encountered them in clusters. That made some sense.

He moved a paper and uncovered a small group of objects. He'd have to start a pile for things that weren't paper. He pushed aside the unchecked papers near his thigh and created a clear spot, then he began transferring the items over: a tuning fork, a pair of kaleidoscopes, a few pens. And then the souvenir clock. He paused as he held it, ready for another hit of its sweet picture. He leaned back against the cabinets as he put the clock on his knee, and then looked at it. The plastic covering reflected the room light almost as sharply as glass would have. The clock was cheap. It was silly. He adored it.

He brought it closer, and his face reflected in the plastic covering, haggard, starkly shadowed and washed of color, but there, superimposed over the picture of his younger self. Photons leapt off the plastic, captured only by his eye. Photons traveled through the plastic, reached the image of the photons that had been captured by a camera years and years ago, and then sent photons traveling back up through the plastic, to be captured by the very same eye in the very same instant. Distances covered so quickly it was almost a form of time travel. Time travel that left all the passengers behind.

He moved the clock until the reflection of his face was gone. The plastic reflected the counter behind him. What angle would he have to turn the clock to see the faceplate image without a reflection on the plastic covering? Which spot offered a clear view? None? He'd seen pictures with no reflections hadn't he? Are they always there and we look through them? What makes a mirror? Light, glass, a dark background, a reflective background. What special qualities did the weak light of the room have to make the plastic clock so effective at casting back images? He turned it. His face, his shoulder, the counter, the wall, the yin-yang T-shirt hanging from the wall.

Its intrusion jarred him. Memories or not, the best part of him or not, it was time to burn that shirt. He went to put the clock down, on the object pile he had just started, when the image on the glass shifted, and again, his eyes, and the photons, performed their tricky little miracle. He saw both images equally: the old photo, and the T-shirt, and the anger left him, though something very close to fear remained.

The dark mass of the yin-yang symbol covered the trees and meadow of the clock. The white mass covered the open sky. The dark dot covered the flying bird, and the white dot covered the faces of him and his little baby daughter, frozen in a moment, looking at each other with love, from opposite orientations, from opposite genders, from opposite ages. In that instant, all his silly terrors regarding the symbol disappeared into that spiral with a speed and a force he could feel. Balance. Harmony. His duty to his child. The symbol just a notion once again.

His wrists trembled. His arms trembled. His heart hammered in his chest. He rose, and felt his right leg burst into pins and needles.

He stood fully, and his feet took a skiing trip on the loose papers. He fell back, and landed on the counter with his elbows, loudly and painfully, but he didn't drop the clock. He laughed, brought the clock up to his lips and kissed it. Then, holding the clock between the pinky and the palm of his left hand, he used both hands to untwist the vinyl-covered wire that held the embroidery hoop to the cabinet latch behind it. He worked, and he didn't drop either item. He worked until the wire pulled free. And then, with his sleeping leg, and his unstable footing, and his hands protecting his two treasures, he made it out of the room, never once coming close to falling, and never once noticing.

As soon as he left the Outpost he saw the Bike Pilots joking and laughing by the fire. *There are close to a hundred people here*, he thought. Enough to sort those papers perfectly in an afternoon. Enough to chart the realmlines and see what's out there. Enough even for some to quit, and make babies, and start that adventure. Where was Nonstop? He saw Krork standing, and watched as Krork ate the contents of a jar of peanut butter in one spoonful — seeming to enjoy it too. Where was Nonstop? There. Sitting on a log... next to Varrage, having a discussion, both men drawing in the dirt with sticks. Would the clock-trick work by fire-light? If not, Norel would just have to light it with exuberance.

He showed Nonstop the clock and the T-shirt, explained what he considered to be the connection, and asked for a ride. A crowd gathered around them, and as Nonstop agreed, and excused himself, and left, Norel told the story again.

Nonstop walked to the other end of the campfire, where Grace, and Skyde, and Diamondsong, along with Sunset and half a dozen other beautiful women, including Brickyard, were giggling over something.

"I'm driving back Grace. A little earlier than expected. I'm taking Dr. Norel. Do you want to go now?"

Grace leaned over and peeked past him, looking down the fire at the crowd around the professor.

"You're taking Dr. Norel? Okay, I'll go. Hold on."

She stood and looked at Skyde, and then extended her gesture to include everybody. "I just wanted to say..." The girls stood up and hugged her, cutting her off with more giggles and more goodbyes. Nonstop stood there watching. They'd be done sooner or later.

Or maybe not.

"The bike's still in the lab," he said to no one in particular, hooking a thumb over his shoulder, "I'll go get it."

* * *

Nonstop returned with the bike. He had equipped it with a spare seat.

"What is that? A saddle?" Grace asked.

"They've got all sorts of stuff in the bike-lab. It's just held on with straps, so —"

"— No riding on road-monsters."

"Dig it. No more tonight."

They got on the bike, Grace sitting behind Nonstop, and they trundled over to Dr. Norel. Nonstop and Grace stepped off so that Norel could place his clock and his T-shirt under the bike's seat. They had to open one of the straps to free the seat back, but that didn't take much time.

On the way up to the landing strip Norel looked around at the trees and the bushes. Trees on another planet, what an absolutely charming idea.

They ghosted out. Norel enjoyed the colors. At least at first.

* * *

June 18th

11:00 P.M.

Rik Ty

**

They ghosted onto a plain, high in the Canadian Rockies. It was night, and it was cold. There was a film of snow on the ground. There was snow on the breeze.

Rattletrap's tire adjusted, and they drove, surrounded by pine and fir and the night's quiet. In the stillness they could hear the engine's whisper echo between the mountain and the tree line.

The cold seeped in, and the hairs on Nonstop's arms stood up. Grace, dressed no warmer than the young man, pressed herself tighter to his T-shirt. As she lifted her cheek against his shoulder, she spotted three glimmers of realm-light as they drifted from his hair and then faded away into the slipstream.

Doctor Norel, the last passenger, looked around him. The tree lines ran along both sides of his vision, reaching above him like two open hands, framing the night sky in a great basin shape that held the stars and the moon.

Norel met the gaze of the moon, and saw, predictably, that it was half covered by clouds. He turned his attention from the sky, and watched the blurring snow beneath the motorcycle instead.

When he thought they must be close to arriving, he looked up past Nonstop's shoulder.

"It's around that curve," He said, pointing.

Nonstop headed for the white trail that hooked into the merging tree lines.

They arrived at a white expanse of snow that seemed to glow in the moonlight, a field that sloped upwards, into a snow covered hill that continued up to the mountain beyond.

On the hill, stood a small, dark cabin. A light shone through its left front window. Nonstop approached the building slowly, advancing the bike until the Doctor tapped him on the shoulder.

"Stop here please," Norel said, some fifty feet shy of the small house. Nonstop stopped the bike and it settled back onto its wheelie bars.

Norel swung off the bike and took a step toward the cabin. Then he took another. He carried nothing. He walked, and the clouds overhead kept pace.

A shadow moved within the window frame, carrying a rifle, or perhaps a broom.

Norel stopped, waiting for the door to open. There on the mountain, he stood, under the heavens, on a tiny patch of snow-covered earth, where his feet offered the world a new axis, a new point from which the rest of existence could turn, forever and ever, if it only chose to.

A bright line formed between the edge of the door and its frame. The line spread. The escaping light leapt along the snow in the dooryard, and expanded until it met Norel and split the Doctor himself into two halves, one, where the glow from within the cabin colored his face, and the other where the dark vistas behind him pressed against his back.

Fully open, the door revealed the silhouette of a woman pointing a rifle, aiming it outward.

"Who..." the woman started to say, until she was cut off by a smaller voice, much higher and much sharper.

"Daddy!" the smaller voice cried, and then the small person it belonged to pushed past her Mother and ran off the porch, into the snow, onto the path the door-light made.

"Sweetheart," Norel said, energy flooding back into his body — into his arms, his legs, his face. Norel bent, and opened his arms, wide enough to catch the moon — and then the moon jumped in, and brought the stars with her.

"Daddy, Daddy, Daddy," the little girl said.

"Hello Sweetheart," he said to the darling child as he stood, and hugged her, and closed his eyes, and then opened his eyes to look back to the doorway.

"Celine," he said to the woman, who was laying the gun down on the cabin floor at the foot of the wall. "I..."

But the woman ran toward him too, running in slip-on house-shoes, running in the snow, wiping her eyes as she came.

"Edmond. It's so beautiful to see you," she said as she drew closer. And then she was hugging him, and hugging their little girl, and she was kissing his scratchy cheek, and his perfect ear — no. There was blood in the folds of it. He had been blee...

"Frank?' Norel asked.

The woman pulled back and smiled at him.

"A failed experiment," Celine said. "Come inside." Her voice broke on the last syllable, and she wiped her eyes again. Then she grabbed his sleeve and pulled.

"One second, I have to say goodbye." Norel turned. Nonstop and Grace stepped into the door-light, cold, but dealing with it.

"Hello," Nonstop said.

"Celine, meet Nonstop and Grace, Nonstop and Grace meet Celine,"

"Hello," Nonstop said, and so did Grace, and so did Celine, but then Celine quickly added:

"Oh, but you're cold. Let me go inside and get you some jackets."

Nonstop waved her off, "That's okay, we're not staying. Thank you though."

Grace huffed, and watched the cloud of mist her breath made. She might have accepted the offer, but didn't press the issue.

"And this young lady is Dawn," Norel said as he bounced the young girl once in his arms. "This is my daughter Dawn."

"Hello Dawn. A pleasure to finally meet you," Nonstop said, nodding. He looked at the young girl. "I've heard a lot about you." Then he turned to Norel. "Doc?" he asked, shrugging with his hands, which held the clock and the embroidery hoop.

"What are those?" asked Dawn, peering from her father's arms.

"Do you like them?" Norel asked.

"Yes, I like them."

"Then they're for you."

Norel leaned, and Nonstop handed the toys to the child. The clock fit poorly in her hand, and so she placed it against her father's chest. She accepted the embroidery hoop from Nonstop, and her fingers wrapped around it easily. Immediately, she shook it like a tambourine, and then smacked it absently against her father's shoulders as she studied the clock-face.

"You staying Doc?" Nonstop asked.

Norel looked at Celine. Celine looked at Norel.

"Yes, I'm staying."

"Forever?"

"I don't know. My wife and I have a lot to discuss."

"What should I tell the others?"

"Tell them to get the camp operational. Tell them to make smart decisions."

"Uhm, I…"

"Come back in a week please. I'll tell you everything you're wondering about then — thank you Lance, now please, please, please, get our young friend here someplace safe."

He turned, child in his arms, and looked at the young woman standing near him with her arms crossed.

"Thank you Grace," He said, making a point of catching her eyes.

She forced herself not to blink, and she thought she probably looked unnatural doing it, but once she managed, she gave voice to the ideas that had consumed her for the last few hours: "Sir? I'd like to stay — really, if anyone ever needed a video-documentarian it's you — uhm — your every move is history, and — I — I won't cause any trouble, I promise... Please?"

Nonstop's eyebrows raised high, and he smiled big.

The doctor kept his eyes on Grace's, though he smiled too.

"By all means," he said, "Let Grace be with us. We'll work it all out. Goodnight you two." Norel smiled at them and turned away, walking toward the cabin with his family.

"See ya after the honeymoon," Nonstop called to the older couple, but they did not answer. They stepped through the doorway and closed it, with only gentle waves goodbye.

Grace grabbed both of Nonstop's hands and pulled him back onto virgin snow.

"Ha ha! You were right," she said. "You were right! Sometimes you have to insist! I didn't want to, but I said 'No. The moment has to happen'. And it did, and he said 'Yes'!"

Still holding Nonstop's hands, she began to run, and twirl, and skip, spinning him with her. He laughed as he trotted to keep up, and then she let go of his hands and twirled alone, spinning with her head back and her arms outstretched.

"Oh, what a beautiful, gorgeous night," she said, opening her eyes to the sky, and looking up to the white snowflakes as they floated among the twinkling stars.

She closed her eyes, and spun slowly in the snow.

"Oh Nonstop, you mentioned something else too," she said as he watched her, ending her twirl, her eyes closed.

"What?" he said, as she stopped.

She opened her eyes, and walked toward him, ignoring all the other sights on the mountain, and taking those last few steps looking only at him.

"There's so much future," she said.

And then she kissed him, and her lips were as soft as the blanketing snow, and as warm as the oceans of paradise.

Nonstop felt the tips of her fingers rest against the back of his head, and in that moment he thought her fingertips were magic, that the briskness of the air emanated from them, that everything in the whole of reality, everything he stood within, emanated out in waves from those small points of contact, broadcasting out to the world, creating the world — the air, the mountain, the snow — Grace herself, her lovely face, her flowing hair, her skin, her moving lips, all of all, all of everything.

They kissed and they kissed and they kissed, and then slowly, Grace's hair began to rise, extending straight out from her head in all directions. Dreamily, she broke from the embrace to see what was happening, and a thousand colored realm-lights escaped from under her hair, followed by a thousand more. She laughed, and so did Nonstop. She squashed her hair down with her forearms and ran to the bike. They got on, and they drove, laughing.

Nonstop circled the cabin as he gave the machine speed. Grace wondered if the move was meant as a tribute to the Doctor, the Doctor whose story she was now going to tell. With those thoughts in mind, she spun in her seat and quickly rummaged through her tool belt until she found her camera.

* * *

She had missed this every other time, and now she would shoot it: *Just what does it look like when you leave a world and a realm-tunnel closes behind you?*

Nonstop drove away from the cabin. The tunnel formed. She shot.

Through the camera she saw the full moon come out from behind the clouds and shine brightly. She saw the cabin in the snow. The tunnel around her darkened, and the image from Earth became hazy as the tunnel lengthened. Finally, she saw the Canadian tree line and the night sky become one dark shape. She saw the snow covered hill and its slope to the plain become one white shape, she saw the cabin become a dark, fuzzy mass, more circular the further they went, and she saw the bright moon, already a perfect circle, lose focus in the dark sky. The scene was framed by the circular opening of the realm-tunnel, and as the light from Earth diffused, she found she was looking at a perfect representation of the image from the Doctor's T-shirt.

And then the image faded to black, and only the realm-tunnel remained, its blackness quickly filling with streaks of color.

"I captured that," she said quietly, astonished.

And after a moment, she noted the color striations, and became equally astonished, and after another moment, she returned her camera to her tool belt, and went back to hugging Nonstop.

"So Hawaii's what? South?" he asked.

"I don't know. Let's find out," she said, resting her head against his back, and smiling over her shoulder as they drove off to invent their world.

*

The End

Under the miracle,
our perceptions.
Under our perceptions,
more miracles.

Rik Ty

To live. To love.
    To cheat. To try.

        To find the truth
          In the fragmented lie.

              To find the Sun
                In the fragmented sky.

                Concurrence

                -In transit

ABOUT THE AUTHOR

Hello,
I used to have a joke: I'm the toy designer who penciled pages for Marvel, the penciler who wrote for Scooby Doo Comics, the writer who designed the entire run of the MONSTER IN MY POCKET line of plastic figurines, and the husband who somehow stayed married. I know how I stayed married: I met the most perfect girl in the world and I wouldn't let go of her. She's been kind enough to hang on right back. We met on Fordham Road, between the RKO and the Woolworth's near the Concourse in the late seventies and we've been very lucky. Once, in the height of summer, we had a bus driver turn off all the lights and give us our own bouncing, rattling, limousine ride home. We have two amazing daughters we couldn't be prouder of, and when times get tough we count our blessings and say "Not bad for two kids from the Bronx."

The RKO is gone. Woolworths is gone.
We're still here.

I wrote a book.

I love you Bethy.

- R

OTHER THRILL KINGS ADVENTURES

If you look at the timeline graphic in the front of this book, you will see that there are several "Bleed Zone" adventures surrounding this novel (there are even a few Bleed Zone adventures INSIDE this novel). The 100 word sequels are tiny glimpses into Thrill Kings adventures, and you can find all of them free on the Thrill Kings Now.com website.

There are several short Bleed Zone adventures available right now that are roughly short story length. More are coming – in short story length, in novella and novel length, even in trilogy length. Stay tuned. In the meantime, here are some details of the short pieces:

In "The Gray Walls", Nonstop and Krork battle an unusual inter-D in a Seattle office tower. The creature may exist by devouring pockets of reality. Worse — it may have already eaten the reality Nonstop and Krork are standing in. Unusual, exciting, maybe a little scary.
Bonus material: an extensive afterword, and the ebook includes a proto edition of the "Thrill Kings for First Timers" sketchbook.

***

In "The Size Of Minneapolis Upright", Nonstop has to evacuate a widow and her foster children from a farmhouse before an enormous Inter-D rampages — but Nonstop can't find any sign of the family, just the heartbreaking corpse of a friendly-looking dog. Where is everyone? What happened? And what was that noise upstairs? Exciting, intense, and by the end, heartwarming

***

In "The Shaftway", Nonstop follows an Inter-D into a condemned factory and gets skunked as he sends the creature home. The skunking has bizarre results, and Nonstop's escape from a ruined elevator shaft is strange, hallucinatory, and DANGEROUS. This one is weird on purpose, and has some fun language experiments, including equating unstoppable rust with Lovecraftian cosmic horror. Fun!

***

In "Not So Bad", the team responds to a Bleed Zone in a small town with a stony beach. Haze readings reveal that whatever came through the portal is moving very fast, and in a lot more than one direction. Nonstop soon finds that he has to somehow stop a herd of giant-leaping-octopus creatures from stampeding the town to rubble - and he has to do it on a bike he isn't used to! Short, but fun!

***

You can catch them all, as well as the novel, and anything new, at the Rik Ty author page on Amazon:

https://www.amazon.com/author/rikty

I followed the release of the novel with a
sequel series of 100 word Bleed Zone
adventures.
You can see the rest at:
http://www.thrillkingsnow.com/100wordsequels

A 100 Word THRILL KING ADVENTURE By Rik Ty

"FIVE WRENCHES"

The spatial anomaly was five phase iterations from defeating Nonstop's tap and thus kaleidoscopically devouring the Earth inside a thousand-year black collapsing.

Nonstop had been late to the Bleed Zone, trying to get a fifth wrench to land in a plastic bucket, but as it was, his hand was in the right spot, at the right angle, at exactly the right moment to fire his tap and avert disaster -- though he never knew it. Instead, he apologized to his team for being late again, and helped complete the mission.

We never fully know,
how many trucks don't hit us.

Some scenes from THRILL KINGS: FRAGMENTED SKY

Thank you,

Please leave a review and help the project grow!

Best wishes,
-Rik Ty

Visit the Rik Ty facebook page for more freebies, and to check for announcements.
Or
Sign up for the newsletter at:
http://www.thrillkingsnow.com/cast-1-1/

Thank You

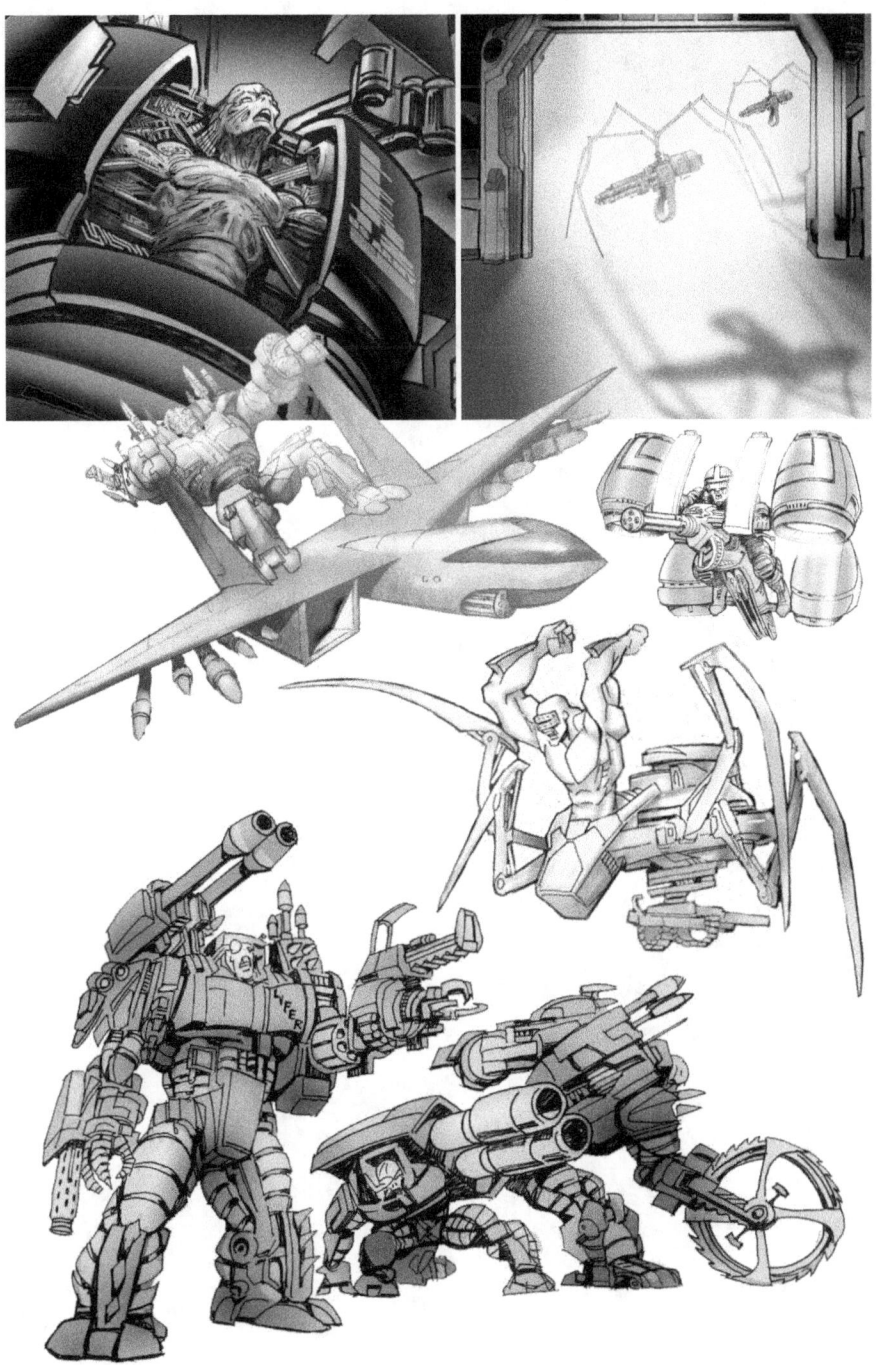

Peace